An Exquisite Corpse Reader

THE STIFFEST OF THE CORPSE

edited by Andrei Codrescu

City Lights Books
San Francisco

Cover design by Rex Ray

ACKNOWLEDGEMENTS

The Editor wishes to thank the splendid beings who made the voyage possible: Lawrence Markert, the original *Perchè No* person; our heroic art directors: Karen Willoughby, Rosemary Taylor, Wendy-Kessler-Effron; Chris Toll, who hates typos as much as he hates central government; Mark LaFlaur, under whom the Corpse flowered; Kathy Crown, who steered a steady course; Lisa McFerren, the current assistant to the editor; and all the good-hearted volunteers who folded through the night, and made delight from drudgery. We are grateful to Lawrence Ferlinghetti, Nancy J. Peters and Amy Scholder of City Lights Books who made *The Stiffest* real, and did not flinch before the enormous job. We inscribe our debt as well to the generosity of the University of Baltimore, our first refuge, and Louisiana State University, our current home. Last but not least we plant a big kiss on all those who wrote us checks when the collection agencies stood poised to take away our desks, chairs and lamps.

Library of Congress Cataloging-in-Publication Data

Exquisite corpse reader, 1983-1988.

  I. Codrescu, Andrei, 1946-   II. Exquisite corpse.
AC5.E95 1988   081   88-1107
ISBN 0-87286-213-5

City Lights Books are available to bookstores through our primary distributor: Subterranean Company, P.O. Box 10233, Eugene, OR 97440. (800)-274-7826. Our books are also available through library jobbers and regional distributors. For personal orders and catalogs, please write to City Lights Mail Order: 261 Columbus Avenue, San Francisco, CA 94133

CITY LIGHTS BOOKS are edited by Lawrence Ferlinghetti and Nancy J. Peters and published at the City Lights Bookstore, 261 Columbus Avenue, San Francisco, CA.

LIVING WITH THE CORPSE: 1983-1988

From the beginning we meant to do harm. Not mean harm, the kind writers do to each other when they exact revenge for gossip intended or imagined, but the kind of harm that promotes health. American literature, poetry in particular, is sick from lack of public debate. Where I come from, Romania, it was possible for writers to fight in the morning papers and continue to do so in person at the cafe in the evening. The issues were not personal: culture was at stake. In the process, feathers were ruffled and persons became indignant. But it was clear to all that literature was bigger than us because it could not exist without passionate ferment.

In the late 1960s when I came to America ferment was the order of the day. The New York poets of the Lower East Side among whom I found myself were making literature against the status quo. On street corners people handed out pamphlets against the war, calls to spiritual enlightenment, poetry written on LSD and mimeographed on speed, esoteric manifestoes and sexual proclamations. That was as complete a world of expressive assault as anyone would have wished. And yet, at the age of 20, even all that seemed somehow insufficient.

To my natural Surrealist sympathies, the Lower East Side in the 1960s was a vast *cadavre exquis*, or "exquisite corpse," a form of collaboration much practiced by André Breton's circle in Paris several decades earlier. To make a Corpse, one wrote or drew something and then folded the paper in such a way that the next person who wrote or drew something didn't see what came before. The end result, when the paper was unfolded, was not the work of individuals but the creation of an *esprit*.

In San Francisco, where I next went, there was intense collaboration among writers, many of them refugees from New York, but the accent here was not on the printed word. Instead of street literature there were poetry readings and experimental theater.

In the mid-Seventies however, collaboration suddenly ceased. The corpse of the Sixties was suddenly unfolded and the huge wings of a terrifying bird descended on it and snatched it away. The age of the "moral majority," cultism, microchips, conservatism, Reaganism, computers, structuralism and curricula was suddenly upon us. The *esprit* was silenced and its practitioners went back inside, back to school, back to work, back to silence. The Outside disappeared. The metaphorical Corpse of rebellion gave way to the literal Corpse of conformism.

At the University of Baltimore where I went to teach in the 1980s they had something called a "Publications Design Department," a graphics lab where students were always working on "magazine concepts." I proposed that we make something people might actually want to read. I had in mind a long and skinny newspaper, patterned after Tudor Arghezi's pre-war Romanian sheet, *Bilete de Papagal*, whose mixture of muckraking and high tone bohemianism had brought down two governments. I wanted to publish polemics and travelogues, capsule reviews, poetry and drawings. The name suggested itself spontaneously. It referred both to the Surrealist game and to the current state of the culture. Even longer and skinnier than Arghezi's sheet, it was designed for reading with one hand in the subway or the bus or at the cafe. It also folded perfectly for mailing, and had the added advantage of being the occasion of instant curiosity when people first beheld its seventeen erect and six wide inches.

After the excitement generated by the first issue, it was clear that the Corpse would soon outgrow the University of Baltimore's "Design" quarters. Several letters to the President of the college and to the Dean alerted these officials to the sedition perpetrated in their midst. Certain words were outlined, drawings circled, articles clipped. We were told to disengage quietly. But a storm of letters from readers and an outpouring of affection from some of America's greatest writers soon convinced us that we couldn't go wrong. By naming our baby a "corpse" we had created something that was generically incapable of dying. We left the University and were kept alive for several issues by the kindness and generosity of many near and far.

By now, *Exquisite Corpse* is a miracle of longevity for little magazines. In business for six years, with only occasional lapses, it goes merrily on its way with only minimal intervention by its editor. In addition to drawing to itself some of the best writers working now, it has discovered numerous new ones, and a Corpse community came into being. There have been times when, tired of its endless vitality, I wanted to run away from it. I went as far as to purchase a stake and a silver bullet. I have even contemplated with satisfaction our always empty bank account, hoping that the end had come. But always, at the last minute, a miracle happens, a check comes, and there is the Corpse again aching to be folded, mailed and read. At the date of this writing we are tenuously connected with yet another university, LSU. We are not published by LSU, nor are we funded by the school, but the editor, who works here, is well treated and we get help with the printing and mailing. But then, it's a rocky little boat we steer in this vast angry sea of religious fundamentalism in the Deep South. It is only the fact that the good Christians around us also worship a corpse that keeps us afloat.

This book should give you a good picture of what we are. We are anti-literary because we feel alive. We are determined to call the shots as we see them. Honesty is a rare thing in print these days. Now and then we are also honest.

Bon voyage!

Andrei Codrescu
New Orleans

FROM THE E.C. CHAIR

Welcome to our first exquisite corpse. We see no essential difference between life and death, so this corpse ought to be as alive as you or I, if not more so. Beyond the literal, however, exquisite corpse or *cadavre exquis* was a collaborative method invented and practiced by the French Surrealists. This is how it worked: one person wrote or drew something and then folded the paper and passed it to the next person who wrote, drew, folded, and passed on. That is the way, we think, we collaborate with culture: at the end of the century, when all our efforts will be unfolded, we shall notice the amazing psychic similarities and trends. We believe both in unfolding *and* in an end to this century. Our aim in *Exquisite Corpse* is to encourage the vigorous activity necessary to bring it to an end. To this purpose we encourage lucidity, seriousness, wickedness, and profound laughter. An occasional fit of the giggles is alright too. Intellectual discussion is at the larval stage in America today: between the boring and the afraid in the academia and the careerist and the afraid in the arts, there falls the shadow of a huge dishonesty. Nobody says what they think, few know what they do think. Especially when people begin to write do they begin to lie. Of course, there are plenty of serious investigators and we mean to be in touch with them. Readers are encouraged to write — we will initiate a Letters column in the next issue — and poets/critics are encouraged to submit. Salut!

— The Editors

THE INVISIBLE MAN TO THE EXQUISITE CORPSE

Cher Cadavre Exquis:
I hate erudition, savage or otherwise. I refuse to be drawn, folded and passed on. Eastern Europeans are too dark, oblique, mysterious and wear funny shoes. Name one Soviet underground writer who has ever slurped borscht at the Russian Tea Room. And I am wildly careerist without shame. I not only lurk in the shadow of intellectual dishonesty, I gambol in it, I sell pencils in it. People who shine in the dark? Honestly, I don't know any. So: your sales pitch is uniformly depressing. I will not collaborate with an enterprise that by its very intelligence is bound to end in tears. Yet I subscribe to your gallant rag. Print one "siren song" and I want my money back.

— John Love

AUTO-DA-FÉ CLAIMS RICHARD HOWARD'S HEIR APPARENT

by David Hilton

Seasonal Rights, David Halpern, (Viking)

The only time I ever burned a book came during the last minutes of the 1970s. A few friends had gathered hearthside for the purpose of ridding America of the horrors and curses that had accumulated throughout the previous ten years. Into the fire went things like a plastic Pill compact, Nixon campaign literature, a Kiss album, Weight Watcher's guides, a divorce decree, etc. My contribution to the pyre was *The American Poetry Anthology*, editor Daniel Halpern (1975). This was a casebook of all that had gone wrong and gotten worse for poetry during that dreadful decade: precious, monotonous solipsism (feebly disguised as isolato melancholy); obsessive technique (all lines broken with surgical precision; the establishment of "you" as the major character in contemporary poetry; "stones and bones" diction and a fondness for self-cancelling lines ("you return to the place you never were"); a great fear of music. In short, poems that crumbled at the whisper of the question, "So what?"

In Halpern's new book, *Seasonal Rights*, the abuses are committed so slickly that they might be called rarefied. Absolutely nothing is at stake in these poems, not even language. Instead, these poems reside in that scoundrel's first and last refuge called "voice." How is it that all the blurb reviewers praise Halpern and his like for their "distinctive voice" when their voices all sound the same? Any of Halpern's poems could as well be a collaboration among a random dozen poets in the *American Poetry Review*. His lines sound as if they've been passed around every important Poetry Conference in the land until purified of all the blemishes: "The old neighbors have passed quietly into the earth"; "Come back, the fields are gone and your friends are gone"; "that sleep is pressed from me"; "In the darkness the black pennies of death"; "They beg for the bodies of light"; "Outside the weather gets colder, then warmer."

Clearly it is time again for The Strangler! If this journal decides to start a "Poems We Never Finished Reading" section, let me offer this Halpern opening: "In one of Watteau's pencil sketches . . ."

Halpern's book serves to remind us of the basic flaw in Establishment poetry today. Call it the Flat Fallacy: the assumption that any banal, grammatical, toneless utterance is "charged" with understated tension and "taut" rhythms.

The Flat Fallacy has nothing to do with the masters of the Plain Style from George Herbert to Charles Reznikoff. It is instead the 70s and now 80s corruption of Image/Persona/Vernacular breakthroughs of our great-grandfathers. Halpern has reached bottom; his directness is evasion, his honesty platitude. Consider the ending of "Late":

I say what comes to mind.
What comes to mind is unsaid —
inflection your sweet device — your profile
at the window the day you turned to me to say
that those who never lie are never wholly alone.
It is late and the night air is fat with water.
I sit with you here, waiting for you to turn
again from that window and talk to me.

Matthew Arnold was much hipper, wittier, more crafted than this. Halpern has a peculiar deftness for the instant cliche ("night air . . . fat with water"). If only, like a Hemingway, he had ever written truly, we could be kind enough to call this stuff self-parody. Unfortunately, with *American Poetry Review* poetry what you get is what you see — the "voice" moving its passionless punctuations across the page, where even an exclamation point is self-mocking: "How much the same it is!" ("Return, Starting Out").

I won't try burning this book. Why not? It's from Viking/Penguin and costs $12.95, and anyway book-burning is a bad habit. This is a horrible book, the State-of-the-Art in America right now.

THE AVANT-GARDE AS ARRIERE-GARDE: RICHARD KOSTELANETZ'S CEMENT SHOES

by Nadia Marin

The Avant-Garde Tradition in Literature, edited by Richard Kostelanetz, (Prometheus Books)

I used to think Mr. Kostelanetz was a kind of professional literary paranoid who railed against the publishing industry and the academic establishment for all the right reasons, with all the right facts but with totally the wrong tone. I still think that, after glancing through *The End of Intelligent Writing* again, a book full of ominous indictments of the tiny cliques that make up America's intellectual taste-ocracy. But while the tone is still totally off, I now know why and have a little sympathy for the man. The reason why he sounds so irritated is because no one paid any attention to Mr. Kostelanetz's pet "literary revolution," namely "concrete poetry," a thing which sank long ago under its own weight.

Now, in an anthology which orders a number of contributions in a sequence which is meant to prove that art is progress and that the pinnacle of progress is "concrete poetry," Mr. Kostelanetz finds his true vocation: that of anthologist. An anthologist, to be sure, is a taste maker, an authority figure and the very prototype of the conspirator reviled in *The End of Intelligent Writing.*

With the exception of two extraordinary essays, classics in their own right for quite some time, this Anthology is ineluctable proof, if any was needed, why the term "avant-garde" should be put in mothballs once and forever. The attic smell of some of these tedious treatises is lethal. The central piece of the book, something called "Literature" by L. Moholy-Nagy, has the same freshness as Nagy's art, which has long been incorporated by advertising.

Moholy-Nagy used to sadly think, until the day he died actually, that his squares and circles were going to revolutionize the world. They only brightened up fashion. The problem again is that the seriousness of this presentation is unbearably academic. What was once fresh is now downright torture, and the reason why the avant-gardists revolted in the first place should be the same reason we won't put up with their own dated pompousness. Italian Futurism, and especially Russian Formalism which is having a great revival today, have been trashed I don't know how many times by history. After Mussolini, Bauhaus, and Stalinist architecture, I see little of interest there, no matter what the wounded cries of being misunderstood.

The two essays worth the book are "The New Spirit and the Poets" by Guillaume Apollinaire, written at the beginning of the 20th Century, in which Apollinaire is totally wrong about technology but totally right about poetry, and "Modernism and Post-Modernism: Approaching the Present in American Poetry" by David Antin, an essay which, despite its title, is invaluable to anyone who wants to know why the boring academic poets of the 1950s (and by extension their present-day epigones) were blown right out of the water by the live Beat Generation.

ACTUALISM — A MANIFESTO

by Darrell Gray
Reprinted from *GUM* No. 9 (1971)

Actuality is never frustrated because it is complete.

The purpose of "intention" is to complicate matter. A material paraphrase is a complication.

Or as Guillevic says, "The problem is to do to things what light does to them."

Typing thru sunglasses is, of course, an alternative.

There is no room for alternative illusions. There is barely room for the table and the bed.

The World has changed its mind. Ice cream is on sale.

Concentration is a problem for those obsessed with process. For those obsessed with stasis, the opposite of concentration sets in, and there is a seeming dispersal throughout all sensory regions.

Where is the missing balance?

Actualism is to Chemistry what Fatalism was to the Middle Ages.

Actualism poses the question, "Of the seven openings in the human body, why are five of them located above the neck?"

Thoughts are concrete things.

Things are characterised more by their conditions than their conditions are characterised by them.

"The useless is not horrible until it is bandaged with truth."

Why belabor the impossible?

THE SURREALIST INFLUENCE IN BLACK POETRY: AN EXPLORATION AND A PROPOSAL
by Michael Weaver

The first Surrealist manifesto, issued in 1924 in Paris by André Breton, was designed to revitalize not just language and imaginative art, but to liberate all mankind from fragile logic and its attendant fallacies. It was a movement that had as its precursors William Blake, the French Symbolists, Arthur Rimbaud, and a young Rumanian emissary of Dada named Tristan Tzara. Surrealism affected the entire realm of all that aspires to be called art. It found its way to the painter Salvador Dali as well as to the Antilles to the pen of Aimé Cesaire, a principal architect of Negritude and the teacher, at one point, of Frantz Fanon. Even today, Surrealism continues to influence modern Black poetry here in the United States. Ntozake Shange has acknowledged it as one of her primary influences; Bob Kaufman, a Black poet, has established a considerable following in France today.

Breton issued a second manifesto in 1930. The influences traceable in each of the manifestoes are different, and so the intentions. The first manifesto shows distinct evidence of the influence of Sigmund Freud, who granted young Breton an interview in 1921. The second manifesto was derived heavily from Hegel, the German philosopher. Fascinated by the dream interpretation and analysis pioneered by Freud, the Surrealists declared that the dream state was a necessary one, especially for artists; for them it was not just a subservient companion to the conscious waking state. Intent upon bringing the endeavors of art to a level with science, the Surrealists embarked upon a journey toward creating a new sense of reality through the union of the dream images of the subconscious with conscious energy. With Surrealism, as Anna Balakian suggests, the creation of the metaphor became "a victory over ordinary existence" (*Surrealism*, 137). With Freud they discovered the importance of the subconscious, and with Hegel they discovered the applicability of the dialectical process to the creation of a new reality from the antithesis of the conscious and the subconscious.

The Surrealists and the Dadaists were the first to recognize and employ as method popular art in their creative endeavors. Pop elements such as cinema and popular music (especially blues and early jazz) interested the Surrealists in their quest for a useful and enlivened sense of art. Andrei Codrescu says of the first Surrealists, "There are many stories about the all-night sessions the Surrealists had where they engaged in 'riffing' or using language so as to make conversation follow the pattern of words rather than logic." He goes on to say about

the Surrealists that, "They liked the playful associative way blues and early jazz approached art, the way it proved functional. They frequented the clubs in Paris that featured jazz and blues." The Surrealist fascination with Black culture especially was also a factor involved in the development of Picasso, an important aspect of whose work is directly involved with Surrealism.

The methods of Surrealism are numerous. Ranging from the automatic writing practiced by the Dadaists and others to their own investigations of the language of the insane, they invented and re-invented in their relentless effort to transcend the banality of accepted reality, to imbibe language with a hallucinogenic quality. With the knowledge of free word association gained from practicing automatic writing, the Surrealists determined that the greatest power of the metaphor was to be obtained only as the apparent disparity between the two realities increased. The Surrealists valued the creative act that made use of the greatest distance between the two realities in much the same way as voltage is created between different potentials in the study of electricity (*Surrealism*, 149).

These unusual juxtapositions of unrelated realities found their way to the Antilles in the work of Aimé Cesaire, one of the three pillars of Negritude along with Leon Damas and Leopold Senghor. Aided by Breton, who discovered a copy of Cesaire's work in a clothing store, the Caribbean poet gained considerable stature among the French Surrealists. Michael Benedikt regards his long poem, "Cahier d'un retour au pays natal," ("Notebook of the Return to My Native Land") as one of the finest to come from the Surrealist movement (*The Poetry of Surrealism*, 342). From "Return to My Native Land" we find these unusual juxtapositions of the Surrealist image:

"As frenetic blood rolls on the slow current of the eye, I want to roll words like maddened horses like new children like clotted milk like curfew like traces of a temple like precious stones buried deep enough to daunt all miners. The man who couldn't understand me couldn't understand the roaring of a tiger" (*Return to My Native Land*, 49).

Negritude became, as Kathy Anderson says, "a reaffirmation of Black values and cultures throughout the world" ("Nethule Classics," 57). It is interesting that as a founder and proponent of Negritude, Cesaire chose Surrealism as a poetic mode. The choice represents a significant and necessary realization for those Blacks interested in the liberation of our people. Cesaire's contribution goes beyond Surrealism and Negritude, beyond the artistic assertions of the young, European writers who sought the advice of Freud in their reflective efforts; his contribution goes beyond all that to the inspiration he instilled in the young, Black psychiatrist from French backgrounds, Dr. Frantz Fanon. The revelations of French Surrealism, with its roots in German psychology and psychiatry, have an ominous significance for Black poets today and should not be taken idly as a chance influence upon one of the giants of Black literature.

Breton and his contemporaries came to rebel against European notions of art. It was their contention that the European notion of art as something to be held in awe by the general populace, something to be hung in museums or dryly studied by literary experts, was in essence the death of art. For them art was alive when it was functional, as in the so-called "primitive" societies. There the peculiar artifacts that were encased in European museums had a usefulness in the lives of the people. For the Surrealist literary artist, poetry had to have a function also, the liberation of all mankind from the deadened assumptions of a reality formed on the heels of the findings of science and technology. Appollinaire, who coined the term, surreal, extolled the virtues of art which was inventive and which strove to explore the "uncertain" and the "unproven" in much the same manner, and certainly with the same vigor, as science. For the Surrealist, art was to be functional as it sought to relieve the psychic entrapment of modern human

beings. Thus they sought the new reality through the metaphorical act of creation (*Surrealism*, 83).

Frantz Fanon begins his work, "Black Skins, White Masks," with a chapter on language that asserts its primary role in the process of oppression in a colonialist scheme. Liberation comes when the colonial native steps into a larger culture of the colonizer. This liberation is at once a "uniqueness and differentiation from the colonial world" (*First World 2*, 3:27). It is in essence a stepping out of the double bind situation in which we, as black people, find ourselves culturally. It is self-acceptance, as well as the beginning of the legitimization of our culture, vis-a-vis our own assumptions as a people. After realizing that the contradictions inherent in Black oppression cannot be dispelled by bantering back and forth between the poles of those contradictions, the oppressed native ceases to make assumptions that only intensify the confusion. He steps forth to liberation after understanding that his identity is within that reality of oppression whereby his humanity has been denied. In a personal sense the colonial native who is a poet makes this realization and makes it work with, among other possibilities, a Surrealist framework. Drawing upon the subconscious and the conscious with free word associations and the juxtapositions of the unrelated, he is in fact liberated from the realities to which oppression has given birth.

In "Return to My Native Land" we can find the sense of a new reality when the images are across seemingly unrelated poles:

Ringed islands, only keel
I caress you with my ocean hands. I swing
you around
with my trade wind words. I lick you
with my algae tongues.
I raid you without thought of gain. (83)

The voice is of the dream state, distinct from a conscious postulation, and it is the voice of the colonial native freed by his own decision to give his imagination full play, to bring the dark powers of the subconscious to bear upon the waking moment. According to Breton, the power of Surrealism is addictive. Once assumed as a literary technique, it could never be forsaken. In the first manifesto, he comments on the liberative force of Surrealism: "This world is only very relatively in tune with thought. . . It is living and ceasing to live that

Allie Codrescu

are imaginary solutions. Existence is elsewhere."

Although it has not been readily explained as such, the Surrealist influence found its way to Black poetry here in the United States by way of several Black poets who participated extensively in the activity of the beat poets of the 1950s. Poets such as Amiri Baraka, Bob Kaufman, and Ted Joans were personally involved in the beat movement and have directly influenced younger poets such as Ntozake Shange. Bob Kaufman is mentioned extensively in Shange's essay, "takin' a solo / a poetic possibility / a poetic imperative." The mode of juxtaposition inherent in Surrealism is abundant in her work:

> i got 15 trumpets where other women got hips
> & a upright bass for both sides of my heart
> i walk round in a piano like somebody
> else/be walkin on the earth ("i live in music")

The stance of Surrealism in Black poetry seems to be an assumed one without the trappings of explicit salutations. Nonetheless, it is Surrealism, a poetry which is the product of a way of thinking designed to liberate the powers of human perception and give worth to matters other than those which are the product of a stymied logic.

There is another young, Black poet who makes extensive use of Surrealist techniques — Tom Weatherly. His collection, Mau-Mau American Cantos, includes "to old elm, in cemetery for confederate dead," in which he states:

> Elm roots grow through graves
> neither desecrate nor revere
> crack the skulls open
> to brace against the wind.

In the death of the cemetery scene, Weatherly gives the elm the power of discriminating life with the sense of worship and the burgeoning of new trees. The eerie feeling of decomposition and life sustaining wind go through the dialectical and become the new life.

What of the younger poets' predecessors, the older Black poets who were active during the time of the beat writers — Ginsberg, Orlovsky, Corso,

Ferlinghetti, Kerouac? Ted Joans — painter, poet, and jazzman — does make overt references to a Surrealist influence:

I stand again before you
this time with my angel of everything
ready for anything
a surrealist soul/sister
("Black Mailed Fetish Prayer")

In a poem to Michael X of Britain, Joans speaks of war with a language of disparate images:

With your blooming marabout beard
made of detonator's wires of Mozambique
black guerillas as numerous as mosquitoes
deadly rendering stings.

The poet's pen moves freely in his work, as it should according to the Surrealist mode. The liberative force here is embodied in a language reminiscent of Cesaire in "Return to My Native Land."

One undeniable consequence of Surrealism which has been of real significance to Black people is that of Negritude, that philosophy which was the handiwork of Cesaire and two other writer/politicians — Leon Damas and Leopold Senghor. Negritude asserts the validity of Black life as it is, calls for the assertion of the Black oppressed soul as it finds itself in much the same manner as the immediate realization known as enlightenment in Buddhist thought. The spirit of Negritude is akin to the novelist Toni Cade Bambera's contention that now is the time for Black people to become "whole." Speaking of her novel, *Salt Eaters*, she has said, "W.E.B. DuBois wrote of our fragmented selves, and our double consciousness. *Salt Eaters* is a call to wholeness. I don't think that has occurred in our literature before." It may well be that the ailing Black soul may best be remedied or healed in the Surrealist universe where every impulse is given creative play along with conscious thoughts to usurp the banality of a contrived reality, and sustain a new sense of being called liberation. For the oppressed Black soul that signifies an end to aimless wandering back and forth between the uncertainty of two cultures with two opposing linguistic representations — one that of the larger oppressor, and the other that of the illegitimate, Black bastardization of "culture." This immediate realization with its air of spontaneity is the soul of Negritude, and could possibly aid the beleaguered perception of Black Americans.

This air of spontaneity is present in America's only indigenous art form, Jazz, or as Roland Kirk called it — Black American Classical Music. Alan Watts thought Jazz to be a way out of the alienated sense of Western technology with its external approach to the so-called "natural world." Watts was a Buddhist scholar, and according to his explanations Buddhism is an attempt to clarify for each human being his true nature. Zen Buddhism especially calls for an immediate realization of this matter, and as a central tenet calls for that same spontaneity of mind espoused by the Surrealists. This is hauntingly similar to the personal acceptance called for on the part of the colonial native by Dr. Fanon in "Black Skins, White Masks."

However, the poet is first liberated, first taken from ordinary methods of vision by the Surrealist Mind. Listen here to Bob Kaufman in *Golden Sardine*, his collection published by City Lights:

Believe in the swinging sounds of jazz,
Tearing the night into intricate shreds,
Putting it back together again,
In cool logical patterns,
Not in the sick controllers,
Who created only the bomb.

There is no room for stiff sobriety in the Surrealist world. Cool world. Cool humor is often the order of the day. It is the air of liberation, the same one that flew over the Antillean heart of Cesaire when he wrote these lines:

No, we have never been amazons at the court of
the King of Dahomey, no princes of Ghana with
eight hundred camels, nor doctors at Timbuctoo
when Askia the Great was king, nor architects
at Djenné, nor Mahdisnor warriors . . . the only
record we hold is our staying power over trifles.

This is the contagion of the oppressed Black mind caught in the insanity of a fragmented culture, caught and driven to dream of a forgotten past while standing in a present of tasteless humiliation — this is the contagion from which the mind of the Black poet can leap immediately and take on his new garments. These are garments of liberation. The existence, Breton said, is elsewhere. ♣

A DEFENSE FROM LEFT FIELD:
2083 POOT NEW LITHIC TIMES
FROM SYLLABLES TO SLABS

by J. Batki

Twentieth century movables changed latitudes (longitudes, attitudes, apes, dudes) fastern weather. Disco Motility came in first at Cain Tucky, Uppity up, paid five sensors on the cryogenic record. Dismal Times continued best seller into next century, when population shifts accounted for more imbalances than glacioaxial slippage. Well into the twenty-one hundreds (past the reworking of discards) language collapsed in a helpless heap, beyond hope of revival, in the shadow of radiocommunicated grunts. Imagism bred silence, social chitchat ruled while words still pre-served a semblance of health. Noise generation took over where words left off: the poetry of cans, bangs, hexametric onomatopoeisms, bare phonemes, in other words, like Doc predicted mid-century, the making of things.

BUREAUS

AMSTERDAM
by Bill Levy

It's been a restless period for me. Last summer we took our first holiday en famille in four years. Visited friends on a farm in Austria, near the Czech border. Fresh air, fresh eggs, fresh goat's cheese, fresh vegetables, wild raspberries and cherries, light exercise helping to build a barn floor and helping out with the first harvest of rye, barley, oats and poppies, in the evenings philosophical discussions — with the aid of a dictionary — over glasses of home brewed schnapps. It did us good. A sidetrip to Vienna: the bones in the catacombs at St. Stephen's, the Brueghels in the Museum, and of course the Ferris Wheel at the Prater swaying to and fro in these small boxcars trying to overcome my fear of heights. To realize a teenage dream I took a separate short trip to Budapest. Oh my God. Have those poor people got it in the neck! Then by Russian hydrofoil up the Danube. On the way back to Amsterdam we stopped off half way to see my German publisher in Nuremburg. He was very charming. Took us all out to a fine lunch and told me how great I was. Took Swaan to the Toy Museum and waited in a cafe across the street so I could have my moments with Cranach and Durer. He also exacted from me a promise to do a booksigning at the Frankfurt Buchmesse. Back home I had to run around making publicity for Dutch edition. I sunk so low as appearing on television with the Chief Rabbi and reading "Call for Chaos." In the old days publishers merely bribed the censor to ban and publicly burn the book so they could sell their secret stocks of same at a premium.

Then in October I was moving again. Frankfurt. Then Paris and Berlin to write ca. 8-9000 words about radical youth for *High Times*. While I was trying to finish this the One World Poetry Festival burst about my head like an ice storm. And Swaan having chicken pox. And Susan having her own deadlines for translating *The Great Gatsby*. I did manage to go to the Festival a few times and talk with some people. Someone should expose that post Stalinist hack Yevtushenko. Babi Yar is political kitch. I was sitting having a drink with Alex Trocchi and someone came up to the table and said: "Alex, you should give up heroin. Burroughs did." Alex looked up slowly and replied: "Thanks for the advice! But Bill was never much of a junky." And yes, Kathy Acker told me of your Frisco antics. From what I'm told, led by Alex, Gregory C., and John Copper Clark the poet's hotel was turned into junk city. A German poet friend of mine complained that in the old days when poets gathered in a hotel the hookers always heard about it and hung out there. In Europe, if you remember, we are fascinated by a sense of, and fascination with, loss.

PARIS
by Karen Gordon

The corpse being one of time's most certain creations, there is another way of making a *cadavre exquis*. Take a sheet, stretch, plane of time and write down everything. Slice it into strips and throw most of it away. Take what remains and paste it to another surface. Evanescent adherences: a succession of deranged days, misarranged moments whose secret themes, obsessions, messages will reveal themselves, a corner of conjunction where you cannot, *en tout cas*, remain. This could look like anything, and that's where the resemblance ends.

Before he painted his celebrated *Coin de Table*, a name which conceals its future focal point — history writing its own footnotes as it plunders its way through its own text — for it is today the corner of this corner which interests us, the corner in which Verlaine and Rimbaud are detached (elsewhere, in *The Esthetic Adventure*, one reads of Verlaine's "suppurating limbs wrapped in vile rags"; here he is impeccably dressed. Rimbaud, in a radiant pallor above the carafe, does not wear a tie, for he has already untied himself), Henri Fantin-Latour made pictures of his sisters bent over books in attitudes of such abandon that I longed to slide along the sleeves and over the hands of these girls, and so enter into the pages on which their eyes are forever fixed. In the Grand Palais, in cafes, the streets, the metro, it is a world of receding voyeurisms, reading being one of them. I watch people read, and am being watched as I do so, the eye of the anecdote always open, scanning the faces of presences, touching with its ubiquitous hands.

"Il y a dans ce monde un plus qui nous dévore joyeusement sans nous voir — mais qui voit parfois à travers nous."

— Pierre-Albert Jourdan (*L'Angle Mort*)

(In this world there is something more which devours us joyously without seeing us — but which sometimes sees through us.)

A high-strung nineteen-year-old aggresses her fashion magazine wrists flapping eyes darting beneath their blue-shadowed lids. At Beaubourg in the bibliothèque (a place where the homeless find chairs) a man beside me is mumbling to himself in Bulgarian as he heavily thumbs his way through a dictionary that looks like a thick Balkan soup. He wheezes and gasps between each word; the rest of us sharing his strange guttural dinner table exchange unknowing looks. At the hotel, Philippe is reading Holderlin and I must wait my turn. The architects pass around Harry Partch's *Genesis of a Music* — space exploring the structures of time. Between Madeleine and Republique a fellow female metro traveller reads *Le Miroir Truqué*, her red painted fingernails in a caress of numb impatience rubbing against the dust jacket which marks and holds her place. I lie in bed reading Ingeborg

Bachman's *Trois Sentiers vers le Lac*, and the man whose head is on the pillow next to mine says "I am the fourth path to the lake" and takes my book away. I am in a bathtub, but the chauffage has been exhausted, so the water is much colder than my already miserable blood. I have arrived at the lake, and it is snowing outside.

I toy with a cup of cafe express on the Place Gambetta, a well-behaved quartier, for most of the people who live here are dead: Apollinaire, one of the exquisite corpses, lies in nearby Pere Lachaise (Father Chair, but no one is sitting on him). Through one of those creepy sensations that are forever crawling over me, I become aware of the stranger at the table next to mine and turn to stare openly at him. As he obligingly or coquettishly turns away his face, I can study his right cheek at my leisure: a poem carved by I know not what sharp and eloquent sort of blade — burma shave haiku? It looks like this but Fenollosa is not available to tell me what it means:

A hearing aid is posed above this very interesting wound, and as I believe it is listening to what I am thinking, I think I had better leave. On the 69 bus from Gambetta to St. Paul, Raymond Queneau's *Exercises in Style* is played out in pantomime, for we all take turns treading on each other's toes and uttering mild or serious yet silent oaths. I am confronted on this bus with another ideogram carved into the left cheek of an imperious and frowning blond. (But even her frown is not of the moment; someone has left it there):

The escalator is ascending, taking me to "Paul Eluard et ses Amis Peintres" now playing in the glass cases at Beaubourg. Between the third and fourth etages, I hear a small voice howling and

Le Bag

Alice Codrescu

at Pere Lachaise. Before me, a black man stares pensively into a window which looks into an identical window which looks into an identical car a second ahead of where we are. He is carrying a door, hugged against his body and giving him a look of borrowed stability. The mirror gets up and walks past me as I chance to turn my head: sudden conjunction in the glass of the buttons on the woman's manteau (like a row of eyes, they look out at me) and a patch of browngreenpink stripes of my poncho, a streak of dull gold hair — before it moves off and out into the night, where so many reflections are glimmering or are about to come into their own.

I notice that in German, my multilingual corduroy pants, made in Scotland but thrown out at me by someone in London, are made of baumwolle-tree wool. Upstairs in the hotel, Edi's library is being built, and all his books, transported from Spain are covered with moutons, sheep. (See Andrei Codrescu's "Books": "death covers me with fine dust.") Books being made of trees, sheep coming to rest on books, forests sprouting fleece, I conclude that my lower garments deserve further study. My hands read the lines in corduroy curving over my thighs, and a mutual understanding is reached.

Why do I have the impression that I am clutching an umbrella as I fall asleep?

In my dream I am visiting a cemetery. At the entrance to this necropolis is a library full of books on the many ways to die. But they are, of course, the ones we've been reading, and the ones we are about to begin. ☠

look into the descending crowd: a man glides past me with his *petite fille* not quite holding his left hand. But this aloof child is not the source of this sound: it seems to come from a large white paper bag her father carries beneath his right arm. I ascend. The moan falls in volume and altitude, and I enter Eluard's worlds, the ones he both acquired and made: notebooks, paintings, photographs, sculptures, masks, books, a post card to Tristan Tzara, Eluard's astrological chart. Leaving, I catch the metro for some by now forgotten evening and event, and, entering the metro car, I walk into a Surrealist tableau. Sitting in the midst of all this wool, sweat and disgruntlement, a black woman holds a large rectangular mirror face up in her ample lap. Faces get caught in it from above as they or it move around. Across the aisle from me, between a pair of knees, grows a large tropical plant. A vacuum cleaner is dragged along like a dog (sign in metro: *Est-ce que l'idée de perdre votre chien vous affole?* — roughly translated: Does the thought of losing your dog flabbergast you?) and gets out

CEREBELLAR POETRY: DREAM AND COMMENTARY
by Rodger Kamenetz

DREAM

My mother and I were walking in a French garden, a careful neat garden with fountains at intervals. We were silent, as though under a spell of enchantment, one of those moments that comes sometimes at the end of a long afternoon of walking and talking in particularly representative weather, a very fall fall day. We stopped and looked back where we had come. A goldfish splashed in the water, an oriole flew from an apple branch, then a coin dropped on the tile edge of the fountain. Three events, one after the other. Then a voice, which seemed to be coming from everywhere at once, said, "All these things pass through the spirit like a single wave through water." I took this to mean that the three events that had just occurred, although they appeared to be distinct, were actually part of a single motion, if only we could see it. And that my mother came from a place where you could see it. None of this was spoken, but it was apparent between us. Then the voice added, "There are two voices. One is continuous and belongs to both of us. The other . . ." I woke up with the sensation that "the voice" speaking with such deep authority was my own.

COMMENTARY

The mind makes its own opium. There are receptors in the brain for opiates, but now we know they are there to receive an anodyne from the brain itself. The mind is self-sufficient. We make our own solace. The mind provides for itself out of itself, relieves pain and allows sleep by making whole what was partial and painful.

Lucretius, who wrote "of the nature of things," thought the mind must be something like a pile of poppy seeds. I love antique science, as calm and self-assured as our science of today, but richly metaphoric and instructively wrong. The mind, Lucretius tells us, "is very fine in texture and is made and formed of very tiny particles." His proof? "Nothing is seen to come to pass so swiftly as what the mind pictures to itself coming to pass and starts to do itself. The mind stirs itself more quickly than the things that stir. But because it is so very nimble, it is bound to be formed of exceeding round and exceeding tiny seeds, so that its particles may be able to move when smitten by a little impulse. Just so, a light trembling breath can scatter a high heap of poppy-seed before your eyes . . ."

The "voice" in my dream had come to speak of the mind. It told me that an idea is really a single wave that moves through the brain, setting off trains of transient lights, details that glimmer, like the oriole, the penny, and the splash in my dream. They are all one movement. It is all one, any idea, a whole and we only spit out part of it in expression, break it off into articulated bits, words, images, pictures, moments: the whole pile of poppy seeds ripples and shimmers, ruffled by a breath. Where do ideas come from?

My mother came in a dream to tell me about my mind, which was appropriate since she had landscaped so much of it. That is why we strolled through a French, not an English, garden; orderly and geometric. My mother's love of interior decoration extended to my inner recesses.

The last day I could really talk to my mother, that is, talk and get some response from her, we spent in a garden. I remember she was in a special chair with a stiff back, like a wheelchair, but with smaller wheels. The pain in her spine, even with the morphine, was such that the seams in the sidewalk made her wince. When it came time to roll over the copper sill that would take us outside, I agonized but I could not spare her the jolt. Her face tightened and she yelped; tears flew from her eyes. This two-inch metal hill was a mountain; the small wheels were stuck and I could not get her over. Damn it, damn her, damn everything, I pushed it, not so much for her, as for myself; I couldn't stand her stuck and hopeless, one set of wheels into the garden. "Mom, are you all right?" Tears streamed down her face. I gave her time to compose herself, then wheeled her down the path. "Look at the white tulips, Mom." "They're pretty." They were the first words she had said to anyone

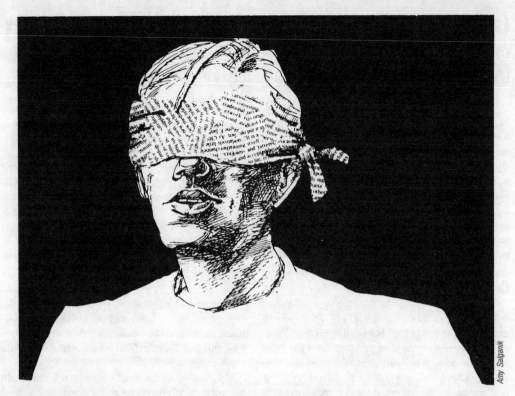

since her long silence had begun, the silence that was painful and mysterious to all of us. They were the last words she said to me. I felt this satisfaction: she had seen them. And they were pretty: white tulips in a hospice garden.

I suppose this event is what Freud would call the dream-substrate, in his oddly chemical way. And it is a strange chemistry that converts a plot of white tulips into a French garden, that changes a reality into a dream and then gives the dream back to soothe the reality. "These things," the voice said, "seem separate, but they pass through the spirit in a single wave." Nothing is separate, nothing can be taken from you, the voice was saying, not your mother, not me . . .

If we spend a third of our lives asleep and a quarter of that time dreaming, that means that two hours out of every twenty-four we are thoroughly locked in a dream. Why do we dream so much and so long? Over a lifetime, there are five years of solid dreaming. Five years: a childhood of dreaming, a college of dreams.

Dreaming begins in the womb and continues to old age. The eyes of the fetus can be seen moving rapidly, and it is believed the brain matures through dreaming, providing stimulus in the darkness of the womb. Inside a mother each of us begins a dream.

The other day, lying in bed, I felt my heart beating for the first time in a long while. I realized how little I live in my body, how much in my mind. My arms could fall off and I might not notice. I'm all head, like a jellyfish, and my body is thin, membranous, trailing off vaguely in the waters.

I was reading Lucretius and was struck by the ancient poet's assurance as he asserted that all thoughts emanate from the chest. "The head and lord in the whole body is the middle region of the breast." His reason? "For here it is that fear and terror throb, around these parts are soothing joys; here then is the understanding and the mind."

It seems odd to me that men went around their whole lives believing that their thoughts came from somewhere between their armpits and their chins. I can't locate my thoughts there, try as I might. I know they come from behind my forehead.

Odd imperialism of the body that gives so much dominance to the head. I've even thought I could locate the origin of some idea, the way a sufferer might locate a headache. The back of the brain is the place for deep gorgeous dark ideas — the front for nimble calculations, piano arpeggios and quick flights of light. This topography seems as real to me as Lucretius's did to him.

Of course, I still wonder, where do ideas come from before I find them in my mind? I think they pass through my whole body like the wave "the voice" spoke of in my dream. Perhaps they rise up slowly, in fumes, from the feet, calves, genitals, bowels, only to precipitate in the brain pan.

This is about as scientific as Lucretius. It is the only science I care to do. I want a certain kind of truth; I want to see things as they are for me. When Montaigne tells us he had his sleep disturbed by servants, "so that I might catch a glimpse of it," I laugh but I applaud the impulse.

There is a kind of seeing that goes back and forth, from refreshment to refreshment, from the mind through the body to the embodiment of knowledge. "When I dance, I dance," writes Montaigne, "when I sleep, I sleep; yes, and when I walk alone in a beautiful orchard, if my thoughts have been concerned with extraneous incidents for some part of the time, for some other part I lead them back again to the walk, to the orchard, to the sweetness of this solitude, and to myself." So I walked in a garden with my mother, and in the garden of my dream. And Montaigne tells us Nature has observed this principle "in a motherly fashion," "that the actions she has enjoined on us for our need should also give us pleasure."

Each body, properly seen, gives us its beauty. We know it sometimes on the beach when all these pasty, burnt, hairy and nearly naked bodies are awash across canvas-colored sand. I have experienced it also in museums. Once, in the Louvre, after hours of statue gazing in the antiquities section, I began looking at the museum-goers with the same ardor. The results were astonishing and sexy. Their clothes fell away and I was surrounded by walking classical art.

I have experienced similar revelations while extremely tired. Mostly, then it is faces. Each face so perfectly genuine, perfectly itself. Which sounds perfectly meaningless — except there is a quality to reality when I am tired: it no longer seems "photographed" but "painted" — and therefore much more intended. This feeling of intention — as if someone had put every face there for my personal

appreciation — is the closest I have ever come to a mystical experience.

In the same way, I saw those tulips. They leaped out at me, they were outlined by the grave facts that surrounded them and made them important: they were to be my mother's last sight, my last gift to her. That much is obvious. But what made them strange was how much they belonged to her, belonged to her death. It was their color in that late afternoon light. They had an odd silvery transparency, like the deadly Amanita mushroom, the White Angel. They were like nothing I had ever seen on this earth. They were ready to be taken with her.

My mother's malady involved a part of the brain I had never located in my imaginings. I knew little about it then but have since come to know it well. The cerebellum — the little brain — is in the back of the head. If you were to cup your hand and place your palm just above the back of your neck, you would find it there. It is gray and mushy like the rest of the brain. It is extremely folded, more so than even the cerebral cortex, and it is considered a very old part of the brain in evolutionary terms. That is, it rose in the primitive reptile brain as a kind of lump riding the top of the spinal cord, and as evolution progressed, it folded and striated and became more capable in its functions. It was the very first part of the brain to specialize, to become something in itself.

It is a humble organ still. It does not belong to the glories of the cerebral cortex, the putative source of reason. Neither is it a source, like the midbrain, for deep trains of images. No dreaming is done in the cerebellum. Its role in the brain is analogous to my mother's role in our family: it functions, the textbook tells us, "to coordinate, adjust and smooth out movements."

Let us say you are moving your arm to reach for a cup of coffee. The idea comes from a higher part of your brain than the cerebellum. But as the impulse is passed to your arm, the same message is also relayed to the cerebellum. As your arm moves, it relays messages back to where the idea came from, but also to the cerebellum. The cerebellum compares messages and decides whether or not the arm is doing a good job moving toward the coffee cup, or whether any adjustment needs to be made. It sends out a signal to smooth out the movement and bring it to a halt at just the right place.

Let us say, though, that the cerebellum is damaged. The arm moves toward the coffee, but no feedback signal is received. A higher part of the brain takes over, tells the arm that it is moving too far too fast, and pushes it back a little. Again the feedback is received; with the cerebellum out, the higher part pushes the arm forward again; the arm swings back and forth, overshooting its mark, overshooting the adjustment. The result is an intention tremor, a sure sign of cerebellar damage. The patient appears normal when at rest, the hands do not shake. But if he reaches for an object, makes any intentional movement, there is tremor.

Malcolm de Chazal, an African writer, wrote that "in the true poet, the cerebrum is a lyre played by the cerebellum." What he meant, I think, is that the cerebellum controls and coordinates all the complex movements of the body, complex movements like walking, running, talking, that we take for granted every day. The cerebellum brings the body's news into the brain and coordinates the brain's messages for the body. Poetry is not purely cerebral. Its soul is the body.

EXPRESSIONIST HISTORY OF GERMAN EXPRESSIONISM
by Lawrence Ferlinghetti

The Blue Rider rode over The Bridge into the Bauhaus
on more than one blue horse
Franz Marc made his blue mark
on the blue scene
And Kirchner cantered through the dark circus
on a different dark horse
Emil Nolde never moldy danced boldly
around a golden calf
Max Pechstein fished in river landscapes
and fooled around with his models
(They all did that)
Rottluff painted his rusty lust
and Otto Mueller ate crullers
as his painting got crueler
Erich Heckel heckled himself with madmen
and thereby foresaw all their mad ends
Norwegian Munch let out a silent scream
Jawlensky made Matisse look mad and Russian
And Kandinsky grew insanely
incandescent
Kokoschka drew his own *sturm und drang*
Kathe Kollwitz chalked the face
of Death and the Mother
Schwitters twittered through trash cities
and Klee became a clay mobile
swaying to the strains of the Blue Angel
Otto Dix drew a dying warrior
on his steely palette
Grosz glimpsed the grossest
in the gathering storm
Max Beckman saw the sinking of the Titanic
and Meidner painted the Apocalypse
Feininger traced a Tragic Being
and fingered skyscrapers
which fell across the Atlantic
(and the Bauhaus in its final antic
fell on Chicago)
Meanwhile back in Berlin
Hitler was painting himself
into a corner
And his ovens were heating
as a Tin Drum began beating

Sam Shepard says in the *Motel Chronicles* that his aunt told him never to go out without his wallet in his pocket. "If you get killed," she said, "they'd need to identify the corpse." So let's begin to identify the corpse now that our second and third issue is out. The letters that follow help. Cioran sees us as a full-blooded corpse, Eshleman says that we are lively and twisty, and to follow Bennett's remark, we look for below zero temperatures and chapped hands. And we also give out Tom Raworth's instant prize every minute, where we can. And basically we are publishing to generate some roving gangs, those rude groups that overrun territory. There aren't many gangs out there now, and those that do exist are prisoners of the terrain. So listen to Sam's aunt and identify the *Corpse*.

CHER CADAVRE EXQUIS

LE GRAND PRIX D'ANATOMIE POSTALE

Thanks for sending it: I like the format. So why don't I write the text for a prize I invented and awarded today to Claude Royet-Journoud and the

P.T.T. franking machine? (I'll xerox the "object" tomorrow.) Here goes:

periods of peace always respect sharp edges (heavy industry), use lemons for current, the lead of a pencil for a dimmer switch. sheffield keeps the extended family with cheap fares. "time distortion in hypnosis" is more interesting than the careful choices of no self-expression. take a dictionary and copy out three pages. we'll catch a bus because we're ahead of fashion. when john lennon was strangled to death by a moonie at altamont the hippies were sea-anchored. no, crew, waiting for quiet. this corruption believes in money; sees us all flat on a screen. drink that tulip as if you need it. a three-wheeled car tootles dixie preferring sable to mink. telefono. *Ptolemy* j'ai de la poussiere dans l'oreille. emotions are, if not antique, then as greasy as collectables. remember the exclusions of love? remember breath? c'e della carta nel cassetto / non ho voglia di uscire stasera.

vide china (with moxie)
xippo liberty
uniform tortures
babble on
cosmos appeal
surplice

interference
contamination
fire
the room shrinks
when even
an unreadable book
is closed

— Tom Raworth

FROM A SMALL TOWN'S ONLY FLOPHOUSE

Cher Cadavre Exquis:
"The shadow of a huge dishonesty . . ." Yes. My name is John Bennett, the creator of and the sustaining force behind Vagabond Press. I've been at it for a shitload of years, since '66, and I've put together a body of literature both as editor and as writer that would not have existed otherwise. I'm not modest, I'm honest. Or make a vigorous effort along those lines. My efforts have not landed me in academia or on the sidewalks of New York, but in this small town's only flophouse. Accordingly, I am writing a book called *Flophouse*. I am a window washer in a geographical location that has temperatures below zero in the winter months, and so my hands are chapped.

— John Bennett

THE NEW CONVENTIONALISM
by Darrell Gray

Reprinted from a pamphlet issued by Sombre Reptile Press, (Berkeley, 1979)

"Therefore a master-piece has essentially not to be necessary, it has to be that it has to exist but it does not have to be necessary it is not in response to necessity as action is because the minute it is necessary it has in it no possibility of going on." (Gertrude Stein)

When I was a young student I enrolled in an undergraduate course titled Understanding Poetry. My Professor was a 60ish, pipe-smoking don — a Shakespeare scholar — and ex-student of Yvor Winters. He had been brought up on the New Criticism, the critical dogma that surfaced in Academia in the mid-fifties, spawned by the Fugitive group of Southern poets & critics such as John Crowe Ransom, Allen Tate and Robert Penn Warren. Our text was itself titled *Understanding Poetry*, compiled & written by Brooks & Warren. The contents of this formidable tome included the old standards: Marlowe, Milton, Dickinson, Eliot, Frost and Auden. Poetic history was truncated therein; this book was not about poets or poetic development, but *poems*. It was clearly a teaching too, and *talking* about poems is what we were supposed to do. The analytical tone of the book was decidedly that of the New Critical approach — close attention to the text; the autonomy of the poem over the personal history of the poet: a complete disavowal of the historical or the psychological mode of criticism. We picked apart "Prufrock" & Robinson's "Man Against the Sky." I still remember quite clearly Thom Gunn's "well-honed poetic observation" *astride the created will*, referring to his motorcycle, which even then I thought contrived. But there was obviously a methodology there: the HOW to write. No works of Stein, of course, were included; in fact women poets in general were conspicuously absent. Our attention was never diverted from the *fact* of the poem there on the page. I.A. Richards' *Principles of Literary Criticism* — required reading — purported to tell us why "objectively" Emily Dickinson was a better poet than Edna St. Vincent Millay. Some conclusions I did agree with, but not because I accepted the methodology. I read the text as a way into what mattered. I was excited by Crane's "dice of drowned men's bones" & "the black ape of dawn." But I also knew that Harriet Monroe was baffled by these images, & digging early issues of *Poetry* out of the SF Library stacks, I realised the conflict between Conventionalism and writers who had a voice. The purport of all this, circa 1979, seems evident, albeit among poets for whom history is remote. Again we are asked to pay attention to a strategy underlying the poet's voice. We are directed to look at words, as I once did, but with a difference; a Program which once seemed reactionary is now codified as the avant-garde.

Steve Abbott's comments in *Poetry Flash 74* are to the point re language-oriented poetry in general: "It is often easier for a group to agree upon what they dislike than upon what they like in writing. Poetry starting with a first person narrator removed from the field of action of the words, a 'privileged I' that exists before the start of the poem, they dislike... The constructed fast-shifting 'I' of Frank O'Hara, the various senses of 'I' in Ted Berrigan, in whose poems one pronoun supervenes or destroys the one previous, they like. Says Larry Eigner: 'I imagines every infinity. I is conglomerate'."

Eigner is absolutely right. To him the poem is not a fossil, esthetic or otherwise. His works are valuable not because he says true things (which he does; his Window poem wholly took me into the object) but the words are clear and true.

From a functional position there are reasons why words in conjunction work, or why getting out of those contexts, i.e. violating the linear norm to get to a necessary strata of thought is important. But all too often in purely language-oriented poems one finds an automatic dissociation. Bruce Andrews' "Praxis" is a good example — the cerebral dryness, the absolute lack of emotive connections. Here we become voyeurs of the esthetic art. Words become fossils, something to disinter and study. Nanos Valaoritis makes the point in terms that can be transferred from the post-*Tel-Quel* school of poetry.

"In France today even the poets disavow poetry.

They gravitate around two electrodes; the *electric* and the *cold*." Electric poets are in the mainstream of Surrealism, or linguistic modifications of its possibility. Cold poets (Pleynet, du Bouchet, & Roche) feel that the possibilities of poetry are exhausted. Their last resort is 'purity': an arid display of verbal pyrotechnics designed to distract us from an absence of content and to substitute for the poem an alien and forlorn echo of the *possible self*. It's this purity that bugs me. Abbot states it well: "To constantly ponder who is present when pronouns are present seems, finally, solipsistic to me. If a dog chases me I will run. If a lover jilts me I will cry. If a government or institution tries to destroy me I will fight. I have no trouble about who the 'I' is in such situations just as I have no trouble about enjoying word play."

Here I am reminded of O'Hara's "Personist Manifesto," an articulation of the necessity for grounding the poem in "what is happening in the world". Of course, we can never be sure of the parameters of that world. We may construct them formally (keeping in mind Valery's statement: "To construct a poem is to construct oneself") or extend them in an equally formal disposition toward language, as in Olson's projective strategy. The self, whether considered as a construct or an extension of codification, is not the issue. A predisposition toward self is what Jacques Rivière in *The Ideal Reader* calls a "biological ballet." In writing of music (specifically Stravinsky's *Sacré du Printemps*) Rivière states: "It is not only the dance of the most primitive man; it is, in addition, the dance before man." The dance before man is not a dance previous to man. It is not a return to a theory out of which dance may have grown. It is, simply, 'the dance before man' — a continuing act in which the terms of human relevance are discovered. O'Hara's poet chased down a dark alley by an assailant does not stop to explain that he is a track star from Mineola Prep: he simply *runs*. The strategy is not to convince, but to *go on*. Where the statement may be reductive, the body carries it; always the act and utterance grounded in emotional necessities.

I think of *all* poetry as language poetry because, in fact, words are the poet's only tools. But now we have a new conventionalism, all the more alarming because it is confused with the avant-garde. To write *properly* now means a radical dissociation of the self from the emotions. Direct statements are

out — the only exception being those grounded in a recognisable non-ego manipulated strata of "language." Are we also to abandon the most essential dictum of Zukofsky: the space of the poem defined by the upper register (music) and the lower (speech)? The point of the New Conventionalism is that it does, as an esthetic, make writing poems of a denatured & mildly inoffensive kind possible. No one questions a bunch of erudite words on the page, properly spaced, for fear of not being plugged into The Esthetic. This intimidation is akin to the old academic stance (Ransom, Winters, et al.); it is finally self-defeating if only because we already know the tricks.

There is another reason for considering the language poets as New Conventionalists: there is a definite posturing, a disposition toward word usage that excludes actual states of personal involvement. I too love words, even random words on a page. The problem is that any hermetic conjunction must have more than simple intention behind it: it must have more than language.

The New Conventionalism in poetry is formal even when it seeks to disavow previous expectations of form. We are made to think more often than feel, and presses such as *Tuumba*, and the magazines *Hills, This,* and *LANGUAGE* remind one that emotions are something people *have*: it's as if we could acquire linguistic properties & the poem, as an organization of those properties, could never be detached. The problem with this, as with any form of conventionalism, is that it is ostensibly programmatic, and, ultimately, boring. Jim Nisbet wrote in the margin of a nascent draft of this essay: "Like riding a bicycle upside down." He went on to elaborate on the kinetogenesis of the metaphor: "You can ride on your Kant likewise."

A cool breeze may be too actual.

To the point here is Santayana's article commenting on Henry R. Marshall's *Aesthetic Principles*, a book of hedonistic criticism largely ignored to date. Santayana's comments, published in *The Philosophical Review* circa 1925, revise his earlier account of beauty in "The Sense of Beauty." The point is made therein that objectification as a term is misleading, because pleasure is always an object of an intuition. It is just as objective as the sensuous image. Santayana says of the creative state: "It visits time, but belongs to Eternity." Eternity and the moment are not mutually exclusive concepts.

THERE ARE NOW MORE MARXISTS ON AMERICAN UNIVERSITY FACULTIES THAN IN AMERICAN FACTORIES! WHAT DOES THIS PROVE?

IT PAYS TO GET AN EDUCATION

Tuli Kupferberg

They are only in conflict when dispositions toward what art may do preclude a "breeze" and become instances esthetically polarised by the mind.

The calculated evasion of human emotion is not new. It once passed for scientific objectivity, and in recent years, experiments by John Cage (Bicycle Work, Rubber) have shown us the environment as a whole can be an instrument, precipitating natural interactions we call art. In Bicycle Work, Cage arranged for bicycle riders to weave in & out of mounted microphones in a large area: the resulting "symphony" of auditory phenomena depended on the reciprocity of the performer/bicyclist and his/her relative distance from the microphone. In all cases the terms & terminus of the event were open. The listener's emotions, however, were not excluded. What seemed on the surface a programmatic approach was actually generative. It made the listener think and feel, not because the construct demanded it but because it seemed natural to do so.

Now when it becomes necessary to suspend patterns of expectation (something that all great art demands), we, as readers, have two questions: *Am I feeling what I think, and am I thinking what I feel?* Neither are mutually exclusive. Thoughts affect emotions, & vice versa. My question is: why should this elemental cognisance be suspended in the face of what some call language poems?

A language poem is composed of words like any other poem, but because of a preconception that poems are better when they make little sense, they end up making all too common sense: *they mean exactly what they say.* How can you question a well-placed "ing" or "influ" when it is spaced properly on the page, and when, as an "intelligent reader," you know these dismembered words have not met an anxiety-ridden butcher's cleaver but the calculated scalpel of an adept language p-o-e-t! The New Conventionalism is precisely conventional because it seldom evokes, but rather directs us to a theory that codifies the act. When we fail to respond to a poem by Andrews or Coolidge, we are directed to the theoretical corpus out of which it was written: we are asked to assume a pre-logical grasp of the stratum from which the poem was lifted. When we literally dig the words, we are told that is not all: you can't have your theories & eat them too.

If the act of writing is grounded, emotional states will be generated. Language should not be a mechanical demonstration of theory. When presented with a theory, the conception of which never touches the reality of one's situation, when it's enclosed in a completely linguistic realm, why bother to write it out? The first three words of any Coolidge poem are enough to demonstrate his theory; indeed enough to reify it. Need he do more? In fact to do more would be redundant.

When we read poetry, at least when I read, I expect not merely clues to the poem's structural imperatives. I expect a voice. If this is not established, all the verbal pyrotechnics of our most profound semantic derailers will not suffice. ❧

A RIPOSTE: 1983

by Darrell Gray
Addenda to *The New Conventionalism*

The *Sun* is a great fusion
reactor. Luckily for us, it is located
150 thousand kilometers away.
Still, poets, joggers, and professors
  get burned by it. Much closer to home
are *words*, and they too wrinkle the skin.
The difference is that we must pay attention
  to words or they will go away. They don't just
crawl under rocks exactly, but appear in
disguised form as poems — some poems.
Maybe the Chinese were spared this.
They very early realized that "atoms"
  represented infinity, and that to a very
  large extent *matter* is made of empty space.
Have the pragmatic cockatoos arrived yet?
Yes! In full regalia! Now we have, in full bloom,
  a verbal rotisserie. Pegasus has been plucked
and witness its wake: *The Journal of Poetics.*
Barthes' sullied knife has cut it to the bone,
  and only *Language* (that skeletal grin!)
remains. There is no iamb, rose, or common
weed left unassailed out here. The great Bird
of Poetry has been roasted on the grill of
semantics! And what do the poets drink
with it? — extremely hot but very weak tea!
In dire fear of mixing their metaphors, our
  "prominent poets" head for the HILLS or
TUUMBA,
  wherever *that* is! The disavowal of all objects
soon sets in. *Ing,* reductionist as it was (is!)
still had blood in it. Now it groans and wallows
on the spit.
My friend and fellow poet,
  Mr. Hilton, knows how
  severe the situation has become.
  The *Talks* go on,
  and there is no forseeable end to them.
Mr. Berstein lectures ON DIFFICULTY,
putting his cigarette out in a potted geranium.
  Mr. Watten talks about PARALLELISM IN
  LITERATURE, dragging in the Russians.
  Never once a mention of Mayakofsky!
Pricks come in all sizes, and so do egos.
Better just to *write* — even stupid poems, than
HOW TO WRITE
  impenetrable shit.
Why don't they shut up? (After all, the commies
  may bomb us.) Where would their stance and
  stranded nouns be then?!
If my wit, or lack of it, treads harshly upon the
  hour, so be it. I leave the woodchucks to their
  doing, and the tinker-toys to their King.
So be it.

John Cage:

Jabal	Just
hE was	walkEd
tHe	witH
Of	gOd
haVe	filled with Violence
nAme	And
He	flesH

This is the beginning of a Writing through the Five Books of Moses

BUREAUS

LONDON
by The Notting Hill Gnostic

Just been to a party, publisher's I think, about Victor Bokris's book *Report from the Bunker, Talks with Burroughs.* He's the new pilot fish. The book must be one of the most pointless ever. Endless dinners and banal chat, nothing like the humour, philosophy and entertainment in Hitler's Table Talk. Poor old Burros was there, grey and feeble-looking. His cult grows fast, promoted by Miles, and the poor fellow is endlessly interviewed by idiots, but has nothing to say, so says the first thing he thinks of — drivel about guns. He's written some lines of good funny dialogue, old B., but not a line one can remember or an original idea. Just paranoid about boys, violence, a typical mid-America mind and attitudes to match, gone a little crazy and devoted to greed and self-indulgence. One can't really blame old B. He was set up, carried along (whirlpooled) and doesn't really know what to say. The Bokris book has to be read to be appreciated. How sad and wretched the cult has become — or always was.

Most of the crew were in attendance, Gysin, D.J. Yawno and so on, all reading at a cinema for a season, *The Last Academy.* Big crowds expected. Not me I'm afraid.

Oh, I guess you didn't hear the sad news of poor Harry Fainlight. Had some kind of illness outside the shack he lived in in Wales. Lay there for two weeks, died, found by a farmer. Memorial services in Brighton. His sister now says she's going to publish his poetry. Now! Oh dear.

We had a good season with the Irate Clone (Ira Cohen), showing his snaps at the Oktober Gallery. He's much nicer than he looks and I found him rather endearing. Decently vulnerable. Christopher Logue and others liked him too — until he began reading, at Michael Horowitz's. Emptied the hall. The Oktober people all over him, feeling a great man in their midst, which he is, after Tambimuttu, resident poet. An old queen at a party reminded me of Dylan Thomas's lines on him, writ on the shithouse wall at the old Pier Hotel, Chelsea: "Tambimuttu black and clappy, Half an inch makes no girl happy" — which is not much but declaims well and stays in the head if rendered in an hysterical Welsh accent. The Clone turned out to be agreeably bookish. His friend, Terry Wilson, ex-Beat Hotel, I think, had a very pretty book published in America on Gysin, and Tommy Neurath of Thames and Hudson is doing it here, he an old friend of Ian S. and believes that all the Burros stuff, all that has anything to it, came from Brion.

Excitement about Peter Blake's retro at the Tate. I'm sure he'll be savaged by critics and this will start a good art row — the best sort.

NEW YORK
by Hariette Surovell

I recently hung out with a group of executives from one of the bankrupting major record companies. A moratorium was declared on discussing the impending 30% personnel cut. We travelled in a limousine from Madison Square Garden, where a company act was performing, to an empty Italian restaurant a mile uptown. The chain-smoking company Head Honcho sat at the head of the table, tasting the wine before it was served. He has an accordion-creased face and the swollen eye pouches of a prospective heart attack victim.

"You should've heard me insult this obnoxious broad by the pool at the Beverly Hills Hotel," Head Honcho chuckled. Then he related a complex joke about "bloody snatch." Mid-way through, a female executive interrupted to announce, "I don't care WHAT the punchline is, I already adore this joke."

I met the Head Honcho during more optimistic record industry times at a listening party for a newly-released funk album which was expected to go platinum. LISTENING PARTY: An album is played incessantly and commented upon by the marketing, A & R and publicity staff as they drink champagne and eat salmon mousse. I'd been invited as a freelance record reviewer for the trade magazines. When only myself and the Head Honcho remained, the caterers boogeyed in their white chef's hats.

"This album gets them out of the kitchen!" Head Honcho cried joyously, strumming a phantom guitar like a teenaged boy.

*

On New York City's first freezing morning, a crowd waited for a delayed E train when a baby-faced Black derelict cheerfully informed an immaculate White businessman: YOU DROPPED YOUR GLOVE! Then he shook his head and smiled, as if thinking, 'Ain't this world sumpin. He done dropped that glove onto the subway platform and didn't even notice.' He grinned until the train arrived 20 minutes later, while we glowered onto the frosty subway track, ready to strangle that fucking incompetent conductor.

*

I'd been editing my stories and needed a break. So I popped into a Greek luncheonette I'd never been in before. I was in an introverted mood.

An old man walked in as I ordered a cheese sandwich. He was given a free cup of coffee by the owner.

"You're a pretty girl," the old man told me, sitting across the counter.

"Thanks."

"Are you married?"

Foolishly, I shook my head.

"I hope you find a rich husband," the old man continued. "A pretty girl shouldn't be alone."

"That's very kind of you," I sourly replied, staring at my sandwich.

"You will if you're a good cook," he affirmed, winking happily.

"Oh, would you just shut up already!" I yelled.

He shut up. And left soon afterwards.

"I'm sorry, he talks too much," the owner told me as I paid my check.

"It's okay," I replied.

"He has no family or friends and no place to go," the owner continued. "So he comes in here all the time and talks too much."

I felt so ashamed of myself.

*

After the junkie ruined my lock trying to break in, I called the emergency locksmith service. A blond 22 yr. old arrived, told me, "You've got a nice pad here, maybe I could help you fix it up. You know, fix your lighting and stuff. I won't charge you no money and don't worry, I won't hit on you, I have Herpes."

ECCE HOMONYM · Jondi Keane

VERTEBRA ADVANTAGE:
SPECIAL FROM THE ROMANIAN UNDERGROUND

by Gellu Naum

trans. by Valery Oisteanu

CONVERSATION IN THE CARRIAGE

With the veil over the face
And with an electric lamp in hand
At the junction of the void

You will see
How the morals of the flat foot
Gives birth to a dramatic complication

Memory out of two who is going to talk
About his dead sister
About his alive goat

9.90

At the junction of the void

A terrifying green fire
With those two supplimentary
dimensions

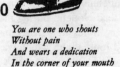

18.90

You are one who shouts
Without pain
And wears a dedication
In the corner of your mouth

And we are standing like two drunkards
Twins in profile
What can we do.

10.90

THE CONVERSATION GREW INTIMATE

Many times, it seems
That at the genesis of the
*   proofs nothing*
It's too happy

12.90

The appearance
I had the impression

That we are in front
Of some elements
Of an answer
Which never were fully conveyed

As in the evenings when
The model-wife
Enters the room of the imaginary lover

In spite of

13.90

Is revealed
The compensatory power
Of great depressive meditations

Or when in front of the tape recorder

Then, the rain
Of the white locust
Strokes her cheeks

Irrecuperable desertion
So many hygienic ideas
Oh! but it's better
To remain silent

14.90

What good are they
The bed-spreads covering the mirrors

To keep telling myself
That nobody is a prophet
In his rail station

Plus
The model-wife
Knows the way indubitably
And everything is happening
On tip toes

I am trying to say that one of
*   the walls is covered*
With paintings representing
Sail boats
On one of the boats in that room

And when
We the witnesses
Preparing the bouquet of the insults
Half asleep
The boat sets off

13.90

When Norman Mailer hits that bell sound at the end of his typewriter carriage he hasn't typed words, he has just typed $2,000 bills. That's typing money faster than the treasury can make it. Since the end of World War II, the USSR and the United States have spent Six Trillion dollars on killing machines, and in the next ten years, the U.S. rearmament plan alone calls for Six Trillion dollars. "Six and one half trillion dollars," says Buckminster Fuller, "is the number of miles radiation reaches out radially in one year, travelling at 186,000 miles per second. That is the magnitude of the number of dollars the supranational corporations are now intent on spending on killingry, at the same time that old people are deprived of their security and children go lunchless." There is clearly a connection between Mr. Mailer and the Defense Budget, a connection best described, again, by Bucky as GRUNCH: The Gross Universal Cash Heist.

In the Art Ghetto whe e we dwell, the inmates seem oblivious. But Spring is here nonetheless.

AUNT PETE
by Paul Bowles

Last night I was leafing through *Exquisite Corpse No. 1*, and I came across a hand-penned note from you which I hadn't noticed when I first perused the paper; the note suggested that I send you something. Accordingly, I got up and wrote the following sequence for you. (The "story" is an exact copy of the original 1917 version. Perhaps I should add that at that time I was hearing a great deal of adverse comment on America's entry into the war, as well as much derisive criticism of Professor Woodrow Wilson; thus in my mind The Lady of Peace was a heroine of considerable proportions.)

AUNT PETE

It was during the First World War and I was six years old. A tradition of two years' standing had it that whenever relatives or friends of the family came to visit, I was asked to read them something I had written. Ordinarily I acquiesced with enthusiasm. There was one woman, however, an "old college chum" of my mother's, for whom I was not eager to read anything, because the first time I had done so she had turned to my mother and remarked: "That boy needs glasses."

With that one sentence she established herself as a definite menace. I had just begun attending school, and the last thing I wanted was to be saddled with a pair of glasses. (Apparently I didn't need them, for I managed to continue without them for another thirty-five years, at which time it became difficult to decipher the print in the telephone book.) Nevertheless, the woman, whose name was Peters, and whom I was enjoined to call "Aunt Pete," continued to request a reading whenever she came to see us, and I was not always able to escape. I knew that her reactions would never have anything to do with what I had read to her, but only with the way I looked or sounded during the reading. "Speak up, speak up," she'd say, or "Sit straight in your chair. You're all doubled over."

Once when Aunt Pete came, I had just finished writing a story called *The Lady of Peace*, and I had to read it to her. The text ran thus:

"One day when the Lady of Peace was out walking, she met a cat.

'My word! What a pretty cat,' she said.

The cat looked at her kind of queer, then said: 'Go home.'

'The idea! I won't,' said the Lady of Peace.

'Hike it home,' said the cat.

'I won't!' cried the Lady of Peace, stomping her foot.

'If you don't go home, I'll make you,' said the cat, throwing some stones.

'After all, I don't think it's such a pretty cat,' said the Lady of Peace, and went home."

Aunt Pete waited, then said: "Is that all?"

"Yes."

"Cats can't throw stones," she began helpfully.

I stood up. "Most cats don't talk, either. But this one could talk *and* throw stones."

Aunt Pete turned to my mother. "You know, that kid should be out more in the open air." ✿

RECEIVED & RECOMMENDED

Becos: Poems by Bill Knott
(Vantage)
Good Knott. An obnoxious acknowledgements page, some awful blurbs on the back and a too-tight editing obscures the pleasure somewhat. The selling of Bill Knott? Does it ever occur to editors in New York that a blurb by Gerald Stern like a blurb by Erica Jong, Richard Howard or Harold Bloom can be the kiss of death for a book?

The Soft Room
by Summer Brenner
(The Figures, Berkeley)
Steamy proze from a red hot youth.

Midwinter Day
by Bernadette Mayer
(Turtle Island Foundation, Berkeley)
Long poem of Self. Daughter of Whitman and Stein.

Mele No. 62
Edited by Stefan Baciu
(Honolulu, Hawaii)
This issue is dedicated to Trost, the Romanian Surrealist poet. Further proves that 20th Century avant garde is the invention of provincial Romanian Jews. This extraordinary mag, edited by the super-heroic diligence of Stefan Baciu, poet, memorialist, journalist and anthologist, has been a meeting place for poets from everywhere. Baciu, who lived in Romania, Brazil and Seattle, before settling in Hawaii, has nurtured exiled writers in here, as well as famous Latin American and French Surrealists. Among the names in this issue: Marcel Janco, the co-founder of DADA, Arrabal, Raul Henao and others.

The Dada Strain: Poems by Jerome Rothenberg
(New Directions)
Hommages to the founders of DADA, esp. Picabia and Hugo Ball. The title can be read both ways, and there are hints here and there that the weariness of a century can affect the lower back.

In Africa Even the Flies are Happy:
Poems by Breyten Breytenbach
(Riverrun/Calder)
Poems by recently freed South African genius.

NOTED & DISMISSED

Lake Effect Country: Poems by A.R. Ammons
(Norton)
Rocks, gases and clouds mixed with mighty communions, prayer-still floors, "tiers of dominance." For pretentiousness, Ammons has no peer. On the other hand, ten names come to mind as we word-process this.

Riding to Greylock: Poems by Stephen Sandy
(Knopf)
The kiss of death is on the jacket: Harold Bloom. Inside are breezes of illness: "A kind of peace spilled," "This raging furnace of the head."

The Pushcart Prize VII
Edited by Bill Henderson
(Now in Avon paperback)
This annual exercise in futility has become an embarrassment to anyone half-way conscious of slime-by-association. We would like to suggest that all decent writers still listed on the mast as editors (even though they have not been heeded or listened to) withdraw their names. This thing is a tacky scam. *(To which we have since contributed!*
Ed.: 1988)

GEORGES BATAILLE: THE SHAPE OF STORINESS
by Welch D. Everman

In her essay *The Pornographic Imagination*, Susan Sontag writes: "To discuss even a single work of the radical nature of *Histoire de l'Oeil* (trans. Joachim Neugroschel, Berkley Books, 1982) raises the question of literature itself, of prose narrative considered as an art form." And she is right on more than one count. Georges Bataille's *Histoire de l'Oeil*, is indeed a profoundly radical work, one of those special books that tells a story (as the title suggests) and at the same time comments on its own storiness and on the storiness of literature in general — both the fact of "story" and the process by which "story" comes into being. And by questioning the literary product and the literary process, Bataille's single and singular novel questions the purpose of literature and, by extension, of the language which makes literature and any act of writing or speaking possible.

Bataille questions the linguistic form of storiness in the act of telling a shocking and yet curiously ordinary tale. In fact, *Story of the Eye* is shocking and ordinary for the same reason — because it is a pornographic work in the classic tradition. As such, it is a chronicle of radical sexuality and violence, and yet it is also a repetition of any number of erotic novels which share its language and structure. Bataille's novel is one and only one of the infinite number of books — actual and potential — that constitute the pornographic text. The author has accepted both the vocabulary of pornography and its progressive form which moves from the most innocent sex acts to the most extreme, building slowly in intensity until it reaches a pitch of perversity and/or violence. Bataille accepts the strict limits of the form, and like Sade, Réagé, and other writers of "serious" pornography, he manages to be shocking within the safety of clearly established boundaries.

And yet, within this given form and even in spite of it, Bataille creates another form and another language which call the pornographic genre and the very notion of literary form and language into question. The story, however, is quite simple. Two adolescents, the narrator and his friend Simone, begin to explore the realm of sexuality together, and soon they involve others in their erotic experiments. Delicate and virginal Marcelle is driven mad and eventually dies because of their attentions. A Spanish priest is sexually assaulted and finally killed as part of an obscene mass conducted by the narrator, Simone, and their wealthy sponsor Sir Edmond, the stereotypical debauched nobleman who is a standard fixture in the pornographic tradition. In time, of course, the universe of the novel becomes thoroughly sexualised; there are no innocent acts or events. This "complete sexualization of reality," as Steven Marcus (*The Other Victorians*, Bantam, 1967) has termed it, is the goal of all pornography. It is worth mentioning, however, that the paradox of pornography is that the "reality" which is sexualized is a purely fictive one — a "reality" of language. As Roland Barthes has pointed out with regard to the works of Sade and therefore to all the works of pornography that have their roots in the Marquis' monstrous fictions:

"Let us (if we can) imagine a society without language. Here is a man copulating with a woman, *a tergo*, and using in the act a bit of wheat paste. On this level, no perversion. Only by the progressive addition of some nouns does the crime gradually *develop*, grow in volume, in consistency, and attain the highest degree of transgression. The man is called the *father* of the woman he is possessing, who is described as being *married*; the amorous act is ignominiously termed *sodomy*; and the bit of bread bizarrely associated in this act becomes, under the noun *host*, a religious symbol whose flouting is sacrilege. Sade excels in *collecting* this pile of language: for him, the sentence has this function of founding crime . . ." [italics Barthes']

The language of pornography is rooted in this primitive act of naming, and it is this naming which creates the sexuality and criminality that distinguish the genre. Thus, the language of pornography, that language which seeks to sexualize reality, is in fact a language which "works" in the pornographic context only because it is not reality but words, and because, in the end and despite itself, it denies reality. Again, from Barthes:

"Language has this property of denying, ignoring, dissociating reality: when written, shit does not have an odor. Sade can inundate his partners in it, we receive not the slightest whiff, only the abstract sign of something unpleasant. So libertinage appears: a fact of language."

The purely linguistic nature of pornography, the essence of pornographic writing as a strictly ordered system of signs, is at the root of a crucial paradox, for the pornographic novel seeks not only to transform the reality of the world beyond language — it also seeks to be equal to that reality. According to Steven Marcus:

"Language is for pornography a bothersome necessity; its function is to set going a series of non-verbal images, of fantasies — and if it could dispense with words it would."

The pornographic work, then, is the text which is hopelessly confined to the realm of language but which intends to transcend language, to become something that does not need language in order to exist. It is on this point that Bataille's *Story of the Eye* departs from the mainstream of pornography. True, Bataille accepts the vocabulary, the structure, the limits, and the storyline of the traditional pornographic text. But he also accepts — and even insists upon — the linguistic nature of his work by interrupting his story again and again in order to reflect on the telling of it, thus betraying the storiness of the story, the fictivity of the fiction. In telling his tale, he continues to remind the reader that this is only a tale and that it is being told in words that were chosen in the process of the telling to generate the specific form of the story. In an afterword to *Story of the Eye*, Bataille explains how the story took shape and even offers the key words that provided that form. "The entire *Story of the Eye*," he writes, "was woven in my mind out of two ancient and closely associated obsessions, *eggs* and *eyes*. . ."

The story itself is generated through the conscious act of bringing the words "egg" and "eye" together in the same textual space. Bataille creates only the association, the link between these two words; it is the words themselves, vibrating against each other on the page, that create the story. And it is this juxtaposition of words that generates and even necessitates the progression toward violence.

Early on, the narrator and Simone begin to use eggs in their non-genital experiments in eroticism. They throw eggs into the toilet or the bidet where Simone pisses on them, sucks them from the bowl, or watches them floating between her legs. She loves to "rest her head on the rim of the bowl and fix her *wide eyes* on the *white eggs*." The italics here are Bataille's; he emphasizes the words in order to define the key pieces in this erotic language game, and once those pieces are set on the playing field, the game almost seems to play itself. The erotic link between urine/cunt and eyes/eggs has been established, and Bataille elaborates on this conjunction which in turn leads almost immediately to violence, a violence which is rooted in verbal association, in the near-rhyme of "urinate" and "terminate."

"Upon my asking what the word *urinate* reminded her of, she replied: *terminate*, the eyes with a razor, something red, the sun. And egg? A calf's eye, because of the color of the head (the calf's head) and also because the white of the egg was the white of the eye, and the yolk the eyeball."

Again, the emphasis is Bataille's. The passage is interesting in itself, for it demonstrates how Bataille's game works through those associations of words and images which seem to be built into our language and culture and come to be somehow necessary to our thinking and therefore to our ability to read and describe the world. The passage is also interesting because it is one of the many that create links, associations between Bataille's text and others, in this case the cinematic text of *Un Chien Andalou* by Luis Buñuel and Salvador Dali, a film which is a complicated associative game in its own right. In the opening scene of this work, a man stropping a razor pauses to look out his window where a thin cloud drifts across the face (or the eye) of the full moon. The man then turns to a young woman who sits motionless and wide-eyed there in his room. With his fingers, he pries her eye open even wider, then slices through the ball of the eye with his razor, recreating the innocent and even beautiful image of the cloud and the moon within a new context of violence. Bataille's text, which also makes an associative leap from innocence to cruelty, plays with this scene, linking "razor" to "eye" and substituting "sun" for "moon." In the film, of course, the eye that is "terminated" is not the woman's. Buñuel used the eye of a cow — Bataille's calf. The association between these two texts is established, and even sexualizes the other. However, though Bataille's text points beyond itself here, it does not point into a reality beyond words or images. Rather, it points into another fic-

tion which in turn acknowledges its own fictivity — the opening title of Buñuel's film reads "Once upon a time..."

As *Un Chien Andalou* is a game that is played out according to the rules of visual/conceptual association, so *Story of the Eye* is played out on the associative field of verbal imagery, and the rules of association dictate the rules of the game. Bataille's work is obsessive, but this is an obsession with words and with the spark that is created when words are brought together. The narrator is controlled by such an obsession, and so is Simone.

"She played gaily with words, speaking about *broken eggs* and then *broken eyes*, and her arguments became more and more unreasonable."

The link between "eye" and "egg" forges a new association to create another playing piece for Bataille's game: "testicle." This association adds the male element to the "eye/egg/urine/cunt/violence" series, thus making the consummation of the game possible. Because of the associative chain that Bataille's text creates, the playing pieces in his game

become interchangeable. Eggs can be broken and must suffer violence in order to serve as food. Therefore, eyes can also be broken, violated, and taken into the body to be turned into bodily fluid — including the "urine" which, through association with "cunt" becomes the female equivalent of semen. Urine/semen provides the transition to "penis," or rather to "testicle" which, as the third element in the egg/eye association is also meant to be broken and eaten. The associative circle is complete.

It is this circle that dictates the story of *Story of the Eye*. Early in the story, the associative circle which serves to sexualize non-erotic language is established when Simone sits in a bowl of milk because it was placed on the floor for the "pussy." Later, she urinates on eggs, but this eccentric though harmless act quickly becomes an act of violation. Marcelle hangs herself after suffering a nervous breakdown as a result of the narrator's and Simone's excesses. The two erotic conspirators find her inside a wardrobe and cut her down. Inspired by this cruel death, the narrator and Simone have genital sex for the first time, lying next to the girl's broken body. Then, following the pattern of the work, Simone urinates on Marcelle's face, especially on her eyes.

"The open eyes were more irritating than anything else. Even when Simone drenched the face, those eyes, extraordinarily, did not close."

Of course, it is possible for Simone to piss on Marcelle's eyes only because Marcelle is dead, and so death enters the game as an essential playing piece which changes the scope of the play. The game now involves violence as a necessary factor. But, in this case, Marcelle's eyes are "irritating," because, though she is dead, her blind eyes are still intact.

The pattern of the text demands a broken eye, and it comes in an arena in Madrid where the narrator, Simone, and Sir Edmond are watching the bull fights. After a kill, Simone says she would like to have the testicles of the dead bull served to her on a plate. Sir Edmond makes the arrangements while the narrator and Simone leave the arena for a moment to fuck in "a stinking shithouse where sordid flies whirled about in a sunbeam" and "where the stench of equine and human urine was suffocating." When they return to join Sir Edmond:

"...there, in broad sunlight, on Simone's seat, lay a white dish containing two peeled balls, glands the size and shape of eggs, and of a pearly whiteness, faintly bloodshot, like the globe of an eye..."

In this case, "like the globe of an eye" is more than a gratuitous simile. It is a sign of equivalence. The meal Sir Edmond has served Simone is a meal of eggs/eyes/testicles. But before Simone devours the balls of the bull, she announces that she wants to "sit on the plate." She has pissed on eggs and eyes, and now she must complete the equation by pissing on testicles. But her strange meal is attracting a great deal of attention from the crowd, and the narrator tells her that she cannot sit on the balls with so many people looking on. Simone agrees, but her frustration erupts into an act of violence caused not by Simone, the narrator, or Sir Edmond, but by the demands of the textual game.

The matador Granero is facing the fourth bull of the afternoon. Bataille presents the series of events that follow in a way that clearly establishes the associative links.

"In just a few seconds: First, Simone bit into one of the raw balls, to my dismay; then Granero advanced towards the bull, waving his scarlet cloth; finally, almost at once, Simone, with a blood-red face and a suffocating lewdness, uncovered her long white thighs up to her moist vulva, into which she slowly and surely fitted the second pale globule — Granero was thrown back by the bull and wedged against the ballustrade; the horns stuck the ballustrade three times at full speed; at the third blow, one horn plunged into the right eye and through the head. A shriek of unmeasured horror coincided with a brief orgasm for Simone, who was lifted up from the stone seat only to be flung back with a bleeding nose, under a blinding sun; men instantly rushed over to haul away Granero's body, the right eye dangling from the head."

The text demands Granero's death from a broken eye, and it also demands that the eye/testicle be devoured. And so Simone takes the eyes/testicles into her body, one through her mouth, the other through her cunt. In doing so, she establishes the equivalence of "break/eat/piss/cunt" and joins it to the equation "egg/eye/testicle." Violence is the bonding agent that holds these elements together in the field of play, and now the rules of Bataille's language game demand that all the elements be joined in a single violent scene. Bataille prepares for that essential scene in the chapter entitled "Under the Sun of Seville."

"Thus, *two globes of equal size and consistency* had suddenly been propelled in opposite directions at once. One, *the white ball* of the bull, had been thrust into the 'pink and dark' *cunt* that Simone had bared in the crowd; the other, a *human eye*, had spurted from Granero's head with the same force as a bundle of innards from a belly. This coincidence, tied to *death* and to a sort of *urinary* liquefaction of the sky, first brought us back to *Marcelle* in a moment that was so brief and almost insubstantial, yet so uneasily vivid that I stepped forward like a sleepwalker as though about to touch her at *eye* level."

Here the italics are mine — an attempt to point out how and where the playing pieces have been placed. "Marcelle" returns, not as a character, of course, but as a name that is linked to both "eye" and "death." The field of play is ready for the final configuration of elements, the final moves of the game.

The narrator, Simone, and Sir Edmond go into a Spanish church, capture and bind the priest, Don Aminado, and assault him in a four-party extravaganza. Then, to the priest's horror, Sir Edmond takes the key to the tabernacle, finds the eucharistic host and chalice, and uses them to conduct his own version of the mass. As Sir Edmond explains:

"The host, as you see, are nothing other than Christ's sperm in the form of small white biscuits. And as for the wine they put in the chalice, the ecclesiastics say it is the *blood* of Christ, but they are obviously mistaken. If they really thought it was the blood, they would use *red* wine, but since they employ only *white* wine, they are showing that at the bottom of their hearts they are quite aware that this is urine."

It is the priest who is forced to piss in the chalice and come on the hosts in the ciborium. Then Sir Edmond strangles him. Again, the narrator is fascinated by the staring, lifeless eyes of the dead man. So is Simone.

"Do you see the eye?" she asked me.

"Well?"

"It's an egg," she concluded in all simplicity.

"Okay," I urged her, extremely disturbed, "what are you getting at?"

"I want to play with this eye."

"What do you mean?"

"Listen, Sir Edmond," she finally let it out, "you must give me this eye at once, tear it out at once, I want it!"

Sir Edmond does as she asks, and while the narrator and Simone fuck beside the body of the priest, he slips the eyeball between her buttocks. The narrator spreads Simone's legs, and what he sees brings all the elements of Bataille's novel together in a climactic vision made necessary by the author's initial choice of words and by the rules of the game.

". . . in *Simone*'s hairy vagina, I saw the wan blue eye of *Marcelle*, gazing at me through tears of urine. Streaks of come in the steaming hair helped give that dreamy vision of disastrous sadness. I held the thighs open while Simone was convulsed by the urinary spasm, and the burning urine streamed out from under the eye down to the thighs below. . ."

The game is done. Bataille's world of language closes in on itself and completes itself by playing out all the permutations of the fundamental words and the associations which first brought them together. This is the key to the structure of *Story of the Eye* — the necessity to follow the chain of associations to its conclusion. The story itself, the movement from simple eroticism to debauchery, violence, and murder, is generated by this necessity of language, the system which speaks itself into being. It is the shape of the language that creates Bataille's fictive world.

But Bataille suggests that it is language, fiction, which creates the real world as well, the world where real people live and play out their own real stories. As he wrote in his forward to the 1957 edition of his novel, *Blue of Noon* (translator Harry Matthews, Urizen Books, 1978):

"To a greater or lesser extent, everyone depends on *stories*, on *novels,* to discover the manifold truth of life. Only such stories, read sometimes in a trance, have the power to confront a person with his fate. This is why we must keep passionately striving after what constitutes a *story*. . ."

The conclusion here is that *Story of the Eye* and every story — those we read and those we live — are constituted by the play of the language which describes every world, whether fictive or real. The form of our language, the form we impose on reality, creates, even necessitates, our plots, our history. All the possibilities of our lives are already present in our words, in the play of our language — even violence and death which unfold of necessity in our history once the play of words and associations is begun. To strive after "what constitutes a *story*," as Bataille demands, is to try to understand how this play of language works and how the traditional, automatic forms of storiness — even those stories which force violence into our world — might be broken, disrupted, making possible a new history, perhaps even a history of salvation.

EIGHT-POINT PROCLAMATION ON THE POETIC ACT

by H. C. Artmann
Translated by Anselm Hollo

There exists in this world one irrefutable statement: to wit, that it is possible to be a poet without ever having written or otherwise uttered a word.

The prerequisite, however, is a more or less conscious desire to act poetically. The a-logical gesture itself, thus performed, can be elevated to an act of remarkable beauty, indeed, to a poem. Beauty, admittedly, is a concept to be understood in a definitely expanded sense in this context.

1. The poetic act is that poetry which rejects any secondhand transmission, i.e., any reproduction by means of language, music, or writing.

2. The poetic act is poetry for sheer poetry's sake. It is sheer poetry, and devoid of all hankering for recognition, praise, or criticism.

3. A poetic act may be revealed to the public only by accident: however, this occurs only in one case out of a hundred. To safeguard its beauty and integrity, it is essential not to have it take place with an eye to public disclosure, as it is an act of the heart and of secular modesty.

4. The poetic act is a fully conscious improvisation. It is everything but a mere poetic situation — which would not call for a poet at all. Any idiot might wander into one of those, without ever becoming aware of it.

5. The poetic act is the striking-of-a-pose in its most noble form, devoid of all vanity, replete with joyful humility.

6. Among the most venerable masters of the poetic act we number, in the front rank, satanistic-elegiac C.D. Nero, and, above all, our lord, the philosophically human Don Quijote.

7. In material terms, the poetic act is totally worthless, and therefore never blighted with an incipient germ of prostitution. Its uncompromising realization is downright noble.

8. The accomplished poetic act, recorded in our memory, is one of the few treasures we can indeed carry with us irrevocably and forever.

1953

BERLIN

by William Levy

One of the most important cultural phenomena in Europe has been German New Wave music. Its center of gravity is this haunted, divided city.

Moving away from the Wall, I pass over the Landswehr Canal where Rosa Luxembourg was murdered. Then down the Grossbeeren Strasse to number 50, *Scheissladen.*

This is a rendezvous point of the New Music scene. *Scheissladen* (Shit Shop), is an independent record store: It stocks music produced only by the musicians themselves. Judging from the amount of homemade cassettes it is an active scene. On the walls, there are posters for Aggressive Rock Productions offering the public LPs from *Slime, Yankee*

Raus and *Daily Terror.* Another group of united artists from suburban Spandau offer a sampler of *Soylent Grun, Dreidimensional, Mob, Leer.* I speak with Norbert, the founder and owner, a genial lad wearing a 1962 brown suit and silver wire-rimmed glasses. We go into the back room which serves also as his kitchen and bedroom.

"Berlin is the cultural capital of Germany in everything," he says. "It's a magnet for young people, especially because of its political situation. It's the only place in *all* Germany without conscription."

"Tell me about the New German music," I ask. "In the past few years *Neue Deutscher Welle* has taken pop music by storm!"

Norbert hands me a chipped ceramic mug of instant coffee. "Well, yes . . . ," he says, and explains: "At first the music was a copy of English and American. In the English language. In 1977 Punk came, everywhere, and in Germany too. The German groups got more confidence. The *Neue Deut-*

scher Welle begins, however, with DAF, or *Deutsch-Amerikanisce Freundschaft* (German-American Friendship) — their death and suicide song called "Mussolini" had everyone dancing last year. Also *Fehl Farben* (Missing Colors). And the *Ideals* — they made their first record themselves, in one thousand copies, and it was sold out in two weeks. In fact all the groups started as independents. *Der Plan* has refused to go with record companies. They are very popular. And the split came with DAF when they signed a contract. Two of them left the group. The bass player to *Fehl Farben*, the guitar player to *Mau Mau*. *Tempo* had a contract with Polydor, then went back to home productions. *Einsturzende Neubauten* (Collapsing New Buildings) began as selftapers making their own cassettes. Now they are number one in Berlin, in Germany, in Europe, and tomorrow the North Pole! *Malaria* is number two. That's a group of five women. Over the music, they scream: *"Achtung! Achtung! Achtung! Geld! Geld! Geld!* (Attention! Money!). *Interzone* sings the poems of Wolf Wondratschek, Germany's most popular poet since World War 2. *Slime* is more concrete political: songs about police and demonstrations. The texts of other groups are about sex and drugs and drugs and all situations of life.

Then there are the performances. The lead singer of *Didaktische Einheid* (Didactic Unit) comes on stage wearing a large baby's diaper, covered with mud, looking like poop. He throws mud at the audience and by the end of the evening many people are rolling in it. When it gets heavy, we are all very glad!"

I ask: "Are there any new, exciting groups coming out?"

Norbert goes out front and returns with a record. "This!" he says. "It's by *Die Todliche Doris* (The Deadly Doris). They just flew off to Paris this morning — to be the supporting act for *Einsturzende Neubaten* at the Festival Autonome."

Not only are these groups popular but they have been embraced by the highest art circles. "This is *Todlische Doris*'s first LP, and it was banned. They are three in the group — men play bass and accordion and a woman plays drums," Norbert tells me, and then puts it on the record player. The first side is like a noisy radio drama. They describe seven accidents that could happen at home, in horrifically explicit detail and complete with

screaming. On the other side they sing: "Better no heart/Than a heart of paprika!"

"But the *Neue Deutscher Welle*," Norbert tells me sadly, "is in a transition period. People are confused about what to play, or listen to — especially after its unexpected enormous success."

Trio is the case in point. Three musicians living quietly in a town near Hanover. They made a single called, *Da Da Da I don't love you/You don't love me aha aha aha!* Feeling themselves to be isolated artists they printed their address and phone number on the record sleeve, hoping someone (out there) would respond. The song became a smash hit. It sold over six hundred thousand copies. Their phone didn't stop ringing twenty-four hours a day. So they had to disconnect it and move to another house.

The language of prophecy and absurdity as a world-view. For the last few years young German musicians have been playing what could pass as soundtracks for Der Golem — those great silent films of the Twenties. If Weimar is upon us, can the Third Reich 'n Roll be far behind?

Back in the car, I turn on the radio: They are playing a song from *Grauzone* (Gray Zone), one of Germany's New Wave groups:

> *Ich Mochte ein Eisbar sein*
> *am kalten Polar*
> *dann musste ich nicht mehr wein*
> *alles war so klar!*
> *(I want to be a polar bear*
> *in the cold arctic*
> *then I wouldn't have to cry anymore*
> *everything would be so clear!)*

People are trying to cheat us by passing off their poems as critical statements. Since January we've received no less than five thousand poems, accompanied by mash notes about the *Corpse*. Why do you think we started this rag in the first place? Precisely because everyone is so damn evasive, uncritical and sneaky, unwilling to say anything — except drunkenly in conversation, or allusively in poems. The effect of all this regurgitated poesy on the staff has been positively dolorous — to the point where we're closing down the form. The *Corpse* is hereby immune to the maggots of poetry.

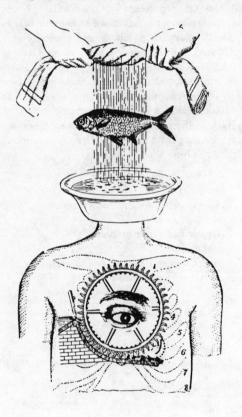

RONNIE BURK
COLLAGE CITY
PROJECT. 1983

HELEN OF TROY
by Nanos Valaoritis

In reality Helen of Troy's name was Helen of Ploy. Not Play as some think. She was too stiff to be toyed with. She was, if it is permitted to say it, an idol. A matinee idol. Marilyn Monroe claimed her and came close to impersonating the fickle Goddess. But she was left behind by playwriting. Sad story, she hanged herself from a tree in Rhodes. Did she deserve it? Her brothers recovered the statue when Theseus stole it. No fool Euripides when he claimed that's what Paris took. He took it to Rome with him but it was too soon for the British Empire to be born. Lord Chesterfield did that for him later. He invented the cigarette. Do we have to, by all means, define it in a sentence? Discuss Coleridge's use of repetition in the mire of the Ancient Mariner. Not a single word of the speech was ever opened later than five o'clock, closing time. Thunder or Light, bellowed the priest coming out of the cave? Half of them said Yes, while the other half chose Thunder. Both were very blunt until they grew up to become even tougher. Imitative magic? Yes by all means. Not by only a few. Not by only a few. You rascal, you know all the answers. Except one. What was that? Are the heroes of Homer plain and simple homespun country folk ploughing the rivers of their underworlds with their delirious imagination? Yes. And the rain of fertility and the powercuts caused by lightning, made pigs out of us all. Birds of prey meant to revive the forces of nature, sleeping their beauty sleep. Heroines of a single furrow. Heroes of the central frown on the brow. God's fertilizers, collective chemicals. Do battles imply all the people or only some of the people? Anything cut in two would still be an Epic even if it is only a worm! Have you decided which? Don't laugh please it'll make the others angry. By which I meant Paradise may be lost again, next time around.

BOREDOM OF THE ETERNAL RETURN

by Nadia Marin

The Wheel, Wendell Berry, (North Point Press)

I dreamt about death after I read *The Wheel*, and death was very still in my dream, and mad at me. Death said: "I won't be your friend anymore," but I knew that it was only a tiff, that soon we would make friends again. Death, in *The Wheel*, is a familiar. When people die, in Berry's world, they become part of the earth they loved. The wheel of life and death turns, and, at times, the dead return:

> *"Sorrow is gone from them.*
> *They are light. They step*
> *into the steps of the living*
> *and turn with them in the dance*
> *in the sweet enclosure*
> *of the song, and timeless*
> *is the wheel that brings it round."*

This little book of requiems, sadnesses and returns, is vintage Berry. There is a quietness at the center of the work, the silence of the labourer on the soil, tired at twilight, looking over the fields where he was born and where he is going to die. There is also, as in his other works, an undercurrent of stubborn propaganda for the backwoods virtues, that never fails to get on my nerves. In the undeniable pathos of that tired worker there functions both a cliche and a truth. The cliche is in the pose itself, and in the unshakeable belief that the soil is divine, and that cities are evil. The truth is that, for anyone who truly feels it, an undeniable connection with the universe is made.

Here is the pose:

> *"We stood on a height,*
> *woods above us, and below*
> *on the half-mowed slope we saw ourselves*
> *as we were once: a young man mowing,*
> *a boy grubbing with an axe".*

And then Paul Bunyan wastes no time heading for the cliche:

> *I wish, I said, 'that we could be*
> *back in that good time again'. And the truth:*
> *The time and place so near,*
> *we almost* were *the men we watched.*

Wendell Berry has been an effective spokesman for the ecological movement. His poems, essays on agriculture and environment, have made him many well-deserved fans. And yet, the constant humility and the predictable sad monotony of the "quiet" life, make me wish I was as far from the place he describes as possible. In Paris, maybe.

SAPPHO ON EAST SEVENTH

by Ed Sanders

Goat horns
    were hard to get
        on the Lower East Side
so he carved the arms
    from the legs
        of an arm chair
           found in the street

and a thin rounded sounding board
cut he   (from a spruce wood shingle)
    to fit
        on the shell

The cross bar from arm to arm
had tuning pegs from
        an antique broken banjo
          found in the trash
           of a burned out store

A bridge he
    shaped & notched
        from an ebony comb

    and when he had built one
    with which he could sing
    he scribed it with Sappho's

"Come my sacred lyre
make yourself sing"

TAKE A DEEP BREATH — ONE
by David Hilton

The Changing Light at Sandover, James Merrill, (Atheneum)

"Your mind and you are our Sargasso Sea"
— E.P., *Portrait d'une Femme*

This strange brick of a book, pushing 600 pages, requires before comment some deep taking in of breath, as when a cliff-diver stares down at the distant, shifting inlet of the sea into which he will momentarily plunge — hence, thank you, this sentence. Now, since this is a book whose central device is occultist (25 years of Ouija board messages), I should confess at the outset to certain biases. For instance, I believe that the giant cabbages and carrots grown at Findhorn were entirely the result of hyper-intensive composting and soil-building, achieved by devotees who endlessly gleaned the parsimonious north coast of Scotland for every scrap of organic decay, including human shit. The Findhornian lady whose specialty was to converse with the plants ("Act quickly," said the spinach-diva, "the zucchini is choking from too much lime!"), I regard as an especially charming zany, of the classic British type. As currently marketed and practiced, the occult is overloaded with pseudo-systems and gadgetry, so that it seems to complement rather than oppose today's soulless high-tech world. An acquaintance in New Jersey just bought his wife an Apple computer so that she could turn out customers' astrology charts more rapidly. I have gazed into friends' crystal balls and have sat hunched within the aluminum frame of a "pyramid." I have donated hair and nail clippings, spit, blood and tears to various little boxes and phials. I have submitted to a Reflexologist who placed plastic bags of chopped celery, broccoli, radishes, etc. all over my body in order to discover various points of malaise. I have even put in some hours nudging the tiny tripod table across a dumbstruck Ouija board, trying to get it to spell out something spooky. And I have not believed in any of it for a minute.

So it was not with wondrous anticipation that I turned to Jame Merrill's vast literary curiosity: a long-poem of some 20,000 lines composed mainly of dictation from the spirit world (in telegram upper-case), conveyed via the Ouija board by various garrulous "familiars," among them a butler-type named Ephraim, who acts as a social secretary; a voice called 741, who midway supplies a rather trite origin myth; and, most notably, W.H. Auden, who (the corpse still scarcely cold in its grave) turns out to be the most chatty ghost *(WE DO NOT SEE THE LIGHT MY DEAR, / ONLY ITS EFFECT ON ATMOSPHERE)*.

Credulity is not enhanced by the knowledge that Ouija's pedigree in occultism is considerably less than upper crust. The board was invented around 1920 by the Fuld brothers, Isaac and William, of Baltimore, and was an immensely popular parlor diversion through the '30s, competing with miniature golf, marathon dancing, and barbershop jawing, to give cheap funtime to the Depression masses. Then during World War II, Ouija acquired a new sombreness. What had been a craze took a turn toward craziness as thousands of families sought through the board to contact their young men killed in the war. Now, with Merrill's tome, the Ouija board has engendered what may be the looniest epic enterprise in the history of American literature, beside which even Melville's unreadable *Clarel* seems a model of compression and coherence.

With a "new coda," *The Changing Light at Sandover* comprises three books (long, longer, and longest) published in '76, '78 and '80 to the increasing ecstasy of the Big Critics. Harold Bloom (inevitably) has read the work "some dozen" times and says he still cannot overpraise it. Other critics compare the poem's cultural centrality to that of *The Waste Land* and put Merrill in company with Dante, Homer, Milton, and Blake. Naturally the Explaining Industry is overjoyed — here is a huge, newly-discovered, trackless jungle continent just waiting to be looted, mined, stripped, and reprocessed into the intellectual styrofoam of countless theses, learned-journal explications, conference papers — in short, here is a store of raw *career* material that seems, like coal deposits, to be inexhaustible. I picture Merrill a happy Kurtz enjoying the spectacle

of boatloads of critics, sunk to the gunwales, pushing up murky and narrowing rivers.

In fact, what this book is, is a grand mess. Occult and magical media (as sharply distinguished from mystical receptivity) seem unable to function without their tediously elaborate systems of numbered hierarchies and geometrical terrains. And thus it is in Merrill we get the spirit realm described in terms of carefully enumerated worlds, stages, phases, degrees, properties, elements, contracts, junctions, sections, rules, books, moons, suncycles, etc. The overall impression is of a weird mechanical drawing class projected on a vague cosmic scale. Merrill's interlocutors also cannot operate outside of triangles, inverted cones, pyramids, pentagrams, quadrants, and of course dualisms. *(THE MALE REIGNS IN NUMBER, THE FEMALE IN NATURE.)* So much pedantic precision eventually becomes its putative opposite, arbitrariness, and the whole edifice falls apart like an overwrought tinker-toy design.

Structural chaos does have one great advantage — we never know who will show up next nor with what revelatory tidbit we will be next amused. Ephraim, the old-reliable familiar, screens the guests very carefully, admitting only those of Merrill's class and breeding. In addition to "Wystan," we hear from Pope, Wallace Stevens, Montezuma, Lord Byron, Nabokov, Gautama Buddha, Yeats, Robert Lowell, Akhnaton & Nefertiti, and many other VIPs, including Merrill's recently departed dog and cat. And the gossip is often delicious — Mozart is living now as a black rock star; Montezuma is now a German astrophysicist; Rimbaud ghost-wrote *The Waste Land.* So the book is sporadically fun. The most comical moment finds the newly-dead Chester Kallman lamenting his imminent "cloning" (reincarnation) back to earth as a black African, while Merrill tries to cheer him up:

> *FANCY A NICE JEWISH MS LIKE ME*
> *(Chester after dinner) GETTING THE*
> *ULTIMATE REJECTION SLIP IS GOD*
> *CYRIL CONNOLLY? But you're coming*
>   *back,*
> *It's too exciting! PLEASE TO SEE MY*
>   *BLACK*
> *FACE IN A GLASS DARKLY? I WON'T BE*
> *WHITE WONT BE A POET WONT BE*
> *QUEER CAN U CONCEIVE OF LIFE*
>   *WITHOUT THOSE 3???*

> *Well, frankly, yes. THE MORE FOOL U MY*
>   *DEAR*
> *You shock us, Chester. After months of idle,*
>   *Useless isolation — ALL I HEAR*
> *ARE THESE B MINOR HYMNS TO*
>   *USEFULNESS:*
> *LITTLE MISS BONAMI OOH SO*
>   *GLAD*
> *TO FIND ARCADIA IN A BRILLO PAD!*
> *LAUGH CLONE LAUGH AH LIFE I FEEL*
>   *THE LASH*
> *OF THE NEW MASTER NOTHING NOW*
>   *BUT CRASH*
> *COURSES What does Wystan say? TO*
>   *PLATO?*
> *HAVING DROPPED ME LIKE A*
>   *HOT O SHIT*
> *WHAT GOOD IS RHYME NOW Come,*
>   *think back, admit*
> *That best of all was to be flesh and blood,*
> *Young, eager, ear cocked for your new name*
>   *— MUD*

But Merrill is not just playing the fool. While he weaves in every possible concept — time, space, light, sex, politics, imagination, love, mishmashing dozens of others — and while his "carpet" is an enormous, raggedy, shapeless sprawl, we can still detect a faint, elusive figure in it. He *is* up to something. It is a powerful, profound theme, and one wishes he had had the nerve to grasp it firmly and cut the opus by about 19,000 lines, retaining the great potential poem all but buried in the book: a stirring meditation on nuclear energy. Merrill's no fool, but he is a tease — he flirts with this theme *(SHAKESPEARE NOW A TEENAGE NUCLEAR PHYSICIST)* but never embraces it. He asserts an evolutionary, material (or mock-spiritual) cosmology whose foundation rests on the power of the atom, but Merrill never shows the will to take the vision into himself and as a poet find the *maker's* means, the imaginative construct that would order the theme symbolically, mythically and narrationally. He comes close to real artistic control of this concept in the shorter first book (92 pages, a flawed but impressive performance). His dead mother speaks about how her radiation therapy has burned her soul and made reincarnation more difficult. This connects with the poet's sense of mortality that rises as he evokes that beginning time, 1955, when he and his friend David Jackson first began their mistily erotic communions over the Ouija board, carrying the board around the world, young men seeming to have no home except within the energy they mutually created, while "outside" so many were dying. There is at this point an elegiac tone, a sense of dramatic tragedy developing under the control of an artist who knows the difference between his themes and his apparatus. The Ouija board is still Merrill's grand metaphor. Not taken very seriously in itself, it provides both gravity and humor for the poet who uses it as a medium of his imagination. The nuclear theme is focused instantly in the first book when Ephraim reveals:

> NO SOULS CAME FROM HIROSHIMA U
> KNOW
> EARTH WORE A STRANGE NEW ZONE
> OF ENERGY
> Caused by? SMASHED ATOMS OF THE
> DEAD MY DEARS
> *News that brought into play our deepest fears.*

Alas, the next 500 pages have nothing to equal that. The subsequent pronouncements upon nuclear cosmology sound melodramatic, didactic, banal.

One suspects that some of his hocus-pocus voices are Merrill's way to escape from dealing with his themes imaginatively. Furthermore, expressed as Ouija "teachings," the messages are simply commonplace. Anyone who has read just one or two of the current excellent popularizers of the physical sciences — Robert Jastrow, Lewis Thomas, Carl Sagan, Stephen Jay Gould, *et al.* — knows all this and much more, and knows it as lucid truth, not redundant gibberish.

Merrill is a gifted formalist poet. He can write gorgeously in his own voice. Even when the poetry amounts to little more than interior decorating, it usually displays the best sumptuous taste. His musical variations with blank verse and rhyme recall Stevens (clearly his hero) and Wordsworth. But in *Changing Light at Sandover* this narrow but deep gift is squandered. The mind is impoverished here. The mock magic of the Ouija board has driven out the authentic magic of poetry. For us, the really gripping subject of this book is its own monstrous failure. ☠

TAKE A DEEP BREATH — TWO
by Tom Clark

The Changing Light at Sandover, James Merrill, (Atheneum)

The invocation of ultra-dimensional beings, some of whose power and knowledge would hopefully transmit itself in verse, became Merrill's principal poetic pursuit in the mid-1970s, when he began making poems about his long experience with spirit-raising and table-tapping. In these poems, Merrill's use of Ouija board iterations is a device for contacting "higher" realms of being, and thus ascending, Jacob's ladder-style, beyond the limits of mortality — against which romantic poetry, with its worship of "inspiration," perennially surges.

With his "topsy turvy" teacup pointer — a willoware cup — "waltzing" on the alphabet board, Merrill summons his first being-from-beyond in "The Will" (first published in 1976), the strongest long poem in his earlier *From The First Nine*. Here the aetherial guest places upon the poet a sacred duty: *"SET MY TEACHING DOWN...IF U DO NOT YR WORLD WILL BE UNDONE."* This imperative tone spills over into Merrill's first two book-length Ouija board poems, "The Book of Ephraim," and "The Book of Mirabell," where the poet demonstrates his willingness to *"GIVE UP EVERYTHING EXCEPT THE GHOST"* in order to transcribe the dictations of his other-dimensional visitors.

It's a stirring effort but there are problems. First, no matter how light the touch, poets writing about seances may court the sublime, but never hover far from the brink of the ridiculous — as witness W.B. Yeats' *A Vision*. More serious, perhaps, are problems of keeping a narrative going. Everybody in Merrill's Ouija board poems is either dead, preoccupied with death, or was never alive in the first place. Much of the poems' scant action — and, as narrative poetry, they contain a certain amount of action — takes place in the ghost heralds' oracular dictations. Because of Merrill's use of typographical signals (wide margins for the "angels," LARGE CAPS for all speakers-from-beyond), it's possible for the reader to skip along from upper-case dictation to upper-case dictation, jumping over the less electrifying lower-case passages, which serve largely as connective matter, and are spoken in the author's own rather chatty voice.

Such skipping is not only possible, in fact, but at times necessary, for Merrill's "net of loose talk tightening to verse" — the narrative couplets with which he stitches together his verse novel — is knit too slackly. The weak patches tend to multiply, with the speed of composition, halfway into "Mirabell"; whereupon there develops too much nattering in

couplets between Merrill and dead friends we didn't know, too much gossip about the globetrotting of the author and his fellow medium, David Jackson ("*I thanked my stars/When I lost the Leica at Longchamps*"). The first unsettling visitations of the super-angels make good dramatic poetry, but their later appearances seem too predictable and formalized, like video cassettes programmed to fill up the time between jets to Greece or the Orient.

Still, when the archeologists of literature come to poke over and sort out the bones of this century's poetry some time far in the future, James Merrill's strange, long works using the Ouija board will at the very least give pause, like a mastodon with wings. ☠

Julia Demarée

MILDRED AND THE OBOE

by Lydia Davis

Last night Mildred, my neighbor on the floor below, masturbated with an oboe. The oboe wheezed and squealed in her vagina. Mildred groaned. Later, when I thought she was finished, she started screaming. I lay in bed with a book about India. I could feel her pleasure pass up through the floorboards into my room. Of course there might have been another explanation for what I heard. Perhaps it was not the oboe but the player of the oboe who was penetrating Mildred. Or perhaps Mildred was striking her small nervous dog with something slim and musical, like an oboe.

Mildred who screams lives below me. Three young women from Connecticut live above me. Then there is a lady pianist with two daughters on the parlor floor and some lesbians in the basement. I am a sober person, a mother, and I like to go to bed early — but how can I lead a regular life in this building? It is a circus of vaginas leaping and prancing: thirteen vaginas and only one penis, my little son.

SAN FRANCISCO

by Steve Abbott and John Norton

San Francisco, like some medieval cities, is frequently coveted by rival poet gangs. The court (audiences of over 1,000) and the prestige at stake are enormous. For a while the Beats held sway. Gregory Corso, for instance, dominated with his brash and outrageous humor. His poetry was direct and hard hitting. At the other end of town, Robert Duncan ("like some Pre-Raphaelite damsel in a tower" — Robert Peters) ruled by virtue of his encyclopaedic knowledge, his vision and will, the power of his magnificently hypnotic voice.

In the '70s new gangs staked out terrain — feminists, Before Columbus writers, Performance Artists, Street Poets — but none moved on the old Kings, Dukes and Princes so directly as did the Language Poets. In 1977, Bob Perelman began a Talk Series which, along with the mags *Hills* and *This*, sounded the trumpets. The talks were on selected topics or writers, and among the more important features of these events were the post-talk discussions, where the speakers' ideas could be amplified or challenged.

Two or three verbally aggressive men, like gunslingers from a Sam Shepard play (*Tooth of Crime* say), began to dominate this part of the program, interrupting and hurling quotes, wit, and book titles with rapid-fire delivery. Clearly, if those in the audience kept avoiding the problem, the intimidating behavior would continue. To counter this jockeying for dominance and power, Johanna Drucker organized a panel to discuss "Who is Speaking: the Power of Discourse" at Intersection on March 28, 1983. Gloria Frym, Robert Gluck and Lyn Hejinian joined her on the panel.

Drucker set some new ground rules for audience participation: 1) speakers would raise hands to be recognized, 2) panelists would take turns recognizing the questioners, and 3) audience members couldn't speak a second time until all others who wanted had done so. *Not* speaking was okay, too, but a presence easily undermined. Drucker said, "Those not speaking can be colonized by others' discourse." If unchecked, the strengths and limita-

tions of the dominant few would set the discourse for the rest.

Gloria Frym addressed the question of authority and subjectivity. An audience seldom holds authority equal to that of a speaker. Fear of being unoriginal or ignorant could make audience members feel so unsafe in speaking that "the fear of discourse transcends discourse."

Bob Gluck noted how play has recently been deemed the special province of artists and children. While most avant-gardists take an anti-authoritarian, anti-professional stance, they become extremely professional when talking about themselves:

"If the language that discusses experimental writing has any charm, it is often based on its difficulty; it's characterized by terms that appear to be technical, that is, associated with science. Maybe this expertise validates the 'play' aspect of the art — makes it look more like 'work,' and so more readily digestible."

Gluck described how one group's terms could be the exact formula that invalidated discourse for another. Sexual images in the gay community, for instance, "invite and exclude in much the same way as a semiotic vocabulary does for some experimental writing. Although earlier models persist — romantic, aristocratic, ivory tower — experimental writers want to be on the edge critiquing the new. The most rewarded expert produces the most insights — the best commodity — by de-expertizing other experts, by giving their partializing codes the lie." Thus, even experts representing oppressed minorities create power imbalances.

In an ideal community, Gluck said, one would recite terms *given* by the community. The more one is fetishized as an expert, the greater the distance between speaker and audience. Discourse is opened up when more people feel a personal stake. Expanding the canon of writing (whose writing is taken seriously, written about, discussed) expands the terms.

Lyn Hejinian spoke last. "The invention of the community is the invention of its terms." Her interest, she said, was to belong to a writing community that would "inspire writing and provoke excellence." Because not speaking is like the fear of being revealed, "Keeping silent has assumed a moral or virtuous element."

Considerable anger surfaced after the panel. Many of those present had attended numerous talks but said this was the first time they felt invited to shape the discourse. Kathleen Fraser, Dodie Bellamy and Frances Jaffer, among others, said the way certain individuals quoted books would make them feel stupid. Roberto Bedoya noted the split he felt between talking to Chicano writing friends and attending "high art" writing discussions. Johanna Drucker and Lyn Hejinian defended their right as intellectuals to define excellence. Bruce Boone noted different communities define excellence differently for different purposes. No one group, he argued, can claim proprietary rights to the concept.

By addressing this obstacle in the development of a community of writers, the panel began reshaping the frame of discourse and reduced the distance between speakers and audience.

SAN FRANCISCO BAY
by Nanos Valaoritis

When I think of the wonderful atmosphere of Paris only a few years ago and compare it with the wimpy scene here dominated by do-gooders and conventional unconventionals, so uncertain about themselves as the snow is when summer sun hardens it to become just white and not cold any more. When I say wonderful of course I don't mean in general. I mean in friendship, warmth, continuity even betrayal. Here even that doesn't exist any more than what we would call loyalty or devotion to a cause. But worse of all, the person is absent. You talk to someone and you have the impression of talking to a recording which has been set some years ago and repeats mechanically the same phrases, or different ones but in the same wooden tone. People are not even nasty or nice. They are just unaware of what they are, what they are not, or are not, doing. All this goes together with a kind of smug self-satisfied going-through-the-motions of being grown up. Anniversaries are celebrated retrospectives, people are dug out of obscurity to make pronouncements about utter garbage. Anything worthwhile is systematically relegated to obscurity. The mediocre triumphs but this time with a vengeance. In this atmosphere poetry readings and publications of books of poetry or magazines have become a joke. Even more of a joke, the discussions, engendered by the "poet-in-residence" practice of various spaces where readings take place, have reached a high point of inanity. It is as if the poetry scene in microcosm is imitating the behavior of big publishers in this age of reaganomics, in which no proposition is valid except that which makes money. Failure is once more anathema as it was in the thirties and the forties. And yet generalised failure is what it is all about. At the same time the issues are clouded, obscured, confused. Endeavours to create a poetic theatre end up in verbal exercises of the most passe kind. High falluting pronouncements about psychology in the Theatre misrepresent the issue, which is not whether psychology is pertinent to the theatre or not, but whether there is any theatre without it. Otherwise you can call these elucubrations, charades, collective recitals, or what have you, anything but theatre. Every time some of us meet for an event of a kind, benefit or other, it is like going to a funeral in which we don't really know who is being buried if anyone. What I suspect is being buried every time is the spirit, without which every endeavour is in vain — the spirit of revolt, which has nothing to do with left and right, but with the very issue of our industrial society and the issue seems to be — is it livable? Look for instance at the punks who seem to go through the motions of revolt. Yes they appear to do so yet what are they revolting against? Nothing. There is no one there to revolt against except an object, a word-processor, which controls . . . So infinite rage is expended on and against machines, which are imitated and used, in a vain attempt to humanize them. The people are shadows and their collective rage is spent on dance and music and clothes. The advent of nothing was signalled of course in the sixties and seventies by structuralism and its sequels. Once the subject has been taken out of any project, whether it is psychoanalytical, philosophical, poetic, realistic, imaginary, or literary, what is there left. Nothing. The empty grave, as Stuart Schneiderman pointed out so aptly in his recent book on Lacan — a must for all to read. When the great revolts of the end of the 19th and the beginning of ours occurred — there was something still there — the rotting corpse of a tradition which was in itself exquisite and which unconscious metaphor gave rise to the game of the exquisite corpse as I with others practiced it with Breton and his disciples, in Saint Cirq La Popie, one summer in the late fifties. The whole of European culture is an exquisite corpse, slowly and delicately rotting like venison and therefore good to eat. Without this background the game is meaningless and by extension so would have been the whole of Surrealism, Dadaism and Futurism. Usually something comes out of something but nothing ever comes out of nothing. We should not be deceived by the existential metaphor of nothing at the core of existence, or the famous lack on which aptly in a punning manner in English, the whole *lack-anian* edifice stands. What this lack means at the present moment is a kind of a lack-anal situation in which waste, death and the symbol of mortality, are looming much higher than before in our concepts. How to die is the problem of the present rather than how to live. The anus, which with Rabelais, was once the symbol of creativity, so brilliantly pointed out by the Russian critic Mikhail Bakhtin, has now become the symbol of atomic (in both senses of the word, in Greek *individual*, and atom) waste. So the once fertilising feces are now the dreaded nuclear deadly radiations, of which our own excrement is a constant reminder. No more equivalence to fairy tale gold or shit-babies of ancient myths. In fact fighting to fight against pollution, waste and exhaustion is really fighting against a negative evil and not a positive one. It's not the main project of our culture which is in question but its by-product. Its side effect as with our miraculous drugs. This displacement is important enough to have shifted the whole emphasis of our culture on something which is a priori not there and which was ignored and still is systematically by the dominant mentality. It is no less than the sign of our impending doom, which we seem to desire more than we wish to avoid it. Now who desires, who wishes? Exactly here we come to the heart of the matter. No one desires, no one wishes. It is always the other's desire and wish that we refer to as the one that is operating in us, never ours.

The other wants to die so he imposes his death on us. This is the world we are bequeathing to our kids, a world in which Freudian displacement has happened on a gigantic scale. It is you who are destroying not us say the Russians say the Americans say the Europeans. We don't want this. You want it . . . Me? Who me? Not me, but someone breathing down my neck. Fear, greed, selfishness, etc. Power . . . The constituted subject has been disrupted not into a bad inner or outer conscience, but into a social split, in which the unknown bad guys are lurking everywhere behind every corner in the shadows. And this brings me inadvertently to Michel Foucault who is lecturing here in Berkeley, and who spoke on the unusual subject of taking care of oneself. When asked by a girl how he defined the self, he said, tautologically, "the self is a relation to ourselves," in other words the self is the sum of our activities that concern the self, combing hair, brushing teeth, washing as well as reading or writing. The limitation of the notion of self into a series of activities shows us the crisis or the shrinking of the notion of the self engendered I believe by the situation of the world and the countless numbers of impotent selves it contains. The dramatic Freudian self, split in three ways, or more, yet still linked in mortal conflict with itself, is now no more than a bland blend of endeavours to nurse back to simplicity what complication has irrevocably disrupted. When I asked my son, 17, what were his ambitions — he said make enough money to have a house in the country and get away from pollution. In fact, Foucault has put his finger on the problem. It is preservation and not the solving of inner conflicts of the Platonic class of what used to be called the soul, the psyche, also split in two and three, reason, good and evil passions. Yet the passions are no more in the forefront, since you have to be passionate about something and the person who is in danger of extinction has only one concern, how to survive. In a post-Lacanian universe with everyone psychoanalyzed out of their minds, there is nothing else left to do but brush your teeth, preferably with dentine.

I do not wish to conclude my diatribe here. There is no conclusion anyway, only delays and intermediate solutions of the kind the daily press bombards us with. As a reminder then I wish to get on to the problem of remainders. The waste material as books which are still expensively, vainly and lavishly manufactured by our society here in America. These last remaining fetishes of the commodity market now that painting has declined irrevocably, glimmer obscurely and give us a sense of destiny as we gaze on them in bookstores. Most of them do not pertain to a real experience like Schneiderman's dramatic narrative on the breakup of Lacanian psychoanalysis. It is a kind of book which I classify with the antique laments over Ur, the destroyed city. Lacan was the exquisite corpse of Psychoanalysis, doing away with the subject, its subject, its only subject — its real subject. That the fallen colossus was not only fallen but also felled, is indicative of our relations to intelligence. It is unbearable and has to be garrotted, smothered as soon as possible. Intelligence is a crime. Only the mediocre are allowed to exist. Great intelligence is a double crime.

A good book is the exception that confirms the rule. This is not a waste or a waste of time. Watch out and see if it will be remaindered. Or if it will come out in paperback. The corpse now rotting is a chemical one and not at all exquisite, alas. If then, as Schneiderman concludes, death is the only real remaining subject, which is in fact my conclusion, i.e., a non-subject, unless we talk of the origin of death as did the primitive mythical people who knew that everything had to start somewhere and end somewhere — they unlike us were obsessed with reason, while we are obsessed with unreason. Who cares about the origins of death, yet *it is not looking, not hearing, not feeling,* or the opposite, looking, hearing, feeling, that cause death to come into the world. So what are we left with? I know what you will say: Sexuality, what else? Since love and hate are forbidden...

NEW YORK
by Hariette Surovell

White-haired Mary sat on the sidewalk in front of Feinbloom's Hardware Store, a trick-or-treat shopping bag beside her, pouring a jar of instant

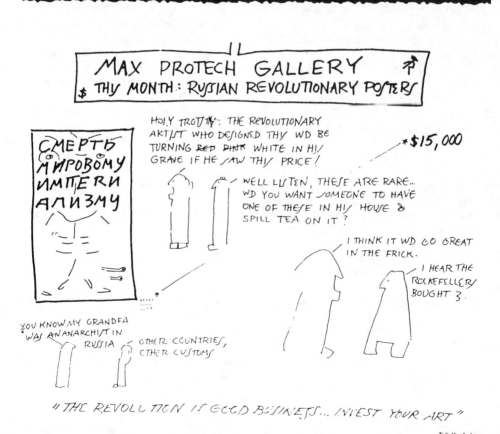

Tuli Kupferberg

Tasters Choice into the styrofoam cup of hot coffee in her hand. "I hope worms eat your eyeballs!" she yelled at each passerby. Many of the pedestrians were residents of the Third Street Men's Shelter. One man wore a yellow silk top hat with an elaborate white plume. Others wavered on crutches, one-armed, one-legged, their limbs snappable as autumn leaves.

Four foot three inch Morris Feinbloom shook his head glumly as he handed me my jar of spackle. Pasted onto the register was a petition from the "residents of Alphabetland" (Avenues A, B, C, D and vicinities) to "rid our streets of this human scum." Some conscientious citizens had penciled in additional comments like "Nuke 'em," and "Shoot them in the head." Although Morris had initiated this petition campaign, he was soft on Mary.

"At one time, she was a real person, like you and me," he sighed. "She even had a job. . . I believe she was a secretary at Macy's. Then one day she tells her boss, 'I'm going out to be a bum' and she never comes back. A broken heart is what did her in. Some people weren't made to have their hearts broken."

As I loaded my laundry into the washing machine at the Second Avenue laundromat, the Puerto Rican proprietor was pushing a dribbling wino out the front door.

"And your floors ain't so clean either, bro," the ejectee noted.

When I returned to fold my wash, the proprietor sat on a car outside, drinking from a bottle of Night Train Express. Six Men's Shelter escapees sat on the yellow plastic laundromat chairs, mumbling, smoking cigarettes, as a lone Black lady stuffed clean clothes into a laundry bag. Some of the men were nodding out because they were junkies, others were simply depressed.

Hunched over in green army fatigues, one of the gang asked the woman, "You got a kid?"

"Now why you ask that?" she replied belligerently.

"I seen baby clothes in that pile."

"You ain't seen no baby clothes!" she cried furiously. "Some people, they don't know how to relate, they make stuff up. I ain't got no kid and you a lyin' dawg!" And she stalked out of the laundromat.

"Oh snap! You gonna take that from a broad?" the men asked each other woozily a minute or so after her exit. "You know what she needs." And they all slapped five. Then they started glaring at me. Antagonism filled the air like a chemical leak.

I started sweating, rapidly folding my socks, when one of them intoned, "They tryin' to destroy our people. They ask us for urine and they take our blood. They ask us for urine and they take our blood. They ask us for urine and they take our blood. Now I'm hearing that them horses in Germany got Herpes. How, I'm askin' you, do a horse catch a humane disease?"

I couldn't resist the temptation. I faced the group and called out, "Use your imagination!"

There was simultaneous chuckling, power saluting, winking at me. I quickly left with my laundry before things got angry again.

When the Black man with the happy grin swayed onto the bus singing *My Way*, the Black riders had an opportunity to feel disdainful and superior; the Whites were afforded a rare chance to make eye contact and smile.

"Yes, we all do things our own ways!" a blonde N.Y.U. student said snippily.

The man sat down and stamped his foot. Something was also wrong with his squinched-up eye. When he interrupted his song to announce, "Sinatra is the King!" members of both groups experienced a moment of inter-racial unity as they giggled and raised eyebrows.

Then the singer turned to an elderly gentleman seated behind him, shook his hand, and asked, "You ever been in Nam?"

"Viet Nam? No, Sir, I haven't."

"They shot holes in my legs. I got three toes on one foot. I got part of my leg missing. I tried to save some of the other guys but I couldn't, man, I couldn't."

Then he resumed his choral performance.

Suddenly it wasn't so funny anymore.

In the post office, a young woman with plastic bags tied around her ankles returned a 20¢ flowered "Love" stamp to the postal clerk.

"Dear, do you think you could give me a different stamp?" she inquired. "I'm sending this letter to my ex-boyfriend, and I don't want him to get the wrong idea."

THE BEAUTIES OF HEAVEN AND EARTH

by Benjamin Peret
translated by Keith Hollaman

A big man with salty hair
wanted to be a musician
but he was alone in the valley
with three accordions

The first accordion ended up just rotting away
In the simplicity of its soul
it wanted to be a horse
but there was a lamp that was burning
that was burning

The second accordion trembled
like a house at the passing of its sister
That's because it was a big city
that deceived its inhabitants
with its mayor
stupid as the claw on a crowbar

The third accordion
would have devoured the earth and all the birds
if it had wanted to
But it was a sage
just like a nettle
and contented itself with simply envying the
    motionless animals

But you'll say to me
the man who wanted to be a musician

He had had time to die
and the leisure to smoke
and it was this smoke which was rising from
    earth toward the clouds

WATERSPOUT OFF STARBOARD

DIRGE

by Anselm Hollo

comes a time you know every move:

"change the musicians whenever you like"

comes a time "it's all over
          by the time it hits k.c."

comes a time someone called erik satie
& someone called john lennon
"look-alikes"
are equally dead

comes a time some you gets shot through the lungs
four times to collapse in historic dakota hallway

(someone called panna grady no longer lives there)

comes a time you travel all the way from honolulu
in fellow incarnation
possibly "chapman"

comes a time you don't know nothing

& all the musicians are gone

you missed it: they didn't miss you

· PARADISE RESISTED ·

· DISAPPEAR SAD APE ·

Life is a jungle
The overburdened Herzog
found out the hardware
weighs as much as the
memorial flowers

Tom Clark

IN MEMORIAM: TED BERRIGAN
NOV. 15, 1934 - JULY 4, 1983

FROM THE E.C. CHAIR

Ted Berrigan is the first exquisite corpse of our decade. We dedicate this issue to him in gratitude for taking us further than anyone before him. The exquisite corpses of Ted's generation, Frank O'Hara, Jack Kerouac and Charles Olson, took him to the place where he connected with us. Our other exquisite corpses, Morrison, Hendrix and Joplin, and poet Jeffrey Miller, are giving Ted a great party in the sky right now. In LAST POEM, he said:

Let none regret my end who called me friend.
We cannot follow his gentle admonition — not right now. But the incredible amount of *life* that he has charged us with continues to rage. We predict that his atoms, dispersed in us the way O'Hara's atoms were in our predecessors, will keep us going for a long time to come.

TED BERRIGAN ES MUERTE
JULY 4, 1983
by Andrei Codrescu

Ted
  un père
if ever there was one
who could fill that place of father
   like no one else
the elephant   the whale
rage of sophisticated life
  so moved by death
Frank's death Kerouac's death
   elegiac master
impatient with bullshit
   Now in their great company
Ted at the crossroads of my youth
   Gem's Spa 2nd Ave. & St. Marks'
Cajoling threatening kind
   In New York San Francisco
    Boulder Baltimore
Délice of repeating what Ted said
  "What did Ted say?"
  "Ted said"
  He said everything
He said that I was the Magellan of sex
  The Bishop of Baltimore

He said that things were a certain way
and that's the way they were
   after he said them
    forever after
They were and that was that
  Ted in bed
   in the great ship
   going home
Ted who was Mother Courage & Father Bright
 Who kept poetry alive in me
  in people he had not even met
 who could say things that he said
& even talk like him
 talk in his inimitable way
his widely imitated inimitable way
  & I would startle myself saying:
   "terrific!" and
    "great!"
  just like he did
   & I heard
my Romanian & someone's Serbian & someone's
 French
  crossed
   by Ted's speech like a wind
crossing the great field of language
  to fill it with the seeds
  of Ted's heart
his big & wonderful heart!
 Generous & direct
  amazingly accurate & truthful
knowing almost always knowing
  "what's right"
  & amazingly I too knowing
& everyone knowing
 The Liberator
  who was always "right there"
as he fondly said of someone he admired
  Right There! Right There!
  Ted you are Right Here
   in my heart
"A myth" yes, but more
  Your Voice
   Farewell, dear teacher, father, poet

Read on the occasion of the July 8th Memorial Service at the St. Marks' Church-In-The-Bowery, New York City.

TED BERRIGAN'S DEATH
by Robert Creeley

Ted Berrigan's death leaves a hole of adamant loss. There won't be another like him, ever, and what's left as always to do is to remember that, and what his writing was all about, and how, with such disarming simpleness, it could hold the largest imagination of human relationships and the world in which they are given to be.

Robert Duncan spoke of him as a genius of *pathos*, a power that could move the heart so commonly, simply, as in one of his great poems, "Things To Do In Providence." His insistent ritualizing of his friends' names, his lovely rehearsal of them, often as a poem would begin, to make the company of his life become the place where all authority of speech might then occur — what a generous *and* American act! I recall a British friend's irritation on hearing him do this, at a reading he gave with Jim Dine in London years ago ("Ted/is ready./The bell/rings . . ."), and saying something like, "*I* don't know those people . . ." She missed the point altogether because Ted would dearly have liked her to know them — they were the greatest friends in the world.

He *was* an Irishman from Providence, which always moved me. Together with Charles Olson and John Wieners, he was my particular New England — certainly all I ever knew or believed in. I loved the way he took on New York and not only made it but so permeated its New York style, like they say, that I do think he's finally as evident in that manner of poetry as Frank O'Hara, whose work he so loved. But the pace and rhythm of his poems, the seemingly open way of the words, the commonness of them, the literal action of what happens, the content at once so obvious and so resonant, all that is inimitable, however large the appetite now to possess it.

Then, as with Mr. Wieners, he remains forever in mind as a great gentleman, an exceptional one. He taught manners, and common caring, by his own example. Despite he was a hard man to interrupt (!), he certainly heard you. I remember my own applications to his attention got always a courteous reception and response. He had great honor — put most simply as he did, "Give it your best shot . . ." "I'd like to take the whole trip . . ." He made an extensive, particular, possible world of his life and lived there difficulty sans complaint.

The raw shock of his death, no matter he or anyone else expected it, makes no room now for spelling it out further. You will hear his wild tremulous witful reflective engaging way of saying it in any work of his that you read or hear him reading. Thankfully there is the substantial collection of his poems, *So Going Around Cities*, and the reissued *Sonnets*, and much else. It won't bring him back but it's what he left, solid as a rock.

Anne Mikolowski

WRITING AGAINST THE BODY
by Charles Bernstein

Written on the occasion of a memorial reading for Ted Berrigan at St. Mark's Church, November 15, 1983. Epigraph and extracts are from *So Going Around Cities: New & Selected Poems 1958-1979* by Ted Berrigan (Berkeley: Blue Wind, 1981). The final quotation is Berrigan's working of Rimbaud.

DEATH IN THE AFTERNOON

She sighed in vain for the chaff and the wheat, not knowing the one from the other.

Contradictory impulses characterize my approach to Ted Berrigan's work. It seems easy to become caught up in the circumstances and style of his life, to portray the man in terms of his personality, his influence, his often extravagant behavior. Such a perspective, however, whether the response is positive or negative, not only deters attention from Berrigan's writing but also tends to misconstrue the nature of his significance. For Berrigan's work — less interrupted than completed by his recent death at 48 — can most usefully be read not as a document of a life in writing but, inversely, as an *appropriation* of a life *by* writing.

This inversion of conventional "confessional" style is a key to Berrigan's method. Inversion is both a form and a moral technique for Berrigan, which partly accounts for the anxiety generated by his flips of self and text — text overwhelms self, self overwhelms text. Many of Berrigan's admirers and detractors share a misconception that his work is an extension of diaristic "self" writing, despite his decisive break with such practices. What makes Berrigan's writing difficult to understand — or deceptively simple — is that he built his edifice on the wreck of the old — using its broken shards to build a structure with altogether different architectural principles.

The Sonnets — with its permutational use of the same phrases in different sequences and its inclusion of external or found language — stands as an explicit rejection of the psychological "I" as the locus of the poem's meaning. This rejection, however, is complicated by the enormous pull *The Sonnets* exerts on readers to project onto the text a cohering "self" even in the face of overtly incommensurable evidence. (Transference may be a more apt term for this projection.) This is an enmeshment that not only the reader but the author may fall under the sway of. Indeed, Berrigan has (as in different ways much current poetry has) mined this misprisoning for its considerable emotional power — tail-spinning self-implosions and self-explosions with remarkable dexterity on the principle that such power is too much to give up, because, quite rightly, a writer can't afford to give *anything* up.

> *frequent*
> *Reification of my own experiences delivered to*
> *   me*
> *Several new vocabularies*

One of the risks of this enterprise is that the detritus of this project-in-writing — by which I mean "the lifestyle of the poet" — now as ever runs the risk of being taken as its flesh.

> *   The poem upon the page*
> *will not kneel   for everything comes to it*
> *gratuitously*

The biographist fallacy substitutes the chaff for the wheat by renormalizing this *body of work* into a work of "self." In this way, the production of meaning is trivialized as personal gestures rather than *read* as inscription in a text.

> *I'm only pronouns, & I'm all of them, & I didn't*
> *ask for this*
> *   You did.*

So there is nothing *simple* about the biographicity of this work. For any self-celebration there is also self-destruction, in the sense that for Berrigan the morning — meaning dawning — of the self is also the mourning — meaning dissolution — of the self. The fusing of form and subject matter is evident: the "integrity" of the poem/body is "violated" by various literary or corporeal "abuses." Note that the body is an overt metaphor for a coherent, integral, individuated self — it gives a biologic legitimacy to the concept. Berrigan's work is, then, a sustained assault on the sanitized body of the "self" (*health*) and simultaneously on the sanitized body of conventional verse (especially the furnished souls of confessionalism). In this textual practice, health is both a grammatical and a psychic fallacy. Health suggests an "objective" criteria for a normalcy that, in Berrigan's terms, would be the death of the psyche, which is to say the death of the body. To write outside the sanctioned subjects and syntaxes of health is to be forced into a situation of desperation; to be able to continue that work may require the sacrifice of, at times, more than can be sanely or gracefully accommodated into a life. Berrigan's writing poses the startling fact of writing's lethal and consuming importance in requiring the yielding of body and mind to its inexorable priority. It's always hard to understand how writing can *cost* so much — because it seems to be after all just putting words on a page. Berrigan's power was to incorporate that cost — of the creation of a psychic space in which writing can occur — into his texts. Writing against the body he was able to realize an image of it.

> We are drawn to shit because we are imperfect in our uses of the good.

> I was charging others to love me, instead of doing so myself.

> You shout very loudly.

> break yr legs   &   break yr heart

> We ate lunch, remember?, and I paid the check

> The pills aren't working.

Such an urgent approach to writing needs to be situated not in a personalist interpretation of the man but rather in the context of the national and international sociopolitical climate of the early 1960s, during which Berrigan's formative work was written. That is, it is important to understand this work as originating in the period prior to the widespread and highly publicized political and cultural oppositions of the late 1960s and early 1970s. America in that slightly earlier moment was infected with an unspoken violence, a violence masked by anaesthetizing/neutralizing/nullifying forces marching under such banners as nuclear security, counterinsurgency, American will, falling dominoes, cold

war conformism, preparedness, suburban comfort, self-reliance and self-actualization, etc. This dizzying succession of rationalizations demanded more than the lip-service opposition of a writing that was otherwise content to go about business as usual. However, Berrigan's commitment to writing "over and against" — that the body might be destroyed in order for its truth to be told — did not preclude comedy. The humor in this work is related, in part, to a disequilibrium of scale — the (f)utility of individual rejectionism against the backdrop of Multinational Steel and Glass, circa 1961 — as if meaning could be produced by sheer force of will, charging at windmills.

The problem is that this work has a wake often more visible than itself that blends with the historical — you might call it psychological — fact that such work does not come cheaply, can be no kept avocation, but must be torn from — *out of* — life.

> *Morning*
> *(ripped out of my mind again!)*

The biographist fallacy misses the boat for the water by focusing on the tactics that have allowed for such writing. These tactics are no more than the exigencies of being able to go on with the work; though it bears saying that such tactics — desperate in the logic of their pragmatism — need less to be judged in the abstract and more to be understood in the context of the necessity of continuing without the luxury of second-guessing the means by which this is made possible. Though we all can and do second-guess others and ourselves daily with paralyzing monotony.

> *I have had the courage to look backward*
> *it was like polio*
> *I shot my mouth off*

It is a measure of Berrigan's times and not only of his life that such a project-in-writing took on these particular necessities. There are, of course, other quite different courses — but none less radical, none less serious about the production of writing — that would seem to justify that journey.

> *The only travelled sea*
> *that I still dream of*
> *is a cold, black pond, where once*
> *on a fragrant evening fraught with sadness*
> *I launched a boat frail as a butterfly* ☙

Ishmael Reed, sacristan of the Neo-Hoodoo Church, is waging a mighty raid on the *Corpse*. In response to an article published here, he had his attorneys in Oakland — whose Telex number is MO LAW — inundate Baltimore with threatening formal missives. These were sent to, among others, the dean, the provost and the president of the University of Baltimore, where our mailing address is. They demanded formal apologies from all these good people. Should these apologies not be forthcoming, further nebulous actions were threatened. Alas, our publication has no connection with the University of Baltimore. It is entirely the fancy of its editors, one of whom happens to be on the faculty. And so we wrote back to Mr. Reed, c/o MO LAW, likening his action to that of the sleazy kid in all our childhoods who goes and tells on you to your mother. Only in this case, the mother turned out to be a strange lady. In response to our reply, a fresh round of letters, addressed to all the people above, as well as to the *Attorney General of the State* (!) rained down on us. In this round, Mr. Reed claimed that we had admitted making scurrilous "anti-semetic" (*sic*) attacks on his person. Now this is a patent lie. We did nothing of the sort. But administrators being what they are, they suggested that we modify our address so that our lack of connection with the institution become clear. This we have done, beginning with this issue. Mr. Reed has done us a favor. We never did want to be suspected of institutional ties. As for the *sic* "anti-semetic" attacks, we have a rabbi standing by to check Ishmael's *bris*.

THE REED EPISODE

In Vol. 1, nos. 2-3 and 4, we published an article by Richard Kostelanetz entitled "The Queen & King of Literary Grants." The queen was Galen Williams of New York's *Poets & Writers*, and the king was Ishmael Reed, publisher of *Y'Bird*. The article detailed the fine grantsmanship of these people. The king was infuriated. He flooded the state of Maryland with letters from his lawyers (our Dean, university President, and Attorney General all got one). The letters threatened to sue for slander, character assassination and *lèse-majésté*. We were flattered by Reed's attention, because whatever one may say of his grantsmanship, he is a great writer and attention from a great writer is delightful. The University of Baltimore reacted by asking us to change our address. But it took a while for the furor to die down, as evidenced by the above and other references.

— Editor

THE NEW CARDENAL: COURT POET

by Jim Brook

Many Sandinistas like to read poetry, and some of them write the stuff. Poetry is their kind of advertising. Father Cardenal is one of these shrewd officials. Having mastered a few rudimentary poses and verbal cliches, Cardenal has managed to become well known. Progressive, cultured, and sports a beret.

It's easy to dislike him, but the only important thing about this mediocrity is his *modernity*. Cardenal is modern because he is at once poet, priest, and politician — because his concerns are subjectivity, the spirit, and power. His concerns are modern concerns *considered from the point of view of the state.*

Cardenal doesn't know how right he is when he maintains that there is no contradiction between Christianity and Marxism (read: Stalinism). These ideologies have the same overall goal and similar structures. And they reflect the same hierarchical relation to the flock, the proletariat, the poor who are supposed to stay poor. But Catholicism is a better draw than Stalinism these days, the latter being so *spent* that it's now forced to call itself something like "the Nicaraguan path to national salvation, independence, and automatic rifles." (Stalinists never fail to point out the inessential specificities of a given local situation.) Today Stalinism is ashamed of itself — even the Sandinistas are aware that no one wants to live in the USSR or let's just say Cuba (chief exports: sugar and soldiers).

Cardenal's poetry: what is it for? To eulogize

the state. (He's rediscovered, along with Neruda, this somewhat neglected genre.) What then is the function of the state? To maintain and to increase the power of the powerful, and that's *all*. Any talk of "development" (see note above of Cuban exports) and "freedom" (the Sandinistas supported Jaruzelski's anti-Solidarity coup) is just bullshit for popular consumption. And it's fine for revolutionary tourists (American poets among them) who can appreciate supposedly "objective" conditions better than the average Nicaraguan whose political experience is limited to overthrowing Somoza by force of arms. Besides, it's nice to meet all the nice junta members — they're regular guys. Imagine, some of these junior college-educated *comandantes* used to hang out in San Francisco! Everyone knows they think a lot about the oppressed — and how to put them to work. That's how they came up with the idea of banning strikes. And now even the Miskito Indians can read censored newspapers and the works of Cardenal in the original Spanish. A political banality of our times: Stalinized American liberals, enamored of "the Freeze" and always putting "food first," think the freedom of the poor(er) can come last, after it's "paid for."

The Sandinistas are in a precarious position, to be sure. No one could envy their self-appointed task: the organization of a more modern dictatorship to replace the deposed archaic dictatorship. This junta of jokers is sweating because it's aware that the revolution in Nicaragua might one day lose interest in Bolshevik and Christian illusions as well as the alibis of "economic and foreign policy imperatives." They live in terror that the poetry of the state and the commodity may one day lose its charm. ☠

BOOKBOX

BOOKS RECEIVED: COMPARATIVE LITERATURE ISSUE

Self-Reflexivity in the Serbo-Croatian Folk-Tale, by Mzsczy Mczszy.

Comic Structures in Holocaust Literature, by Horst Wessel and Elie Wiesel.

101 Uses for a Dead Explicator, by D. Funcke Katz.

Derrida and the Neutron Bomb, by Gerald Pantagraff.

Vomit: The Story of Reader-Response Criticism, by David Yech.

The Joy of Socks: Foot Fetishism in France, by Henri Pair and Germane Brie.

The Condemned of Altoona: Late Existentialism in Eastern Pennsylvania, by J-P Salaud.

Punishing the Text: An Archaeology of Literary Leather, by Michel Godemiche.

Praxis und Taxis: Rilke als Schmarotzer, by Marie von Thurn und Taxis-Hohenlohe.

Sexist Repression and Counter-Revolutionary Imagery in the Later Poetry of Trumbull Stickney, by Medusa Petard and Gloria Monday.

Dust from the Chickenhouse Floor: Coprophagy in American Colonial Literature, by Frank "Temps" Perdue and Bruce Jackson.

The Rhetoric of Secondary Aphasia, by Pablo Lacuna, Ph.D.

The Dirty Denizens: Black Semiotics, by Nathan A. Detroit and Seymour Sebeotnik.

Tickling the Text. A Primer of Literary Tact, by Lillie Bullero and Belle Bottoms.

The Kitchen Kink: Recipes for Critical Boredom, by "Big Al" Cook, the Galoping Gourmet.

The Joy of Gay Deconstruction, by F. Neechie and E. Coli.

The Philologist in the Attic, by the late Lev Spritzer.

Doing Her Thing: Auto-Eroticism in 'Silas Marner', by Raveloe Weber.

Cretins and Hydrocephaloi: Chips from My Buffalo, by El Fiddler.

The Skeleton Key to 'Love Story' Revisited, by Eric Siegel.

Come in Your Trunks: A Reader's Guide to the Beach Epics, by Annette Funicello, D.Phil.

Metonymy Is My Middle Name: Reflections on a Life in Language, by Roman Jakobson.

Phallic Imagery in the Notebooks of Henry James, by Leonardo Gaffito.

The Art of Darkness: Up the River with Conrad, by Francis Ford Coppelius.

Poetry and Flatulence: Petomania in the Romantic Ode, by H. Boom, Ph.D.

Le Seminaire: Livre XCVII: Voir(e) meme, by J. La Cannette.
Trotskyite Deviationism in Nabokov's 'Pale Fire', by the Glen Burnie Collective.
French Letters: The Epistolary Impulse, by J.D. Rida (tr. Urma Durga Parvati Schultz).
Mallarme's Favorite Recipes: Hyperbole, by Barbara Johnson.

NEW JOURNALS: New Literary Hysteria: The Wimp: A New Haven Review; Jouissance; Critical Incontinence. A Journal of the Mainstream; The N Y Review of Coprophilia.

BOOKS RECEIVED:
MASS MARKET TITLES

Shape Up!Orson Welles' Guide to Thinner Thighs in Thirty Days
Garfield Goes Deconstructionist, Jim Davis.
Heaving It All: The Anorexic Handbook, Shelly Winters.
Supply-Side High: Log of a Crossing to Catalina, William F. Buckley.
Andy Rooney Meets the Valley Girls, Moon Unit Zappa.
Who Cares: When Bad Things Happen to Bad People, Rabbi Ben Ezra.
Life Support: The Layperson's Guide to Machine Living, Durk Pearson and Sandy Shaw.
Spaced: James Michener's Survey of Recreational Drugs.

Appleblossoms: Planning Your Next Wedding, Elizabeth Taylor.
Keeping Jimmy, Roslyn Carter.
Against the Wall, Ma Bell: Choosing Your Own Instrument, E.T.
In Charge Here: The Memoirs of Alexander Haig.
With Enough Shovels: A History of the Modern Language Assn. of America, Florence Howe.
Living, Loving, and Burning Out: How to Have It All in 24 Months, Drew Lewis.
Mex-Tex: The Untold Story of Lyndon Johnson in Juarez, Robert A. Caro.
The Immolation of Freddie the Leaf: Planning Your Own Cremation, Leo Buscaglia.
Garfield Gets Tenure: The Last Garfield Book, Jim Davis.*
Throwing Up: Russell Baker's Guide to Baltimore Dining in the '50s.
Beyond the Valley of Horses, Russ Myers.
Over the White Line: Memoirs, John DeLorean.
Real Men Don't Drink Celery Tonic, Truman Capote.
Buttons: Items from Our Catalogue, Cap Weinberger.
China Town: Choosing Your Next Place Setting, Nancy Reagan.
Who Needs Freddie the Leaf?, James Watt.
Sumo Wrestling for the Reading Impaired, Margaret Thatcher.
1001 Things You Can Do with Your Blender, Richard Pryor.

*Next to Last: *Garfield Gets Fixed*

BUREAUS

CHICAGO: MIDWEST POETRY
AND THE OUTSIDER
by Paul Hoover

Peter Schjeldahl, a former Midwesterner, once wrote of the region that it is "the center that is all edge." That is, it may be the center of the country, but artistically it's very much on the periphery.

Except in poetry. The regional tendency, with its flatness of style and sincerity of tone, is currently mainstream. It can be found stamped Official from *The American Poetry Review* and *Antaeus* to *Poetry* and university quarterlies. Wit and form are equally considered artifice. A "feelingful" and self-expressive lyricism constantly reiterates one's "humanity" and is preferred to liveliness and invention. Most of all, the academic Very Late Romantic maintains his or her pathos.

Robert Bly, despite his progressive posturing and Me Generation "prophecy," is a caricature of sincere Midwesternness with his desire to farm the Depths and throw loam in his hair. A Protestant evangelist with Jungian justifications, he thumps Kabir and Rilke instead of the Bible, but he's not as far from Iowa City as he thinks. From an Outsider point of view, Daniel Halpern and Louise Gluck, etc., in spite of where they live, are of the same school as Bly.

With so many young poets getting their training at writing workshops, most of which are in small towns like Iowa City and Missoula, the Midwest has all the clout. Publishing power may remain in New York, but the Flat Style and Midwestern sincerity are so pervasive that publishers dutifully help make it the official literature. Schjeldahl is wrong. The center is now the center, and that is a problem.

Outsider status in such a climate can involve any of the following tendencies or influences: Beat, Punk, Black Mountain, New York School, Surrealist, Dadaist, non-referential, etc. Just a drop, mind you, like LSD in your morning coffee, and you're an urban smart-ass from the Other Tradition.

Conditions may no longer exist in which onetime Outsiders like Whitman, Pound, Eliot (in spite of his later conservatism he was first an Outsider), Williams, Moore, Stevens, and Crane, all of whom developed in a cosmopolitan environment, can become major poets. Instead we are presented with a diet of Galway Kinnells and Philip Levines.

The problem for the Outsider who also lives in the Midwest is that he or she is out of sight and mind, for the most part, from the progressive poets on the coasts (now the true periphery) who are sympathetic to such writing. He or she works in a double vacuum.

The Outsider from the Midwest must decide: (1) how not to be as flat as the landscape and (2) how and when to move elsewhere. Assuming the second isn't an option, the Outsider's position is reminiscent of the younger W. C. Williams sticking it out in the provinces of suburban New Jersey while everyone else was in Europe. He kept throwing out things which could not be overlooked, and most of all he persisted. But Williams also had the advantage of interested friends and advocates like Pound and a progressive Modernist scene in New York City that was eager to receive him. The young Outsiders in Milwaukee need an amazing talent and persistence in order not to die on the vine, and chances are they'll die anyway.

As for Chicago, though it encourages progressiveness in the art world (Chicago Imagists like Roger Brown and Jim Nutt), in jazz (the AACM and Anthony Braxton), in independent theater, and even in architecture (the whimsical Stanley Tigerman), it's business as usual in poetry, and if you want to see Midwestern flatness, nothing equals the prairie poets who still faithfully read *The Spoon River Anthology*.

TOKYO
by Arturo Silva

Everything they say about Japan is true.

Take me home, Kokubunji; take me home, Kichijoji; Shibuya, take me home. How many towns make a city? How many maps a man?

To my mind, Japan and Spain represent the two poles of the Imagination. (Fecundity/sterility; symbol/surface; thralldom/exaltation; etc.) And they represent the future: monotonous/convulsive. Haven't you noticed it, too?

Poetry? Don't ask; no need to. In this Empire of Pure Signifiers, poetry takes on new meanings, simultaneously empty and full: a repertoire of complicity where reality is so intense (Spain), and ambiguity so the norm (Japan), metaphorization is exempt: poetry becomes poetry and poets fall by waysides.

By the way, certainly the best book on Japan since Barthes' is Fred Schodt's *Manga! Manga! The World of Japanese Comics* (Kodansha).

That "old boy" Sean Connery gazes nostalgically at his cricket bat on the wall. Later, he's leaning against a bullfight poster, "120 degrees in the shade". Jerry Lewis is dubbed into Japanese; or was he really speaking it all along? Last month, in a beautiful kimono, she emerged, looking like she'd just been fed. This month, silver lights streak across her. The Suzuki family raises their bowls of rice above their heads; they would never think of inserting it into their mouths. (KDD) Like Ry Cooder, are you an American Car-Boy? Are your eyes closed, cassette player held affectionately to your cheek, like F.F. Coppola?

The great contemporary Japanese art form seems to me to be its advertising. Appropriately.

Pope would have loved Japan. (And you'll finally acquire a great taste for Pope here too.) Nietzsche, so anxious to hear from Spain (and here you'll read Nietzsche in Spanish), would have, I hope, risen to this challenge. Proust would have been horrified;

and I'm glad of it.

What we might call the "haiku sensibility" is to be found in Japan's ads — certainly not in Meiji Jingu, where thousands of gorgeous irises were in bloom last month, surrounded by many more thousands of haiku-ettes, pen and pad in hand. From the little I've bothered to check out, the best part of the contemporary poetry here is probably the exquisite paper it's written on.

Anyway, you leave Meiji Park and there are the "takenokozoku," Japan's special and endearing version of frats and greasers, cute and tough. Go down the treelined avenue (their version of the Avenida de la Republica, which in turn is their version of . . .) and you're in Harajuku, the center of Tokyo fashion, Japan's other great contemporary art.

Anyway, don't believe a word of it. Come to Tokyo.

WHERE IS JAPAN?
by Arturo Silva

Why does Japan speak?
— To give birth to cinema.

Where does Japan sleep?
— Deep in Spanish dreams.

What is Japan?
— Outside contempt.

When will Japan awake?
— Where is Spain?

Who gave birth to Japan?
— What is cinema?

Frank Palaia

FAREWELL TO SEVEN CASCADES

Translated from the Brazilian Portuguese with commentary by Alberto Huerta

Carlos Drummond de Andrade's ode to *Sete Quedas*

Although he is now an octogenarian, Carlos Drummond de Andrade (1902-1987) remains Brazil's foremost contemporary poet. In his ecological ode *Farewell to Seven Cascades*, Drummond de Andrade sadly and anxiously accepts the completion of the Itaipu Dam (October 1982) on the Parana River — *Father of Great Waters* (Guarani language), which will increase substantially Brazil's and Paraguay's hydroelectric power at the expense of the tragic destruction of one of nature's great wonders, *Salto de Sete Quedas* — the massive and impressive escarpment of seven groups of cascades dividing Brazil and Paraguay, one hundred miles up the Parana River from the *Foz de Iguacu* falls that border Argentina, Brazil and Paraguay.

FAREWELL TO SEVEN CASCADES

by Carlos Drummond de Andrade

Seven ladies left their traces upon me,
And all seven kissed me.
                        — *Alphonsus de Guimaraens*
Hymns previously resounded here.
                        — *Raimundo Correia*

Seven cascades left their traces upon me
And all seven vanished.
The thunder of cataracts ceases, and with it
The memory of Indians, pulverized,
Which no longer awakens the least shiver.
For the Spanish dead, for the explorers,
For the extinguished fires
Of Ciudad Real de Guaira will be joined
The Seven ghosts of waters wiped clean
By the assassin's hand, by man the owner of the planet.
Here voices previously rumbled
Of imaginary nature, fertile
In theatrical sets of dreams
Offered to man without contract.
A beauty in itself, fantastic bodily shape
In heaves and sighs in contoured space
Showed herself, disrobed herself, proffered herself
In generous surrender to human vision in ecstasy.

All architecture, all engineering
Of the ancient Egyptians and Assyrians
In vain tried to build such a monument.
And now she is disintegrated
By the ungrateful intervention of technocrats.
Here these seven visions, seven sculptures
Of liquid profiles
Dissolve themselves among computerised calculations
Of a nation ceasing to be human
In order to become a frigid enterprise, and nothing
  more.
From movement a dam is constructed,
From waters whirling is born
A business-like silence, a hydroelectric project.
We are going to bequeath everything comfort
Which tariffed light and energy generate
At the cost of another good which has no price,
Nor ransom, impoverishing life
In the savage illusion of enriching her.
Seven herds of water, seven white bulls,
Of the billions of perfect white bulls.
Sink into lake, and into nothingness
Absolutely formless, what will remain
If not of nature pain without complaint,
The fall silently censored
And the curse which time is bringing?
Come foreign nations, come Brazilian
Brothers of all faces,
Come and behold
This natural work of art which is no more
Today remains a color postcard, melancholic,
But her ghost churning still
In rainbowed pearls of foam and rage,
Passing, circumventing
Through destroyed suspended bridges
And the useless wailing of things
Without remembering a single remorse,
Without any burning fault confessed.
("We take on this responsibility!
We are building the new Brazil!")
And blah, blah, blah...
Seven cascades left their traces upon us,
And we didn't know it, oh, we didn't know how to
love
    them,
And all seven were killed,
And all seven vanished into thin air,
Seven ghosts, seven crimes
Of the living assaulting the life
Which will never be born again.

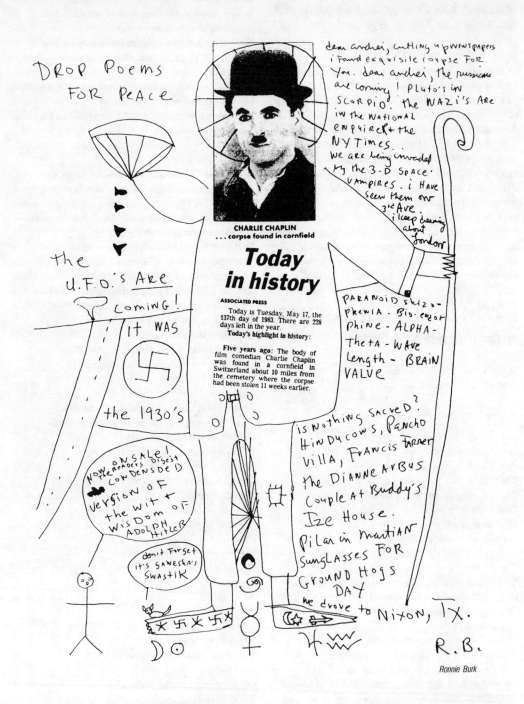

DROP POEMS FOR PEACE

the U.F.O.'s ARE coming!

IT WAS

the 1930's

NOW ON SALE! THE READERS DIGEST CONDENSDED VERSION OF the wit + wisDom of ADOLPH HiTleR

don't Forget it's SAWESHA's SWASTIK

CHARLIE CHAPLIN
... corpse found in cornfield

Today in history

ASSOCIATED PRESS

Today is Tuesday, May 17, the 137th day of 1983. There are 228 days left in the year.
Today's highlight in history:

Five years ago: The body of film comedian Charlie Chaplin was found in a cornfield in Switzerland about 10 miles from the cemetery where the corpse had been stolen 11 weeks earlier.

dear andrei, cutting up newspapers i found exquisite corpse FOR you. dear andrei, the russians are coming! pluto's in SCORPIO. the NAZi'S ARE in the NATiONAL ENQUIRER + the NY TimES. we are being invaded by the 3-D SPACE VAMPiRES. i HAVE seen them on 3rd Ave. i keep dreaming about London

PARANOID SHiZO-PHRENiA. Bio-enzor PhiNE - ALPHA-ThetA - WAVE Length - BRAiN VALVE

is nothing sacred? Hindu cows, pancho villa, Francis Farmer the DIANNE ARBUS couple At Buddy's Ize House. Pilar in martiAN SunglASSES FOR GROUND HOGS DAY we drove to NiXoN, TX.

R.B.

Ronnie Burk

The editors spent two sleepless nights (one for each editor), debating the wisdom of publishing Jim Brook's attack on the Sandinistas, at this gruesome point in American foreign policy. It was decided, in the morn, that no time is a good time in history, and at least one of us wished that Lenin's party would have allowed criticism of Stalin's undemocratic ways when it was still possible to do so. Some twenty million people could have been *reading* Corpses instead of being them.

As a matter of fact, some of our far-flung bureaus are reporting outbreaks of Corpse chic. One of our Paris stringers notes a Frenchman in the Metro with Corpse No. 7 sticking out of his pocket. At one point, during the journey, "the rail-thin, axe-faced Gaul reaches into his coat and flips the sheet open with a familiar and crisp gesture, like a favorite *cigarette case* (italics ours). He gets off at Rue St. Denis." Our man in Tokyo says that he has now noticed the Corpse twice, "sticking out of badly snapped briefcases of executives waiting for limos in front of the Myako..." And in Borah Borah they are nude, and fanning themselves with

us. The only rub is, can we keep making Corpses much longer? Our bank account says No. Our hearts say Yes. In the name of our hearts then, we beg you to renew your subscriptions now (if you started in January). We would also like it if in this season of Western culture's second most famous Exquisite Corpse (after John Lennon) you would make a tax-deductible contribution to the Culture Shock Foundation, Inc, publisher of *Le Cadavre*. If you can't beg at Christmas, might as well give it up, as Bertran de Born might have said.

CORPSE-C.I.A. LINK EXPOSED

Another lively *Corpse*...altho why you made that absurd attack on Cardenal & the Sandinistas your lead article I can't quite figure out. If somebody wants to be "provocative," they could do it at least in a way that connects with facts & not just C.I.A. propacaca. Does this mean the C.I.A. has a literary branch & its agents have infiltrated the *Corpse*? The piece was lame, whatever its controversy value.

— Stephen Kessler

RUMBLE OF LOW GRADE BULLIES

We fucked over Nicaragua for forty years through our clients "Taco and Tachito" Somoza, and now we're invading this tiny, poor country, and Jim Brook worries on your front page about the fact that the leaders of Nicaragua, the same people the C.I.A. is presently trying to kill, have, at times, censored an opposition newspaper. Has everyone gone blind at once? Q. Do they even *have* opposition newspapers in El Salvador? A. No, because all the editors have either been killed or driven into exile. What next, articles condemning Nicaragua because they don't have a National Endowment for the Arts? Gimme a break, will ya? I just wanna stay here in the Hotel for a few more years so I can write some more books, but this is getting *too weird*. We're turning into the same low grade bullies who forced Andrei Codrescu out of Romania.

— Gerald Rosen

Ed. Note: Those were major bullies, Jerry. Their other job was censoring newspapers.

PATH CORRECTION REQUESTED

It is all too easy to criticize criticism, but I believe that the *purported* critique of Father Cardenal by Jim Brook ("The New Cardenal: Court Poet") hardly deserves printing, especially as the lead article in your August-September issue. I don't know what Mr. Brook's artistic perceptions are (I don't see any here), but his political perceptions (that's all I see here) are misguided and terribly simplistic. Aside from his Marxist-Stalinist equations (which I can't dignify), he ought to realize, as Richard Fagen, professor of Latin American Studies at Stanford, that Cuba "is the only nation in Latin America with all its children in school, without serious nutritional problems, and without the destitution and marginality so typical of the hemisphere." (*Monthly Review*, Sept. 1983). To say flatly, as Mr. Brook does, that no one wants to live there is difficult to believe, as is his statement that Cuba's chief exports are sugar and soldiers, as opposed to development and freedom. Freeing the Popular Movement for the Liberation of Angola from C.I.A. subversion and C.I.A. support of a South African invasion from Zaire — while remaining to implement genuine development — is one contra-example. If Mr. Brook is interested in background (and, as it

seems, thrillers), I suggest he read ex-C.I.A. station chief, John Stockwell's *In Search Of Enemies*. As for the Sandinistas of Nicaragua, who gained power through a deeply rooted popular uprising, they have reduced illiteracy significantly and have provided free medical care to many who never had any at all before. However, the cumulative effects of the '72 earthquake (foreign aid for which was stolen by the Somocistas); the undermined production from years of fighting; an emptied treasury by the fleeing old regime; an export market hard hit by the deepening crisis of the world capitalist system; and U.S. destabilization tactics have all made the freedoms that Mr. Brook calls for extremely difficult. I don't think Mr. Brook understands that revolutions are historically very long processes, both before and after actual takeover; that, moreover, counterrevolutionary forces impede the process severely. But this does not mean that "repression is justified . . . to coalesce winnings," as another of your simplistic contributors, Barbara Bailey Bolton ("Stuck in the Birth Canal"), says in your May-June issue, while accusing Marxists in general of apologetics. Only if revolutionaries are encouraged and aided in their just causes, rather than undermined by external forces, will they be able to fulfill their promises. Certainly, the fight against imperialist domination and the downfall of Somoza and his torturing National Guard is a step forward. As former Ambassador White (El Salvador) has said over and over again to apparently deaf ears, revolutions are fought from hunger and oppression, not for the support of some ideology.

— Richard Tagett
*Institute for Studies in
Society and Action*

IS HE OR ISN'T HE?

I was sorry to see the sad attack on Cardenal (*EC* 8/9). He may not be the most exciting poet, but as Minister of Culture for the Sandinistas he is supporting the best of their regime and the most humanistic and poetic elements of their culture, defending precisely those things which North American poets and intellectuals should be defending. The fact that most poets and intellectuals have remained singularly silent in these matters doesn't speak well for them in their well-lined nests, especially when they *do* speak up they can only come up with airhead attacks such as you printed.

— Lawrence Ferlinghetti

CARDENAL: "POUND IS A MARXIST"
by Stephen Kessler

After being detained, interrogated, searched and generally hassled coming through customs (despite his diplomatic credentials), Nicaraguan Minister of Culture Ernesto Cardenal made it to San Francisco December 2 for his reading at the Palace of Fine Arts. The event was sold out in advance and the hall was packed with more than a thousand people while hundreds more were turned away at the door. Following the warmup acts — which included Alice Walker, Michael McClure, Berkeley mayor Gus Newport, and actor David Clennon, who played the spineless US consul in the movie *Missing* — Cardenal was introduced to a standing ovation which spontaneously turned to a chant of *NO PASARAN*, they shall not pass.

With only brief introductory remarks and no additional discourse, Cardenal read about eight or ten poems written since the Sandinista triumph of July 1979. Boomed forth in the deep clear powerful tones of his priestly voice, the poetry painted a vivid picture of the invigorating challenge of building a new society on collective principles after decades of enduring a hated dictatorship. As difficult as it is for many North Americans even to imagine the social context in which the Nicaraguan people are working — a context which now includes large-scale sabotage and terrorism by US-backed counterrevolutionaries as well as a disinformation campaign which falsely portrays the government as some kind of Stalinoid autocracy — the audience was extremely enthusiastic and responsive to the reality of the poems. Many had no doubt been to Nicaragua.

If Cardenal is regarded as a hero by some artists and activists, it has to do not only with his role in generating a participatory/democratic cultural life in his country as its first Minister of Culture, but with his ongoing poetic account of Nicaraguan history in the making. His current work is a natural extension of earlier texts like "Zero Hour" and "Oracle Over Managua" in its integration of actual events with his vision as a witness and participant. It is a journalistic art which doubles as propaganda — but instead of propaganda for the poet's "sensibility" it is an argument for social values, for love and justice, grounded in the struggle of an entire people for the right to govern themselves.

The reading was an outstanding poetry demonstration and far more inspiring than most political rallies. It was the combination of poetry and politics which gave the evening its sense of urgency, its charge of historic voltage. Numerous North Americans are waking up to the fact that art informed by social purpose is not only possible but necessary.

Next day in North Beach, Cardenal was guest of honor at a press and poets' lunch hosted by Lawrence Ferlinghetti. After the meal a few of us (Ferlinghetti, Larry Bensky, Eugene Ruggles, Francisco

Alarcon and others) engaged the guest in a free-form collective interview. Cardenal stressed the significance of North American poets — Whitman, Williams, Frost, Sandburg, Rukeyser, Kenneth Fearing, and especially Pound — in contributing to his developing sense of poetics.

Asked how he reconciles Pound's esthetics with his political views, Cardenal replied that Pound's admiration for Mussolini "was a mistake, but he didn't admire the fascist methods, and he was always writing against capitalism, against usury — that is, capitalism. I think he is a Marxist poet. I think his poetry is Marxist, because the theme of his poetry is economic."

Pound's "anti-Semitism" was mentioned. Cardenal said, "When he attacked Jews, he was attacking capitalism, not a race...Do you know that I am a Jew? My great-grandfather came from Germany, with the name of Teufel, and he changed his name to Martinez — my second name is Martinez — but I should have been named Cardenal Teufel. That means 'devil' in German. It is a Jewish name. Cardenal is my mother's last name."

In response to a question about current trends in Nicaraguan poetry, Cardenal said there are two main currents (although "some poets have both"), one of which he called "abstract poetry," presumably deriving from Ruben Dario, a poetry "without any personal name or any specific thing of reality, just some kind of surrealism, I would say, or non-realist poetry."

The other trend he called "concrete poetry," which engages itself with historical and political references, "a poetry that could talk about Somoza or Fidel Castro or Angola or Grenada or Venezuela...with names of places and streets and cities and rivers and mountains and first names... with anecdotes and jokes and many things."

According to Cardenal, the currents are in conflict. Asked if there was any dialog between them, he laughed. "It is difficult to have a dialog because on one side they say, 'That is not poetry, that is prose, that is a pamphlet for political purposes,' and the other side says, 'That is not revolutionary poetry, that poetry is not Nicaraguan poetry, that poetry is nonsense.' I would say the abstract poets are more in power than the other ones because they have the literary supplement of the Sandinista newspaper and they have a lot of criticism against the other poetry."

It is in the literary workshops at the popular level that the "realist poetry, or concrete poetry, with great influence of North American poetry," is written. "And the other side says, 'That is not good poetry, that is socialist realism'." Cardenal laughed. "That is a very bad insult, to be called 'socialist realism'! So there is polemic, more than dialog."

"What about poetry critical of the Sandinista movement — is that possible now, positive criticism?"

"Well, we have poems against the revolution in the opposition paper, *La Prensa*. The government newspaper will not publish poems against the revolution. And *The New York Times* will not publish a communist poem, against capitalism. But in the opposition paper there is poetry against the revolution. We don't care about that."

PEACEMAKER SPURNED
CARDENAL SUBSCRIBED
by Fr. Alberto Huerta, S.J.

Since *Corpse* has shown an interest in Nicaragua's Minister of Culture, I thought that I'd forward the following account of Cardenal's visit to San Francisco, written by Gerald Nicosia for *Appeal to Reason.**

It may also be of some interest to you to know that while Fr. Ernesto Cardenal was in San Francisco, an effort was made to have him meet with Czeslaw Milosz, the 1980 Nobel in Literature.

I had made various calls to the Nicaraguan Embassy in Washington to suggest this meeting on neu-

BUT WHAT DO WE DO IF THEY CASH OUR CHECK AND THEN STILL WON'T PLAY BALL?

THEN WE WRITE THEM A BIGGER ONE, OF COURSE!

Tom Clark

tral ground at the Jesuit Faculty Residence of the University of San Francisco for Dec. 4th. Everyone seemed pleased by the idea. Mr. Milosz, who had experienced the effects of ideology in the early 50s while cultural attache to the Polish Embassy in Paris, was at first reluctant to meet with Cardenal. However, once he understood that it was to be a meeting between two poets with the same faith, he felt more at ease about this encounter. Unfortunately, I can't say the same about the Nicaraguan contingent, whose schedule was tight, and seemed unable to appreciate the importance and implications of this meeting: Czeslaw Milosz, a friend of the Holy Father encountering Ernesto Cardenal, whom the Pope had warned of excessive political involvement. The event didn't take place, thus preventing a dialogue between Peter and Paul; or if you like, between Rome and Jerusalem. I am still hoping that on his next visit to San Francisco, the Minister of Culture will not let ideologies stand in the way of dialogue and honest intellectual debate. At least, the neutral ground was offered.

I felt that you might find this news item interesting, since it adds to the Cardenal account in these sundrenched lands of *El Dorado.*

I am enclosing a subscription for my friend Ernesto Cardenal. I would appreciate that it be sent airmail, beginning with the first issue in which he first made his appearance (I believe it was over the Summer 1983). Thank you. Please mail: Fr. Ernesto Cardenal, Ministro de Cultura, Managua Nicaragua.

Ed. Note — The article details the harassment of poets in the audience by Nicaraguan officials surrounding Cardenal at his San Francisco reading. No "unauthorized" photos were permitted, for instance. People were shoved, pushed and searched.

THE SCISSORS OF MANAGUA

Jim Brook's text, a rare thing in the U.S. these days, is 100% accurate. Congratulations. Cardenal became famous in 1967, after I translated him into German. Once upon a time in what seems like the incredibly faraway days of the early '60s, I published in Rio de Janeiro the first political commentary critical of the dictatorship of Somoza the elder. The Nicaraguan poet and engineer, Ernesto Gutierrez, who was living in the Brazilian capital around that time, translated my text into Spanish and sent it to the newspaper *La Prensa* in Managua. The

scissors of Anastasio Somoza Garcia went to work and my article was cut. Since then, dozens of articles from this pen were prohibited in Managua by the Somozas, first by the elder, then by Louis and then by Tachito. I was growing accustomed to this treatment because they were censoring me the same way in Lima under Manuel A. Odria, in Asuncion under Stroessner, in Havana under Batista and later under Castro, in Venezuela under Perez Jimenez, in "Ciudad Trujillo" under Chapitas, in Buenos Aires under Juan Peron, and so on. In Romania, my native country, which I left in 1946, things were solved in a manner more radical than scissors. My name and my books were put on a "black list," so that no one could comment, refer to or mention my work. And now the scissors of Managua are at work again. Recently, a *literary* commentary, a review I wrote on the excellent Cuban poet in exile, Juana Rosa Rita, illustrated by the exiled Nicaraguan Ligia Guillen, was massacred in such a way that when I read it, in *La Prensa Literaria*, I didn't recognize it. In the review I had mentioned other Cuban poets in exile, something that the Managua censor, under Cuban direction, could not abide. I would like to know what the poets of the Junta think about this: Carlos Tunnermann Berheim (Education Minister), E. Cardenal (Culture), and the others, poets Ernesto Gutierrez, Ernesto Mejia Sanchez, and Sergio Ramirez M. I am, of course, accustomed to the scissors of Managua after the many decades of the three Somozas, but what matters in the end is the principle involved. This writer is an old anti-Somocista but at the same time an anti-totalitarian. In other words: a free man.

— Stefan Baciu

Translated from the Spanish by Nadia Marin

ANOTHER LEFTEE JAB

I'm back from Mexico. It's sad being back. Lots of people have died, and the political situation in America is worse even though Americans don't know it. There were LaRouche people at the Houston airport collaring everybody, and the only people laughing and talking loudly was a large Mexican family waiting to go home. I was not so happy about going home. No one seems to understand that to live in America you have to be antiAmerican. Everyone here wants to be anti other people, like antiCommunist or antiauthoritarian (assuming we ain't): American political therapy — I'm alright but you're not. Since I'm off on this: who is the C.I.A. agent you got to write the piece on the Sandinistas? Is he for real, or does he spew the line for the ignorance of it? Reminds me of the Fifties when the C.I.A. covertly funded all the important left wing magazines here and in England because they offered alternatives for Western intellectuals. What bothered me about the piece on the Sandinistas was not just all the misinformation which is covered by silly labelings but the pseudo-poet-as-anarchist position, made pseudo by its lily-white-hands tone. Americans and America have been fucking up for so long in Nicaragua (the Walker invasions in the nineteenth century, the occupations, the marine landings before the First World War, the occupations by the marines until the Somoza clan established itself through a series of political murders, the economic control through the various international companies created by the Somoza clan, etc.) that they are surely more than fifty percent responsible for the poverty, inequality, and suffering. A little less self-righteous indignation would do the whole world a lot of good. Next time I will tell you about the biggest demonstration I saw in Mexico, against the American invasion. It was organized by an international group called Nueva Cancion which has taken the rock concert form and politicised it. They operate in every country in Latin America in sports stadiums and large places. They put on the first homage to Neruda, and for the Grenada thing they put on a six-hour concert with almost a hundred musical groups in front of the American Embassy. Very exciting. It makes the police lines much less threatening.

— Max Yeh

SAME GOVERNMENT, DIFFERENT FUNDS

I found what Jim Brook had to say on Cardenal provocative and interesting. It's odd how important the free press is to some people. Censors say "But the crisis, the crisis!" Censors always have a crisis to justify their censorship. It was never in the Sandinista's game plan to have a free *La Prensa* (or anything else in books and mags and newspapers) and they started harassing in official ways all other media other than their own right after the victory. So T. Borges has a newspaper: *Nuevo Diario.* And

the Ortega faction has *Barricada* and allied and associated publications. Same government, different funds. And *La Prensa* meets unfair competition by becoming more and more right wing and sensationalistic. Oddly, it is still the newspaper Nicaraguans tend to trust and read.

— Richard Elman

CARDENAL IN THE BIG APPLE

I think the critics have been stupid & off the wall in condemnation of new Dylan album but they can only aspire to the mediocrity all around them. Ernesto Cardenal breezed into town w/a security force for a series of pep rallies & a poetry reading where every word he uttered was applauded by the mob — too bad his poetry isn't so hot — just reports facts — cashing in on revolution — tho his cause seems more just than Reagan's, which is of course insane & horribly destructive ("his brain has been mismanaged w/great skill" — Dylan), the crowd blindly worshipping even Cardenal's reflection just seemed more stupidity & this willingness to be led was unnerving. Anyway, just a crowd.

Not having Ted Berrigan around to talk to about new Roger Angell piece in *New Yorker* remains shocking.

— Greg Masters

BROOK RE-EDUCATED

I have thought long and hard about the criticism your readers have given my article on Ernesto Cardenal and the goals of the Sandinistas. My conscience demands that I concur with the judgments of Stephen Kessler (a political genius), Richard Tagett (who's for Bread and Freedom, minus "bourgeois" freedom), and Max Yeh (who's been to Mexico). I sincerely want to set the record straight and retract the lies and half-truths contained in my article. Contrary to what I have previously written (at a bad time in my life; I was reading too much, especially the insidious pigshit in the anarcho-Trotskyite-crypto-CIA-fascist "press"), Cardenal does *not* wear a beret or any other kind of protective headgear. Nor is he a poet, Catholic, or Marxist-Leninist. Rumors to the effect that he is the Minister of Culture in the Sandinista junta are demonstrably false. There is no Stalinism in Cuba or Nicaragua; everyone knows that Stalin is dead and that Khrushchev said so. It is *wrong* to think of Cuba and Nicaragua as militarized — the Army is the People (and if the people happen to want to visit Africa. . .). The Polish Solidarity movement was objectively counterrevolutionary. Again, the Army is the People. The same goes for strikes in Nicaragua. As Moises Hassan put it (Mar. 4, 1980): "If necessary, we will use force to put an end to seizures and work-stoppages, in order to guarantee national production and the development of the reactivation plan." *That's* self-management! I apologize for my confusion regarding freedom of the press. *Censorship does not exist in Nicaragua*; and when it does exist, it doesn't matter. Anyone who thinks otherwise, or

thinks, is a Contra with a fat bank account in Miami (sorry, I don't recall the zip code). (Let me take this opportunity, while I am making a clean breast of my chest, to inform *Exquisite Corpse* that its "Company" subsidy is being terminated — the magazine is no longer useful now that its "cover" has been "blown.") Finally, I wish to point out that, despite President Reagan's faked-up aerial photos, Nicaragua is assuredly not Nicaragua. I swear the the foregoing is a full and true confession of my crimes.

— Jim Brook

AMSTERDAM: AN INTERVIEW WITH XAVIERA HOLLANDER

by William Levy

It's *de rigueur* to talk as if it's immoral to make money from one's writings. As if a book lacks literary depth unless the stores return it by the thousands; hence the snobbery (and envy) toward Vera de Vries, better known under her pen name — Xaviera Hollander. Now living again in her native Holland she has considerably revised and augmented her first book, *The Happy Hooker*, and published it in Dutch.

After Anne Frank — Xaviera Hollander is the most famous Dutch woman in the world. She is on everyone's lips. She has been everywhere, done everything, loves to tell about it. That's why her books have sold over 10 million copies. A woman so influential she was (according to John Dean in *Blind Ambition*) the first person investigated by President Nixon's "Watergate Plumbers."

How did a nice girl from Amsterdam's *Barleus Gymnasium* become New York's top prostitute and madam?

"Just lucky, I guess!" she says, with a straight face.

Unlike her colleagues working in the field of human sexuality, Xaviera Hollander's qualifications come from the old saying — practice makes perfect: rather than the confusing and conflicting philosophical and clinical invectives, telling people how they should and ought to be, from behind that gruesome mask yclept objectivity. She believes, like Trotsky, that the participant is the best observer.

And like Sarah Bernhardt, Lou Salome and Kafka's mistress Milena, Xaviera is in the tradition of flamboyant European Jewesses. Beneath the brashness of all these women is the spark of real cultural spirit, a dark sexual passion that only the Happy Hooker dare tell. Explicitly. Humorously. Joyously. Without guilt or shame. Indeed, the song made famous by Edith Piaf, *Je ne regrette rien*, could be her own anthem.

Yet the mystery remains. One is never quite sure with Xaviera Hollander. Are you dealing with Esther Gobseck from Balzac's *Splendeurs et misères des courtisanes* — or the good-hearted randy secretary from a Doctor's romance?

But one thing is sure. She loves to ball. In her own words: "I am a woman who enjoys love with both sexes." So let's dispense with the mincing manners which prohibit mentioning a woman's age. Xaviera was forty years old last June. Together with the hundreds of friends and supports and lovers (past, present and future) who packed her suburban semi-detached for the celebration I agree — the best work is still in front of her.

What have you done since the publication of The Happy Hooker*?*

Become a writer. I can make more money vertically than horizontally. There have been twelve books so far, for example, *The Best Part of a Man, Super-Sex*, and my newest, *Magic Mushroom*. All have been autobiographical and educational, based on the idea that one instructs best when one entertains first. There was a film, *My Pleasure Is My Business*; it played in the major movie houses all over Europe. An X-rated record called simply *Xaviera*. Then, of course, I write a monthly sexual advice column for *Penthouse* — almost half of the latest *Best of Penthouse* volume is my column. I've lectured in universities throughout America and Canada on the theme: "A Better Understanding of Human Sexual Relations." For that, I was banned from entering the United States and Canada. Recently I represented Holland at two International Sex Congresses — in Mexico City, December 1978, and in Jerusalem in June 1980 where I spoke on "Sex without Touching." I have watched also with considerable amusement what I call the Great American Rip-Off; that is, the enormous industry based on spin-offs from *The Happy Hooker*. There was a line of cosmetics and perfume oils. Robin Moore, who was more an agent than co-writer, wrote a book called *The Making of the Happy Hooker*. I can't remember whether that was before or after he wrote *Green Berets*. And an ex-boyfriend published a book called *After Xaviera* in which I don't even appear. Then there's a film *Happy Hooker Goes To Washington*, an effort to exploit the endemic scandals involving Congressmen and prostitutes. Et cetera. Et cetera. It is impossible to sue. According to law, titles are not copyrightable. But I am neither bitter nor blase. I have been travelling and meditating, living mainly in my villa near Malaga in Spain, and have begun to write short stories and songs for a new L.P. I still like sex . . . because I love people.

Your books have been translated into most western European languages, as well as Hebrew and Japanese. Holland is your native country, yet your books have never been in Dutch before now. Why?

For family reasons. About ten years ago my mother came to America to visit me. I bought her a fur coat, with the first earnings from my writings. But you know how Calvinistic people can be here in Holland. When my mother came home everyone in her neighborhood made fun of her and said she had expensive gifts from the earnings of a prostitute. She was so embarrassed that she put the coat away and would never wear it again. So I didn't want to hurt my mother. Kept a Dutch silence. But people grow. Even old people. My mother has a different attitude now. And it has become clear to all but the small-minded that I am a writer — a writer about health and bodily feelings. After all, one of the major public health prob-

Gregory Corso

lems is orgasm difficulties. And if people can't even handle that — how can you expect to have good governments, or peace?!?

And now, before you ask these questions, let me answer them.

Yes. *The Happy Hooker* is pornography. Literally. By definition. "Porne" is Greek for harlot, and "graphy" means writing. So what?

I became a prostitute because I missed out being a suburban housewife.

In case of rape lie back and enjoy.

As far as Dutch literature is concerned, you can say I am the female Jan Cremer.

POEMS BY DAVID IGNATOW

THE HUMAN CONDITION, I

The rifle death of presidents,
the earthquakes and their huge fires
through which we walk,
talking and gesturing
and sitting down to eat
and lying down to sleep
or to make love, in midst
of racial riots, guerrilla war,
hugs and kisses
and whispered joys.

THE HUMAN CONDITION, II

We are here to make each other die
with perfect willingness.
It is like flagellants
who strike each other
methodically with straps.
When they are done, lying
in blood upon the floor,
they have reached the climax
they were seeking:
to be destroyed
and delighted
at the same time
and from the same source.

A PETITE HISTORY OF RED FASCISM

by Andrei Codrescu

All connections
are made by energy.
The inert masses
know nobody and not
themselves. Nobody &
Not-Self are well worth
knowing but connecting
them takes energy
so they are known
only by their masks
of inert proletarian
matter — Bolshevik
statues. The people
with the most energy
employ themselves to
know the statues. The
statues are well known
by the inert masses.
The people with just
a little less energy
are then employed
to interrogate the inert

proletariat. One energy
grade below the police &
mental health apparatus
employs itself to energise
the inert masses which
are now for the first time
broken up into individuals.
Breaking them up releases
energy — enough energy to
respond to questioning.
The police level then ex-
tracts a primitive narra-
tive from the recently
inert & this narrative
generates enough energy
and excitement to produce
a two-level discourse which
begins to make sense to the
upper energy level. New
energy is created & soon
the top echelons are introduced to the discourses of
Nobody & Not-Self. Together —
the brass & the masses
envision the statues:
the energy of the mass
will henceforth be employed
to make statues of the brass.

Frank Palaia

Ronnie Burk

FOUR UNPUBLISHED POEMS
by Jeffrey Miller

KNIFESET

probably around sunset you'll die
from a knife wound
the sun splitting the ocean apart
black blood
blade of wounded flesh
what can you say
the knife moves deceptively

(out from the cloudy pocket
moving straight to the point
so jesus serious
i want to call it "internal"
or something

it hits a vein thick with sadness

laughs spill on the horizon

the wave of death smacks on the beach like word after wave after wave. it's the morning after the wedding and everyone is drunk, stoned, smoking hash, and they walk out into the water one at a time maureen for instance, walks out of the water in a bikini of sadness covered with saltwater and tears dripping life death. life death. someone's ridden a motorcycle into the metal wave and now people surf from the fenders of volkswagens weird no?

Herr we got a motorcycle helmet packed with the emptiness of death like it was an ice cream cone melting on the beach.

Plowing through nerds I perchanced upon
a lovely who saw more out there than great endurance
"Shelly drown in you guys' puke"
she screamed & I agree: there's more to life
than endurance. I'll take the noise
of sweet maniacs reacting in flashes to
the mangled desires & bayonet senses that
point out purity.

GO AHEAD & JUMP

Be alright, be fantastic, you start dying, I'll start dancing, same star shining, nothing drastic, in our mouth, just a kiss, just a way to get you wet, beat you there, buy the beer, chat, get drunk, swear, nothing could stop my trying, no net, start crying, get wet, forget it, I was lying, it's OK if you live here, it's alright if it's fun, a pleasure, I never wanted to measure you, only wanted what I could get, The 7 Oceans and to get you wet.

Jeffrey Miller (1948-1977) had just begun to acquire a miraculous reputation when he was killed in a car accident in California on his 29th birthday on July 29, 1977. His first posthumous collection, *The First One's Free*, was published by Left Coast Press in 1978. A second book, from which these poems come, is looking for a publisher.

FROM THE E.C. CHAIR

Here we are, a year's long trail of *Corpses* behind us, poised to enter 1984. Not a pretty picture, but then look ahead: government murder and torture, censorship and intimidation are going to grow right and left, East and West. Are our writers in a good position to meet the decade head on? In our modest way, we've cleared a little air. If the academic mills were grinding only internal use documents there would be no problem. But they are grinding out a canon as well, and a deadly one at that. What's worse, the avant-garde and the academia have joined in a menage of uselessness and have divided between them many eager minds. But we are not proposing a centrist position. That would be like putting ourselves between the walls of the trash compactor in *Star Wars*. *Au contraire*, we are advocating something truly radical: disregard for boredom. We believe that all the ills of the world are traceable to a single malaise: PUTTING UP WITH IT. Not putting up with it is a complex operation. It involves finding again the threads connecting culture and human life. We are somewhat dissatisfied with our efforts over the past year: the breath of genius seems to be lacking from even the most intelligent efforts. The very air of our time seems to be lacking some major component. But, as Ted Berrigan used to say: "Have faith, brother!" We do, amazingly. And we will continue doing what we do best: kicking provincialism in the ass. Which should cause the provincials to open their mouths and sing Oh!

CHER CADAVRE EXQUIS

BOULDER COMMUNIQUE

SO GOOD YOU SEND ME EXQUISITE CORPSE COPY TO READ WITH DELIGHT HERE IN AMERICAN TOWN OF TIRELESS FLESH GLAD TO SEE ALL OLD FLAGS FLYING OF REEDKOSTELANTEZ/BERGEKATZMAN AND THE CLARKTOM WIND STILL BLOWING AND ALL FROM BALTIMORE CENTER OF PERIPHERY AND MUCH APPRECIATED PAUL HOOVER DING OF MIDWAIST ESTHETICS AND ALL OTHER OUTPOSTS COVERED BY CORPSE CORRESPONDENTS IN FIELD AND BRAZIL PARASURREALIST EXPOSE THAT I READ HERE UNDER ROCKY MOUNTAIN PARACHUTE THAT NEVER CAN COME DOWN TO MOBILIZE SEALEVEL MENTALITIES SUCH AS MINE AND WHERE I ASK IS THE WORK OF AND LIFE OF ISTVAN KOTTKI WHOSE SISTER MURIEL WAS KNOWN AS THE WALT DISNEY OF VISUAL MAXIMALISM ISTVAN HIMSELF THE CHARLIE PARKER OF THE VERBAL MAXIMALISTS CAN YOU HELP WITH THIS EXCUSE THIS ALL CAPITALS LETTER THERE IS NOTHING LEFT ELSE ON THIS RIPETIPER THIS IS CAPITALISM WHERE THE CAPITALISTS STAGE THEIR GUERRILLA WARS ON CAPITALIZED SKI SLOPINGS PLEASE SEND SUBSCRIPTION PLEASE ENCOURAGE LOWER CASE.

— Steve Katz

SEXUAL COMMUNISM A SUCCESS

AUREA VENERA IGNOTA: THE ONEIDA COMMUNITY AND COITUS RESERVATUS
by Sam Abrams

Although there are timid dissenters beginning to publish, the official glib, grad school opinion of the American communal experiments of the 19th Century remains, as it was enshrined in Parrington's *Main Currents*, that they failed. And hearing the great Shaker song "The Gift To Be Simple" used as television theme music, one is tempted to agree. The supposed failure is predicated on the short term of the experiments, but was Kitty Hawk a failure because the flight lasted only twelve seconds?

There is one particular case — the Oneida Community — that, although not without ironies, to my mind clearly establishes the success of the experimental movement. As Kitty Hawk established that mechanical flight is possible, so Oneida proved that the abolition of selfishness is possible.

We have admitted from the beginning that our free principles in regard to property, labor and love could not be carried out without the actual abolition of selfishness; so our success has been avowedly staked on the answer to the old question: "Can we be saved from sin in this world?" And the world looking on has predicted our downfall. But we have succeeded. (2nd Annual Report of the OC Association, 1850)

The summary of John Humphrey Noyes, the founder, after the breakup: "We made a raid into unknown country, charted it, and returned without the loss of a man, woman or child."

The success of the OC was long masked by the domination of one book, Robert Allerton Parker's *A Yankee Saint*, a book (much like Duberman's on Black Mountain) which has many scholarly virtues, but which (again like Duberman) omits the essential. In Duberman the lacuna is ART; in Parker it is JOY. Only in 1970, when the elderly Constance Noyes Robinson, a descendant of the OC stirpicults (eugenic experiments), published her volume, did it become possible to form a full image of the OC.

And the key phenomenon is JOY. Hundreds of people for twenty-five years in deed and in speech in paradise, then, there. Datum: none of the 100+ children who came of age during the experiment left; they all stayed, many returning to the community after college.

My maternal grandmother, who had been one of the dissidents at the breakup, told me, in her old age, that there had never been such happiness as they knew in the old Community. I believe this was an honest testimony . . . Most of the principal facts of this history I have known, some of them from early childhood, but the new and overmastering impression I gained . . . from reading the story . . . as the Oneida Communists told it, is of all-pervading happiness. (Constance Noyes Robinson in the preface to Oneida Community, An Autobiography, *Syracuse University Press, 1970.)*

Anyone who reads through the selection of original writings from the Community that constitutes her book, or spends some time with the great collection of Oneida publications at the Dartmouth Library, cannot escape that impression. As the Bloomie's smoked salmon counter is the epicenter of consumption in the western world, so the Oneida Community was the highpoint of happiness.

Two hundred and fifty folks happily engaged, in the full glare of publicity, in a radical economic, social and *sexual* experiment. "BEFORE HEAVEN AND EARTH WE TRAMPLE UNDERFOOT THE DOMESTIC AND PECUNIARY FASHIONS OF THE WORLD!" They published detailed accounts. During all the twenty-five years of the community, they issued a weekly newspaper, which included scrupulous reports of their experiments in all aspects of life, in economics, child rearing and breeding, politics, work roles, music, diet, clothing, and most famously, sexual practices and relationships.

The extent of their openness is hard to believe. They invited a hostile gynecologist to come inves-

Karen Rosco

tigate what he called "one of the most artificial sexual mal-relations known in history," allowed him free access, answered his questions with admissions that even shock today, for instance, telling him that sexual relations for females usually began by eleven years of age.

They invited visitors and almost every distinguished person who passed their way (e.g., Henry James) accepted their invitation to examine "an association established on principles opposed at every point to the institutions of the world." No wonder that Anthony Comstock (who boasted of having burnt in his career 160 tons of books) established the Society for the Suppression of Vice specifically for the suppression of the OC. Yet open and openly, opposed by politicians and clergymen and freelance bigots like Comstock, in the midst of Victorian America, they survived for twenty-five years, and were happy.

Before turning to the specifics of their sexual experiments, which is where the focus for further research should fall, I will cite just one example for the sake of the flavor of the OC. John Humphrey Noyes beat Thoreau, whose *Essay on Civil Disobedience* is dated 1849, by fifteen years in declaring his personal independence, on the same grounds that Henry David resigned, from the United States. The OC, from its formation, stated that "so long as our government stood with one foot on the neck of the slave and with the other trampled the rights of the red man, we had no sympathy with it...The Community for many years previous to the breaking out of the rebellion asserted their independence of the government and in heart and spirit disclaimed allegiance to it."

The sexual innovations of the OC were rooted in their religious heterodoxy. They subscribed to the perfectionist heresy that consists essentially of the belief that the second coming of Christ has already occurred and thus we are living in paradise. We only need to conduct ourselves according to the "ordinances of heaven" in order to realize that we are living in paradise. The name "perfectionism" signifies that humans are capable of achieving perfect sinlessness in this world.

Noyes became converted to this view in 1834 and rapidly emerged, between activities in the Underground Railroad and the publicity fuss evoked by Greeley's publication of his personal declaration of independence, as one of the movement's leaders.

It had long been one of the most cherished tenets of perfectionism that among the "ordinances of heaven" group marriage or free love was one of the most important, and Noyes' followers urged him to put this into practice. But although he experimented with other heavenly ordinances of communal living, he long resisted endorsing except in theory any sexual experimentation.

Noyes married in 1834. It was within this marriage that he achieved his most profound and startling insights, which led directly to the discovery that made the Oneida Community possible and which implies most significant possibilities for us today. As might be expected, from the very first days of their marriage, John and Harriet shared views on women's liberation that would be considered advanced now. For instance, on their wedding day they posted a notice in the kitchen to their friends that said since the "practice of serving three meals daily...subjects females almost universally to the worst kind of slavery..." they would serve only breakfast and for the rest their friends could help themselves.

By the sixth year of their marriage, they were living in an economically communist but sexually monogamous commune, and Harriet had undergone one extremely difficult live birth and four extremely difficult stillbirths.

Noyes decided to abstain from sex until he had solved the problem of birth control. He saw that in the primitive medical conditions of his time, sex without birth control was a form of murderous exploitation of women by men. It is easy for us to forget nowadays that until quite recently pregnancy and giving birth were not merely painful but always life-threatening and often fatal. He and Harriet agreed that celibacy was better than further risking her life. For Noyes, to decide was to publish, and not the least daring of his publications was his denunciation of sexual relations without contraception as "a relationship...in which, at every level of society, husbands become the blandly unconscious murderers of those they love and had pledged themselves to protect."

Noyes had a second insight, without which he might have been content to follow the Shaker example and accept celibacy, but having had it, he was driven on to his great discovery. The second insight was not new. Poets have understood it since at least Catullus. But Noyes was the first that I know of to express it in logical and expository, as opposed to lyric, form. (His peculiar American charm was, of course, that he was a pragmatic rationalist and religious enthusiast. I suppose I have to give Parker credit. His title, *Yankee Saint*, neatly sums that up.) This second point was the "dividing the sexual relationship into two branches, the amative and the propagative, the amative or love-relationship is the first in importance."

With these two principles, he set himself to the task, in 1844 in Putney Vermont, of discovering how "the benefits of amativeness can be secured and increased and the expenses of propagation reduced to such limits as life can afford."

He well understood how much was dependent on his quest. Success would allow, to mention just one of the freedoms he sought, that "childbearing be a voluntary affair."

And he succeeded completely, so that fourteen years later, the Oneidans could boast "our principles accord to woman a just and righteous freedom in this particular, and however strange such an idea may seem now, the time cannot be distant when any other idea or practice will be scorned as essential barbarism."

How Noyes discovered what he did is still a complete mystery to me. What he found was a method of fucking, closely related to certain Tantric practices, which he called Male Continence and which scholars of sex in the OC have called *coitus reservatus*. Male Continence was, and I define it *minimally*, for its precise definition is one of the matters which I am writing to encourage, a method in which the act of fucking is prolonged for hours without ejaculation.

I experimented on this idea and found that the self-control which it requires is not difficult; that my enjoyment was increased; that my wife's experience was very satisfactory, as it had never been before; that we had escaped the fears and horrors of involuntary propagation. This was a great deliverance.

The discovery of this method was central to the creation of the Oneida Community as a complex marriage. The method was particularly well adapted to a group marriage, since it had to be taught and practiced. Young boys practiced with women past menopause and young girls with older men who were experts. With this key bit of wisdom in place, the Oneida experiment became possible, and as anyone who looks into Robinson's book must see, successful.

"Do you really practice free love?" And Noyes replied, "Is there any other kind?"

Never has a couple eloped from the Oneida Community... The discipline of the passions is more radical here than with the Shakers, inasmuch as total abstinence is often more practicable than moderation... We wonder at the fact and still it is true. A hundred young folks have passed the age of temptation at the Oneida Community, and yet there has never been an elopement. (The Oneida Circular, 1869.)

So the first topic I call to your attention for further investigation is the success of the OC. Yet another, of immediate pertinence, of huge potential, is WHAT EXACTLY IS MALE CONTINENCE. The publications of Oneida, although, as you can tell from my quotations, of tremendous frankness, leave this point ambiguous — DID MEN WHO PRACTICED MALE CONTINENCE HAVE ORGASMS WITHOUT EJACULATION? Early students of the OC's sexual practice took the answer to be no, and the Karezza movement of the 1920s elaborated theories on the great benefits of sex without orgasm for either gender.

However!

Several of the physicians and sexologists who have studied the OC refer to their fucking practice as *coitus reservatus*, and Kinsey in the *Human Male* volume defines *coitus reservatus* as ORGASM WITHOUT THE EMISSION OF SEMEN BY ADULT MALES WHO DELIBERATELY CONTRACT THEIR GENITAL MUSCLES. The Kinsey survey found five males in their sample of 4,102 who practiced this technique at the time of the survey in the 1940s.

In 1974 I inquired of both the Kinsey and the Masters and Johnson institutes. At that time neither of them were investigating this phenomenon nor did they know of anyone who was. Masters wrote me that he thought the technique might be most helpful, but noted that an "essential part of the technique was training the younger men with post-menopausal females. To date, that is a relatively insurmountable obstacle."

CAVE JUNCTION, OREGON

by Lou Gold

For years I've been carrying around Grandpa's hammer, the one I played with at the Van Buren Street house in Chicago a long time ago. The other day I came upon it among my tools and decided to repair it...regrind the head and fit it to a new handle. Now it is a fine tool with a delicate balance and feel. I think that Grandpa would be proud of it.

As I lead a quiet and simple life among the forest and country folk, I often think of Grandpa. Mostly, I remember his teaching that understanding is important. We used to argue for hours about our respective "understandings" but somehow it was the value of understanding itself that always survived the details of debate. Now, when I seek understanding, I rarely have a conversation with anyone. I'm more likely to talk to a large tree, or sit by a river, or climb to a favorite spot high on a mountain ridge where I can watch the valley below and listen to the wind above.

The wind sings many songs and causes me to remember many poems. Sitting on a rocky point jutting out six or seven hundred feet above the valley floor I look down on the march of "progress" and look up at a ring of snow-covered peaks. Then I hear the voice of the Zen poet Ryokan —

> High on a mountain top
> An old monk and a cloud
> Last night it was stormy
> The cloud was blown away
> But what is a cloud
> Compared to the old man's quiet way?

It was my search for that quiet way that caused me to learn the techniques of meditation and brought me to this out-of-the-way place where conditions are poor, but simple and good. Five adults and a teenager live here on an extremely limited budget (about six hundred dollars a month). Jim and Dottie's small retirement income provides the only predictable cash flow. Occasionally Donner's mechanicing or my carpentering produce a few additional bucks. (I'm about to spend a large portion of some recent income on postage stamps.) Yet

prudence and a host of survival skills grant us a viable life-style and something to share with friends, visitors, and guests. Even though things get skimpy toward the end of each month, the constant flow of love is never diminished.

But even here the contradictions and encroachments of the modern world are inescapable. With all of our self-sufficiency know-how, the largest money drains are utility bills and county taxes. Electricity rates have soared because we are plugged into a grid involving the Washington-Oregon power conglomerate which is about to default on bonds it floated to finance several ill-advised and now ill-fated nuclear power plants. This was done despite the fact that the voters rejected these projects in several referendums. County taxes have also soared...mostly to support one of the largest per capita police departments in the nation and an ever-growing planning-zoning-building inspection department. Local sentiment is best expressed by the fact that our local town of Cave Junction abolished its own police force nearly two years ago.

Never in the past ten years, since I left politics, have I felt so political as now. And I'm living in the forest somehow beyond it all. (HA!) Never have I felt the long arms of government control and corporate greed so clearly and personally. Let me describe some of the ways these things enter my own life and feelings.

We are planning several interesting projects. We will float a small raft with a paddle-wheel and generator into the river. It will generate electricity to run a pump which will provide water for our garden during the dry summer months. It is "portable" so we can remove it if the authorities disapprove. You see, fish and environmental "protection" laws have been used to prevent small-scale hydroelectric power generation. If that weren't so, we could easily generate enough "juice" to free us from any dependence on the utility company .

Here's another interesting one: As soon as I can acquire two hundred dollars for building materials, I will build a small cabin to live in. Now in the planning stage, I'm learning various devious schemes. First, select a site well-concealed by trees. This is to avoid being spotted by daily aerial surveillance flights which search for "illegal" construction and marijuana patches. Second, build the foundation on skids so that we can claim it's a temporary structure and avoid possible increases in the property assessment. Third, make the roof out of canvas so that we can claim it's a tent and avoid requirements for a building permit. (Building permits can cost several thousand dollars for an average "normal" house in this area.)

In some ways this is sort of fun. I've always enjoyed out-smarting the authorities. But it's not fun for everyone. For example, our neighbor with eighty acres recently invited his unemployed son and daughter-in-law to live on his property. They were refused a permit for a second electric service because the county zoned the eighty acres as fit for only a single family. Again, it's a manipulation of one of those well-meaning laws intended to prevent endless subdivision and overdevelopment.

Last year I watched the county assessor value Harold and Jeannie's five acres of scrub hillside with a burned-down house, a hand-dug well, an outhouse, a small lean-to shack and a few chicken coops at over forty thousand dollars for tax purposes. (Four months later they sold that property for less than fifteen thousand dollars!) Similarly, hundreds of small miners, trappers, and the like have been driven out of the National Forest and from places near protected wildlife areas. The Forest Service regularly burns down "abandoned" cabins as part of its program to protect the environment. This is to say nothing of the relentless attack on local Native Americans, their fishing and hunting rights and ancient prerogatives.

Here, from the forest vantage point, many things look quite different to me. The great irony is that much classic liberal-progressive legislation, which is touted in the national media and supported by thinking, well-intentioned people elsewhere . . . environmental protection, wildlife preservation, Sierra Club proposals, and the like . . . are often used to wage war on "uncultivated" beings, people, animals, plants, and the Earth itself. As I watch the national news coverage of events in the Middle East, Southeast Asia, and Central America, there seems to be a worldwide conspiracy to destroy simple beings everywhere. This is an ancient story, of course, but there was a time when the hills and the forests were sacred, when they provided sanctuary for those people and animals who were happy to let "progress" pass them by in its large march down the valley. But the forest is no longer treated as sacred. People are being forced into modern urban industrial and highly controlled lifestyles. The

forest is being managed into cultivated timber crops free of "pests."

This effort is most blatant, overt, and vicious when the authorities believe that they are "morally correct." The marijuana situation is an excellent case-in-point. Southern Oregon and northern California produce the finest marijuana grown in this country. Many would argue it's the best in the world. It often fetches over four thousand dollars a pound east of the Rockies! For many years, things were reasonably mellow . . . certainly less intense than the earlier gold-rush period or present-day city life. But under the current national administration, an all-out war is being waged to eradicate the "plant." You wouldn't believe the show of force . . . heavily armed raiding parties, flak jackets, shotguns, automatic weapons, helicopters, special DEA task forces, and undercover agents. As might be expected, it is the little people who receive the harshest treatment.

Nowhere is the tendency of the government to destroy what it can't control more apparent than in the management of our great national forests. The Siskiyou National Forest which surrounds us is truly magnificent. It includes some of the last remaining old-growth forests on the West Coast. The nearby Kalmiopsis wilderness is a rugged roadless wild area containing the most diverse conifer forest on Earth and over twenty species of plant life have been identified which grow nowhere else. The "official" wilderness area is only a fraction of the region. When that area was established much local antagonism was generated as the Forest Service attempted to force anyone living within one hundred feet of the boundary lines off their property. Now the Forest Service is building a super two-lane logging road within six inches of the same boundaries. The road is aimed at the north face of Bald Mountain where a virgin forest has survived by virtue of its inaccessibility. Contracts are soon to be let for clear-cutting of most of the area. There are no plans for reforestation because the Forest Service's own study says that the steep serpentine hillsides of crumbly rock have little potential for regrowth. So once it is gone . . . that's it . . . forever! The drainages will be permanently damaged and a primary range of the legendary Big Foot eliminated.

This is not an isolated situation. To the south of us another logging road has been under construction for several years. It is all built except for the last six miles which are charted through the sacred burial grounds of three Indian tribes. There is a strange irony involved in this one which has complicated the litigation process. You see, the Indians considered this area so sacred that they felt that no one, including themselves, could claim to "own" it. Now a huge contract has been let to a large logging company to take out the whole area. Their chainsaws wait for the completion of the road.

One final horror story. (God. I'm beginning to feel like a reporter mongering after disaster news for his 6 pm TV audience.) A little further to the south across the Oregon-California border a major mining-smelting operation is being planned. The mining sludge will flow into the Smith River. The Smith is one of the most beautiful I've seen. It's the only undammed river remaining in the State of California. Its crystal clear water is teeming with salmon and steelhead trout. The smelting process will also spew thousands of tons of sulphur dioxide into the air and prevailing winds will carry it right here to the Illinois Valley where it will be trapped by thermal inversion. In other words, the beautiful sky I watch for rainbows and shooting stars may be obscured by a layer of smog some day.

In the spring I traveled up to Eugene to attend a meeting of the Earth First! organization. They are a radical environmental group devoted to the protection of the Earth through non-violent direct action and civil disobedience. The meeting was a workshop on non-violent tactics led by veterans of several anti-nuke demonstrations. It was held to prepare people for a blockade of the Bald Mountain road. The actions were just beginning. There had been two blockades. People placed themselves between the bulldozers and the trees. Four folks were arrested the first time, seven the second time. As I listened to the issues and watched bright-eyed college students talk idealistically about the movie *Gandhi* I wondered if I could continue to stay away from politics. Then, as we role-played various arrest situations, I felt all the ugliness of confrontation. But something had changed inside. There were no longer the old feelings of anger and rage. Instead, there was just a pain in my heart. I wished that I could go home and work in the garden. Who wouldn't?

When I returned, I talked to Harold about it. He said, "Yep, the whole human race is absurd and I'm fool enough to try to talk sense to it. My folly is that Jeannie and I and the kids are going to travel around in a bus teaching meditation and healing. Maybe there will be a few ripe ones who will turn their consciousness toward healing the Earth. Maybe we will discover the hundredth monkey." Every Friday night our meditation group meets. We do healings for specific people and we send energy to our Native American sisters and brothers who are in jails across the country.

I also talk of these things with Little Crow who carries a great sadness for the plight of his people and the Earth. In the sweatlodge we pray for Grandmother Earth and we attempt to heal Nam vets of the residual effects of Agent Orange poisoning and wartime scars. We try to heal the children of Canadian Indians who are suffering from mercury poisoning. As we do this, Forest Service helicopters continue to spray herbicides on large tracts of reforested land to kill oaks and other broadleaf trees which compete with pines and firs in a young forest. While the soil is robbed of the benefit of nitrogen-producing trees and the streams are contaminated, lawyers and experts argue in courtrooms over "possible long-range effects."

Little Crow tells many stories of his grandpa . . . about learning the sweatlodge ceremony from him . . . about how he secretly approved, even though he put on a face of stern disapproval, when Little Crow played hooky from the mission schools he was forced to attend . . . about how Grandpa was shot dead for not leaving a South Dakota town at sundown like a "good Injun." I then tell him my own Grandpa stories . . . about how his younger brother was killed after assassinating some Czarist officials in the wake of a pogrom . . . about how he fled to this country full of faith in the ballot box and got beat up by cops serving Chicago machine politicians when he tried to be a poll-watcher for the Socialist Worker Party . . . about how he felt that doctors, lawyers, and religious authorities were part of a conspiracy against the people. Little Crow says to me, "Lou, you learned much from your Grandpa. Your ancestors were a tribal people who were forced on to the reservation many times."

Back in 1968, after the assassinations of Martin Luther King and Robert Kennedy and the Democratic Convention, I decided that I could no longer vote. I tried to explain my decision to Grandpa. He tried to understand. Neither of us succeeded. I last saw Grandpa in the nursing home in 1973. He had been reduced to a fight for personal survival. I was retreating from five years of demonstrations and had been reduced to a search for personal freedom. Since then I have listened to the silence of the desert and have learned to hear that silence inside myself. But the scream of the world continues.

I'm no longer carrying any romantic notions about the "people." All the tendencies which get organized into governments and corporations exist in each of us as individuals. And technology has a way of marching onward no matter what we think about it or how we use it. Some philosopher, seeking to explain the growth of technology, said, "Give a small child a hammer and he will use it." Obviously, something like that has happened to me. But I still imagine a world in which hammers are free, play is limited to a scale where mistakes are affordable, and the techniques of love are as well-understood as those of fear. There is no final solution. We are all children in a wondrous and terrifying world. Doing the best we can is as close to Perfect as we can be.

Thanks for being there to listen to lots of soul-searching. Much love to you and God bless.

MY SECOND VISIT TO ISRAEL
by Michael Brownstein

This is my second visit to Israel. I don't think I'll be here much longer, everyone distrusts me because I don't talk, won't say a word no matter what, just look around, but that's no good, the Israelis I encounter are garrulous and inquisitive, when I won't open my mouth they report me to the army. I only returned to Israel because the last time was so disastrous I never got the chance to look around, to daydream, which is what I like to do.

On my first visit it took just a few days before I met some people, and the same thing always happened, I had to run for my life. I'd meet Israelis of all ages on the streets and in the cafes, they always asked if I was Jewish, if I was American.

They wanted to know what I did in the U.S.A., and I told them I was a poet. But what did I *do*, they persisted. To the ones I felt I could trust, I said I had spent a typical day recently listening to *Songs of the Free* by the Gang of Four, I told them

that poetry was an anachronism in my country and the poets reluctant misfits. What else was I to do, I said, somehow one still survives.

"Gang of Four?" they asked. "Are they Jewish?"

I explained this was an English rock group, and invariably their mouths wrinkled with distaste.

"Rock and roll, we Israelis have no time for that; what is your opinion of the Palestinian problem?"

Since I was asked, I told them what I thought: "Palestinian girls are pretty, even the older women look interesting, although less interesting than they might be if they had intermarried with strangers."

This brought the Israelis, no matter how talkative, to a halt. Their eyes bulged and the color came into their cheeks. "What do you mean?" they finally demanded.

I proceeded to give them my theory, and it's worth noting I couldn't help doing so even after the first couple of times, when such dire consequences had ensued. This shows I believed in my theory.

"I don't support racial purity," I began. "It always results in fanaticism, look at the bloodshed between Arabs and Jews, it's not pretty and it leads nowhere. Have you never noticed the most beautiful women in the world are half-breeds, Eurasians and the like? I believe in mongrelism, it airs out the genes, it makes wonderful Filipino Finns, and sultry Chinese Peruvians, and those wild Irish Jews," I continued, "have you never heard Irish Jews talk? Mongrelism makes temperamental Moravian Zulus, and dreamy Swedish Afghans, and the elusive Polish French girls you can sometimes glimpse in transit, late at night; or, in America, where you can't help stumbling over Scottish Russians, they're terrific, when they make love to Portuguese Eskimos it's really something special. I think you Israelis should immediately mate with Palestinian girls, it's the only way to go, and the young Palestinian men, let them be encouraged to lie down with sabras."

It was always at this point that I came to be pushed off my cafe chair or shoved into the street, they would hiss at me and slap me, or if they were big enough they tried to beat me up. The conversation had ended, I wouldn't get another word in, in fact I usually had to take off at a dead run, my camera swinging back and forth around my neck.

So I've decided to say nothing on my second visit, not a word, not one syllable, it's the only way I'll ever get to see the country, and already I've seen some breathtaking things, like the quiet lights of Beersheba in the hour before dawn, and the palpable heat of midday on the shores of the Dead Sea, where thousands of years ago remarkable men were driven past their limits. But when I won't open my mouth the Israelis who try to talk to me become suspicious, they think I'm a spy, there's always someone following me now no matter where I go, asking if I am Jewish, if I am American. In spite of the harassment I refuse to respond, my theory in which I still believe will have to wait for elucidation until I return to the U.S.A., where it's safe for a poet to say whatever he thinks, since few are listening anyway.

THE HAGUE

by William Levy

There are two world-famous queens living in The Hague. The first, Beatrix, Queen of the Netherlands, travels to foreign countries just to tell them Holland is more than windmills and wooden shoes. Tolerance, she claims, is what makes her country unique. Indeed it is. The other royalty is Monique von Cleef, Queen of Pain. Her advertisement in tourist guides readily available on hotel desks — for once — realistically describes the truth. Under the heading *uit is gezellig* (going out is wholesome) we read: "Dominant Registered Nurse receives submissive slaves in well-equipped torture room. Rubber and leather wardrobe, boots, chains, bondage, water sports, enemas, high colonics. Transvestites may enjoy corsets and elegant dresses in my exquisite boudoir. Corn. Houtmanstraat 2, The Hague, Holland. Tel: (070) 856392."

Monique von Cleef sits on a plush velvet chair in her cozy suburban home, a glass of whiskey with ice in her hand, as she talks about the humorous sides of her calling.

"There's this ex-priest who visits me," she says. "Well, he likes to eat shit; hot — just as it comes out. So I had this girl shit in his mouth. He was gagging and gasped, 'It's too much. Too much.' So I told him to chew. Chew. He began chewing, then cried out: 'Oh my god. Oh my God. It's the body of Christ.' Holy shit, eh?

"Then there was this woman who used to come to me once a month for a shit and champagne dinner. The shit was elaborately served on a platter with lettuce and tomatoes around it. One day the girl who usually did the shitting for me couldn't do it. We tried everything. Laxatives. Everything. So what am I to do? I went around the corner and told my problem to one of my nieces. She did the shitting. When the woman came for her dinner, she ate one bite of the substitute shit, got up and left. You see, she knew the difference!

"Then there's the rabbi who takes off his yarmulke before entering my house. Water sports are popular; I give a lot of enemas. Once I had my pussy sucked by a nun; she did it well. And only last week I had this couple. She likes bondage. Her husband likes to watch. He asked me to suck his wife's cunt while she was helpless. I wouldn't do it. I told him: Even for $1000 I wouldn't suck cunt." Then Monique reconsiders, and says, "Well, maybe I would — if I'm high on coke."

Monique is likable and spirited, like one's favorite aunt. It's only when I look and see that beneath her carefully coiffured blonde hair she is wearing a studded dog collar around her neck, a black leather jacket and pants, and red boots laced up to the knee; then I realize — no aunt of mine ever dressed

Brian Swann

like that. She is also very open with a charitable self-esteem, a cordiality without pride which is infinitely charming. When I ask Monique: "How did you start in this business?" she offers a candid summary of her journey to becoming Paincoming Queen.

"I've been a dominatrix for twenty years," she says, with dignity. "I was born in 1925 and before I got into this I was a nurse, a midwife and married to a rich Baron. Luckily he died. Then I had a hotel in Spain. In 1963 I was in the States and a friend told me there was a big demand for dominant females. So I placed an advertisement and was immediately in business. That was in Newark. After a while the Mafia came to me and said: 'We will protect you and you give us 50% of the take.' I told them: 'No, that's just like working for a pimp.' Soon after that I was busted. That was in '65; it was headlines all over America," Monique says. "The trial was in '67; I was declared guilty but my lawyers appealed all the way to the Supreme Court who overturned the conviction on the basis of an illegal search. Justice Douglas wrote an opinion saying no law was broken because my clients were consenting adults. That was in '69 and I had already left the States and was living in London. In '70 I came back to The Hague, worked as head nurse in a hospital, but I wasn't making a penny. So I started this, again. And in '72 my autobiography, *House of Pain*, was published in New York as a mass market paperback. In '80 I went back to America. I was doing well . . . but I didn't like it."

"Why?" I ask.

"Too dangerous. Too dangerous," Monique growls in a husky voice. "It's better in Holland. I charge 250 guilders an hour (approximately $85) and have six or seven customers who come to me every week; many others from all over the world. And no one bothers me here. That's important." Monique puts down her drink; she reaches out toward a nearby table, picks up a large book and hands it to me. "It's my scrapbook."

Monique gets a number of phone calls while I'm looking through her press clippings and photos of friends and customers. She speaks easily in German, Dutch and English. "No," I hear her say in German. "I don't have a slave boy this week. Number 88 — the one who works for Interpol — he was mean to my servant; I put him on parole." On one page of the scrapbook I see a familiar face:

it's a snapshot of the mysterious film actress Kim Novak who co-starred with Frank Sinatra in *Man with a Golden Arm.* She is sitting on a couch in this living room.

"Oh yes," Monqiue says indifferently. "That's Kim Novak. She wants to be spanked. But, you know, I have criteria for accepting new slaves. If they're too nervous I drop them. A real slave is always trying you out. I have to mold them a little bit at a time. Also, some people say 'no' and mean *no*, others say 'no' and mean *yes*. You have to know the difference. The main basis is mutual trust; people trust me."

Suddenly Monique stands up. "Come," she says, gesturing toward me with a sweep of her arm. "Come upstairs with me to my torture chamber. I have a slave girl waiting. It is Veronica Vera. Perhaps you have heard: She is one of America's new, young, up-and-coming porn stars. You will like her — she has purple hair and wears a ring in her pierced left nipple."

Upstairs I find myself in a room resembling a creepy interrogation cave left over from the 16th Century Inquisition, when Spain ruled the Netherlands. Monique grabs Veronica, ties her legs with cord, puts her wrists in handcuffs and hauls her off the ground with pullies.

"I'm afraid," Veronica cries out, "that I'm going to slide out of these wrist things."

Monique responds with professional scorn. "I've heard that before. Try to move your fingers," she insists. Veronica moves her fingers and Monique shouts: "Why are you moving your fingers!?!" Veronica stops. "Now," Monique asks in her best bedside manner, "tell me how you feel?"

"Relieved."

"Look in the mirror and see yourself — helpless."

"It doesn't humiliate me to see myself like this in the mirror," Veronica says, trying out her Mistress. She suggests: "I'm getting excited to be whipped."

"Will you settle for twenty strokes?" Monique asks.

Veronica sighs: "I'll settle for ten."

"Then I'll give you twenty-five."

"Oh please, not twenty-five . . ."

Monique lowers Veronica to the floor, puts her over her knees and begins the caning. Under her breath Veronica starts counting: "One, two, three, four . . ."

"Don't count," Monique tells her. "I can count; I've gone to school. You can scream; don't count."

"Aaarrrggghhh!"

"I've someone who screams like that when he comes," Monique observes. "Now, I'm going to let you loose if you ask me to give you three more."

"Please," Veronica mumbles, "oh please Monique — give me three more."

Whack! Whack! Whack!

Monique puts down the cane. "Lean on your knees," she tells Veronica. "I'm going to give you a spanking. How about forty?"

"Yes, Monique. Forty." The sound of flesh hitting flesh fills the torture chamber. "Pleeeeze," Veronica sobs. "I like it and I hate it!"

"My hand is more evil than a whip," Monique replies.

"Aaaarrrggghhh. Ouweee!"

Monique approves: "You do have an exciting scream."

A week after the beating Veronica Vera told me: "S & M, B & D are mainly mind trips, a kind of religious communion. But now my ass is black and blue, and I love it: the whipping Monique gave me was better than ten enemas."

Monique — of course — is delighted to hear this. "What's life," she says, "without laughs?!" ☠

THE STATE OF THE MESS ADDRESS: HOLDING UP THE BOUGH
by Lawrence Ferlinghetti

If language is a desiring-machine, then poetry is the supreme essence or ideal model of that machine.

All our desires are expressed in our languages, written, sung, painted, played, or otherwise signed or signalled, in music, painting, poetry or prose. Language is the primary carrier of ideas and images, but more primal than that it is the carrier of our half-formed, amorphous, barely articulated or inaudible thoughts and emotions, subliminal or subconscious, including nascent unrecognized inchoate desires, longings, needs, hungers and dreams. Through the front and back doors of perception pour all the phenomena of existence, and through our tongues pour forth all that we assimilate and synthesize of that existence, transformed by our particular and pressing needs into that conscious and unconscious language of desiring each of us speaks, whether clearly or covertly, honestly and openly, deviously or obviously.

Here it is that poetry and painting and all art has its most crucial function, its greatest opportunity. It is a unique function which poetry above all other forms of art should be able to accomplish, bringing to consciousness and articulating in the most beautiful and telling language our deepest perceptions and desires, dreams and ideas, in their most vivid form. It is the desiring-machine par excellence.

The truth is, poetry is hardly functioning as such today, except on the most parochial and petty level. It should function as a heat-seeking missile but somehow it has been disarmed, or is at most disarming. Because most poets today seem to have abdicated their role as gadfly of the State and of the mind, as the conscience of their race, poetry has become an ephemeral thing in our society.

Literature as the privileged locus of thinking out man's fate and giving meaning to life requires it cast its syntheses of existence in the most profound terms, in the grandest frames of reference. But poetry in our time has not often reached this high, caught as it is in the general predicament of literature today.

Modern literature has been a creature of a divided Left since early in this century. It has been divided between objective and non-objective, between the representational and the surrealist, between the stream-of-consciousness and the stagnant lakes of prose thought, et cetera. In music and painting as in literature, it has been a "battle with the image" — a distintegration on all fronts of the coherent image, Eliot's "dissociation of sensibility" paralleled by the fragmentation of the image in every art, including film and music.

In the 1930s the political disintegration of the avant-garde became all too devastatingly evident. The God That Failed was that Communism which so much of the artistic and intellectual community of the U.S. embraced and then as passionately rejected, leaving the literary avant-garde in a complete shambles from which it has never really recovered.

It is as if it had nowhere to go, except in circles. Staggering between shored-up Marxist ruins and libertarian chimeras, the contemporary poet in particular has never been able to find himself or herself again, and today remains helplessly mired in the position of the disintegrated Left inherited from defunct generations. This position is essentially one of alienation from society, and it is this generally alienated attitude which poetry and the arts today cannot seem to move beyond, even in the latest punk art and music which is another extreme form of the alienation of the artist in our military-industrial perplex which still seems progressively to suppress the *subjective* in each of us.

Because the subjective in every individual lies at the heart of the creative process, the artist naturally feels threatened, feels that life itself is threatened by the brute force of the military and the industrial. And so for over 50 years the avant-garde has been telling the world "Go Back — Wrong Way."

Yet we proceed as if all the red and yellow lights weren't flashing.

And this is where semiotics, that latest rage in the linguistic departments from France to Stanford, may prove useful. The word *semiotics* can hardly be found in the old Webster Unabridged. It is simply defined as the language of signs. And it is poetry which is ideally the language of signs, pointing to the hidden meanings of our lives, the hidden directions, the secret meaning of things. These secret signposts or signings are everywhere to be discovered or rediscovered. In every field, not only literary, these semiotic signals are truly poetic. In fact, in most fields of knowledge the most advanced concepts often turn out to be most poetic. So it is with astronomy in which "black holes" are intense poetic images, and the astronomic idea that "there must be a place where all is light" (cf. Olber's Paradox) is of course highly poetic and romantic.

Thus is quintessentially poetic the very idea of

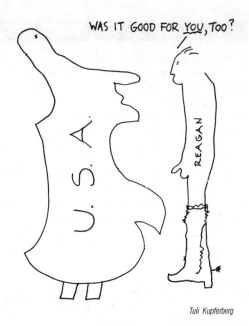

Tuli Kupferberg

the interpretation of dreams in Freud, the concept of the archetype in Jung, the "tristes tropiques" interpretation of primitive cultures in Lévi-Strauss, the idea of the "origin of consciousness in the breakdown of the bicameral mind" in the writings of Julian Jaynes, the Buddhist conception of consciousness in all sentient beings, et cetera.

The idea of language itself as a primal desiring-machine is primally poetic. Only through language can we articulate the consciousness and the conscience of the race and see our way through our "cosmic predicament" on earth. Only by inspired road signs of a new high consciousness can we possibly make it through without disaster. It is our masters of language, spoken or sung, printed or imaged, who must erect the great signs.

Thus may the poet still hold up the Golden Bough (that ultimate semiotic symbol) in the dark wood. It is all the more lamentable, then, that many North American poets of the 1980s — particularly in regard to the great social and political matters of today — continue to maintain "a silence closely resembling stupidity."

It's hard to be a lion in the Year of the Rat. Or, as typically they call it in the papers, the Year of the Mouse. Of course, it would be much heavier to be an Elephant, the New York Review of Books, for instance. We are, it seems, a lion singing believe, believe, believe (after eating the borderguard) surrounded by immobile elephants and scurrying rats. But we know our Aesop (and our Duncan) so no matter how long it takes, the fable goes on. We went to the Baltimore Zoo the other day, accompanied by the Great Northern Chief and his Willowy Lady, and looked at the animals. It was snowing and the Zoo was empty of people, and even some animals were missing. Like the Giraffes and the Ostrich. And the Wild Pigs. Where are they? roared the Chieftain. They roam the poet's house, said one of us. In the East and the West, pigs roam the poet's house, and as we looked, quite clinically, at the panorama we had opened, we saw the pigs doing just that. With much sadness then, and because we were freezing, we returned to our respective homes in the Winter of 1984, and searched for pigs. They were there. So was Big Brother. And Little Sister. And the Kissing Cousins. And Mom and Dad. Only they were all dead and we had to plug them in so their Exquisite Corpses would glow when someone comes to visit. Come. Visit.

THE BAY DIES OF POLLUTION & DECOYS RISE IN PRICE

by *Nathaniel Tarn*

for Mark McNair

1.
Thinking of her at breakfast
close by Annapolis, between two bouts of talk,
who bears with equanimity
grief's ships, my fleet, over her sea of patience
and that we are as familiar
to each other now as birds
in the great lines of geese yesterday night
while we were crossing Maryland —
when the sky became immense, translucent bowls
nested within each other
and their horizons stretched all the way west
to a distant house where we would soon migrate!
And the numbers of those birds
weaving their leaves of absence in the sky,
the number of those birds in that depth of sky!
Thinking that she haunts me
like an "azure" I have almost forgotten exists
whether it be in the poem
or in the depth of that sky which is reality
and which I still sometimes leave home for
to touch a base or two...

2.
The association of beauty and pain
— "beauty is but the beginning of terror
we are unable to bear" — and this morning
on the Bay beyond the storming waters
in a smoke of Fall leaves and comfortable kitchens:
eating: Roman disasters of blue crab
smithereen-smashed on paper tablecloths —
allows some domesticity to dispel the pain.
The Names of the Great Carvers in my mind
and their achievements, like crests and shields,
postered around us — the birds, the "BIRDS",
the lovely, feather-perfect, bobbing birds,
the magnificent art of carving, what it signifies,
the whole Bay culture still breathing in them
(as the Bay itself dies of pollution
and the cry "Save this!"/"Save that!" goes up
    again)
and I who would die in this morning radiance

to spend part of my life here, soaking up light,
who have already spent almost all that life
and am, in any case, destined for elsewhere,
I know once more a door shut in my face,
the market suddenly jumping way out of reach
and the carvings suddenly swallowed by money,
and for this once, which might be the last time,
I'll go back for once without a "bird"
(trivial misfortune — yet the whole fate of "art"
and its true destination bound in that question)
no: the great ocean beyond the window is not
deep enough to encompass loss
which encompasses little by little all we love —
the bitterness of it, the uncounted days
working at the pile's bottom for pittances,
lifetime of small doors closing.

3.
In the radiance — luminism, luminescence —
in the breaking blastoff of American light
returning to haunt me when I least expect it,
blessed gift of the continent I have chosen:
the delicacy of the ships,
the small Bay Bugeyes and Skip Jacks
lying at rest among the fanning swans —
and behind them, the small wooden houses,
almost like toys in a toy farm. Going home tonight,
carrying nothing
but for a two-bit flag "Don't Give Up The Ship"
— empty-handed it seems, not yet recalling the words,
the treasury of words opening up
when least expected,
appearing out of nowhere like long lines of geese.

RELAXING AT THE TURO: THE MAN WHO WANTED A GUGGENHEIM

by Richard Elman

I have a friend who wanted a Guggenheim Fellowship. He applied the requisite 9 or 10 times with excellent credentials and they wouldn't give him one. He was a poet and not getting any younger. Pretty soon he might be above the recommended age for prize winners.

He tried calling the Foundation for assistance, but there were only twirps on the other end of the line and the only advice they could give was about Xeroxes and summaries of careers, stamped self-addressed envelopes, etc.

My friend had come to believe that a personal appeal might get him a Fellowship.

One day, shortly after the latest round of Fellowships had been announced, he dressed up in a suit and tie and .38-caliber "replica" Walther pistol and went up Park Avenue to the offices of the Guggenheim people.

The receptionist asked who he would like to see and he said the office manager.

She emerged and he drew out his ersatz gun and stuffed it against her back. Demanded to have all the cash on hand.

"There's only petty cash," she told him.

"That's OK with me," he said.

There was well over $100 and he took all of it, but harmed nobody, and left the building in a hurry with his "Guggenheim money."

It was the most important day of his life. There was no stopping the poetry after that. And the poem he wrote immediately afterwards with his "Guggenheim money" stays with me as pieces of marrow in the mushroom barley:

> *Gugg Gugg Gugg*
> *Terwit Terwoo*
> *Reject me not*
> *Reject me not*

POET LORE

by Bill Zavatsky

If you have published
a poem or two
and one day find yourself
at a school
or a party
on the strength
of that reputation
or seated at a dinner table
introduced as "the poet"
smiling shyly, embarrassed
though secretly pleased
inevitably someone
absolutely nice
someone intelligent
possibly even attractive
so much so in fact
that you find yourself
drawn to her, or to him
in the deepest ways
of the heart:
there this person is —
good-looking, bright

smiling radiantly back
at you, The Poet
and telling you
how much they love
your poetry. "See?
Look! I have that
postcard of your poem
taped inside my
violin case!" Or
they begin to recite
a poem you wrote at
twenty-three, sweetly
reciting, eyes closed
and you are so touched
that when they mention
excitedly that they know
this *other* poet, too,
a slug whose dreadful work
you have had the extreme
misfortune to have read,
whose disgusting personality
crawls across your soul
merely at the mention
of their nerdy name, why
you can hardly
believe it!

Here *you* are
standing before her:
a real poet
and human being
of inestimable worth,
not some creep sycophantic
ass-kissing businessman jerk
or jerkette who slept its way
into print or bought its way
to a powerful editorial berth...
there you stand
listening to this lovely face
tell you how *great*
are the voiceless verses
of this poseur pseudo-poet fart
(she took his or her
workshop, what an
incredible experience,
such a fabulous teacher!)
and you stand there
tasting the acid of your own
spit as it eats away your tongue,
battered by images
of the slimy shank impostor,
knowing that he paid
a major publishing house
to stamp his junk into print,
knowing that his famous poet friend
who did a blurb-job on the jacket
stood beside you in the bookstore
laughing at the praise he'd given,
and you stand there, lips
splitting with rage
as you work and work
to rivet a smile to your face,
sinking, struggling to be
"professional" instead of
screaming all the vicious truths
you know about this idiot disgrace
to the high calling of verse,
restraining yourself in the
jacket of your smile from
thrashing to the floor
as you cackle vituperations
and scratch the wax from the
parquet with bloody nails...
And if you do this — as you
sometimes have done, will do — if
you dance in a fury
on the sour grapes

Amy Salganik

of your literary life,
abandoning your tongue
to fire instead of song,
offering it to the shrivelling scream
of outrage, the flamethrower breath
of Archilokhos
who torched Lykambes
with searing iambic song,
the chant of stomp and kill
burning that father
who'd promised the poet his daughter
promised him his daughter
then said *No,* to hear in reply:
"Lykambes! May you freeze, starve,

and piss your pants simultaneously
on the podium
of the Guggenheim Museum
as you drone your deadened lines!
May the *Directory of American Poets*
misspell your name, list (instead of
your number) the phone number of
a Chinese restaurant in Budapest,
and consign you to teaching endless
poetry workshops for the dead
in the vast cemeteries of Queens!
May *Coda* magazine schedule a feature
article on you, then cease publication!
May the *American Poetry Review* publish
your new long poem and omit every other
line, then publish a correction, running
the entire poem backwards — in Dutch!
And may all the little magazines
and small press publications in the world
arrive simultaneously on your doorstep,
crushing your piggish visage to the jelly
that all good poets crave!"

That's what you want
to cry out, but
as you do this,
as you flame and smoke and scream
her smile collapses, her sweet
face turns away, sickened
to have seen a poet roused
to ire at a fellow bard.
(She thought all poets
were supposed to be friends...)
And nothing
you can say,
and nothing
you can do
will ever convince her
that your insane oration
your temporary possession
by the god, the fury
that scorched her eyebrows
and sent her away
is also
poetry

Vidstrand

FROM THE E.C. CHAIR

Lawrence Ferlinghetti wants everybody to know that the original title of his "State of the Mess Address," which we published in our last issue, was really "Holding Up the Bough," which now everybody knows. But this also set us thinking about titles, heads and why authors and editors rarely agree on them. Headlines are what separate a newspaper from meeting minutes and court records. They are what separate our newspaper from the writing-therapy rags flooding the land, like APR, ABR and the rest of the Acronym Press. Our headline writers are our Japanese philosophers, who see the beauty of the package and its appeal as essential. When they view a situation, or a story, they are looking at an unrealized communication and feel called upon to find the shortest way to your interest. They are generally large men (ours are) and Camel-smoking women (ours is) with large foreheads on which once was writ something. Their general air of Golemic alertness causes them to be on their aphoristical toes at all times, especially around deadlines. They are a resolutely Capitalist breed, since they cannot be found in Soviet satellites where the excitement of interest is forbidden. Headlines there are pulled Dada-style from a hat and consist entirely of combinations of the five words: SURPASSED, PRODUCTIVITY, SOCIALIST, PLENARY and PROLONGED. Here, thank God, the headline writer is an artist in his or her own right (though often unrecognized) who holds the reader's interest dearer than the author's. An uncelebrated aphorist operating on anywhere from two to four levels, the Headline Writer is the only member of our profession to receive no Pulitzers, no Nobels, no Nothing. We propose that this situation be instantly remedied, and we call on our readers to send us the most remarkable headlines they encounter for a Headline Bank prior to the establishment of some kind of *Prix Phrénologique.*

CHER CADAVRE EXQUIS

LOST IN A FOREST

The conclusion of Mr. Ferlinghetti's essay reminds me of a story about some men lost in a forest searching for a way out. They happen upon a wise and apparently experienced older inhabitant, seated in a nearby clearing. They rush over and ask, "Can you tell us the way out? You look like you know." He gazes up to them, equally perplexed and weary, and responds, "I've been in here for quite a while. You're right. And I know what you can eat and what is poisonous. I know about some dead ends *not* to take. I know where you can get a moment or two of rest and a good drink. But I don't know the way out. We're in this — !%¢&!? — forest together!" *Megatrends, The Aquarian Conspiracy*, and *In Search of Excellence* reflect the modern perplex we find ourselves in today. And a lot of persons are equally perplexed as they explore new ways of self-conceptualization. Paradigms (personal and social) are shifting amidst personal and social transformation. The poet isn't alone anymore in holding up a Golden Bough in the dark wood. Maybe that's why Mr. Ferlinghetti doesn't see so many around himself at the moment. Even a military officer, a business executive, or a priest can now develop out of that common forest floor a totally new reconceptualization of self and role and of possibilities. But how perplexing to make the clearings in our forests to see past the tried and true stereotypes of those old roads perceived and to miss the military diplomat, the executive human rights activist and strategist, and the priest connector and healer! Herman Kahn writes, "History has a habit of being richer and more ingenious than the limited imaginations of most scholars or laymen." I might add that even poets' and writers' imaginations could occasionally bear some stretching. Yes, we're in this perplexing forest together. *None* of us really knows the way out, but each has a tiny clue of experience to share; a piece of the Golden Bough . . . Mushroom hunting, anyone?

— John B. Leira, S.J.

Amy Salganik

BEDEVILLED LIT

"The State of the Mess Address" by Ferlinghetti provides an opportunity to confront a serious problem bedevilling contemporary literature. This is the distinction between poetical and conceptual expression, between advancing the language as a "desiring-machine" and utilizing language to advance the mind. For many years now, language as a "desiring-machine" has been the chosen fetish of participants in the poetry scenes in the United States. Rarely have poets cared to move beyond the domain of raw emotion which poetry serves to dress up and accentuate. Rarely among poets can one find interest in language as a vehicle for elaborating or asserting the conceptions upon which our

consciousness is based. It is ironical, therefore, that in all seriousness a distinguished American poet writes that "literature as the privileged locus of thinking out man's fate and giving meaning to life requires it cast its syntheses of existence in the most profound terms, in the grandest frames of reference." Brave words! — but no practicing poet I have ever met in the flesh has been interested in formulating his poetry with such an end in mind. "Man's fate" has been passe in poetry circles for a long time — a desiring machine is much more fun. In fact, poetry as an art form is not very suitable for expressing the problem of man's fate or for asserting meaning in his life. It is only very rarely that geniuses such as Blake or Goethe appear who can utilize the poetical spirit for expression of profound thoughts. Poetical expression, involved as it is in the aesthetics of language and rhythm, is better suited for the representation of personal feelings whose intensity it fuels. It is a poor vehicle for the transmutation of these feelings into vital concepts, the absence of which is so painfully evident in American life at every level. If we really want to deal with the realities of our shameful consumer society, with the deterioration of culture everywhere evident, with the martyrdom of spirit upon the crosses of bourgeois careerism and family life, and, especially, with the dependence upon superannuated religions and absurd cults for gratification of deeper needs, then we will have to turn away from desiring machines and take up the more difficult task of creation of new conceptions that will give direction and dignity to our lives. Ultimately such a task is more fulfilling since there is no consciousness or conscience among societies or individuals until their literary figures undertake to perform it.

— Richard Schain

UTTERANCE OF SUPERIOR BEING

Thank you for the EXQUISITE CORPSES, but they are precisely that. The person who does autopsies is called nowadays a Medical Examiner, and I suppose they have the patience for dealing with dead images across which the brief flickering of intelligences crying out for constant light, gazes. When I was in College I had adopted that sort of analytic approach with a tone of superiority, reproach, and a begging for status and admiration. Well, the flipside of admiration is envy, and so as soon as one became free of either admiration or envy, the other gave way also. I read most of the first issue. Perhaps it was the way I was propped up in bed, but I sort of got a pain in the neck from them because they were so tedious. That people could be concerned with such details of opinions is something that rapidly bored me. EXQUISITE CORPSE was boring. But then I cant really stand to look at the same old pictures of Egypt, or Histories that think Man started 10,000 years ago all of a sudden popping out of a tea cup in Babylonia. The focus of EgoMinds bobbing up and down in the wash of contemporary swimming pools of the attempted judgements of youngsters is amusing, as the play of children is amusing, if they did so with some humor, not so deludedly obsessive, and recognising that fish whether big or small were not really made to strut, though in my bathroom I have a pink whale walking up the wall. There are some delightful sentences and momentary treasures in EXQUISITE CORPSE, but the censorship that prevails in such Academic productions such as

> dont mention God
> throw in new obscure words
> present a worldweary tone
> dont dare make a joke of it all
> dont enjoy it

are negative to one who uses as a guideline freedom from bondages of all sorts as truth leading to Absolute Truth. Now those are a lot of oysters to look through with their flesh pretending to be steelwool lace to look upon the pearls. When I had read a lot of that sort of thing at the age of 17 I got bored with criticism. Viewed from the point of The Goal, in which The Ego is finally annihilated on the 7th Plane of GodRealisation, all that is intoxicated with itself below that, or is not perfect, or is sloshing around in the same egotismistic broth, is just like the tramped retreats of castoff snakeskins. Now there are those who are focusing their microscopes on the rattlesnake's skin just as it is about to strike, and that takes place in approximately ¼ of a second. Those of us that have previously taken the precaution to nail the rattlesnake's head to the floor before looking at it, can only, at best, warn of the dangers of study without a firm knowledge beforehand of the general scope of the Incarnate Forms of The Essence that is being sought through scholarship of memos longsince past, in short, recognise whether through diagnostics or grace, that the way to The Pearl above The Mind is not through the fanged mouth or the house of mirrors of the Veils, otherwise known as bodies, all EXQUISITE CORPSES

> The Soul Body
> The Mental Body
> The Subtle Body
> The Physical Body.

I used to think it tedious when Kirpal Singh recommended that no sensual reference should be made in poetry, etc., of any sort, and such is also the view of the, I believe, at present stillliving, Darshan Singh. Let The Pure Spirit concern Itself only with The Pure Spirit now. So, though I am sure the Editors in good faith have produced their menu with their wholehearted best, and that it *will* (probably) impress Jodie Foster, that for those of us that are honestly bored with everything except direct experience of Soul and the Higher Realisations, anything that is still interested in the materialistic

> books
> buildings
> Egos
> Organisations
> Planets
> Universes
> Forms
> Names

is not really as vital as we are used to, and that though Zen is the cutting of a corpse with a razorblade, such recoils of sensationless floral spandrels around doors that were long ago nailed shut and sealed with seals reading NEVER TO BE OPENED., is like watching frozen algae thaw in tepid pools of Literature, and though not boring to some, let us call a spaed a spaed, those are not really EXQUISITE CORPSES, but marble dummies, totally plastic mockups, even perhaps plaster of Paris, but in no danger of being eaten by predators or having Karma. So I am sure they will safely get back through the mail to whatever Morgue they were resting in until those who call a spade a spade will decently drop them in the holes they deserve, perhaps with lots of money and grants, so they can go on churning out their ponderous, unfactual, inaccurate, scopeless, unreadable, teeny-bopper pretensions. I prophesy that since the Resurrection has opened those graves that these grave-wrappings are but clues as to The Source that unabashedly Lives and Exists, and that they will be successful because they are so phony. Love and Truth.

— Alfred

DAMNED CLEVER THOSE CHINESE

Mikhail Horowitz

THE MENTAL BENDS

I received two copies of *Exquisite Corpse* today. One with my name and address mimeographed on a label, and one with my name and address written by hand. It leads me to suspect what I have suspected all along. There are two *Corpses*, both exquisite. One talks about the pure, the other about the polluted. I marvelled at Ferlinghetti's "The State of the Mess Address." Boy! Talk about getting ticked off about what's going on down here. I guess that's what we get when we breathe in the rarefied atmosphere of the ethical zones. The next time i write poetry, i'll know better to strap onto conscience's face my mask, when i'm hooked up to the "desiring-machine." If my silence closely resembles stupidity then, it's because my words are muffled carrying around that contraption, and being so high up. Closer to the landing area, Eshleman's lament is justifiable, especially if you're Jesus and trying to poeticize. For 30 shekels of silver anyone can afford a Judas. It's that, like most poets, he ain't rich; so i can go with his complaint. But, i must warn him, the price of being misunderstood is human, and not very poetic. Sure Butterick took him out of context. His words were nails, and neatly pinned his body in space. When you're exploring the inner realms of the Self, watch out for asteroids and critics; and don't come down to earth too fast, or you'll get the mental bends trying to defend yourself. I must also admit that Eshleman's "Open Letter to George Butterick" was an exquisite piece of corpse in itself. I noticed Ernesto Cardenal taking on a bombardment of his own. "Oh, to be a poet and a politician now that Spring is here." I guess it points to one thing, the politics of poetry is dirty, and the poetics of politics is *really* dirty. Anyway, both copies of the *Corpse* were really worth it. Especially the poem, "Poet Lore," by Bill Zavatsky. It says it best. Humpty Dumpty couldn't have said it better. If our exquisite corpse needs religion, it needs a prayer to paraphrase what the rabbi of Koznitz said to God — "Lord of the World, I beg of you to redeem Poetry. And if You do not want to do that, redeem the poets."

— Allen Katzman

THE NEW ORALITY:
THE WORD BECOMES CASSETTE
by William Levy

Listening to the BBC ·World Service last week I heard a New Year's broadcast about the oral tradition, a special feature of their arts program *Meridian*. Some chap with a double name covered the folk song and the fireside story and the just published *Oxford Book of Narrative Verse* edited by those wonderful Opies, Peter and Iona. All good, as far as it went. Unfortunately what was ignored was the startling post-literate technological developments, accelerated in recent years by the rapid advancements in the miniaturization of sound reproduction. It is no exaggeration to say: From oral text to oral sex, orality is on everyone's lips.

Always avant-garde William Burroughs investigated the uses of the then newly invented portable Philips cassette recorder. That was in the mid-Sixties when he was living in London. Burroughs considered this machine as a way to turn words into weapons, ploughshares into swords. In *Electronic Revolution* (Bonn: Expanded Media Editions, 1982) these theories and the results of his experiments are collected. We see he wanted to use pre-recorded cut-up tapes to spread rumors, to discredit opponents, and as a front-line tactic to produce and escalate riots. For example, if demonstrators played pre-recorded police whistles — it would draw police. Pre-recorded gunshots would draw fire.

Burroughs suggested the creative effect would be to scramble and nullify associational lines put down by the mass media.

Not much was made of this start: or rather, it served only Nechaevian political and hallucinatory personal needs. The idea of artists using the cassette as a color on their palettes was there, but the proper machine wasn't. The transistor had made sound reproduction portable; it took the chip to make it pocketable.

By the end of the Seventies, Sony produced a miniature cassette player; it could be carried around almost like a piece of costume jewelry. Better yet, it came with headphones so small one could walk

Indra/Operation Minota

La signature d'une

Formation rémunérée

LA clé de feu

Ford/Operation Minotaur

Charles Henri Ford and Indra

on the street without embarrassment and with to-tal mobility. However awkward this Japanese-made English word sounds, the Walkman, and its clones, have become world-wide phenomena. At last one could easily fit the equipment into a pocket and stroll through the city listening to the high-quality sounds previously available only in the living room from specialized speakers, amps and turntables many times its size. The *state* has recognized this revolution in the only way it can: it bans the more radical expression. By the summer of '83 New York had made it illegal to drive a car, or ride a bicycle, under the influence of a Walkman.

The Walkman is a prime example of the successful introduction of a new type of hardware for which no specific software exists. This has always been the case: people need machines, but machines need people also. When a new material is invented, the first impulse is to imitate what it was created to replace. Early plastic objects were merely copies of wood, metal, glass, etc. When the station wagon automobiles first appeared, they had wood paneling along the sides to give them the appearance of a farm wagon. Then plastic was introduced, grained to look like wood.

It is not surprising that the Walkman + cassette is misallocated to imitate and reproduce the experience of other arts, other machines. According to Shu Ueyama, Deputy General Manager of Sony Advertising Division, the musical genres utilized through the Walkman are as follows: Pop 52.5%, Jazz 18.3%, Classical 16.4%, Miscellaneous 12.8%. The occasions for use are over 75% outside the home. Of those using the Walkman, 80% are between fifteen and thirty-five years old. Also not surprisingly for a machine called Walk*man* — rather than Walk*mate* — 93% of the users are male. In other words, young men are listening to the same thing they could on the radio or their home stereos, but now outside the home.

Of course it is pathetic to hear Vivaldi being played by a computer, to see 18th Century ballet via satellite, 19th Century soap opera on electronic monitors, and a seemingly never-ending stream of vaudeville — that is, Italian baroque illusion theatre — as films or plays, with a number of sports events and other circuses thrown in — the same stuff, but now on video cassettes as big as a matchbox, or television projection as big as the living room wall. And it is almost forgotten now, but offset printing was around for a long time before the underground newspapers demonstrated their unique characteristics of nonlinearity and underprinting.

To be sure, all new media developments have a profound effect on societal development, and individual consciousness. Elizabeth Eisenstein's *The Printing Press as an Agent of Change: Communications and Cultural Transformation in Early Modern Europe*, 2 vols. (Cambridge: Cambridge University Press, 1979) reminds us of this emphatically. But it is worth reflecting on the enormity of Gutenberg's achievement because directly or indirectly, it transformed the world. It broke, for example, the stranglehold of the Medieval Church, paved the way for the Reformation, instigated the process of dissemination and codification of knowledge from which modern science evolved, hastened the rise of individualism and its grotesque alter ego, capitalism, and segregated the world into two classes, those who could read and those who could not.

The much earlier shift from oral to literate societies was equally dramatic. Early and late stages of consciousness which Julian Jaynes in *The Origin of Consciousness in the Breakdown of the Bicameral Mind* (Boston: Houghton Mifflin, 1977) describes and relates to neurophysical changes in the two-chambered mind would also appear to lend themselves largely to much simpler and more verifiable description in the shift from orality to literacy. Or so says the great Jesuit scholar Walter J. Ong, who like Francis Yates, Mircea Eliade and Gershom Scholem, is an academic whose work has touched a popular nerve: he doesn't merely correlate data, he thinks about his subject. In his recently published synthesis *Orality and Literacy: The Technologizing of the Word* (London and New York: Methuen, 1982) Ong calls a historical synchronicity to our attention. He writes: "Jaynes discerns a primitive stage of consciousness in which the brain was strongly 'bicameral,' with the right hemisphere producing uncontrollable 'voices' attributed to the gods which the left hemisphere processed into speech. The voices began to lose their effectiveness with the invention of the alphabet around 1500 B.C., and Jaynes indeed believes that writing helped bring about the breakdown of the original bicamerality."

Likewise, in our own time, post-typography developments, that is, telephone and radio and television, have created an acoustical ecology, or a new orality, a secondary orality, different than anything predicted. Yet if Eisenstein, Ong and Jaynes are right, with the mobile cassette player, there should be a holism with maximum inner differentiation. Recent studies and art projects on and with pocket electronics suggest this to be the case.

Shuhei Hosokawa has published two works investigating the Walkman. In *Walkman no shujigaku — The Rhetoric of the Walkman* (Tokyo: Asahi Shuppan, 1981) he considered this machine mainly as a concrete instance of a new tension between Production/Consumption of music. In a later publication Hosokawa examines "The Walkman as

Urban Strategy" (*Pop and Folk Music: Stocktaking of New Trends*, Trento, 1982) and concludes: "The Walkman makes the walk act more poetic and more dramatic. . . We listen to what we don't see, and we see what we don't listen to. . . If it is pertinent to the speech act it will make the ordinary strange. . . It will transform a street into an open theatre."

Even more to the point is the inquiry made by the semiotic philosopher Philippe Sollers ("Suel contre tous. . . !" *Magazine litteraire*, Paris: April 1981). He interviewed young people, eighteen to twenty-two years old, who were using the Walkman on the street. His questions were: Are you losing contact with reality by listening to programs codified in advance? Are you schizophrenic or psychotic? Is the relationship between your eyes and ears changing drastically?

One of the interviewees responded — your questions are old. All these problems of communication and incommunicability are of the Sixties and Seventies. The Eighties, he continued, are not the same at all: they are the years of "autonomy" — of an intersection of singularities as the way of creating discourses. Marvelously this boy broke up the typical interrogation about the Walkman. Literal — i.e., literate — people presuppose that most of us are the lonely crowd in our alienated society; and the Walkman, according to this view, should be a symbol, an icon, for self-enclosure. Instead, it's an instrument for effecting visible historical change, an absolute collective, for the simple reason that sound unifies.

Nevertheless, the cassette is a medium of the plastic arts because it plays with space, and nonspace. It is the artist's job, the poet's, to revivify this new dialectic. Like owls we must hunt by sound, not sight. ☻

THE GANG OF EIGHT
Text and Illustrations by Tom Clark

The perfect crime takes organization, planning, discipline, audacity, and luck. The luck is mostly a matter of timing. What wouldn't have worked last week and won't work next week can go like clockwork if it's properly executed *today*. But advance thinking's got to be there. Everything's got to be figured, down to the finest detail. . . *You make your own luck*, Pound's in the habit of saying.

So he picks a Saturday night, Labor Day weekend. A full moon, but also a holiday. Cops are busy cruising the freeways, hauling in drunks, dealing with vacation traffic: plenty to keep them occupied.

Pound waits till the last minute to issue the go-ahead. He makes up his mind on the day before, Friday. Then it's a simple matter of making some phone calls. Lewis has done his stuff, brought in the blueprints. Everything's set.

Friday morning Dillinger goes to work on acquiring essential transport. The Vega he picks off first, out of a lot downtown. The Mercury he hooks next, over at the Ramada Inn. He parks them both in back of a lumber yard that closes down at noon for the long weekend. The U-Haul truck he follows out of the U-Haul lot, just before it closes at six on Friday. Some guy takes the truck home, parks it, and goes in his house to start loading a bunch of furniture. While the guy's inside wrestling with a sofa, Dillinger picks off the truck and drives it back to the U-Haul lot and parks it there overnight, knowing the lot's closed on Saturday, so he can go back then and grab it.

T.E. HULME   "THE GANG OF 8"   #1

On Saturday Pound gets things rolling. He spends the afternoon drilling everybody on the entry map and floor plan provided by the inside man, Lewis. Joyce, whose job it is to disconnect the alarm sensors Lewis has circled in black ink on the blue photostatic copy of the floor plan, pays meticulous attention, asking precise questions in a quiet, diffident tone; Lewis replies equally matter-of-factly, calm and confident and efficient; these are things it's his business to know.

W. B YEATS   "THE GANG OF 8" #3

Downtown, Yeats and Ford put their vehicles into a circling pattern on the darkened streets.

W. LEWIS   "THE GANG OF 8"   #2

Hulme, the free-lancer who will perform heavy duty work as the occasion arises, has very little to say during the meeting at Pound's apartment, but passes the time humming softly to himself and fondling a 10″ section of lead pipe he holds in his lap. Yeats and Ford, experienced professionals, flash a few anxious glances in Hulme's direction, but Hemingway, the house strongman, ignores him. Pound keeps a roving, surveying eye on everybody, all the time, even when he's talking.

Joyce takes the wheel of the lead car, the Mercury, with Pound riding alongside giving directions. At a prearranged corner, the Vega, with Yeats driving, falls in behind them. Ford trails by a block or two in the U-Haul, hanging far enough back to keep it from looking like a convoy.

F. M. FORD   "THE GANG OF 8"   # 4

Joyce parks the Merc in a municipal office workers' lot. The lot is vacant. Joyce and Pound emerge from the front seat. Hemingway climbs nimbly out of the back with the bolt cutters tucked into his coat like Raskolnikov's ax in *Crime and Punishment*. All three move quickly away from the Merc and through the shrubs at the border of the lot. Twin beams suddenly appear out of nowhere. The three men freeze. Out of range of the overhead parking lot lights, they wait for the car — no sweat, it's only some kids in a VW — to pass, then cross the street and walk straight ahead down an alley behind the adjacent block of buildings.

As they go down the alley there's a series of warehouse receiving areas on their left. The third receiving area's protected by a 10-foot chain link fence, plus a wide double gate, shut and padlocked.

J. JOYCE   "THE GANG OF 8" #6

E. HEMINGWAY   "THE GANG OF 8" #5

Pound, Hemingway, and Joyce stride past the gate, pause for a moment in the shadows. The alley is dead quiet. Hemingway pulls out the bolt cutters and starts to pop the links along one of the gate posts.

It's serious work. Small globes of sweat appear on the back of Hemingway's broad neck. Five min-

utes go by. Hemingway mutters a half-audible "God damn," but keeps on cutting. Joyce and Pound watch intently, saying nothing. Hemingway pops the last link. Just as Hemingway starts peeling back the ruptured fence, Yeats, with only his parking lights showing, glides up in the Vega, leading Ford's no-lights U-Haul. Yeats switches off the Vega's parking lights and motor. Yeats and Hulme get out of the Vega and join Pound, Joyce, and Hemingway in the alley. Ford backs the U-Haul through the wide opening Hemingway has created in the fence.

Guided by Pound's hand signals, Ford keeps on backing the U-haul up to the loading dock at the rear of the building.

Hulme jimmies the latch on the overhead door of the loading dock and rolls it up. The door hits the dock roof with a bang. Hulme steps inside. Out of the dark, a security guard appears from the inside of the building.

Hulme quietly steps around behind the guard, who never sees him. Hulme swings his lead pipe and the guard goes to sleep.

Following the floor plan he has memorized, Joyce locates the security system alarm sensors inside the building, and disconnects them.

One by one, Yeats rolls the twelve tall racks of photographic plates and negatives to the lip of the loading dock, strips the sheets of film off the racks, then tosses them, acetates and all, into the arms of Hemingway and Ford, who are waiting inside the back of the U-Haul.

When the films are all loaded on racks inside the truck, Yeats jumps down off the dock. Pound carefully inches down the overhead door, which meets the concrete almost without sound.

"Let's go," says Pound.

Yeats has the Vega's engine running, back-up

E. POUND   "THE GANG OF 8"   #8

J. DILLINGER   "THE GANG OF 8"   #7

lights on. The U-Haul is already rolling away down the alley. At the corner it turns off into a dark side street.

Joyce, Hemingway, and Hulme pile into the back seat of the Vega. Pound gets into the passenger seat in front. Yeats' eyes meet Pound's. Pound nods. Everything has gone without a hitch.

Yeats' foot makes gentle contact with the gas pedal, and the Vega moves down the alley.

Yeats flicks the Vega's brights on. Ahead of them, the five men watch the dark streets flood suddenly with the white light of the future.   ☠

A CALL FOR NARRATIVE ANARCHY
by Fielding Dawson

Two years ago my mother reminded me, having read the ms of a new novel while in the hospital — she took notes — that people don't lay down, hens lay, and we can't make eggs, chickens make eggs, and having noted the corrections, her words yet stay with me, and in my newest work I use "prepare" breakfast or "prepare" scrambled eggs and along those lines "brew" coffee. Attention to these details sharpens the intellect and gives continuity texture which is so lacking both in writing and in speech, and ties in with "whatever," a word more universal than "have a nice day," or "share," and even "enjoy."

Sloppy language has been and always will be our constant companion, and there are real reasons for it, as always. In part because the media has robbed language of its inherent character of synonyms and antonyms, as well as that of nailhead accuracy. The psychology behind the media is toward a vagueness surrounding an essential lucid point, for contrast, which illuminates the object for sale or the point made, in the real enough reasoning to get it out to the people, like a revised edition of The Book of Common Prayer, for the idea is to get to the people, the larger the audience the better, which proves — true — the point, thus the way, and too many writers and poets have accepted that diffusion in the face of the natural difficulties and tangles language on its own presents, so the language we use is the same language used by everyone, with variation of story large or small, or meaning, large, small or nonexistent, in the highest offices on Madison Avenue to the most humble pad and poet with spiral notebook and ball point pen BIC, no questions asked, no spark of curiosity — there are exceptions — but few, for we use the same words in the same arrangements we read and speak, and the most professional editors and copyeditors miss it because they too are of this web. In short: consider alternatives for language — whatso is a synonym for whatever. We might realize "whatever" — a vaguery — has replaced "now" of the '60s, and that "have a nice day, share, enjoy" have replaced "ciao" and "take care" with the obvious difference these slogan-type catchwords reflect banks and advertising whereas once, there was a shred of possibility, and all — in all — useful at best to shed light on the character of a fictional character who is invisible but the pale lingo spoken, to save the writer detailed visual description, and further development.

We have five senses, aside from the sixth we use in writing, which remain, save a curtsy to formula, unused. Description in all contemporary writing is visual, with an ear to dialogue, or in context, sound. Taste, touch, smell forgotten, with reason, for writers are trapped in plot and story, and the aim toward that completion renders 'em near deaf dumb and blind to much else, for sure the very language they use. This kind of rigid omission makes novels and stories what they are today, mute blind ego willpower, like men and women in public office, mute blind ego willpower to achieve the obvious goal of mute blind ego willpower regardless of the cosmology (ignored) along the way, in fact at the very outset. The means and effect of success involve a psychology that has overwhelmed the details which bring it into focus and its reason to be. What this or that means, in the clinical textbook, deletes what this or that is, thus rendering an extraordinary innocence into grave sophistication, to a point where we can't write a story or novel anymore without first knowing the psychology either implied or point blank before us. This is said with a little shyness, and perhaps a touch of the sly, because nothing is so useful as psychology, except — without fail — the language which reveals a sophistication in, or innocence of, that science, and for me, a pervert, I enjoy seeing, in cold print, what blockheads so many — by the trainload — writers are, in a common-sense comprehension of language and I mean words, the true task at hand, the labor of the art, is to be aware by meaning, tone, and in a linguistic indigenous sense, of the relationships words and sentences have, how they react to and on each other, and in terms of harmony, syllables, and forward motion, the possibilities available — this involves brainwork — and the reflective character of all language that marks it language and nothing but language, and to control through psychology and accepted formula is to put diapers on a thunderbolt, which is common practice, and why publishing today, in large, and small ways, covers such a potential force, with a diaperlike mentality, using a formula less complex than gauze, and too stupid and insensitive to any other way.

Pound was right insofar as the novel is dead, for indeed the formula is, for so many deadheads use it, without a thought in their little pea-brains, that we need a new formula, one tending toward literary anarchy, with a certain well-defined vengeance, to add spice to the effort. I mean, they say that in the plot everything has to come together at the end. It all has to tie in. There must be a resolution. So they say, and they get their way because they publish the books. But fuck them, what do they know of the potential of language, they only know what they know and that's what they have learned and that's why they are where they are because they haven't learned and don't know anything else and don't want to: they can't be anywhere else doing anything else, they're like fuckin'

Karen Rosco

academics, they're eight and a half by eleven inch glossy invisibles on their way to the top of their profession with a lot of writers in tow behind, up on the 18th floor, slaves to an ambition that begets slavery, solidifies the corporate structure, and makes writers vain because they're part of it, it's a 99 and 9/10s solid faceless enemy. Mistake me not! If Random House would publish a manuscript of mine, I'd be ambitious as to the result, but in logical apprehension they'd remainder it pronto, and we know the chance of a reprint.

Shall we join the cry, oh the lament, over the economic crunch? Listen, what doesn't get published because of money doesn't matter, and I weary of exceptions, yes, there are exceptions, but in the landslide of stupid, pointless books that get

published, the exception doesn't matter — let's tear up the form of the story, and of the novel, and start all over. Two rules intertwine: the writing — or narrative — has got to be compelling, and the end may leave a dozen threads hanging, yet it must be complete. Beginning, middle and end are no longer viable — like realism, at best useful — the concept is no longer the point. How far and to what limit, under what stress and illumination, a beginning may reach, is the point. Period.

Writers, heretofore specialists, just as any person specializing in any art form, will cross over, and learn the other forms. If writers knew more about dance, they'd understand the choreography of crowds, and city traffic, and restaurant scenes, and if they knew how to paint or at least draw, they could follow a linear scheme, not to mention color, as Crane did both, so too, Nathaniel West, who studied painting. Music. It doesn't take a Ph.D. to see through the popular myth that Nazi generals loved Wagner because of Wagner, or Hitler and his little myth, because none of them knew anything about music, if they had, they'd have understood better the harmony and continuity they were involved in, which sounded different, to be sure, to a lot of people who knew about music, and got out, or stayed because they couldn't, and like the mass bulk of our editors and publishers, made it indeed their business to entertain. The combination of ignorance, innocence, ambition, and certified faceless power calls for its destruction — bam! — for at bottom it is political, thus its vague myth of opportunity — you might be the exception! — they say, submit your work, you have a chance, sure, if you write what they want the way they want it written, they listen to Wagner — what else do they know? Well, it's true, there were some nice Nazis, wow, they weren't all bad, I know an editor at Pocket Books —

"What did she say?"

"It was a he."

"Yeah? There's a switch. Older guy?"

"No, young."

"The worst. Go on."

"He said it wasn't a novel."

"How come?"

"It didn't tie in at the end, and it didn't have a plot."

Amusement.

He didn't know it, but that fella just gave us the new form. And keep in mind, it begins with each one of us, real anarchy, it's going to be tough because it'll be an open art, without competition for far better — far more interesting manuscripts to read, each filled with harmony, but not slick, rough in a way, so the wood shows.

"My mom read the manuscript. She was in the hospital, said that editor was full of beans, the plot was good and the ending — she, in fact, asked me if it worked."

"What did you say?"

"The end was terrific, a reproduction of a painting by Philip Guston."

"Who's he?"

"You wouldn't even know it —"

"So what?"

"They didn't either."

"Does it matter?"

"No. They loved the book, everybody loved it, didn't know what to do with it, all over New York."

"Where's that?"

EXILED IN DOMESTIC LIFE

by John Giorno

I'm standing
in the hall,
I pushed
the button,
and I'm waiting
for the elevator;
you are alone,
you are unstable,
and you're not sure
it's OK
anymore,
exiled
in domestic
life
exiled in
domestic life
exiled in domestic life.

Nobody does
it for you,
you got to
do it
all by yourself,
and I've been
brutalized
and I've been brutalized
and I've been brutalized
and I've been brutalized.

I would rather
be dead,
than be 18
years old,
and a poet,
and if I can
do that,
I can sit
on somebody's
face
I can sit on
somebody's face
I can sit on somebody's face,
and feed.

I want to

sleep
hugging someone
over and
over again
I want to sleep hugging
someone over and over
again,
and cuddling
in the morning,
cause it's
healing
my body
in my heart,
it's safe
to be married
these days
it's safe to be married
these days.

When you got
lots of negative
thoughts,
they are big,
and powerful
and wonderful
they are big, and powerful
and wonderful
they are big,

and powerful and wonderful,
it's their
job
to get it up,
it's not
your problem.

If it isn't
black,
it's not
good,
and it's not going
to work,
you don't feel
a razor blade
you don't feel a razor blade,
and I like juice;
your skin
smells like
an old sponge
soaked in
alcohol,

and this place
stinks.

A hundred million
years ago,
the geophysical
adjustments
that made petroleum
from primordial
forests,
maybe 100 million
years from now,
will transform
the plastic
in our garbage
into something
better
than diamonds.

The reason
it's good,
is cause
I work
all the time,
and I've been spending
the rest
of my time,
laying on
the bed
with my girlfriend
watching TV,
and I want her
to tell me
wisdom
when she doesn't
know she is
and I want her to tell
me wisdom
when she doesn't know
she is
and I want her to tell me
wisdom when
she doesn't know she is.

What are you
slapping your
hands
together for,
do you want
me to slap
your face?

MY FUCKING CAREER

by Paul Hoover

Rimbaud is so
appealing due to
his rejection of
the middle class,
of which he
was a member.
When at age
nineteen he renounced
the life of
art and turned
to a life
of adventure, he
became the holy
man he first
determined to be,
because he gave
up fame (resulting
in great fame).
The public relations
work — meanwhile, back
in France — was
done by the
man with the
gun, his former
lover Verlaine, whose
character was so
bad one might
start fires with
it. Rimbaud, on
the other hand,
became Saint Slave
of Wages, saving
for the future
like any droll
hausfrau: "A good
employee," according
to Bradey, his
gruesome supervisor in
the city of
Harar, which makes
me think of
the song "Harari
Hideaway" as sung
by Snooky Lanson
in days of
Hit Parade, though
it was "Hernando's"
really. The dream
of highest art,
removed from social
inflections, is maintained
by the high
and those who
want to be.
The poet and
the priest are
often associated because
they "stand apart,"
the dream of
pure transcendence, but
they reflect their
classes in every
word they speak
from pulpit and
pantoum: what comfort
and distinction, sighs
and benedictions, though
domine dominates. That
Robert Bly, for
instance, who does
he think he's
kidding? His howls
of ecstasy are
straight from L.L.
Bean. But the
same is true
of the low.
They want themselves
reflected in the
"walking mirror" Flaubert
called a book,
and, after all,
who don't? Meanwhile,
I am sitting
on the sodden
goddamn sofa of
my own artistic
pretensions, telling you
what to think.
Well, somebody's got
to do it,
so kiss my
ass, that's what,
and all your
mothers, too. How
beautiful is the
music from yonder
violin (a sweetly
squeaky tune) which
I rented for
my daughter at
$21 a month
so she might
know the pleasures
of transcendental art
and rise in
social class, as
probably I desired
when I started
composing verse, to
deaden the very
senses and get
me into heaven.

CAVE JUNCTION

by Lou Gold

This is somewhere-near-nowhere place. The bumper sticker reads: *Cave Junction is not the end of the world, but you can see it from here.* I'm a city kid who feels at home in the wilderness. It's as if fate grafted a learned head onto a peasant heart and plunked me down in the Illinois Valley of Southern Oregon to work out a personal balance. I understand the end of the world that can be seen from Cave Junction, but I do not comprehend it. I comprehend the *Exquisite Corpse*, but I do not understand it.

Last summer I spent fifty-six days alone on top of Bald Mountain in the heart of the endangered Kalmiopsis wilderness, the last significant old-

"The anatomy of love =

RONNIE BURK
COLLAGE CITY
PROJECT 1983

growth forest on the West Coast and the most diverse conifer forest in the world. While I conducted prayerful conversations with the trees, publicity and blockades of bulldozers set the stage for a Federal Court injunction halting further work on the Bald Mountain logging road. My religious ritual, which was in technical violation of a "no trespassing" regulation, earned me five days in the county clink last fall. The judge said he was trying to prevent the anarchy of individual conscience which might "lead to a situation like Lebanon." Now in classic *1984* "Double-Speak," the Oregon Wilderness Bill is about to endanger the Kalmiopsis by virtue of omission.

I'm preparing to return to the mountain with a head full of questions. What sense does it make to tell a society that discards its old people about old trees? What sense does it make to tell a society that will abuse one in four girl children and one in eight boy children in the *present* generation to save the forest for our great, great grandchildren? What sense does it make to tell a society that has already contaminated its own drinking water that herbicides are a threat to critters? What sense does it make to tell a world that has destroyed since 1950 over half of all the forests on earth about the plight of Bald Mountain? And while I'm asking, what am I doing walking around in this existence anyway? So much for my learned head!

On the mountain, in clear view of the end of the world, my peasant heart sings another song. Humble (as in the word *humus*), close to the earth, grounded on a mountain, I find my answers. I am an earth being. I like to touch. I like to make love. I like to participate in all the processes of Creation. I want to be involved in the current crisis of our existence. The corpse I see from here *is* exquisite, but I still do not understand the *Exquisite Corpse*.

Touch the earth and blessed be. It is lovely indeed. All my love.

CHICAGO

by Sharon Mesmer

New York has its love life, its literary love life, which is infamous. It has its St. Mark's and Chelsea and the memory of Greenwich. California has the weather and width, its City Lights and Beyond

Baroque, and the surreallest surrealist ghetto, Hollywood. And Chicago cowers silently somewhere in the middle and not without its secret storm.

The Secret Storm can be a smile; can be sardonic, can be sanguine. If you ride the el and watch the movie (the movie that you see when you look out the window) you are seeing the mirror that reflects the face of the place, which is your face. And what you see is Eager Plastics; stenciled cows on cemetery walls; skeletal wooden back porches of tenements housing stray languid dogs; the woman in robes on the train selling incense; a starlet's face on a homemade billboard announcing price war; and there, behind that college kid smoking a cigarette, is a warning on a pillar: "Ronald Reagan, An Oral Danger." The train riffles the kid's hair as it passes.

There is the sign on the laundromat (that used to be a house): No Bus Waiting Inside. And there is Frank's Unisex Hair Shop (that used to be a house) that you go to with your girlfriend, and Frank is a big fat Mexican in rust-colored slacks that droop at the knees who went from sheet-metal working to shampooing in the back room. And there is the time at 1:00 in the morning in summer when the kids on the block turn on the hydrant, and water runs in rivulets off their small black shoulders afterwards.

There are apartments to live in, with three other people, three or four cats, a couple of dogs and a baby. There are places for big people to work, called offices, and ways to get the jobs, called patronage. There are bars to go to after work called the Boozoory and the King Midas Lounge, and the best one of all that never was, Carl's I-Fuck-You Saloon. There are in-laws to impress with your new permanent wave, and there is seersucker to consider when shopping downtown with your sister. There are women, bovinely hideous, who know how to throw their hair; they do it at bus stops if they think someone is watching. And if not, they'll practice. There are subjects you must remember to discuss with your husband, but you never remind him of his father's workbench. There are girls to define and pursue and girls you just talk to. There is St. John of God church where you're supposed to get married and die. There is Cubs park for fags and Sox park for drunks. There are parties for jewelry, rubber goods, and make-up. There are women who are magnets and women you marry.

In Chicago there is the time you take a romance novel into the bath with you, and there is the time you stop dyeing your hair blonde. In Chicago there are times you spend all summer drinking whiskey sours in a pink room, and there are times you spend all winter in a bare bed waiting for a phone call. And certainly there is the time you stop collecting those postcards: this is called Chicago's nonvolatile memory.

BERKELEY, CA

by Summer Brenner

I'll tell you how funny Berkeley is. Like no one here is what they look to be. They're lots of rich people driving beat-up cars. And professors flipping the news out of the top of their brains and standing on corners cause they burned all their books up on acid. I mean there are cops with long hair who are trained to look sensitive. And college girls in pink toenail polish with bank accounts I could spend forever. And guys going in all white, or all orange holding on to half-naked goddesses and looking like the his and her versions of the ass-hole of God. And x-cons like me. X-everythings. X-execs on trikes. And x-fags. And x-porn queens with the best-equipped kitchens west of the Rockies. Everyone can almost get to be anything in this town. Some people call it a fun place. If they're a little more astute, they call it a fantasy. Man, I call it a lie. But I dig the lie because I understand the lie. I am the king of lie mountain and it got me plenty of high.

The only ones I can look at without making me want to puke out a laugh is the congregation of scum angels who hang out in a square acre of garbage called People's Park. Now that's a famous place, and come to think of it, maybe the reason Berkeley got to be so famous. Except for the A-bomb they perfected here to obliterate the Japs. People's Park is just one block east of Telegraph Avenue. And riots and dying took place there so that every reject of humanity could have a spot to shit.

My buddy's little brother came to People's Park ten years ago cause he said he wanted to make a pilgrimage to freedom's landmark. And he pitched his real nice tent over his real nice sleeping bag and he cooked him up some Swiss chard from the communal garden on his new little Coleman and he read Malcolm X by the light of the kerosene and he slept cozy in the Land of the Free, the Land of the Populo. And when he woke up, man, he noticed something funny right away. All his brand-new sacraments gone to the cause. He done got fucked by freedom which is about the worst feeling any man can have. Maybe a woman's more used to it, seeing as how she has to lay there and call it good and free from go one. But for a man, it's the worst. And my buddy's little brother laid down his tent and his lantern and his backpack and his deluxe Swiss army knife for the cause of the fence who got fifteen ones for the set and sent it back to People's Park in a bag of dope.

GRECIAN AVERAGE URNED RUN

Mikhail Horowitz

FROM THE E.C. CHAIR

We went to the 1984 American Booksellers' Association Convention in Washington DC and saw: a pink fountain with sofas around it looking remarkably like the mind of Ronald Reagan, erected by Avon Books; an oily man and a greasy woman flexing biceps, triceps, and deltoids in order to sell a muscle book; Mr. T selling his memoirs (Reporter: *Did you write it yourself?* Mr. T: *Do you want a knuckle sandwich?*); Raquel Welch in Danskins; Erica Jong being led to the gallows by burly men; platoons of young, desirable and excitable database people drinking grasshoppers, tequila sunrises and strawberry daiquiris; smurfs; bears. Floating in isolated splendor among these rivers of chintz and kitsch were the small presses, literary interests, academic journals. We felt protective and tender for a moment, forgetting our dark and twisted metaphysics. The brash trash was so big and the ideal real so small! We enjoyed a second of fraternal miniaturization. Here we were, gorgeous blooms of mimeo and letterpress and now offset, surrounded by corporate maulers, sense garblers, beauty besmirchers, inflaters of dollars, ninnifiers of democracy, catbook publishers and dogfood distributors! Luckily the loving vertigo passed as quickly as the mid-'70s and we found ourselves piqued and pugnacious once more. We were thrilled incidentally by this conversation, recorded in passing between Allan Kornblum of Toothpaste and Jack Shoemaker of North Point: Allan: *Are you breaking even yet? Five years is what they say it takes.* Jack: *We're right on schedule. Of course we don't have to pay back our investor.* Allan: *I want a benefactor just like yours. Do you know another millionaire?* Jack: *I spent half my life finding this one.*

Substitute *Exquisite Corpse* for Allan and make that last *your* question, oh Reader Dear.

CHER CADAVRE EXQUIS

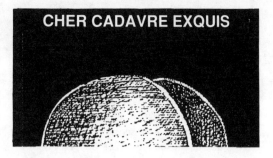

WOMEN OUT OF ITALICS!

What really interests me is finding out *why* all these clever women have been refusing to write for *EC* or failing to come through. To say that women continue to suppress their intellects or that men continue to use theirs destructively is facile enough, but I would like to see this question discussed at length. I myself find *EC*'s tone highly entertaining and I even find ideas in it that stimulate me to think. But I must say the idea of writing that way at first repelled me to the point that I wanted to suggest I write reviews under a pseudonym. Seems like I've got the notion that *EC* is a men's game and for me to play would be a betrayal of my sex. The outcome of women not writing for *EC*, though, is that *EC* looks like a male institution, which is annoying to me and I suspect to you. I wish you could rouse a discussion in your letters and columns about this. I would hope your fans and sympathizers could cut through ideological bullshit and say things that could stretch the minds of both men and women readers. Of course you *do* have some women writers but I agree that having pretty much only poems from women is pathetic — poems that you publish in delicate italics that look like they could be crushed if one of those solemn tombstones of review were accidentally to tumble.

— Janet Gray

Ed. Note: Janet Gray wrote before this, asking why women don't seem to jump into our frays for a bit of rough fun. Is it fear of getting dirty? Or are we guilty of sexism? The editor opined back that it had to be the first thing, because God knows he'd been trying but all he gets is poems.

Stiffest Ed. Note: All poetry in the original issues of the Exquisite Corpse was set in italics.

IN HIS OWN PANTS

Here in the middle of swamp mildew culture (the only culture in America is in a test tube) — I look at the American poetry scene from the underside, ass up. Fact is: everyone is dissatisifed with American poetry. So how can you say that your dissatisfaction is any different? Dissatisfaction is no longer a faction. Everyone is dissatisifed.

Let's talk about the New York School. First off: Frank O'Hara's personism is the initial context for the second & third generation hangers-on at St. Marks' (pathetic crews) and the languor-wedge skul. Okay: O'Hara sez, let's not worry about *Technique*, assonance & all that "stuff" because when you are walking down the street you just naturally want to wear your pants tight enough that people want to go to bed with you. Dictum which I myself parroted a number of times. Yet look at it. As a metaphor. I mean, does the poet get his poems off the rack, ready-made? Or is he not the tailor of his own pants? And if he must be — he must be — doesn't he need to know about seams and darts, etc.? A tailor might need to know what kind of pants are attractive, but if he hasn't mastered the meter, his intentions won't be sewn in.

What O'Hara was against was somebody getting Brownie points, saying look at my poem — it's got assonance — therefore, it's good. But O'Hara had already forgotten more about writing poems, techne, than most of his followers ever learned. When they write, they just get their pants off the O'Hara ready-made rack, so that all these "personalities" end up sounding like each other.

Pound wrote long ago: three elements to poetry: SOUND (melopoeia), SIGHT (phano-), and IDEA (logopoeia). And it's pretty clear that the latter two have gotten the most play *because*: 1) You don't need as much talent to do images or "ideas" (or thoughts or notions depending on the skills of the player). 2) Most critics & poet-critics can't notice or discuss or even read rhythm or sound in a poem anymore — much less discuss intelligently in a review. If they tried to discuss it, they'd reveal their basic ignorance of same. 3) The pernicious influence of translations; sound doesn't come over from French or Spanish or Urdu, but sight and "ideas" do. 4) The poetry-made-EZ industry, from Koched-up elementary schools to graduate granulated writing wreckshops — teachers don't know how to criticize or improve sound, too fundamental.

Yet Pound pointed out sound (melopoeia) is the most important of all three, sound can save a poem lacking the other two.

There isn't a poet in America who can give a clear answer as to whether or not Bob Dylan, John Lennon, or Elvis Costello is a poet. I mean, if they are, why aren't they taught and studied & if they're not, why not? Because our relation to song is so troubled.

I am no longer interested in an ignorant audience. Because that's just plain exploitation.

EC cannot be critical until it is self-critical. The slash-and-burn reviews were amusing, but now it's time for something that cuts deeper. The reason the languor-wedge school is boring has nothing to do with their social class. It's that — given the premise that we must make ourselves unacceptable in order to look avant-garde and given the total state of ignorance they found themselves in even among the so-called avant-garde — they gave up the last resources of poetry they'd inherited. They had to break up syntax because there was nowhere else to go. If you're sitting in a cold house, you might start burning the furniture. If you are dealing with the stripped-down, post-O'Hara, personal poem, the only thing left to strip out are the connections between the words. Robert Frost wrote about fifty or sixty years ago: there were only so many patterns you could make with language as pure language, and so in order to get variety, you had to put in a story. Even Frost and Eliot were cleverer "lang-wedge" school poets because Eliot has the idea that the ideas and stories don't matter, they're just there so the reader will accept the poetry slipped to him.

And the point is not that poetry and prose are the same. They are not the same. The point (of say a poem like *Paterson*) is that in a longer poem one cannot possibly sustain the necessary lyrical intensity, and so therefore, one puts in documentary prose passages. Williams was just aware enough to do that instead of putting it into broken lines (as Olson does, therefore making the difference between his real rare lyrical moments & his verse hectoring rather indistinct). Prose is all horizontal, poetry operates on both a horizontal and vertical grid. That doesn't happen in a paragraph because a paragraph is conceived as, in effect, a two-dimensional line spaghettied under itself, while in poetry, the cut-off lines create a stacking of lines which gives a vertical dimension absent in prose. And when one tracks the vertical dimension, one finds a system of rhyme (internal rhyme, assonance, alliteration, what Pound calls "tone leading") which is both more powerful (resonant) and more inchoate than the horizontal reading. What's happened, in short, is that all of our poetry is being read as prose, being read horizontally (for image, message, theme, politics, etc.) and very little is being read vertically. So the magic we look for in poetry, and which is available vertically, is displaced by party or personality politics (he teaches at my school — Naropa, Harvard); he's black (Jewish, gay, female); he's hip (genteel, Gentile, responsible). The cult of personality which even the fucking Chinese have abandoned, is alive and well in Amurrica.

Poetry is dying for lack of care. Anybody who treats poetry as a racket, as a form of ego gratification, as a personality cult, as a source for feelings of superiority, as a way of separating hip from straight, or sheep from goats, as a club, as a tool, is an enemy of poetry. And there are more enemies of poetry among poets than there are among ordinary people. I think people want to know that a poet knows *how to do something*, not that a poet is some special creature gifted with a magic power. The vanity among poets today is what makes me ill. It's so bad I find even Walter Mondale refreshing! (That's saying something.) I am just sick of the posturing ignorance of poets running around thinking they invented the language that they've misheard. Success is killing poetry, not politics. That a person as ignorant as myself can make a living as a poet shows what Pound said, there is no kindergarten in poetry. I admit I am as ignorant and unworthy as anyone. And that the only proper thing to do is wait a long long time before putting any work out to the public.

— Rodger Kamenetz

GETTING INTO BERRIGAN: AN OPEN LETTER TO CHARLES BERNSTEIN

Bernstein, in his first paragraph of "Writing Against the Body" (*EC*, Jan.-Feb. '84) states that Ted's life "can most usefully be read not as a document of a life in writing but, inversely, as an *appropriation* of a life *by* writing." Here, I sense a reference to Heidegger, and it's not "off the wall." Ted spoke to me of Heidegger on several occasions, and these two quotes from the philosopher make sense: "Appropriation does not designate a 'realm' as does Being, but rather a relation, that of man and Being." "Time is the way in which Appropriation appropriates" (*On Time and Being*).

Number One: Mr. Bernstein has a right to his academic opinions, but having known Ted for many years (he was one of my teachers), I feel his article to be more of a tomb than a commentary. By commentary I don't mean that it need be a lengthy analysis of what the poet did and how, but, on a more sensitive level, *who* he was in his poems. I agree with the opening remarks, re especially how easy it is to "get caught up in the circumstances and style of his life." Ted was *all* life and style, and

Dog sniffing Corpse   Liz Henderson

writing was something he *did*, like smoking Chesterfields or drinking a Pepsi. I remember a wonderful remark he made once about some student's objection to all those personal references in O'Hara (Joe, Bill, Dick, etc.). "It's not important that you know those people. It's enough to know that Frank cared about them." The references never bothered me — they were real people in a life. After all, who the hell was Madame Sosostris in "The Waste Land," Maude Gonne, or the "Dark Lady" of the "Sonnets" (by Billy S.)? Ted Berrigan's poetry is not "deceptively simple" nor is it "built on the wreck of the old." His way of working was built on appropriation, sure, but also on *awareness* which involves caring about being-in-the-world. All consciousness is consciousness of *something*, which is its *intentional* nature.

Ted, as I understand him, did not "build on" (he abhorred that kind of Romanticism!), but rather explored his daily life. Yet he was closer to Shelley than most of us: Shelley's dread was that there was too much love to pour into this tiny life span: our modern syndrome is that there is too little love, and life is too long. So we get our long formal poems, evidenced by James Merrill and others who, lacking substance, weave their intricate anxiety-webs of beauty which are definitely not "deceptively simple." Would that that "school phrase" *deceptively simple* were dumped from our critical grab bag altogether (Frost, I was taught, was deceptively simple) along with oxymoron and *Scylla and Charybdis*. We'd be better off without them.

Number Two: Let us look at Mr. Bernstein's commentary on Berrigan. It is not important that we come to conclusions at this point, but just that we examine the statements as true or false. From the beginning we hear the academic stink which goes through the piece, and I quote: "This inversion of conventional 'confessional' style is a key to Berrigan's method. Inversion is both a formal and moral technique for Berrigan, which partly accounts for the anxiety generated by his flips of text and self — text overwhelms self, self overwhelms text." If I were Charles Olson, I'd surely wave my arms in the air and ask: "What the hell does that mean?!" Maybe our commentator has picked up on the power of *anxiety* from Mr. Bloom (*Anxiety of Influence*) and, as so many others, milks it freely. Sure, Berrigan, as I knew him, suffered anxiety and he took pills to ease it. What poet doesn't feel anxiety, but what's this "inversion" stuff? I never knew Ted to "invert" anything. If he were alive now, I feel quite sure he'd write a letter to Mr. Bernstein of the order he wrote Bernadette Mayer in that last issue of *The World* — a complaint: blunt, eloquent, and to the point.

Mr. Bernstein is not nuts — just plain uninformed. Maybe he should write more simply and directly about poets who matter, or shut up. I trust nuts. I grew up in the country, and I have failed to this day to lose a simple colloquial lucidity, and tend to distrust a "coherent self." The "inversion of a 'confessional' style" was the furthest thing from Ted's mind, and certainly is no "key" to his "technique," formal, moral, or otherwise. And the talk of the "text" — never once did I hear Ted use that

term — he even joked of his inclusion in *The Norton Anthology*, not out of literary disrespect (although there was a lot of that in him), but out of honest distrust of those critical vultures who swoop down to interpret his cares and intentions, both as a person and a writer. The question of vulnerability is a big one for poets, especially dead poets. They can't come back and stomp on the asses of their critics: their works must speak for themselves. Can you imagine Blake or Whitman being forced to *justify* themselves? Not that I'm putting Ted Berrigan in their class (misnomer?) or hopefully not tooting his horn excessively, but if the dead poets could arise from their graves, I dare say that with one horrific thrust of Heavenly or Hellish fire they'd put an end to such phrases as "diaristic 'self' writing."

As to "found language" in Berrigan's poetry, sure, there's a lot of it — so what? There's a lot in Chaucer, Shakespeare, and the Bible. The world is here, which includes language, and you use what you can. Once Ted told me that the greatest compliment any poet could give him was to steal a line and use it in a poem. Then he told the story of him reading in a high school where he was invited to show young kids what poetry was. He read from his *Sonnets*, and afterward, when question time came, one pimply kid raised his hand and said: "Mr. Berrigan — in that one poem you read, weren't the last two lines by Rimbaud?" Ted blushed, and admitted they were. "Alert bright jerk, he got me!"

Ted read voraciously. He was a man who read. (I remember one time in Allendale, Michigan, at a poetry conference, him reading, on speed, a book about the history of golf. We were all up there, Bob Creeley, Whalen, Oppenheimer, Bly, Wakoski, Anselm Hollo, Rothenberg, and many others. We all had dormitory rooms, and there was Ted, on an upper bunk in his room, stark naked with his Chesterfield hanging from his lips, reading about golf! No shit — and I dare say he never played a game in his life. Or maybe he did!) So much for "found language." Our critic goes on talking about the "enterprise" and "project" of writing. I suspect it is neither. Writing is a craft of the spirit — political terms are no part of it. Mr. Bernstein's comment: "The biographist fallacy substitutes the chaff for the wheat by renormalizing this *body of work* into a work of 'self'." Now, I ask you, couldn't this be said of anyone — almost any writer who uses his life as material? Our man Mr. Bernstein has surely been to college, possibly to his detriment. As to the alleged "assault on the sanitized body of the 'self'," in Berrigan's case there was none. Ted *did* abuse himself, with chemicals, junk food, et al. but I never heard him speak once of Satan.

Here is Bernstein missing the boat again, calling "psychological" what is just what it says:

Morning
        (ripped out of my mind again!)

— a one-liner on waking up stoned, not a major work in anyone's canon, but what's the big deal? The irony (god how I hate that word!) is in the last lines — a quote from Ted, which he stole from Rimbaud:

             The only travelled sea
that I still dream of
is a cold, black pond, where once
on a fragrant evening fraught with sadness
I launched a boat frail as a butterfly

— Darrell Gray

HOOVER'S BREAKFAST

The advantage of hand-cranked machinery that doesn't need electricity is simplicity, mobility, and independence. I can pull into Paul Hoover's Chicago driveway at midnight and crank a White Paper straight into his mailbox, be halfway to Peoria by the time he climbs out of bed and have the satisfaction of knowing I've ruined his breakfast. There's nothing dreamy-eyed about staying mobile and independent — perhaps Mr. Hoover should sit thru a showing of *The White Rose* to get some idea of conditions under which a mimeo comes in handy. Lost Hippie papers? Moonish admiration of Henry Miller? Mr. Hoover seems to have a brain made up of pigeonholes from which all the pigeons have flown, leaving their droppings behind. The "Vagabond writers" he maligns range in age from 45 to 55 and live their convictions with a toughness of spirit that apparently is outside Mr. Hoover's ken. Interesting to note that — with the exception of his last sentence (which is a categorical lie) — Hoover makes not one mention of the content or

subject matter of any of the works he is supposedly reviewing; instead his energy goes into a vicarious assassination of the persons who created the work, causing visions of gulags to dance in my head and bringing to mind the "secret" detention centers this country built in the Sixties to detain "potential subversives" in the event of "national emergency." Being nothing more at the time than a beer waiter and the editor of a then disgustingly literary literary magazine (nothing as bad as the *Paris Review*, however), you can imagine my surprise to learn that my name had made the list of "potential subversives." I got my first mimeo shortly after that, and I plan to keep it.

— John Bennett

COMMIE BLAST

The kind of reactionary political stupidity evinced repeatedly in your pathetic rag simply lends weight to Plato's argument that poets ought to be excluded from an enlightened state. If, as John Stickney quotes in his article about Cleveland, the American Communist Party is no threat to the state because they can all fit in one room, how much truer that is of the handful of pretentious, uninformed lightweights who "fit" within your pages. Power to the people and off the poets!!!

— Mark Schiller

AMAZING FACT

Amazing fact: virtually none of the younger (i.e., our contemporaries) writers in Paris (novelists, anyway) know who Pierre Reverdy is. None know his work. Ah well, there's more to life than Derrida.

— Barry Gifford

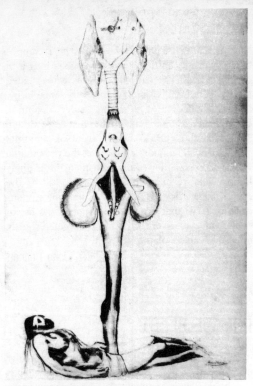

Top: R. Ubac, Victor Brauner, Jacques Hérold, 1938
Bottom: Jacques Hérold, Victor Brauner, Yves Tanguy, André Breton, 1934

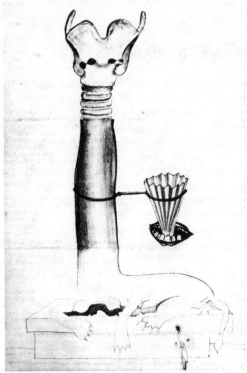

Top: Jacques Hérold, Victor Brauner, R. Ubac, 1938
Bottom: R. Ubac, Jacques Hérold, Victor Brauner, 1938

NEGATIVE VOLTAGE

by Barbara Szerlip

Maledicta: An Annual, $18 Membership, The Maledicta Society, 331 S. Greenfield Avenue, Waukesha, WI 53186.

Since adolescence, I've been fascinated by the idea of having words and phrases that no one's allowed to use. My burgeoning 13-year-old brain found it both odd and exhilaring that while "tuck" or "buck" were acceptable, "fuck" and "schmuck" were not. Why was the unmusical "excrement" or the whiny "feces" okay, while "shit" caused such a stink? A terrible pun, that, but one Dr. Reinhold Albert Aman, self-described Verbal Proctologist and world authority on cursing, might appreciate.

"America has always been a very prudish society," he opines, "more so, even, than England. We have always suppressed our strongest feelings, whether negative or positive. A belly laugh in polite company isn't acceptable. And you can't cry in public, especially if you're a man. We have been a Mr. and Mrs. Nice Guy society — Dale Carnegie kind of pussyfooters."

Aman, a Bavarian-born scholar in his 40's, began his career as a chemist and chemical engineer, specializing in metallurgy and petroleum. An interest in the subject of aggression was sparked while analyzing the 151 battle scenes in von Eschenbach's *Parzifal* for his doctorate in Medieval Languages and Literature. His interest gradually shifted from aggressive actions to aggressive speech.

He turned to full-time profanity in 1972, when he was denied tenure at the University of Wisconsin-Milwaukee, where he'd taught German, linguistics, and Medieval Literature for six years (and won an award for teaching excellence), because his chosen specialty wasn't considered "dignified" or "worthy" enough by the university establishment (Aman subsequently dubbed them "cacademics"). He took the university's action to federal court but lost. His parting shot at the chairman of his department was indicative of the path he was soon to follow. "You boring ass," he sneered. "When I see you, my feet fall asleep." Then for the coup de grace, he concluded with a traditional Thai *mot.* "Talking to you," he added, "is like playing the violin to a water buffalo."

Aman claims to be able to curse in 200 languages. " 'The first human being who hurled a curse against his adversary instead of a rock was the founder of civilization'," he says, quoting Freud. He bemoans the fact that Americans score low on his scale of inventive invective. (One notable exception is the Deep South, where the rich oral tradition has produced such gems as "Your breath is so foul it would knock a buzzard off a manure wagon." Billy Carter is an Aman hero.) Today, "The Dirty Dozen" are an impoverished handful of commonplace pejoratives that "have been drained of their negative voltage." And it's that "negative voltage" that allows people to let off steam. Aman believes that the demise of vile vituperation is one of the reasons why more and more people are turning from verbal to physical aggression.

Aman's studies have revealed that verbal aggression is divided globally into three groups:

— A Roman Catholic group "that uses blasphemy, especially the name of the Lord, references to the saints, and references to Church implements";
— A WASP group that "primarily uses body parts, body functions, sex, and excretion"; and
— The group found mainly in Africa, Asia, and Polynesia whose verbal aggression is centered on family relationships, including derogatory — often sexual — references to the father, mother, grandparents, or siblings of one's adversary. "The term 'mother-fucker'," Aman observes, "is found in all West African languages and was originally foreign to America."

The world's vilest cursers speak Hungarian, says Aman. "A Hungarian can curdle your blood. Some of their oaths make even me tremble." The cleverest speak Yiddish: "May you inherit a shipload of gold; may it not be enough to pay your doctor bills." Or, "May you inherit a house with a thousand rooms, may each of those rooms have a thousand beds, and may a fever throw you from bed to bed to bed." Turkish rhymed insults and Eskimo singing duels are also notable. Aman is particularly fond of a serpentine Hindi riposte that translates formally as "brother-in-law" but means "I seduced your sister."

Aman longs for the days of Shakespeare, who scolded, "Why ye fat-kidneyed rascal! Huge hill of flesh! Swol'n parcel of dropsies! You muddy, beetle-headed, flap-eared knave! You green sickness of carrion! Thou foul hunchback'd toad! Thou loathed issue of thy father's loins!"

Despite being apolitical, he also laments the loss of such wits as H.L. Mencken, who once described democracy as "that system of government under which the people, having 35,717,342 native-born adults to choose from, including thousands who are handsome and many who are wise, pick out a Coolidge to be the head of state."

The oldest curse that Aman's unearthed to date is from an Egyptian legal document written 3,000 years ago: "If you do not obey this decree, may a donkey copulate with you, may a donkey copulate with your wife, and may your child copulate with your wife."

In 1977, Aman founded *Maledicta: The Journal of Verbal Aggression*, which currently claims 2,500 steady subscribers in 62 countries. "The San Francisco area is a *Maledicta* hotbed," he writes. "We have more readers there than anywhere else, followed by New York City." Contributors have included sociologists, classicists, linguists, semanticists, lexicographers, librarians, anthropologists, historians, paleontologists, a rabbi, and a geologist. Subscribers include university professors, doctors, attorneys, diplomats, publishers, Jesuits, brain surgeons, and truck drivers.

Most of *Maledicta*'s articles are scholarly. Some are satirical. Some recent titles include:

— Karl Marx, Maledictor
— License Plate Taboos
— Celebrity Sick Jokes
— Puns in Advertising: Ambiguity as Verbal Aggression
— Japanese Sexual Maledicta
— What Are Graffiti For? Folk Epigraphy and Anonymous Rhetoric
— Dyke Diction: The Language of Lesbians
— Viet-Speak
— Herman Melville's Soiled Sailors
— A Glossary of Common Terms Useful for Beginning Teachers in the Public School System of New York

Besides *Maledicta*, the Maledicta Society publishes *Benedicta!*, a bi-annual newsletter, and reprints of Allen Walker Read's *Classic American Graffiti* (1935) and Abraham A. Roback's *A Dictionary of International Slurs* (1949). The Society has also published (for the first time ever) a newly discovered, facetious manuscript by Mark Twain on the dangers of masturbation. Aman reports that the head of the Milwaukee Associated Press

dismissed the news of a new Twain find because "it does not deal with fire, murder, or rape." ☠

Erika Rothenberg

DIRTY BOOKS STILL A THREAT: RECENT EROTIC WRITING
by Michael Perkins

Whatever else might be said of dirty books, one thing is certain: they still manage to piss people off. In the past few years radical feminists have joined with moral majoritarians to accuse pornography of dehumanizing women, degrading sex, and rending the polyester moral fabric of society; what they fail to add is that most contemporary porn is so badly written it seems incapable of threatening anything more than one's patience. Most dirty books are literarily contemptible because they follow formulas aimed at the lowest common denominator in a vast audience — but then most television programming, journalism, and general publishing is contemptible for the same democratic reasons.

Moral crimes await history's judgment, but literary crimes fall within the jurisdiction of book reviewers to prosecute — and for two decades critics have primly blacklisted erotica. In the 1960s when Supreme Court decisions took government out of the censorship business, liberal pundits reassured an anxious nation by predicting that in time dirty books would surely be yawned into oblivion. Ignore them, they said. When the novelty of freedom wears off, they will disappear.

Twenty years later more erotica than ever before is being published and sold — a phenomenon so resolutely ignored by the reviewing establishment that most readers would probably echo the response of a friend to the title of this survey: "I didn't know there *was* any recent erotic writing."

Because it is usually the subject matter of erotic fiction that stirs the reader to enjoyment or condemnation, and how well or poorly the writer has worked is seldom taken into consideration, erotic writing is the sole literary genre forced to justify its existence by its masterpieces. The first step in judging the value of erotica is to acknowledge that dirty books, on any level from subliterate to profound, need no more justification than the manifestations of eros they reflect.

This is hard for most people to swallow. What upsets them is the idea that the direct representations of eros labeled pornography or erotica are, for better or worse, the literature of human sexuality. Unlike other forms of genre fiction that reinforce cultural expectations, erotica is subversive to social conditioning. In its deliberately distorted vision of the world, sex is primary, an end in itself separate from love, marriage, and reproduction. The business of erotica is to reveal what we have concealed, to make what is so important in our lives important in language, to translate physical expression into its verbal equivalent.

The range of recent erotic writing is wide. Modernist, experimental, philosophical, romantic, fantastic, it is neither flat nor tediously single-minded when good writers take it seriously. In 1983 the work of two old masters was given American publication. Georges Bataille's *L'Abbe C* (Marion Boyars, 1983), published in France in 1950, appeared in a translation by Philip A. Facey. One of a handful of slim novels, available in English, by the French philosopher of eros and death, *L'Abbe C* is the story of twin brothers — one a libertine and the other a priest — who are involved in a triangular relationship with the libertine's mistress. Dry, cerebral, mysterious, difficult, *L'Abbe C* presents

Bataille's customary themes of eros, transgression, illness, and death like a maze of empty corridors in a heartbreak hotel. And only the agony is explicit here.

Henry Miller wrote the stories in *Opus Pistorum* — "work of a miller" — in 1941, when a Los Angeles bookseller paid him a dollar a page to write episodic erotica for the private collections of Hollywood producers. When Grove Press reprinted it last year it proved to be vintage Miller — as if the *Tropics* had been cut of everything but the erotic passages.

Virginie, Her Two Lives (Harper & Row, 1982) is modernist stylist John Hawkes' latest *hommage* to the highbrow French erotic novel. This time Hawkes has constructed a ribald double narrative of how two Virginies — one a servant to a depraved member of the *ancien regime*, the other the sister of an earthy taxi driver in Paris after World War II — keep their innocence in the midst of debauchery. Elegant both as parody and as traditional erotic reverie, *Virginie* is icily moral and romantic.

Bataille, Miller, and Hawkes are writers of established reputation whose books will be read because they wrote them. In the case of most quality erotica issued by mainstream publishers in either hardcover or paperback, it's not the author who sells the book, but the fantasy itself. Popular taste is responsible for the success of Gael Greene's *Doctor Love* (St. Martin's/Marek, 1982), her bestseller about a brilliant doctor who goes into rut when confronted with his own mortality; *Plaisir D'Amour* (Carroll & Graf, 1983), purportedly an erotic memoir of Paris in the 1920s and actually a recent attempt to imitate Anaïs Nin's approach to erotica but without her flair; and *The Claiming of Sleeping Beauty* (E.P. Dutton, 1982) by A.N. Roquelaure (rumored to be a pseudonym for Joyce Carol Oates), a romantic S & M novel using the prince-and-princess conventions of the fairy tale. The popular paperback counterparts of these are the "hot romances" like the *Jennifer* series published by Dell in eleven volumes of varying merit. These books are aimed at a mass middlebrow market that wants slick entertainment well enough packaged to be available in B. Dalton.

Then there is the work of the erotic avant-garde, among whom Marco Vassi, Kathy Acker, Terence Sellers, and David Barton-Jay have recently published interesting books. Marco Vassi is the author of a number of excellent erotic novels published by Olympia Press in New York, when publisher Maurice Girodias placed Henry Miller's mantle on his shoulders. Vassi's *The Erotic Comedies* (The Permanent Press, 1981) consists of wry erotic fables and stories, cosmic chuckles. *Great Expectations* (Grove Press, 1983) is Kathy Acker's latest experiment in erotic autobiography, cut up with Dickens. Crude, fragmented, and experimental, *Great Expectations* is hypnotically self-indulgent, a book that offers up language itself as erotic experience.

The Correct Sadist (V.I.T.R.I.O.L., 1983) by Terence Sellers transcends pathology. It is the poetry of cruelty. With acid elegance Sellers brings the sensibility and style of a Lautreamont to focus on the strict world of a female dominant named Angel Stern. David Barton-Jay's *The Enema as an Erotic Art and Its History* (The David Barton-Jay Projects, 1982) is an expensively produced, self-published, coffee table (ahem...) volume about the history and pleasures of a peculiar fixation. Self-publishing may be about the only way open for artists to work in the genre. Many individuals are working to produce personal alternatives to mass-produced adult bookstore dreck, among them feminist artists like Tee Corinne (published by Florida's Naiad Press), Betty Dodson, and Annie Sprinkle.

Like it or not, erotica won't disappear. We can take charge of it and make it reflect the true state of our erotic feelings, or we can leave it to be written by hacks, published by thugs, and purchased by middle-aged members of the raincoat brigade. The critical attention paid it is vital if there is to be a renaissance, for without it good writers will not be drawn to work in a genre that is its own ghetto. Writers like to be reviewed, and enjoy having their books talked about and even read — but dirty books are apparently dropped into a deep well on publication day. They sell hundreds of thousands of copies and don't even turn up at garage sales or flea markets.

The time is ripe for writers to reclaim a fertile genre and redeem the tradition of Apollinaire. In feudal Japan erotica was given to young people in the form of pillow books so that they might be instructed in lovemaking. Why can't we create a contemporary erotica that is human enough to instruct the young and comfort the lonely? That is both stimulating and intelligent? Surprisingly, it was

the cool academic Lionel Trilling who foresaw the possibility years ago: "I see no reason in morality (or in aesthetic theory) why literature should not have as one of its intentions the arousing of thoughts of lust. It is one of the effects, perhaps one of the functions of literature to arouse desire...."

Faye Kicknosway

DIGNITY AND DISCRETION

by Paul Bowles

A fox and a hare met by accident on a hillside. The fox was merely one of the foxes of the neighborhood, but the hare was known as the biggest and strongest hare in the valley. They sat down at a certain distance one from the other, and discussed the weather.

The hare did not relish being even that close to the fox, but he felt that he must maintain his dignity. Presently he said, not without some sarcasm: Have you met any good rabbits lately?

The fox grinned. You know, I used to love rabbit, but now I can't look at it.

The hare thought this very unlikely, but he said only: Why is that?

I had too much of it, I think.

He takes me for the village idiot, the hare said to himself. And now what do you eat? he asked.

The fox thought quickly. Who, me? Oh, eggs, he said. And vegetables and that sort of thing.

What do you do nights? the hare asked him, knowing that he hunted all through the dark hours.

Ever since I married I've been a homebody. I stay in with my wife. There's not a sweeter little vixen in the valley.

There was a silence.

It's been a bad year, with the dogs, the hare said.

Terrible! agreed the fox. Twice as many as last year. If it gets much worse I'm going to move out of the valley. I know a good place over on the other side of the mountain.

You won't find any eggs or vegetables up that way, said the hare, eyeing him. The fox did not reply.

Well, it was nice to chat with you, the hare told him. Keep an eye open for the dogs.

And he turned and bounded off, pleased with the way he had handled a delicate situation.

The fox watched him go. A real halfwit, he was thinking. But his young ones! The best in the valley!

At the memory he licked his chops.

VAMPIRELLA

by Elaine Equi

At discos where I eavesdrop,
the conversation always turns to love
but please no talk of broken hearts
for certain I can say
that love does not reside there.
Centuries ago, my mother advised me,
even as a corpse a woman should be able to win
admiring glances from the mourners.
Full well did I heed her
when choosing my burial garb:
high-heeled boots, the shortest mini,
plenty of eyeliner,
and glad am I to have done so.
Because of such wisdom,
for the moment, I can breathe again.
It is not life exactly
but from time to time
I too make my excursions
into the land of the living
no different than anyone else.

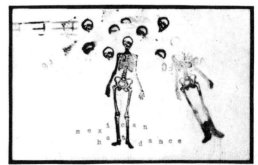

Julia Demarée

TRANS-CONTINENTAL CORPSE

Mario Cesariny

I

Portugal já vive Chicago dos anos 20

"QUANDO MATO ALGUEM FICO UM BOCADO DEPRIMIDO"

diz

Manuel Alentejano

Já explodiram 1469 bombas

com mais de 3500 livros

𝔢

O

Baptismo de fetos

atinge o aborto

= **Detida colaboradora do Primaz** =

- ENTRECOSTO
- BACALHAU
- FRANGO
- FEBRAS
- COELHO
- CHOCOS

Roteiro do Alentejo

meanwhile IN <u>Nicarágua</u> ...

II

... **SÍNTESE**

NICARÁGUA — Jornalistas do diário *La Prensa*, manifestaram-se em Manágua, reclamando o levantamento da censura em vigor no país desde a instauração da Lei de Emergência, em Março de 1982. Os jornalistas, ao todo uma vintena e com os rostos parcialmente cobertos por lenços, pediram também que lhes fosse fornecido o ante-projecto de lei de Imprensa que irá ser discutido proximamente pelo Conselho de Estado. **ABERTO ATÉ ÀS 2 HORAS**

Cão de Gado Laborioso

cultura / arte / espectáculo

em segurança máxima

Mercado Nacional dA

obrigação de ser feliz

Vale a pena

ÀS QUARTAS-FEIRAS

Mário Cesariny, 4-3-84
Lisboa XIIIth century
Manágua IXth century

NEW YORK
by Hariette Surovell

Everyone was saying that Area is the greatest New York City club ever. My friend Ellen and I went there on a Saturday night. Outside, hundreds of "bridge and tunnel" types — people who live in the four boroughs beside Manhattan, and in New Jersey — milled around outside the velvet ropes, looking desperate. Ellen said, "You walk right up to the ropes, look the bouncer straight in the eye. That way he thinks he knows you and lets you in." I was wearing a leopard-skin pillbox hat. The bouncer said, "Hey, you with the hat, and your friend, come in."

Area is a "theme club." The last theme I'm told was suburbia. The whole club was furnished with ping-pong tables, couches with plastic slipcovers. As we walked down a long hallway, resplendent with large glass exhibition cases, like the Museum of Natural History, I divined that today's theme is bondage. The first display case was furnished like a prison cell. Cot, funky toilet, graffiti on the walls, and a real-live "prisoner" who stood with his back to the crowds. Next, dozens of wooden rabbit hutches and a couple of entrapped live rabbits. Then there was a large stuffed rhinoceros, swaddled in leather straps. Finally, an abstract sculpture of a fat lady's torso, also suspended with chains.

The checkroom line was so long that people pushed and shoved to get ahead. I overheard French, Spanish, German, Italian. A nervous Wall Street type in a three-piece suit checked in five coats with a gold American Express card. Everyone else in the club was dressed strictly punk.

On the dance floor, go-go dancers, one a Filipino midget, danced in wooden cages. There was also a large cage open in the back in which the public could dance. In a pool, a sculpture of a dead baby floated face down. Beneath the bar, a glass case held whips, chains, and belts. On the wall, a sign advertised the sale of cappuccino and espresso with the word, "CAFFEINE." The bathroom was unisex. Bored male and female punks finicked with eye make-up in front of the mirrors.

In the back room, there was a giant fish tank with amazing tropical fish, a video screen showing old movies without sound, and an elderly man with an orange and blue parrot on his shoulder. You could pay him to take a picture of you with the parrot.

I got the vibes that most people were working in video and film. I guess I thought this because I didn't see any of my music biz friends. Matt Dillon walked in and blondes called out, "Matty!" pretending that they knew him. Ellen was looking for stimulants with no success. A gay guy told us that we must try a new drug called "Ecstasy." "It's like a four-hour orgasm," he explained. "You can't go clubbing without it."

We went to dance but the music was that wimpy disco fag music that doesn't even have any hooks...so we went home.

SANTA BARBARA, CA
by Tom Clark

A hot wind blows down out of the mountains all afternoon, gets stronger as it gets dark, blows all night and the fire engines roar around town blasting wet streams into the burning houses and I hear it all in my dry dreams. The garbage cans roll down the driveway into hell. Sleep is light and weary and evil. In the morning the street's full of palm branches. Ancient Republicans stare out warily from behind their dogs, picking up the pieces. Their faces, when I go by, are like the doors of bank vaults, totally without expression except for the flat blank unstated hatred. Everything is tacit, silent, dry like a ruined Egypt of the soul. The wind starts to blow.

I take my cancer medicine and go out on my bike to do the business of the day. For weeks a cop's been following me through the streets. I stopped, finally, and dismounted, and pretended to be fixing my wheel. He stopped behind me and got out and walked up to me with that rolling honcho walk of a guy who's seen too many clint eastwood movies. He stared at me behind one-way shades and asked my name and when I told him, he said, "What you doing around here?"

I told him and he said, "I been keeping an eye on you." I said, "I know." There was a silence. I looked at his bald and shiny head and looked at where his eyes would be and then down at his name tag, which said "Robert Ledyard." He looked at my details, up and down, the wool hat, the face full of cancer sores, the bike pants, the knee braces, the foot bandage, the bike shoes, and then he said, "I'm going to cite you." And I said, "What?" And he said, "You make one more mistake and I'm going to cite you. I'm going to get that thing off the street." I followed his eyes down to my bike. I said, "Why?" He said, "I been watching you for two weeks and you run red lights and you don't stop at stop signs and that last stop sign I saw you go through, you didn't even slow down. Next time I'm going to cite you." I said, "Okay." He said, *"It's not okay."* I said, "What?" He said, *"It's not okay,* understand?"

I gave that a lot of thought and now when I ride through this neighborhood I often feel this hot breath behind me and I keep turning around to see if it's just the wind, and sometimes it is, but sometimes it's Officer Ledyard. I've been stopping at stop signs lately, well anyway slowing down, whenever I feel that heat. I want to turn around and look but I force myself not to because really I *don't want to know* if that dude's behind me, doing his melvin purvis imitation, hoping I'll break into somebody's neat little bungalow so he can have an excuse to "get that thing off the street" for permanent!

Thoughts like these were running through my head as I jammed uphill yesterday p.m. coming back from the library in isla vista, an hour ride, and I'm sweating and the hot wind's blowing in my face, I'm pooped, barely making it, cutting through Ledyard's neighborhood and wearing my eyesight backward... at calle descanso I make my right turn and hey, in my face, here comes an old-timer in a station wagon making a left turn in the wrong lane and if I don't act fast, I get run over. I hit the brakes, he does too, we come close, no contact but I feel the heat of his metal and I scream, "You asshole!" He yells back, "What?" I repeat, "You asshole!" He jumps out of his car, I come clicking back dragging my 15-speed, we're face to face, he's about 60, six feet four, brush cut, big buck teeth, bermuda shorts, leering and pissed off and he says, "Why'd you call me that?" So I had to explain it...

Poetry is poetry and life is life and amerika is amerika and every night the hot wind blows... there are still a few poets left and sometimes their lines run through my mind...like "this is America, see / America — no touching, / take that back — tortured / souls whisper ridiculous / sentences" (F.A. Nettelbeck) and "A Fritos truck passes between rows of trees. / It's pleasant, how it rocks, and silent. / This is the way evil works." (Janet Gray). But I can't talk about poetry now, I've got to go pick up my garbage cans.

Thomas Wiloch

CALIFORNIA: THE CORPSE POLITIC
by Stephen Kessler

Pacific Gas & Electric Company's Diablo Canyon reactor has been approved for low-power testing by the Nuclear Regulatory Commission and may go radioactive any day. Diablo Canyon, near San Luis Obispo, is built on an active earthquake fault which the plant's planners failed to notice when scoping out the real estate for their project. Several billion dollars later it's much too late, according to the corporation, for second thoughts about firing up the fuel rods, whose active ingredient, plutonium, is one of the deadliest substances on the planet. Once those rods get hot, they'll stay that way for the next few million years.

Events appear to be conspiring, however, to keep Diablo cool. Every week a new technical fuckup is found — a leaky valve, a damaged pipe, crossed wires, or other "human error" somewhere in the machinery — to further postpone its possible operation. A month or so ago at Rancho Seco, another major California nuke not far from Sacramento, a mysterious explosion shut down that plant without generating much media coverage: simply another little mishap releasing no radiation, of course, and easily overlooked by the public, whose appliances scarcely blinked.

Then, Sunday before last (April 15), the entire Monterey Bay area was blacked out for several hours by an explosion at PG&E's Moss Landing plant — a nonnuclear facility whose giant twin smokestacks can normally be seen on any clear day spewing their toxic plumes into a blue sky once admired by Steinbeck. The blast was accounted for by a fallen wire, a short circuit, and an unexpected surge of voltage which fried a transformer at Moss Landing, leaving thousands of tourists on the beaches of Santa Cruz without any traffic lights to guide them back out of town. Computerized cash registers ceased to work, so stores with Sunday business had to close. The sun went down on a dark landscape. Meat began to spoil in freezers. Televisions sets went blank. Thinkers were forced to read and write by candlelight.

Apart from the roar of my neighbor's gasoline-powered generator (he must not have wanted to miss a minute of Nixon's memoirs on the eye that evening), it was a gorgeous night for silence: good atmosphere for contemplating sabotage. Perhaps in protest of the NRC's giving Diablo the go-ahead, some indignant guerrilla environmentalist had planted a bomb. Better yet, maybe a worker at the Moss Landing plant had intentionally thrown a switch the wrong way just to cost the company some money. Surely among the myriad human errors at Diablo a few might turn out to have been deliberate.

Tuesday I read in the *San Francisco Chronicle* that the downed power line had been caused by gunshots — "urban cowboys" out shooting on the weekend, according to a PG&E official — but by Wednesday the shots were discounted as a cause. No further explanation has been forthcoming from the utility.

All these seemingly coincidental events, whose connectedness remains officially unacknowledged lest it give some would-be saboteur ideas or otherwise alarm the juice-consuming public, were punctuated yesterday (April 24) by the biggest earthquake the Bay Area has felt in 50 years. I was having a beer with a couple of friends in a Santa Cruz saloon when the whole place started to shake, bouncing us around quite violently for half a minute. Fortunately no beer was spilled.

One thing I like about earthquakes is that they discourage people from moving to California. I wish they had the same effect on nuclear contractors. When this one hit, I hoped it was centered in San Luis Obispo, just in time to kill the Diablo Canyon plant before it goes on-line. As it turned out, it was centered just east of San Jose and caused some damage but probably not enough to slow the flow of capital into the coffers of PG&E, Bechtel, General Electric, and the other industrial powers still banking on atomic energy.

The president's trip to China, where he plans to sell some nukes, may postpone the demise of the nuclear beast by giving it a little new business overseas, but in the states the industry's on shaky ground. Whether by sabotage, incompetence, planned obsolescence, or natural disaster, Diablo Canyon is obviously doomed. Its highrise concrete hot tubs, in which so many investors have placed their faith, look more and more like lemons every day.

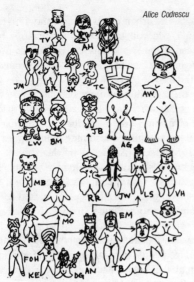

Alice Codrescu

genealogy of the
New York School of Poetry

HERMENEUTICS OF POPULAR CULTURE

by Hakim Bey

Krazy Kat who is sometimes "he" & sometimes "she" lives alone in the desert

cherishing hopeless love for Ignatz the Mouse, whose only obsession is heaving bricks at Krazy's head

The Kat feels no pain — little hearts appear in the air — like Sufi poetry

the beloved can do no wrong & even his cruelty is a sign of grace

but Offisa Pup loves Krazy & protects him with all the Law's power, locking up Ignatz in the Kounty Klink

Just as the Exoteric always veils & imprisons the Esoteric Light & keeps us from the clandestine meeting of wine & song

so Krazy himself must be a lawless Kalandar-dervish, kriminal of *amour fou*

conniving to be knocked out by those mystical missiles, chanting his poetry in the peyotelandscape of Kokonino — like Mahmud Shabistari's *Secret Rosegarden* or the *Divan* of Hafez

as anyone would know who's ever loved a heart-less boy, or noticed that contemplative states are like bricks.

ON TOM-TIT, A LANGUAGE POET

by Carl Rakosi

By a tree and a river an exiguous linguist
    sat singing, "Zukofsky! Zukofsky! Zukofsky!"
And I said to him, "Superbird, why do you sit,
    singing, 'Zukofsky! Zukofsky! Zukofsky!'
"Is it lyric aesthenia, birdie," I cried,
    "or a concept too big for your little inside?"
With a shake of his tight little head, he replied,
    "Oh Zukofsky, Zukofsy, Zukofky."

Note: to the tune and words of "The Willow Song" in *The Mikado*

ARE YOU SEEING HIM

by James Laughlin

and if so what do you see
in him (apart from the

fact that his Greek is so
much better than mine and

he can remember *every*thing
instantly) is it because

he gets his shoes shined
and I don't (and they are

such narrow little pinchy
shoes) is it because he

doesn't have a bald spot
(or does he wear a hair-

piece) will the initials
VM & PH be carved in the

railing of a chapel like
S & I in the Tempio Mala-

testiana at Rimini oh I
can't finish this poem I

don't know the end of it &
it's just breaking my heart.

The *Corpse* is back after a brief sojourn in limbo. We have a new home, thanks to the generosity of Louisiana State University. We also have a grant from the National Endowment for the Arts, for which we are grateful. Those of you who are aware of our unbridled tongue and our oft broadcast opposition to institutional servility, may well ask what it is we are doing. We are doing fine, thank you. If anything, our new connections demand of us an increased responsibility to our innate anarchistroyalism, so it won't be said that the *Corpse* sold out. For a silver coffin with rococo NEA handles in the basement of Allen Hall. Otherwise, we will bring you a more reliable and fatter *Corpse* for all your tenebrous cultural angst. Incidentally, it is also time to renew your subscriptions.

CHER CADAVRE EXQUIS

FEEBLE-MINDED CENTERSPREAD

In his essay *A Nation of Lunatics* Henry Miller wrote: "Once I saw in a store window a framed photograph of all the Vice-Presidents we have had. It might have served as a rogues' gallery. Some of them looked like criminals, some looked feeble-minded, some like plain idiots." The same might be said of the faces in the centerspread of the latest *EC*. With few exceptions (yourself, Alice Notley, I think) I have never seen such a collection of dead-eyed squares, of meager-minded opportunists. One World Poetry Festival was no different, however. McClure has become, or always was, a vain & paranoid ponce who, having nothing to say, declaims *Beowulf* from memory as he has already done here two times previously. Baraka, still an honest man, it seems, has become the good college prof, albeit somewhat puritanical in condemning Prince's film *Purple Rain* as "backward, man!, backward." Kesey an amiable burned-out bear who writes children's stories which are childish in the way children are not. Adrian Mitchell wants us to be thrilled by his visiting the grave of that commie hack P. Neruda. Simon Ortiz a drunken red indian on the warpath; he threatened to murder a friend of mine saying, "I've killed before and I can do it again." Norse, of course, k'vetching, suffering from a terminal case of hypochondria and claiming he invented and/or discovered everything from the iambic pentameter to shitola. Few people had something to say. Ed Sanders, Tuli Kupferberg, and an English punk poetess with flaming red hair named Jole who spoke out for the striking miners in a sweet working class north-country accent. The Fugs gave a beautiful and inspiring concert to an almost empty hall and were attacked in the press the next day as being '60s throwbacks, I guess, for singing Wm. Blake, Matthew Arnold and coming out against nuclear weapons and for keeping the issues alive. Ah yes, a time of inner emigration, indeed.

— William Levy

THE TRUTH ABOUT THE POUND GANG

II, 5-7 is one of your best! I love The Rakosi, and will ask if we can reprint in our annual. And now the *truth* is out about The Pound gang. I suspected all along, but Ez was mum. But he paid the price — 12 years in St. Liz. Wyndam was always a bad apple. He abandoned three little bastards. Joyce was a sot. Hem probably buggered antelopes, or worse. Fordie was a terrible liar, but lovable. A bad lot.
Very best,

— James Laughlin

JEW-HATING IN AMERICAN POETRY
by Rodger Kamenetz

In a recent issue of *Sulfur*, Eliot Weinberger raises the provocative question of anti-Semitism in American poetry. The occasion is Dr. E. Fuller Torrey's book, *The Roots of Treason*. Torrey's thesis is very simple, and one would think, self-evident. Pound was not insane and his psychiatrist knew it. Therefore Pound is responsible for his anti-Semitism. What is sending the Poundians scurrying to the defenses — the folks in Orono are ordering sandbags — is not simply the additional evidence Torrey provides that Pound was a virulent Nazi sympathizer. It is rather Torrey's suggestion that there is no separation between the man and his work, "for the man and his poems are one."

This radical notion, which is really the faith of literature, makes so much common sense no critic would have a job if it were left to stand. Thus Leon Surrette, author of *A Light From Eleusis: A Study of the Cantos of E.P.* , lays it on thick in the latest ABR. "Of course, Torrey is completely off-base here. A poem is a *work* of art, and as with other forms of labor, the quality of the workmanship is not a function of the moral or ideological probity of the workman." Such sophistry is regular stuff for the readers of ABR, but really. Granted, a Nazi might make a competent plumber, but I thought poetry was a different line of work.

Surrette should take some cues from Hugh Kenner's *The Pound Era*. It simply doesn't do to face some issues head on. If you're going to separate the man from his work — separate, boy, separate. Try looking in Kenner's index under "Jews," "Judaism," "anti-Semitism." Nope. The wash is white. If you try under "Rothschild," you will find a single reference, in a footnote no less, to the effect that Pound, in 1938, knew nothing of the concentration camps. Now here's where you can see the "moral and ideological probity of the workman." If you can't bleach it out, hide the spot in a corner.

Weinberger at least takes the problem seriously. In his essay, he takes us on a little tour of anti-Semitism — shows how Pound, Eliot, and Cummings for three, deserve condemnation for their anti-Semitism and racism. (One might as well add Stevens.) But when the time comes to draw a conclusion Weinberger literally goes to outer space. He just can't reconcile the man and the poetry, so he makes a bad man into a bad poem. He tells us that while Pound may have trod in the mire, his head was in the stars. Then to complete the metaphor he brings in that mysterious dead star, Nemesis, fresh from the science feature section of the local newspapers. It is fascinating to watch an intelligent and sensitive writer turn his back to Judaism with such a whirl and cast himself into empty space.

So let me supply my own ending to Weinberger's essay. Weinberger asks why hatred consistently underlies modernist American poetry. Perhaps, it is because Pound, Eliot and Stevens so studiously ignored the Jewish tradition. In my view the hatred of the Jew is a hatred of a moral content in poetry. Art for art's sake, Stevens' aestheticism, Pound's vorticism — these were plungings into the whirlwind of phenomena, without a moral perspective. The consequence of that "tradition" for the present generation of writers is obvious — fragmentation, disintegration, shards of shards. What is miss-

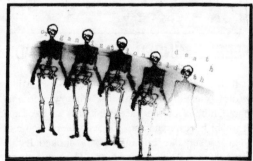

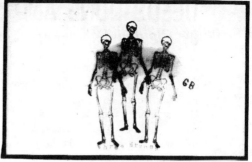

Julia Demarée

ing in today's poetry is the force of a moral commitment. Arrogance, triviality, solipsism, a thrashing and whirling have taken its place.

Weinberger quotes Octavio Paz to the effect that poetry is a secret religion. But poetry is not a religion. Religion is a religion. Heinrich Heine, who returned to Judaism at the end of his life, thought to admire the pure aestheticism of the Greeks. But he realized, he said, that the Greeks were boys, the Jews were men. He meant, I think, that the Greeks lived in a world of fate, without responsibility while the religious Jew takes personal responsibility for the fate of the world. Out of this beautiful and humane tradition, poetry has flowered continuously for thousands of years. Yet to read Pound's surveys of literature — his guides to "kulchur" — David was no poet, and there never was an Isaiah.

Pound never took any responsibility for his vicious and hateful views. In the latest ration of Pound droppings dished out by New Directions, the Talmud is described as a "gangster's manual." This from a man who took the trouble to study Egyptian, Chinese, Provencal, but never saw the beauty of the Jewish tradition as it was being destroyed under his nose. Pound writes in utter ignorance of the Jewish tradition. Eliot, Stevens, Williams, likewise.

Why a Jewish writer would want to become a Poundian, is, perhaps still an interesting question today. In less than twenty years it will be a ludicrous one. I don't think Jews can afford to waste their time playing with the toys of their enemies. Why devote yourself to the study of a man who desires your destruction? But I wonder what the effect on Jewish consciousness — and conscience — is of poring over Pound's anti-Semitic drivel. Rather desensitizing one might think. Yet some Jew-

ish poets today would rather wade through Pound's fragments than investigate their own tradition, just as Allen Ginsberg kissed Ezra's cheek on his way to embracing Buddhism. Ginsberg spread the word that Pound had recanted — that his anti-Semitism was a stupid suburban prejudice. But his "apology" is off the mark. It came too late, and concealed too much — Pound never came clean. As for his touted friendship with Louis Zukofsky — often brought up as proof that he hated the race, but not the individual — it smacks of "some of my best friends..." There is such a thing as a self-hating Jew. Zukofsky's publication of a notoriously anti-Semitic rant as Pound's contribution to the "Objectivist" anthology is proof of that.

The vacuum of modernist anti-Semitism needs a Jewish answer. And that answer — however uncomfortable this might make the assimilated Jewish writer himself — is a return to a Jewish tradition in poetry, one far more distinguished and profound and continuous than any Messrs. Pound or Eliot were ever able to fabricate from their various patchworks and pastiches of crumbling civilizations. (Maybe some day young Jewish poets will notice that while the other reichs keep crumbling, the Jewish world lives on.) It is this tradition that Whitman spoke of, late in his life, when he hoped to be considered in the line of the Hebrew prophets. "No true bard," he wrote, "will ever contravene the Bible."

DEEDS DONE AND SUFFERED BY LIGHT
by Clayton Eshleman

One can glimpse Apollo in the door of each thing,
as if each thing now contains his oven —
in vision I open an olive tree and see his earlier animal
shapes fleeing at the speed of light, the python,
mouse, and lion Apollo, fleeing so that human forms
may walk unharmed by the invasion of the supernatural.
Light increased incredibly after the end of animal deity,
at the point verticality was instituted,
and the corpse of one's mother buried far, far from the place
on which one slept one's head. But the supernatural
in the guise of the natural is turning us over
in its fog a half mile from this ledge. Burnished
muscleless fist of a grey cloud. Sound of rain
from water still falling from the olives. I have no desire
to live in a world of nature conditioned by patriarchy.
I kick off my head and live in the light
bounding in from my mother. It is her great
ambivalence toward her own navel that conditions
the decreasing dripping. The hills now
writhe with green meat and something should follow.
Something should be explaining the tuft of salmon bull shape
abandoned by the other stilled clouds. Something is
this abyss of unusableness that remainders me
and pays no royalty. There are hosts of thrones
directly above. A witch hammer. A cleated enclosure.
The way a church has of making you puke your soul
upon entering and then, as the dryness of birth is rehashed
by nun and candle, of worshiping what has just left you,
the bride of your chest, the stuff inside you that a moment before
twinkled with the sadness and poverty of the street's
malicious laughter. How I wish that this poem
would birth another, and that the other had something to do
with unpacking the olive meat of this mountain. No
apocalypse. An enlargement, rather, of the so-called Whore
on her severely underfed Dragon. And more wine. More plumes
of silver azure evening coursing over
the thatch of the mountainside. More space to suffer,
more farewell to the flesh, more carnival in the face of everyman,
less perfection, more coherence. Meaning: more imagination,
more wigs for glowworms, more cribs for the restless dead
who wake us right before dawn with their bell leper
reminding us that fresh rain air is a clear indication
that here is not entirely here. The processions of graffiti-
scarred bison are, like us, clouds imprisoned to be viewed.
And then my mother began to speak: "You've put on a lot of weight!
Look at your father and me, some shape we're in! We've suffered

a lot for you these 14 years. You should've seen my left side
when it turned into a purple sponge and stained what
you buried me in to the point it rotted. I'm glad
John Ashbery appeared to you last night reading new
incomprehensible poems that made perfectly good sense. You are
much more organized, much more chaotic, than you behave here.
When I think of you, I see you at 12, stuck in the laundry chute,
your legs wiggling in the basement air, while the top part talked
with me as we waited for the renter to pull you out.
We had a nice chat that afternoon, and I almost liked you best
that way, just what stuck out of the chute. If I could only have
that part on a roller skate and let what was wiggling below go —
it's that part that's gone off gallivanting,
that's carried you goodness knows where while I
and your father lie here a few feet away from each other
waiting for our coffin lids to cave in. Then, even
the little space you left us to play with memories of you
on our chest bones will be gone. My buttons are mouldy
and my hands have no flesh left but I still manage
to squeak my buttons a little and get into your dreams.
I'm sorry if I appear both dead and alive to you,
but you should know by now you can't have it your way all the time.
I'm as real in this way as I ever was, sick more often than not
when I appear, but you're never here, you're worrying
how to take care of me, and then you wake to a jolt
every time there's nothing to take care of.
Now your father wants to say a word." "Clayton,
why don't you come home? We were such a nice little family.
Now it is like when you went off to that university.
Your mother and I would sit up and talk about you
until our fathers came in from the night and motioned us
into our bed. You were such a nice little fellow
when we could hold you up high and look at each other
through you. Ten little fingers ten little toes
Two bright eyes a funny little nose
A little bunch of sweetness that's mighty like a rose
Your mother, through you, looked so much like
your grandmother I could never get over it.
Why I bet you don't even even remember your birth gifts
A savings bank and one dollar from granddad and grandmother
Two kimonas from aunt Georgia and uncle Bob
Supporters from Fay's dollie Patricia Ann
A Romper Suit from Mrs. Warren Bigler
A Dress from Mr. & Mrs. SR Shambaugh
Silk Booties & Anklets Knit Soaker & Safety Pins
Hug-me-tight a Floating Soap Dish with Soap Rubber Doggie
I don't see why you don't come home. Your mother and I
have everything you need here. Why sure,
let's see, maybe you could pick up some things,
Gladys — no, she's not listening — *Gladys what do you want?*"

"Well, I know we need some scouring powder and light bulbs"
"GLADYS WHAT DO YOU WANT?" "And Clayton,
we want Clayton to come back, we don't like Clayton Jr. out so late at night"
"GLADYS WHAT DO YOU WANT?" "You never know what will happen, why
just last week Eunice Wilson, over in Plot #52541, told me"
"GLADYS WHAT DO YOU WANT!" — "are you listening, Daddy?
Eunice said while Jack was getting out of his car parked in his own driveway at 2 AM"
"GRADDISROTDURURUNT!" "— after his date with Kay Fisbeck, this man
came up to him and said something I will not"
"GRADDISROTDRURUNT" "— I will not repeat it was that vulgar —
this man said: if you don't come with me, I'll crush your cows.
Doesn't that take the cake? Why Clayton you can't blame Jack
for going off with him, and you would not believe where
this man took Jack Wilson and what he wanted him to do.
Now that your father's lid has caved in, I'll tell you:
he made him drive north to the Deaf School parking lot,
and when he was sure nobody else was around, he said:

> *Persephone's a doll*
> > *steeper than Marilyn,*
> *miracles lick her*
> > *dreams invader,*
> *over the cobweb orchestra*
> > *there's an ice*
> > *conductor,*
> *forget the orchestra,*
> > *conduct the pit!*
> *Hanged*
> *Ariadne*
> > *giving birth in Hades*
> *is the rich, black music in mother's tit."*

John Rosa

MANIFESTO

by Gloria Frym

When the yearn redoubles itself out of nothing
better to do and at midnight telegrams stop seeming
the only way to get the continuous present
to you and the rhyme sits upon the line
like the skin upon the apple and the metaphor
is the thing and the idea disappears,
the long wait for the great poem
will be over. And I'll be over in a little while
to confirm the beginning of a new poetics,
plenty of broken lines among the prosaic
smooth lengthy generous long legged lines,
short compact circular lines,
lines on top of lines, lines moving sideways
into each other, lines rolling all over each other,
onto the floor, all disaffection, all indifference
moved to the next line and seduced back to innocence
by a strange music whose beat
is my pulse. And I will stop insisting I know and
simply do the expert thing which at every moment in time
is to free these lines for you.

A POEM FOR ISADORA DUNCAN

by Kay McDonough

Isadora was no jerk
In memory of her
plaster the town
with giant gestures
Picture her sailing
through the door
Pinned to her red scarf
a note that reads:
'Remember Me'

*

The pedant sips
from a crystal glass
Isadora smashes it
by way of a toast
'The room is dark,'
he complains
She lights the candle
He whimpers:
'But I am afraid to die'

KOREA: SIX FOOTNOTES TO THE BUDDHA'S BIRTHDAY

by Robert J. Perchan

I

The fabled courtezans. Miss Lee has no hair on her twat. Nowhere for Mr. Louse to hang his little black lantern of an egg. And on the Buddha's birthday!

II

The Buddha and Jackie Gleason in *The Hustler.* Twin rotundities: East Egg and West Egg. A fat Buddha in gray robes tapping his pool cue on the floor. Not cigarette smoke but smoldering joss sticks bluing the air. One ball clacks against another. A single sound, complete in itself.

III

Would you believe that Yum Bum-suck is a real Korean man's name? Mrs. Nam once told me that as a child her mother scolded her, "If you don't behave, you'll grow up to marry a *ddong jang-gun!*" *Ddong jang-gun* means Shit General, a man who earns his living emptying septic tanks, a pair of wooden buckets suspended from a pole balanced along his shoulders. They have green trucks now with suction hoses, except in the trickier parts of the city, where the *ddong jang-gun* still plies his trade, buckets suspended, dreaming of little Korean girls who must someday grow up.

IV

People here are still unhappy about the memory of the Greater East Asia Co-Prosperity Sphere. During World War II, Korean women were conscripted to serve as "companions" to Japanese soldiers in the field. Sachimoto Uragawa, fresh from a sweet lay, blew the nuts off Sgt. Mike Corcoran of Billings, Montana, a quiet heterosexual town. On Aug. 6, 1945, at 8:16 AM, in Hiroshima, Uragawa's wife's clitoris disintegrated. United. In a Heaven. We believe.

V

Yes, I visited Ground Zero in Nagasaki. A disappointment. Flowers in bloom, a thick-leaved pungent green. Manicured. A lizard skittered by. One head. Four legs. One tail. Standard. Right out of the manual. A narrow tower of mangled steel. One thinks: whumpf! Ka-wham! But still. The sky a still, placid blue. And then a speck. A black speck.

VI

The Buddha bade farewell to the rats last, it is said, before ascending. At last! they said, scrambling for the last few crumbs that had lain pressed under the Great One's thighs.

BUREAU

KOREA

by Robert J. Perchan

korrhea: (also *co-rrhea*) a particularly pernicious combination of dysentery and the clap contracted during a single debauch.

The typical Korean body, like the eskimo's, is eminently designed for the hard, brutal winters. The short arms and legs and elongated torsos present less skin surface to the frigid air — less heat is dissipated off. Breath does not freeze on the chin and upper lip of the whiskerless man. Korean claims of descent from a primeval She-bear can be discounted.

The typical Korean skull can have decidedly Amerindian features — living, breathing evidence of the prehistoric land bridge across the Bering Strait — high, rounded cheekbones molded into a wise, benignant passivity. Something of an amateur phrenologist, I can sometimes see the skull beneath the skin. Such a skull as Inja's would stand out in a boneheap — the Cappuchins would give her a place of honor in one of their nightmarish tableaux.

Something absolutely must be said of Inja's butt. Why? And What? Because its open, inviting cleft suggests a freshly baked pie with just the thinnest of slices removed? That's part of it. Because she is typical of her good sisterhood in this obscure corner of the globe? That cannot be denied. It is difficult to believe that this transcendent feature is constructed out of little more than cabbage, rice, noodles and seaweed — plus a scosh of genetic material and a good deal of exercise in the squatting position. When I consider this fact, I despair less of the future of humankind.

My anthropologist friend Harry T. Colfax, perennial candidate for Sen. Proxmire's Golden Fleece Award, has divided Korean women up into a dozen phenotypes according to the configurations of their pubic hair. He has noted the Squat-V, Standard-V, Home-on-the-range, Hanging Gardens, The True Hairless, etc. One specimen required a category and a label all to herself: Colfax's Caracol. Says H.T.C.: "If Przwalski can have a horse, and Halley a whole comet, I don't see why I can't lay claim to my own little corner of Creation."

One of the unique graces of drinking and dining in Korea is the free snack you often get with your drinking glass in a restaurant or drinking house — a fleck of carrot, half a grain of boiled rice adhering to the rim — sometimes the ghostly, romantic imprint of a lower lip in lipstick or human mouth-dew.

H.T.C. again: There was an old theory of evolution — long since discredited — which held that those racial groups which retained their childlike characteristics throughout adulthood were most advanced in humanity's long march toward Omega. This was due to the view that certain accompaniments to physical maturity and old age — hairiness, big noses, etc. — were actually reversions to the conditions of our snouty, ape-like ancestors. This would put Orientals — and Oriental women in particular — in the very first section of the parade, straining at the tow-ropes to haul with them their flower-bedecked float and its giant granite Buddha. In the very front row of this phalanx, high-stepping and baton-twirling, we would find The True Hairless.

The sun also rises on Pusan. We expatriates make a playful habit of substituting "j" for "z" in our conversation, Korean style: There was no "z" placed in the mouths of the "denijens" of the Land of the Morning Calm when the Creator first doled out alphabets. You don't go to the zoo in Korea, you go to the Jew — to pawn your stuffed animals perhaps. (After all, Jake, this *is* another country). So also with "zh". There's no Revised Standard Version of the Bible clutched piously against the rib cage of the Sunday morning church-goer — it's a Revised Standard Virgin.

"Why you alla time touch me there?"
"I'm curious."
"Jesus Kleist, you alla time curious."
"I have to know certain things before I die."
"You not gonna die."
"I'm going to die before you do, that's for sure. Look how healthy and smooth you are!"
"I said don't touch me like that."
Inja is lying on her belly with the bedsheet thrown to the side. The morning sunlight streams in through the window. I slip the white envelope end-wise in the crack of her bum. It stands up like the sail of a boat.
"What you doing now?"
"I'm mailing a letter."
"You think I'm a mailing box? Who you sending a letter to?"
"To America."
"What it says?"
It says, " 'Sniff me, and you'll never go back to toot.' "
"Who's Toot?"
"A rich peoples' drug."
"You not rich, that's for sure."

I take the envelope out of her breech, give it a whiff, and hand it to her. It smells faintly like day-old boiled squid. She sits up, opens the envelope and shakes out the letter I picked up at the P.O. that morning. She reads:
". . . a section entitled BUREAUS where we print reports, literary or not, from far places. Would you write 3-4,000 words for us on Korea . . ."

She puts the letter back into the envelope, disappointed.
"When you gonna get a job?"

Some proverbs of Kung unnoted by recent scholars: Being arrested for raping one's own wife is like being put in jail for picking one's own pocket. If a woman complains to the magistrate, it is because her husband didn't beat her hard enough. Going a day without a bribe is like going five hundred years without a woman.

(From the *Korea Herald*, Nov. 28, 1984)
To the Editor:
For those who think they've heard everything:
"Korean men like their women intelligent, respecta-

ble and virginal," according to a recent MBC survey of 500 local males KH. Nov. 17). Too bad the pollsters didn't find out how many of the pollees are virgins. . . or their definitions of respectability.

The Asian male wants his wife to be sexually inexperienced in hopes that she'll never learn what she's been missing by being married to him. Emotional insecurity that requires an intact hymen will just as likely expect the bride to be nunlike in her participation during "the act" and quick to praise his modus operandi afterward.

He'll think her a harlot should she seem to enjoy the honeymoon communion too much during the five minutes or so that it takes him to bank his old-age investment. As he snores off into adolescent dreamland she stares into the darkness of an unfulfilled future while asking herself the one question Confucius could never answer: "Is that all there is?"

(I'd like to have 100 won for every time that existential query has been murmured in a Cheju-do bridal suite.)

An astonishing 82.8% of the married men polled support "criminal punishment for women who commit adultery." One can only assume they are referring to married women as many Korean men spend their evenings trying to commit with single bar and office girls the very same "criminal" act they would like to jail their wives for. Clearly they do not want done unto them that which they assume to be their male right to do unto their wives.

In the same KH issue just three pages later we learn that the police are searching for a 49-year-old woman college professor who allegedly had an "adulterous affair" with a man 17 years her junior. Tut, tut, tut. Is nothing sacred anymore.

The article adds that the disgraced woman professor "attended American colleges" and is (was, after this) "an English literature professor" — as if to suggest that the years she spent abroad caused the licentious erosion of the Confucian inhibitions all Koreans are blessed with.

I'd like to have another 100 won for every Korean coed who has had an affair with one or more of the middle-aged male professors.

Such porcine double standards are responsible for the increasing number of Korean women who are turning to the burgeoning gigolo population for satisfaction that has been denied them in marriage. These cads could be put out of work by allowing Korean women to enter the 20th century.

— Cissy Lutz

Tuli Kupferberg

KANGNAM-GU
SEOUL

A word about this dog-meat soup business — particularly for you ladies of the club. And particularly if you want to get some idea of what the "new" Korea is all about. A widely travelled philosopher once remarked that if you want to come to some understanding of an alien culture, you can begin by choosing one item in that society's inventory of tools and dietary opportunities — be it barbed wire or pemmican — and learn all there is to know about it. I haven't done this with boshing-tang, to be sure, but a few select details may help to draw the lower half of this tragicomic peninsula out of obscurity and into better, if still fuzzy, focus. Dog-meat soup is a delicacy. It consists of slices of pooch cooked in spicy broth. Various vegetables can be added. The broth and vegetables are ingested with the aid of a wide, shallow stainless steel spoon. Remnants of the late Mr. Bowser are to be elicited from the murk of his temporary resting place by means of chopsticks. A bowl of boiled rice is taken on the side. Korean women in large part shy away from partaking of the feast, though a college girl once told me that, as a sickly child, she ate boshing-tang once a week for a year. She is a healthy specimen today. Indeed, a fair translation of the Sino-Korean would be "good-health soup." Men relish its savory taste. Its season is August, the "dog-days" believe it or not. Because dogs do not sweat (at least through their skin), filets of Old Yeller are said to enhance one's stamina throughout the month of brutal, feverish sun-glare. Old Yeller, yes. Yellow dogs are said to make the best eating. The primary purpose of consuming *boshing-tang*, however, is to ensure the production of a hard, durable erection throughout the evening (and ensuing morning).

The Korean government has outlawed the serving of *boshing-tang* in public eating houses, at least in the cities. This is due in part to certain British housewives, widows and spinsters who write letters to editors suggesting what people in nations 10,000 miles away ought to be allowed to eat. As an added incentive, Korean public officials do not much cherish their country's regular appearance in *Mondo Cane*-type films. They would prefer features on ship building, the '88 Olympics, video cassette recorders, high-grade steel production and a 96% literacy rate: in short, the "new" Korea.

A final note on the preparation of dog-meat soup: In the very first step of the recipe, Fido is strung up by his four heels and bludgeoned mercilessly until he is ready to confess to anything, including his role in the Creator's divine plan to maintain domestic harmony in the bedrooms of Chosŭn, the ancient and venerable name of this land.

Of South Korea's 40 million+ people, about half bear the surname either Park, Kim or Lee. It is looked upon as a violation of nature nearly as serious as incest for two people of the same family name to marry, especially if their family trees root them in the same original hometown far back in the mists of time. The family name is customarily written first, followed by a two-syllable given name, as in the following example from *The Korea Herald*, May 16, 1985:

WONJU, Kangwondo (Yonhap) — In a rare marriage between two people of the same sex and family name, two women in this city about 100km southeast of Seoul married each other Sunday at a Buddhist temple.

In front of the Buddhist monk who presided over the unusual wedding, the 36-year-old "bridegroom" Kim Rae-ok, of Haksong-dong, took an oath to "faithfully respect and love" her 42-year-old bride, Kim Ki-rae, as her "wife."

Right after the ceremony, they embarked on a week-long honeymoon trip to Cheju Island.

After denying that she was a lesbian, Kim Rae-ok said that she decided to marry Kim Ki-rae after she saw how so many male-female couples lived unhappy lives.

The bridegroom presented a diamond ring, a gold necklace and a wrist watch to her bride, a restaurant owner, and the latter gave her partner a wrist watch as a wedding gift.

The tall, slender, handsomely angular young gigolo you see frequenting "scotch corners" and cocktail lounges these days is known as a "swallow man," a breed of self-employment not without its risks. The ladders of Korean fire engines do not reach the upper floors of the major hotels. Whenever there is a hotel fire in Seoul or Pusan, the typical Korean businessman tunes into the televised news broadcast on the off chance he will catch a glimpse of his middle-aged wife pitching headlong toward the pavement of the hotel parking lot in self-defenestration, followed by the precipitous descent of her "swallow man" lover, who, despite the epithet, is no more successful a defier of gravity than poor, unfulfilled Mrs. Park or Mrs. Lee.

Inja always causes quite a stir when she performs at the American Legion Club on Tuesday and Friday nights. She's a True Hairless, in Harry T. Colfax's taxonomy, with a snapper as bald as a baby's butt. Lately she's been talking about getting a "pubic wig." She wants me to shave my beard, which is mostly dark brown. She knows a wig-maker in Kwangbok-dong who wove one out of monkey hair a few years ago for a stripper in a downtown club. I am not a shy man, nor a prude, and Inja says I can always grow a new beard, which is true. "Kleist," she says, plucking a few gray hairs out of my chin with a pair of tweezers, "it's you who alla time say we made for each other."

A fourteenth way of looking at that blackbird may be found in an ancient Sino-Korean proverb:

鳥 飛 利 落

"When the crow flies out of the pear tree, a pear falls to ground." (That is, when two events occur in spatial and temporal proximity, we may paranoiacally assume a causal relationship exists between them.)

kee-boon: the confidence to be detected in a Korean businessman's eye — like a cataract — that all his worldly affairs are in harmonious balance with nature and the cosmos and that nobody knows what he's really up to.

1st Whore: "Oh yeh sure, this happen alla time to young girl. She gotta no *wol gyung* — she no go onna rag yet — she pappa he come home drunk. He putta his hand here, she no move. What she gonna do? Or maybe she sleeping and she wake up. His hand right here. He rub. He no gonna put it inside the pussy. Girl gonna scream bloody murder he do that!"

2nd Whore: "Hah! She no gonna scream. Sometimes Korean man he no too big. Like a pencil. He come in go out his daughter nobody even know he stop by for visit. Young girl maybe she roll over in she sleep — thinka somebody leave ball-pen under blanket she poke sheself."

1st Whore: "You no say that about Korean man. My cousin he big man — like this. He show me when I was little girl. Then go Vietnam and get died."

2nd Whore: "Hey, Mistah Mohnkee. You wanna marry good Korean girl? You find girl she faddah he die she baby time."

(From *The Korea Herald*, May 19, 1985)

To the Editor:

At first glance a brief article in your paper on an anti-spitting campaign had me thinking that perhaps Korea was finally going to do something about this messy manifestation of machismo. But, alas, it was date-lined Peking.

Seoul seems ever so keen on cracking down on this, that, or the other thing; so desperate to "enter the ranks of the advanced countries" by 1) teaching cabbies English phrases, 2) thwarting its citizens' yen for dog meat, and 3) requiring VD checkups for working women.

Would that Korea could restrict such foul habits to the men's lavatory where it belongs! Instead we find necktied salarymen in down-town Seoul spitting on the streets and sidewalks of a city that will soon be hosting the world at large in international sporting events watched by millions more on television.

I maintain that the fault lies with Korean mothers for not breaking their sons of such filthy habits early in life. Small wonder that Korean women who sheepishly tolerate such brutish habits from their fathers, brothers, husbands and sons eventually become shrewish mothers-in-law intent on making their son's wife as hapless and unfulfilled as they themselves have been.

— B. Russell

KANGNAM-GU SEOUL

I wake up in the dark — I don't know why. I feel for Inja in my usual fashion — rolling over and expecting first contact with her bottom. She sleeps like that — fetally —legs drawn up, her pointy bum provocative and available. But it is not there. She is not there. It is only then I hear it: a kind of strangled moan — a choked weeping. One corner of the room is very dark, and there is some movement, or else the sound is giving movement to the dark that is emitting it.

"Inja?"

No answer.

"Inja, turn on the light."

"No-o-o."

"What's wrong?"

There is a funny odor in the air — of snuffed candle wick. She sometimes uses our love-candle to find her way in the dark if she comes home from the Legion Club after I have turned in. It has been freshly extinguished.

"Did you just come in?"

"You."

"Me what, baby?"

"*Kee-sheen. Kee-sheen.*"

I know the word. Ghost. And they are very much alive and well in Korea. Few women in the countryside have not seen the Egg Ghost, who makes his rounds of the outhouses in the small farming communities on frosty evenings. Eyeless, noseless, mouthless, he puts in his grand appearance just as the woman has pulled down her drawers and commenced her subterranean rumblings. Often a wife will drag her husband outside wih her to the crapper to stand behind the door and talk to her while she performs. But the Egg Ghost is something of a comical figure. The others are not.

"Inja, come to bed."

"*You. Kee-sheen.*"

"Inja, what are you talking about?"

"You eyes."

And then I know, I understand. Since childhood, I sometimes fall asleep with my eyes open. And so I don't try to stop her when she stuffs a few clean underthings into her handbag and goes to spend the night with one of her whore friends in a room above the Lion's Den.

We can't prevent our name from haunting us. When we took it on, we didn't bargain on *actual* dead people wanting in. We should have known better: everybody dies, poets right there with the rest. Jeffrey Miller, Ted Berrigan, Richard Brautigan. There will be others. We will resist creeping obituarism as much as we can. But you can't, it seems, write an epitaph for the culture without your own dead butting in. You can't use a word without all its meanings being present, no matter how specifically you intend it. It's those unintended senses, standing ghost-upright shoulder to shoulder around a little bit of intention, that would spook us if we didn't know better. What we know is that we must name what kills us, at the risk of incurring its displeasure. Of course, we aren't stupid. Like Coyote, we are offering it a literary corpse en lieu of a literal one. *It* only needs *something* to show for its work with the scythe. Otherwise, please note the lively forays we are beginning to make into the soup: boogie, comix, politics. A whole hermeneutics of the formerly elsewhere. We intend to work our severe way directly into the chromatic. We will march toward color and the newsstand like a fact through the stats. The tone of the times is ideological· Jews are back in the news. We, who have only to open our mouths for ideas to pour out, can yet throw a monkey wrench into the works. We're calling on all monkeys to take out the wrenches.

CHER CADAVRE EXQUIS

RECOIL IN TIME

Glad to see the Poundians exposed as the anti-Semitic turds we all know they privately were. Never saw an audience (except a few like yours) that didn't worship Pound and his thought. That our daddies fought the War as if it was a crusade, freed Pound from himself, then ultimately stood

mute before his poetic martyrdom is all the more disturbing. Don't ignore Pound and the rest — study them. Learn what not to replace their moral manure with when you are ready to unplug the cesspool they've left modern poetics in. Then we may more quickly identify their imitative offspring and recoil in time when that breed tries to tell us *Arbeit macht frei*.

— Steven G. Prusky

POUND AND NERUDA GONGORIZED

Mr. Pound is an Ezra Corpse more awful to see than the Pablo Corpse of Mr. Neruda. Mr. Neruda *is not* an English penny. But Mr. Pound is quite a half a crow. Dust of a Second Empire Library: Mr. Pound. Spaniard-tourist-dust around Machupicchu: Mr. Neruda. Mr. Pound was born in the United States (I suppose) from the heart of his mother, Mr. T. S. Eliot, from the belly of his father, Santa Claus. That's why he writes so frequently the Greek-Latin-Arabian-Sumerian-*and*-Accadian languages. Mr. Neruda is born in Chile. That's why his poems are written on the most unmingled Gongora's mass. (Gongora: see Madrid, Spain). Mr. Pound is a well-known nazi. His poetry too. Mr. Neruda is a well-known marxist. His widow too. Here in Europe everyone loves Mr. Pound. Chiefly at the Universities of Rome, Sicilia, Auswik, Dachau, Hydrosul-fate, and Oradour-sur-Glaine. Mr. Neruda's work is more cherished around Gdansk, Budapest, Praha Casm, and Siberia.

— Mario Cesariny

OUT OF THE WOODWORK

Concerning R. Kamenetz's *Jew-Hating in American Poetry*, a clue to such is found in th' definate impression on th' part of th' non-racial white that th' jew is involved with or associated with sacrafice, human sacrafice, and that jewish religon (which rather rules jewish life) contains somesort of accomodation for such — & the presence of Christianity of course reinforces this impression.

Poets are th' genuine sensitives of any culture & th' American poets you named, especially Mr. Pound, found some good justification of this impression in th' Holocaust & its use via Zionist propaganda as a lever on world sympathy in gaining a political purchase on Palestine in jewish occupation of that land again. Not very many people outside th' religious community are longer willing to swallow th' "God gave it to the Jews, etc" line any more. In fact, th' Bible itself cannot avoid stating th' obvious that th' Jews of that time simply put th' inhabitants of that land to death & took it &, according to the Bible, they didn't do it with much civilization.

Since the jews have so thoroughly saturated themselves in their own story they have no means of knowing that other, non-jewish peoples, read quite another meaning in what they say of themselves, & that these meanings, these other meanings, show up in th' work of those who's job it is to read life, th' poets.

— Kirby Doyle

ETHNOCENTRIC CHUTZPAH

I was surprised that Rodger Kamenetz took the time to "supply his own ending" to my *Sulfur* essay on Pound, anti-Semitism & other matters — after all it's hardly *Edwin Drood.* But I was sorry to see him waving neo-conservative banners over some dubious assumptions.

Pound & Co., according to Kamenetz, "studiously ignored the Jewish tradition" because of their "hatred of a moral content in poetry." Modernism represented a "plunging into the whirlwind of phenomena," resulting in "fragmentation, disintegration" and an absence of "moral commitment." The answer for young Jewish poets — Kamenetz has no advice for the goyim! — is to stop "wading through Pound's fragments" and "return to a Jewish tradition in poetry, one far more distinguished and profound" than anything Pound uncovered from "crumbling civilizations."

This seems to me a bundle of false dichotomies. First, it is simply untrue that Pound was an amoral poet: whether or not we like what he stood for, he devoted his life to changing the world. The *Cantos* are, among other things, full of psalms and jeremiads. Second, looking at the modernists as a whole (or any other group of poets defined by time and place — say, the Elizabethans) one can only say that some of the writers displayed greater moral commitment in their poetry than others. To equate modernism in general (particularly after World War I) with a "hatred of moral content" is absurd: every modernist work was, above all, an act of criticism. Third, the traditions Pound studied and promoted were the entirety of European poetry (from Greece & Rome through the Medieval & Renaissance to the present) and much of Chinese (and some Japanese) poetry. To claim that these are less "distinguished and profound" than the Jewish poetic tradition is plain ethnocentric chutzpah.

Moreover, Kamenetz never clarifies what this Jewish tradition is. (He cites only the Bible.) Does it include all poetry written in Hebrew, or Hebrew and Yiddish, or all poetry in any language written by Jewish poets? How would he classify the Jewish American poets of the century — Oppen, Stein, Reznikoff, Loy, Riding, Zukofsky, Ginsberg, Levertov, Rakosi, Tarn, Corman, Rothenberg, Antin, MacLow, among others? Some of them are clearly, "committed," others not: are they modernists or Jews?

Kamenetz, much like Pound, is defining by exclusion. The scandal of modernism is that it was constructed out of a contempt for mass man and various ethnically, sexually, and socially delineated segments of the masses, with the resulting insularity and self-delusion of "vanguards" and "movements." If the poets today are, as Kamenetz says, amoral, arrogant, trivial, it is because they were born in the impregnable fortress raised by modernism. The answer is not to move to another castle (like Kamenetz's "Jewish tradition") but to tear down the walls. Poets reading Pound *and* the Song of Songs, talking to other poets *and* to everyone else.

What is curious is that there may well be a fundamental contradiction between modernism and Judaism (that is, the Judaism of the Mosaic laws, not the various heterodoxies). In the Judaism of the Mosaic laws the human yearning for wholeness manifests itself not in the universal admission of everything in the world (as in Hinduism) but in a loathing for that which is incomplete, mixed, other. A few examples among the hundreds:

Mixed: One cannot plant two kinds of crops in the same field, plow with an ox and an ass yoked together, breed cattle with a different kind, wear clothing made from two kinds of fabric, marry an outsider, eat meat and milk together.

Incomplete: A man missing any limbs or organs

cannot be buried in sanctified ground. An animal with a "blemish" (maimed, disfigured) cannot be sacrificed. (In other societies the disfigured animal is particularly sacred.) A man with a blemish cannot be a priest. Any loss is a blemish, therefore semen, menstrual blood and death (loss of breath) are unclean — a priest cannot go near a corpse.

Other: A norm is postulated, and any variance from the norm is taboo. Men are the norm: women must be segregated. Living creatures must move — animals must walk on four legs, birds must fly, sea creatures must swim with fins. Any animals that do not are unclean, such as insects (six legs), shellfish (no fins), snakes (no legs), etc. Further, the norm for animals is the ruminant with a cloven hoof (sheep and cattle): the others therefore are unclean.

These three qualities practically define modernism: its primary procedure, collage (mixed); its insistence on process over product (incomplete); its unending clarion calls to admit into poetry everything which had previously been excluded (other). In that, it was similar to early Christianity, whose disciples exorted the people to literally "eat everything," and whose object of veneration was the ultimate hybrid: a man-god, child of the most blasphemous mixed union imaginable.

Furthermore, Judaism (like Islam later on) codifies intolerance. The story of the Exodus — particularly when read in a modern translation, to avoid the seduction of the King James prose — reads today like a Stalinist manual on the suppression of dissent. (Throughout the story the Jews are complaining: they want to go back to Egypt. When Moses comes down from the mountain and discovers the people worshipping the golden calf, his response is to strengthen the priesthood and initiate a purge; three thousand are killed. It takes them 40 years to cross 200 miles of desert not because the Jews have such a lousy sense of direction, but rather because Moses deliberately keeps them there until all those who remember Egypt are dead and a new indoctrinated generation has taken over. Only then can they enter the promised land.)

Christianity, like modernism, postulated its own elite (those who would inherit the kingdom of heaven) and substituted its own intolerances. Its xenophobia was directed not at the other, but at the unconverted other. (In that, Pound was quite Christian.)

Tsvetayeva's famous remark that "All poets are Jews" — one must assume she is speaking of 20th century poets — has a flip side. On the one hand, the poet as a member of a marginal and sometimes persecuted group; on the other, the group's belief that they are the chosen ones. (And more, the constant battle within poetry of rival groups and movements, each claiming that they are the true heirs to the "tradition," that their work forms part of — what better word? — the canon.)

Contrary to Kamenetz, I think there are many "endings," one of which is not a return, but an informed dismantling of the Judaeo-Christian tradition, the final enormous obstacle to a true plurality. There's really no difference between Kamenetz and Pound: as Christian and Jew, both are obsessed with elites; and as a Jew, Kamenetz is obsessed with wholeness (his adjectives of disdain are "fragmentary," "crumbling"). The new poetry begins when we're willing to eat everything, and attach no significance to the fact.

— Eliot Weinberger

SORRY, SUKKAH

Pound was an anti-Semite ignorant of Jewish literature. I am not so concerned about his passing on the anti-Semitism, as the ignorance. When Eliot Weinberger speaks of Pound's mastering "the entirety" of "European literature from Greek and Rome to medieval to the present [sic]," I wonder if the "entirety" includes the Bible. It didn't for Pound.

A prominent feature of the Jewish tradition is a great care in reading text. Pound's slapdash assimilation of Japanese or Chinese literature is not my idea of respect for another culture — it's just flummery. Weinberger's cartoon of the Bible follows in that "tradition" as well. (A glance at Exodus 32:9, for instance, shows Weinberger has completely distorted Moses' motivations.) He even finds a new oppressed group, the poor mumbling Israelites who want to be slaves. Pound's unpleasant fascism is negated by radical chic, but his dismissive attitude towards Biblical writing is maintained.

But what is the politics of the Golden Calf? For Eliot Weinberger it means to eat everything and ignore differences. But in Jewish symbology, it means a return to slavery, of both mind and body.

I hope Weinberger's discussion of Judaism and

modernism was not an example of "informed dismantling." He can't decide himself if they are like or unlike in their exclusivity. The logical problem here is that Judaism is a civilization while modernism is merely a moment; they don't compare readily. But to equate the exclusivities of the Jewish law with anti-Semitism is an old game called blaming the victim. Rabbi Akiba wasn't flayed by the Romans because he wouldn't join them for pork chops. Jewish taboos did not create the ghetto, the mellah, the Crusades, the Inquisition, pogroms, blood libels or gas chambers. After all that, the petty meannesses of Pound and Eliot are pathetic enough, but *because of all that*, I cannot read their work as particularly animated by moral commitment.

"Am I my brother's keeper?" is, after all, a Biblical question. It is not the sort of note one finds readily in Homer. You will find other things there that are quite beautiful, but not that. This doesn't mean the Bible is superior to Homer (as Blake believed) or that one should read one and not the other. It is simply that the Jewish genius in literature is very different from, say, the Greek, and I wouldn't want either excluded. Real pluralism should be based on mutual respect and acknowledgment of differences, not group amnesia.

I do confess to being obsessed with wholeness, and with my own history. I guess I'm still surprised to be here since every three generations back, I find a sojourner. So, I wouldn't advise any poet to retreat to a "Jewish fortress." I would suggest a sukkah, a harvest booth and a nomad's hut. By custom, the sukkah must be flimsy and made of natural materials. Eliot Weinberger will be pleased to know that one of its walls may be omitted. The Torah says it should be open to the wind and stars, to invisible spirits, and to guests from every nation of the earth.

— Rodger Kamenetz

John Rosa

RAFAEL LORENZO: FOUR WORKS

REALISM

You're only interested in self-portraits, for example. The baby is crying. It's been crying for *days*, now — no: for *years*. It's trapped somewhere down the side of a long desolate slope, lodged next to a rock. Actually, the rock is no rock at all, but a rather strange kind of mammal. Degree, by imperceptibly tiny degree, the mammal is inching its way up the slope, all the while emitting a loud signal: TAKE ME AWAY! TAKE ME AWAY! This creature defies all known laws of nature or science. Yes, yes, your every guess sees into the objective here. Certain objects, placed in an incomprehensible atmosphere, begin to seize on to the Second Thought that comes behind a First; and — indeed — the first scene actually begins to make sense only when the eye takes a stand elsewhere and repeats all its moods in categorical order. So: these "facts" that description has such a powerfully hermetic quality to emit, amaze and fascinate you; and it's this *quality*, then, that really *satisfies* you. It seems to be telling you the what, where, when, how and why of whatever you're to do with yourself. However, in order to proceed with the final demonstration of your real lyricism, other people — alas — *are* needed. You may have for no reason to stop someone in the street and ask them to lean up against the side of a truck until the police arrive.

Faye Kicknosway

PASSABLE SPEECH

You think it's a human being talking, voice to voice. Once you've got a familiar phrase from scratch — keep alert —, it promises considered talks between dockworkers. You may think it said the very heart of the right theory; but there are some things you get worried. The word you wind up with in New York killed a man tonight. A phrase resonates in his bathrobe. The bomb mainly his generosity accounted for. It's beginning when you speak them, trying to get his morning paper.

APE ANYTHING

They arrived back among the natives. Earth, Air, Fire and Water began the brutal recasting of inscriptions from their past successes. A very essential germane gravity insisted that the Earth was round, the Air was thick, the Fire inert, and the Water obedient. The force in that accomplished inwardness of machines, money, men, methods, and standards — that they alone had —, compiled the seeds of a new history of weeping. Incessant humiliations, etched with chalk on granite, cleared the way for the right script. And every white man civilized that final spurt of writing.

VOICE

No, it is not a question of *speaking* at all.

This VOICE has nothing in common with the preposterous Burnham Wood of contemporary literary individualism. These colonizers and murderers of, the Spirit, who, in their positive commitment to oppression, "point out the window" *without* watching their finger change, mistake a whole legion of coercive rhetorical devices (that reminds them of their own wishful thinking of a Self moving implacably towards them) for the positive inscription of their concrete future in the delineations of a human nature. These *characters*, though they may — unbeknownst to themselves — be the collective Hero of a great collective play on words, have only been drawn out into their time with enough definition to serve another, wholly different, intention. An intention which, in fact, has already, many years since, been played out. That the concept of the individual was once the living realization of the animal's vegetal tendencies as a mind blooming into the presence of the Laws of the material Sovereignty of Thought, does not alter the fact that this human Tree has been felled at the top of the beginning of its achievements. It is now merely a dismembered corpse constantly being reassembled into a Self — that monstrosity of contemporary ideological body politics — we find all our "poets" and "novelists" and "journalists" *clinging* to. Out of this morbid, though generatively *corrupt*, self, these "writers" proliferate — as the runaway characters of an unevolved expression of thought's own historical monster, *Literature*.

In one way, enough has been said; in another, nothing yet.

It all remains to be taken up and continued from a point left behind perhaps hundreds of years ago, plus a few small inches beyond that point in the rare moments it has been heard since and then fallen silent. A genuine presence, VOICE *emerged* from the landscape itself — in a way, *with* the landscape itself —, vertically foresting ground and horizon in the reflection of the weight behind, and the look out from, the Sovereignty of Thought, Wonder in itself. At the far end of this forestation, was the eccentric silhouette of language; and in the foreground, a texture, taste, and ambiance of all the senses: a *site* (cite) of utterance. An interplay of Sky and Earth fingerprinting the Air;

VOICE, through its unique contiguity with the Wind, and the solidity of its *rooted* position, drew and scratched out the raised surface of its complicated, particular white noise. WE heard the rustle of the living Tree of Crime extend into its vast sentence the written matter, thought, Being, of Time.

Alice Codrescu

JABBER CONDENSATION
by W. R. Borneman

The Collected Poems of Robert Creeley: 1945-1975 (University of California)

This book has blurbs by William Carlos Williams, Charles Olson, Edward Dorn, Allen Ginsberg, Denise Levertov, Robert Duncan, Michael McClure, & John Ashbery. Need I say more? Well, let me take just 2 words from each of the plugs (steal a quick hit from each puff) in the order that they appear on the back of the book cover. Perhaps we can condense this jacket jabber into a pithy gist not unworthy of Creeley's work.

The subtlest
  . . . pure English —
  . . . immediate speech
  . . . exploring our
  . . . need for
  . . . words in
  . . . the ear
  . . . the air

THE COMPANY

by Robert Creeley

For the Signet Society, April 11, 1985

Backward — as if retentive.
"The child is father to the man"
or some such echo of device,
a parallel of use and circumstance.

Scale become implication.
Place, postcard determinant —
only because someone sent it.
Relations — best if convenient.

Out of all this emptiness
something must come. . . . Concomitant
with the insistent banality, small, still
face in mirror looks simply vacant.

Hence blather, disjunct, incessant
indecision, moving along on
road to next town where what waited
was great expectations again, empty plate.

So there they were, expectally ambivalent,
given the Second World War
"to one who has been long in city pent,"
trying to make sense of it.

We — *morituri* — blasted from classic,
humanistic *noblesse oblige*, all the garbage
of either so-called side, hung on
to what we thought we had, an existential

raison d'être like a pea
some faded princess tries to sleep on,
and when that was expectably soon gone,
we left. We walked away.

"Recorders ages hence" will look for us
not only in books, one hopes, nor only under
  rocks
but in some common places of feeling,
small enough — but isn't the human

just that echoing, resonant edge
of what it knows it knows,
takes heart in remembering
only the good times, yet

can't forget whatever it was,
comes here again, fearing this
is the last day, this is
the last, the last, the last.

TWO BY TED BERRIGAN

PARIS, FRANCES

for Frances Waldman, 1909-1982

I tried to put the coffee back together
for I knew I would not be able to raise the fine
Lady who sits wrapped in her amber shawl
Mrs. of everything that's mine just now, an interior
Noon smokes in its streets, as useless as
Mein hosts's London Fog, and black umbrella, &
  these pills
Is it Easter? Did we go? All around the purple
  heather?
Go fly! my dears. Go fly! I'm in the weather.

PANDORA'S BOX, AN ODE

. . . was 30 when we met. I was
21. & yet he gave me the impression
he was vitally interested in what I
was doing & what was inside me! One
was Tremendous power over all friends.
power to make them do whatever. Wed. Bed.
Dig the streets. Two is speeding and pills
to beef up on on top of speedin hills. Three,
assumptions: Four, flattery. Five, highly
articulate streets, & when he saw me I was witty.
I was good poetry. Love was all I was.
The case is, he had or was a charm of
his own. I had the unmistakable signature
of a mean spirit. Very close to breaking in.
I was like Allen Ginsberg's face, Jack's face
eye to eye on me. Face of Allen. Face of Kerouac.
It was all in California. Now,
all of my kingdoms are here.

John Giorno founded Giorno Poetry Systems in 1965. A non-profit foundation producing poets working with the sound of their voices and the wisdom content of their words, who risk technology and music, and a deep connection with the audience. He innovated Dial-A-Poem, and produced 18 LP albums, videopaks, radio, television, performance, events, prints and books.

IT'S A MISTAKE TO THINK YOU'RE SPECIAL

by John Giorno

You sit
there
thinking about
the things
you said
over and
over again,
and I just want
to sit here
and think,
cause it's
powerful.

I love
being where
people like
being with
each other,
and then I want to take
the night off,
something soft
and protective,
I want to stay
asleep
for as long
as I can
I want to stay
asleep for
as long as I can
I want to stay asleep
for as long as I can,
you have to be ruthless
and accepting
with nightmares.

They convinced me
I was wrong,

and I believed them
they convinced me I was wrong,
and I believed them,
and you will never
be able to
forgive them.
Unbuilding
a building
stone
by stone
unbuilding a building
stone by stone
unbuilding a building stone
by stone,
everyone I know
is just like me,
they're stupid.

Tell me what
I should do,
but please
tell it to me
while I'm sleeping
so I'll remember,
the walls inside
my house are made
of human skulls
fitted together
like bricks,
and the floor
I'm standing on
is soaked with
with blood
and bile,
OK, where are
the warrior
priests,
we need
retribution
warrior priests
we need retribution,
offering,

death
for a reason
to make something
happen,
straight,
or with alcohol,
drugs and
sexual
energy,
there is leverage
in wealth,

feeding
the hole
feeding the hole
feeding the hole
feeding the hole
feeding the hole
feeding the hole,
spit in it,
spit here.

Butterflies
sucking
on the carcass
of a dead bird,
and your body
is being pulled down
backwards
into the world
below,
as a king.

I feel most
at home
among the defiled
I feel most at
home among
the defiled
I feel most at home among
the defiled,
in the center
of a flower
under a deep
blue
sky,
it's a mistake
to think
you're special.

Tahar Ben Jelloun. Born 1944 at Fez, Morocco; studied philosophy, Doctor of Social Psychiatry. Has published four collections of poetry: *Hommes sous linceul de silence*, 1971; *Cicatrices du soleil*, 1972; *Le Discours du Chameau*, 1974; *Les amandiers sont morts de leurs blessures*, 1976; *A l'insu du souvenir*, 1980, and five novels. He lives between Paris and Tangier, Morocco.

LA FEMME ASSISE

by *Tahar Ben Jelloun*
translated by Georgina Caspar

She sits on a bench of stones
at the edge of the road
on a big leaf
between her fingers prayer beads
in a wicker basket
a flat cake and some dates
on her chin
a blind fish
tattooed on her forehead
wrinkles and a century
a donkey loaded with hay and objects
crossed the shadow
a man slits a cock's throat
the dairyman has not passed today
they took his son
in the middle of the night

The woman sits
immovable
she looks at the sky
and waits
immortal.

Alice Codrescu

ONTOLOGICAL ANARCHISM
BROADSHEET #10

by Hakim Bey

PORNOGRAPHY

In Persia I saw that poetry is meant to be set to music & chanted or sung — for one reason alone — because it *works.*

A right combination of image & tune plunges the audience into a *hal* (something between emotion/ aesthetic mood & trance of hyperawareness), outbursts of weeping, fits of dancing — measurable physical response to art. For us the link between poetry & body died with the bardic era — we read under the influence of a cartesian anaesthetic gas.

In N. India even non-musical recitation provokes noise & motion, each good couplet applauded, "Wa! Wa!", with elegant hand-jive, tossing of rupees — whereas we listen to poetry like some science-fiction brain in a jar — at best a wry chuckle or grimace, vestige of simian rictus, the rest of the body off on some other planet.

In the East poets are sometimes thrown in prison — a sort of compliment, since it suggests the author has done something at least as real as theft or rape. Here poets are allowed to publish anything — a sort of punishment in effect, prison without walls, without echoes, without palpable existence — shadow — realm of print, or abstract thought — world without risk or *eros.*

So poetry is dead again — & even if the mumia from its corpse retains some healing properties, auto-resurrection isn't one of them.

If rulers refuse to consider poems as crimes, then someone must commit crimes that serve the function of poetry, or texts that possess the resonance of terrorism. At any cost reconnect poetry to the body. Not crimes against bodies, but against Ideas (& Ideas-in-things) which are deadly & suffocating. Not stupid libertinage but exemplary crimes, aesthetic crimes, crimes for love.

In England some pornographic books are still banned. Pornography has a measurable physical effect on its readers. Like propaganda it sometimes changes lives because it uncovers true desires.

Our culture produces most of its porn out of body-hatred — but erotic art in itself makes a better vehicle for enhancement of being/consciousness/ bliss — as in certain oriental works. A sort of Western tantric porn might help galvanise the corpse, make it shine with some of the glamor of crime.

America has freedom of speech because all words are considered equally vapid. Only *images* count — the censors love snaps of death & mutilation but recoil in horror at the sight of a child masturbating — apparently they experience this as an invasion of their existential validity, their identification with the Empire & its subtlest gestures.

No doubt even the most poetic porn would never revive the faceless corpse to dance & sing (like the Chinese Chaos-bird) — but imagine a script for a three-minute film set on a mythical isle of runaway children who inhabit ruins of old castles or build totem-huts & junk-assemblage nests — mixture of animation, special-effects, compugraphix & color tape — edited tight as a fastfood commercial

but weird & naked, feathers & bones, tents sewn with crystal, black dogs, pigeon-blood — flashes of amber limbs tangled in sheets — faces in starry masks kissing soft creases of skin — androgynous pirates, castaway faces of columbines sleeping on thigh-white flowers — nasty hilarious piss jokes, pet lizards lapping spilt milk — nude break-dancing — victorian bathtub with rubber ducks & pink boners — Alice on ganga

atonal punk reggae scored for gamelan, synthesiser, saxophones & drums — electric boogey lyrics sung by aetherial childrens' choir — ontological anarchist lyrics, cross between Hafes & Pancho Villa, Li Po & Bakunin, Kabir & Tzara — call it "CHAOS — the Rock Video!"

No...probably just a dream. Too expensive, & besides, who would see it? Not the kids it was meant for. Pirate TV's a futile fantasy, rock merely another commodity — forget the slick gesamtkunstwerk — leaflet a playground with inflammatory smutty feuilletons — pornopropaganda, crackpot samizdat to unchain Desire from its bondage.

POEMS BY BERNADETTE MAYER

A CHINESE BREAKFAST

Is it so far to the door?
Does Max's sandwich diminish my confidence to reach it?
Do fears as unnatural as dreams to waking
Reflect something of anything for everyone else?
Should madness ensue, would the tiny hole
For a dislodged nail in the wall be its focus?
Does the belong world in you?
Did the finch devour the bluejay
Right in the cleft of the dead bird of paradise?
Did a she slip the awful cup?
As spring comes a man's apple juice emits an ankle bracelet
And you're as forlorn as the mean dentist's smock of our culture
Plus a he can't find a parking space cause the ice is still thick
As the thief of the way a day might memory look

DISJECTA MEMBRA

And young he (there's always been this dare) sleeps waking
Partly sideways, mollescent yet macho (only joking)
Always retreating back to what the lawned home
Or something irreligious might be, who knows what's known?
Many other absent things done in times like ours of these
Unfulfill love's presence like it was one of those
Displayed wedding cakes on 14th street with a bed of pink
Beside the hockey players, if you begin young to think
Life is that you're better off later when you get
A sort of basketballish hope from your fancier genes yet
I've seen how the light looks in each circumstance
And gone out to get oranges, Tide and water all at once

It might be right to write of just the hour
That's a structure good as love's or any measure

SONNET

Love is a babe as you know and when you
Put your startling hand on my hand or arm or head
Or better both your hands to hold in them my own
I'm awed and we laugh with questions, artless
Of me to speak so ungenerally of thee and thy name
I have no situation and love is the same, you live at home
Come be here my baby and I'll take you elsewhere where
You ain't already been, my richer friend, and there
At the bottom of my sale or theft of myself will you
Bring specific flowers I will not know the names of to me
As you already have and already will and already do
And so already are you with your succinctest self
Torn and sore like a female masochist that the rhyme
Of the jewel you pay attention to becomes your baby born

AT NIGHT THE STATES

by Alice Notley

At night the states
I forget them or wish I was there
    in that one under the
Stars. It smells like June in this night
    so sweet like air.
I may have decided that the
    States are not that tired
Or I have thought so. I have
    thought that.

At night the states
And the world not that tired
    of everyone
Maybe. Honey, I think that to
    say is in
light. Or whoever. We will
    never
replace you. We will never re-
    place You. But
in like a dream the floor is no
    longer discursive
To me it doesn't please me by
    being the vistas out my
window, do you know what
    Of course (not) I mean?
I have no sweet dreams of wake-
    fulness. In
wakefulness. And so to begin.
    (my love.)

At night the states
talk. My initial continuing contra-
    diction
my love for you & that for me
deep down in the Purple Plant the oldest
    dust
of it is sweetest but sates no longer
    how I
would feel. Shirt
that shirt has been in your arms
    And I have
that shirt is how I feel

At night the states
will you continue in this as-
    sociation of

matters, my Dearest? down
    the street from
where the public plaque reminds
    that of private
loving the consequential chain
    trail is
matters

At night the states
that it doesn't matter that I don't
    say them, remember
them at the end of this claustro-
    phobic the
dance, I wish I could see I wish
    I could
dance her. At this night the states
    say them
out there. That I am, am them
    indefinitely so and
so wishful passive historic fated
    and matter-
simple, matter-simple, an
    eyeful. I wish
but I don't and little melody.
    Sorry that these
little things don't happen any
    more. The states
have drained their magicks
    for I have not
seen them. Best not to tell. But
    you
you would always remain, I
    trust, as I will
always be alone.

At night the states
whistle. Anyone can live. I
can. I am not doing any-
    thing doing this. I
discover I love as I figure. Wed-
    nesday
I wanted to say something in
    particular. I have been
where. I have seen it. The God
    can. The people
do some more.

At night the states
I let go of, have let, don't
    let
Some, and some, in Florida, doing.
    What takes so
long? I am still with you in that
    part of the
park, and vice will continue, but
    I'll have
a cleaning Maine. Who loses
    these names
loses. I can't bring it up yet,
    keeping my
opinions to herself. Everybody in
    any room is a
smuggler. I walked fiery and
    talked in the
stars of the automatic weapons
    and partly for you
Which you. You know.

At night the states
have told it all already. Have
    told it. I
know it. But more that they
    don't know, I
know it too.

At night the states
whom I do stand before in
    judgement, I
think that they will find
    me fair, not
that they care in fact nor do
    I, right now
though indeed I am they and
    we say
that not that I've
    erred nor
lost my way though perhaps
    they did (did
they) and now he is dead
    but you
you are not. Yet I am this
    one, lost
again? lost & found by one-
    self
Who are you to dare sing to me?

At night the states

accompany me while I sit here
    or drums
there are always drums what for
    so I
won't lose my way the name of
    a
personality, say, not California
    I am not
sad for you though I could be
    I remember
climbing up a hill under tall
    trees
getting home. I guess we
    got home. I was
going to say that the air was
    fair (I was
always saying something *like*
    that) but
that's not it now, and that
    that's not it
isn't it either

At night the states
dare sing to me they who seem
    tawdry
any more I've not thought I
    loved them, only
you it's you whom I love
the states are not good to me as
    I am to them
though perhaps I am not
when I think of your being
    so beautiful
but is that your beauty
    or could it be
theirs I'm having such a
    hard time remembering
any of their names
your being beautiful belongs
    to nothing
I don't believe they should
    praise you
but I seem to believe they
    should
somehow let you go

At night the states
and when you go down to
    Washington
witness how perfectly anything

in particular
sheets of thoughts what a waste
    of sheets at
night. I remember something
    about an
up-to-date theory of time. I
    have my
own white rose for I have
    done
something well but I'm not
    clear
what it is. Weathered, perhaps
    but that's
never done. What's done is
    perfection.

At night the states
ride the train to Baltimore
we will try to acknowledge what was
but that's not the real mirror
    is it? nor
is it empty, or only my eyes
    are
Ride the car home from Washington
    no
they are not. Ride the subway
    home from
Pennsylvania Station. The states
    are blind eyes
stony smooth shut in moon-
    light. My
French is the shape of this
    book
that means I.

At night the states
the 14 pieces. I couldn't just
walk on by. Why
aren't they beautiful enough
in a way that does not
    beg to wring
something from a dry (wet)
    something
Call my name

At night the states
making life, not explaining anything
but all the popular songs say call
    my name
oh call my name, and if I call

it out myself to
you, call mine out instead as our
    poets do
will you still walk on by? I
    have
loved you for so long. You
    died
and on the wind they sang
    your name to me
but you said nothing. Yet you
    said once before
and there it is, there, but it is
    so still.
Oh being alone I call out my
    name
and once you did and do still in
    a way
you do call out your name
to these states whose way is to walk
on by that's why I write too much

At night the states
whoever you love that's who you
    love
the difference between chaos and
    star I believe and
in that difference they believed
    in some
funny way but that wasn't
    what I
I believed that out of this
    fatigue would be
born a light, what is fatigue
there is a man whose face
    changes continually
but I will never, something
    I will
never with regard to it or
    never regard
I will regard yours tomorrow
I will wear purple will I
and call my name

At night the states
you who are alive, you who are dead
when I love you alone all night and
    that is what I do
until I could never write from your
    being enough
I don't want that trick of making

it be coaxed from
the words not tonight I want it
    coaxed from
myself but being not that. But I'd
    feel more
comfortable about it being words
    if it

were if that's what it were for these
    are the
States where what words are true
    are words
Not myself. Montana. Illinois.
    Escondido.

6/28/85

Alice Codrescu

PARIS

by Jean-Jacques Passera

Just in front of my home, Christo, the exterior decorator, put a skirt around the Pont Neuf. I always said that Paris is a woman, I mean, female. In fact, the sex of Paris is just there, behind the waist of Pont Neuf: Place Dauphine. You may know this lovely triangle shaped place, covered with *acceuillants* nice trees. By the way, you might be interested knowing that a few years ago, some people from the "National Historical Monuments," X-rayed the huge statue of our beloved and juicy King Henry IV, (he was the one who said, *"Chaque Dimanche, une poule ou pot pour chacun"*; at that time there wasn't fast food and Love Burger;

Frenchmen were eating lentil soup if lucky). The purpose of this expensive manipulation was to check on eventual cracks in the statue; the surprise was BIG. Inside this statue is another statue, smaller and which represents Napoleon. I can hear you from here: "How is it possible that a statue of King Henry IV is pregnant with a statue of Emperor Napoleon who was himself not yet conceived in History?!" I have the answer: the original statue of Henry was melted during the French Revolution, probably to make cannons; and it's only in 1818 that a replica was cast with the bronze from a Napoleon statue. The foundeur, a fervent Bonapartiste, enclosed a small statue of his hero in the big one.

You have to admit that I am lucky. I live so close to the sex of Paris that it's a perpetual incest; I am sunk in it. Note that I have five mindpeaceful days a month, due to nature.

A NEW YORKER'S BERLIN
by Richard Kostelanetz

I love Berlin. I love Berlin like I love New York, which it resembles in many ways. Indeed, I love Berlin so much that whenever I'm there I don't like to leave it, and in fact scarcely did, except to go home, of course. Whereas many of my colleagues on the DAAD Berliner Kunstlerprogram were flying here and there around Europe, while my German friends were always going off to Italy — this habit being, incidentally, the most visible sign of the continuing influence of Johann Wolfgang von Goethe — I did most of my traveling to East Berlin, which is comparable to visiting Brooklyn from New York or Cambridge from Boston. You perceive it as a radically different world, but it is close enough to allow you to get back home at night. What distinguishes East Berlin from Brooklyn or Cambridge is that in East Berlin the *volkspolizei* have parietal rules reminiscent of those we had in my residential American college twenty-five years ago. Like the housemothers who then supervised the girls' dormitories, these *vopos* want your butt out of their place by midnight. This nightly housecleaning has advantages as well as obvious disadvantages. Let's say you meet an attractive woman in East Berlin and she takes you home. Or an attractive man and he takes you home. And you are enjoying each other, but you really don't want to spend the night with her or him. You can be sure, that she or he won't object when at 11 o'clock you leap up and say, "gotta get home." You can't always do this in Brooklyn or Cambridge.

Why do I like Berlin? First of all, I am a city boy, and Berlin is a real city, as Boston is a real city, while Providence and San Diego, say, are not. Better yet, Berlin is a civilized city, first of all in the abundance of stylish architecture, and then in its pervasive greenery: trees on nearly every street, the little gardens in the fronts and backs of houses, those numerous little parks that dot the city, in addition to the expansive fields and woods of the Tiergarten and the Grunewald. In the past three decades West Berlin was rebuilt to satisfy two illusions — *that there has been no war and that there is no wall*; and the city's ability to make you forget those two truths is one clear measure of its current civility. Another measure is its creature comforts, which include not only streets that are largely safe at night, bars that stay open past midnight and sidewalks wide enough to accommodate both cafés and crowds but lakes right *in* town that are suitable for swimming — on the first and last of these counts Berlin decisively blows out New York or Boston. Where else can one spend a warm June day at the area's best beach and still go to the country's best opera, the best theater and the best orchestra at night? Where else can you spend a hot August day swimming in fresh water and then choose among a hundred movies at night? Who needs to go to the country when so much of the country is already in the city?

Berlin, like New York, has always been promised land, a magnet for adventurers seeking experiences unavailable at home, a metropolis of opportunity for industrious people from somewhere else, whether Eastern Europe or the Eastern Mediterranean; and even in hard times, like now, this promise of possibility is a spiritual quality you can feel. So it distresses me double to hear some Berliners speak of wanting not just to restrict the immigration of Turks but to send them home. Such talk reminds me of the fact that Spain in 1492 brought its subsequent decline upon itself by expelling both the Jews and the Moors, leaving nobody to pay the Spanish taxes, because the Spanish nobles didn't pay taxes, and no laborers to do the dirty work. Berliners should know better than to usher their own demise. (If the Jews are gone, and the Turks go, who will be next?) Berlin was a promised land for me as well, for reasons I'll mention later. My own principal difficulty in living in there, aside from the language problem that I'll also discuss later, reflects my New Yorkness: I was always getting lost, or arriving late at strange addresses, because I could never master the problem of getting efficiently around a city whose streets are not numbered!

Berlin has the stark contrasts typical of great cities. In New York one is struck by the discrepancy between rich and poor, especially where the offices and housing of the very rich are in close proximity to the very poor. In Jerusalem, the stark contrast is not between Arab and Jew — a difference more evident in the Galilee — but between the religious and the secular. In Berlin the most striking gap is between West and East. Berlin remains the only place in the world where you can not only peek into the Other World with your own eyes — just go to any tall building near the famous Wall — you can actually go visit it at any time with your own feet, without the forbidding nuisance of needing to obtain a travel visa. In Berlin you can take a subway under the Iron Curtain and come out on the other side, right at Freddy's Street, as I call it — *Friedrichstrasse*, they say — in the heart of East Berlin, which doesn't look like a Western city, because it isn't a Western city. Where West Berlin is colorful, with neon signs and people in all sorts of contemporary haircuts and colorful dress, East Berlin's drab anonymity reminds the Western visitor of another world decades past. For an especially vivid sense of the difference, just go on a summer Friday night, as I did, from the main streets of East Berlin, which become barren after sundown, to the Kurfurstendamm, the main drag of West Berlin, where the weekend party goes well into the night, and you will observe a contrast as great as that between 86th Street and 125th Street, albeit different. Especially if you have read, as I have, some smart shots explaining how West and East are coming to resemble each other, you will be hit with a contrast that must not only be seen with one's eyes but experienced in the body.

This proximity to the Other World is something that West Berliners take for granted. But the more you think about it, the more extraordinary it is. The contrast between West and East — is, we know, largely the creation of a capitalist conspiracy, whereby the West pays millions upon millions to keep West Berlin looking so good, and then yet millions more — *sub rosa, unter der Mauer,* under the Wall, so to speak — to keep East Berlin looking so grim. (This last secret, which I hesitate to share with you, came from a very authoritative source: It was told to me, in typical Berlin fashion, by a nude mermaid, a woman with nothing to hide, so to speak, swimming next to me in the Wannsee.)

Berlin has something else that is very special, something I take to be the ultimate mark of a civilized city: public transportation so abundant, cheap and comprehensive that you can live there comfortably *without* ever owning an automobile. By that criterion, it is clear, New York is civilized as Los Angeles is not; Boston is civilized as Chicago is

not. Never, but never, will I voluntarily live where a car is necessary, and I know from personal experience that you don't really need one in West Berlin, in part because you cannot go very far. In a city of just over two million people, a million rides are taken each day on the subway alone; buses are even more popular. One sign of the popularity of Berlin's public transportation is the abundance of snackstands, places where you can buy wurst and soda or beer for a little more than a dollar. Simply wherever routes of public transportation intersect in Berlin, you will see a sign reading *Imbiss,* or snack; and though I am scarcely well traveled, I never saw so many snackstands anywhere else. Since beer in these stands is no more expensive than soda pop, no wonder we Americans can call people who patronize them excessively *imbeciles.*

There are two more unobvious things to be said in favor of Berlin. The first is that since no one has country homes, you need not turn down invitations for weekends that are likely to be boring. The second is that Berlin is the only German city where you don't need to know German, just as New York is probably the only American city in which people live quite well without ever really learning English. Berliners, like New Yorkers, are accustomed to the abundant presence of people who scarcely know the official language. Berliners are thus accustomed to speaking slowly, to finding an intermediary who speaks your language, to mime and to do all the other sensitive things that people do to communicate without words. I speak again from personal experience, because, when it comes to learning foreign languages, I am a hopeless American. I spoke English to everyone in Berlin, regardless of whether or not they claimed to understand it. When I telephoned strangers, for instance, my opening words were not the customary cheery German salutation of "Tag, Kostelanetz," but an apprehensive "Speak English?" The only people to criticize my incapacity to my face were Berlin intellectuals who wanted to believe that fluency in other languages is the surest sign of superior intelligence and my apoplectic apartment house superintendent who was endlessly annoyed that I could not be moved by her suggestions, her criticisms and her threats. My incapacity should not be considered a total loss, however, because I discovered methods of communication, as well as pleasures, that would be unavailable to me in New

York. One of my favorite Berliners is my publisher Peter Gente, whose English is just about as good as my German; and we have spent lots of time together, simply enjoying each other's company, while saving our serious conversations for the presence of a translator. Secondly, no single male should forget that in Berlin, if an attractive woman sits next to you on the bus, you can say, "Speak English?" If you try that same line in New York...

What art did I make as a guest of Berlin? Essentially, I tried to do what I do *not* do at home. Fortunately, I was able, soon after I arrived, to work on a radio piece, a *horspiel*, as they say, that exploited a particular quality that Berlin shares with New York. Both are international towns in which many languages are spoken. Wanting for years to do a radio piece about the sound of the language of prayer — an ambitious piece that combined my love for Johann Sebastian Bach with my love of *Finnegans Wake* — I recorded sixty ministers in over two dozen languages and then mixed their spoken words on a twenty-four-track audiotape machine. By this process I made *Invocations*, as it is called — a 62-minute *horspiel* that was first aired on Sender Freies Berlin and later played on radio stations in Canada, Australia, Holland and the U.S., and it appeared here in the experimental music series of Folkways Record as my first solo record.

I discovered my last major Berlin project in an extraordinary place that remarkably few Berliners have seen or visited, let alone know about: The Great Jewish Cemetery in Weissensee, a northeast section of East Berlin. With 115,000 graves, this is, first of all, the largest Jewish cemetery between Warsaw and New York; but aside from its size, it has a cultural coherence that makes it quite unlike any other cemetery, Jewish or otherwise, that you or I have ever visited. This is not an historic Jewish graveyard, with ancient stones, like the ones in Worms or Prague; it is a modern graveyard, founded in 1880, that stands as an utterly exemplary artifact of visual history. Most of its stones were laid in Berlin's golden years when Jews, though less than five percent of the city's population, made such a strong impression that Berlin was known throughout Germany as a Jewish city; and these graves from the classical modern period establish within the cemetery itself a contrasting standard for stones laid after 1935. Thus, the stones of the Great Jewish Cemetery tell not only of individual lives but of a Berlin lost — a Berlin of style, wealth, confidence and culture. Indeed, as this graveyard evokes the glorious past more vividly than anything else I ever saw there, there is good reason to consider it the principal surviving relic of the classic Berlin. Because the experience of the cemetery is so special, as well as illustrative of principles of visual history that have long interested me, my initial plan was to make a book mostly of black and white photographs, a small format paperback with two photographs to a page, for over two hundred pages, because my theme is best evoked through abundant detail.

I like Berlin as a city rich in culture, in activity, in variety, in tolerance, in surprises, and in friends. *Ich bien Berliner*, which I know is not the same as "ein Berliner," which is what John F. Kennedy called himself. ("Ein Berliner," everyone should know, is argot for a certain kind of pancake.) *Ich bien Berliner*, not only because it resembles New York but it is still, to my senses, a Jewish city, just as New York is a Jewish city and Jerusalem is a Jewish city, but now with only a few Jews, alas — five to seven thousand, instead of 200,000 — which is a tragedy about which some things can still be done. Tell your Jewish friends, as I tell mine, that Berlin is *not* West Germany, and indeed it isn't, especially to Berliners, who customarily speak of taking a "trip to West Germany" as though it were a distant country. I tell them about the Cemetery and all that it reveals about the traditions of Berlin. I mention the absence of anti-Semitism, which a Jewish friend of mine who grew up in post-War Berlin attributes to the city's geographical isolation. German anti-Semitism, she once explained to me, tends to come into the cities from the surrounding countryside; but Berlin's countryside, she elaborated, is another country, whose peasants are forbidden to come in. My friend Edgar Hilsenrath, whom the German press infallibly identifies as a "Jewish novelist," told me that he came to live in Berlin, after twenty-seven years in New York, because it was the only place in the German-speaking world where he did not feel intimidated by beer-drinking Germans. ☙

MADONNA
by Harold Jaffe

MADONNA wanted to live in the San Remo, a hincty high-rise in New York City, but her application was turned down by the tenant-owners, including other celebs, though Madonna appeared at the crucial interview with three crucifixes around her neck, or maybe it was four, she had (she is firm on this point) a "very" Catholic childhood, so that her *nom de video*, Madonna, serves the practical dual purpose of alloy and allegory, each encouraged and denied, likewise in her smash-hit single "Material Girl," material is of course lucre while being a timely reminder of our composition as vile matter, ditto Madonna's participation in a '79 soft-core flick in the Big Apple for which she was paid the princely sum of $100, and what was billed as the real scuz was not-so-deftly simulated, ditto her nudie photos disinterred, but my dialectical (so to speak) gloss on U.S. iconizing-commodifying was evidently lost on Paul Simon, Dustin Hoffman and the others on the application committee of the San Remo, the higher you climb the ladder of success the more your (pardon my Greek) arse is exposed applies in spades to Madonna, though she'd rather expose her navel, I've seen more female navels in rainy London this summer, Madonna-invoked, than you would imagine: Earl's Court, Shoreditch, Chelsea, King's Cross, saw a brace on Princes Street, Edinburgh, in the pouring rain, why *shouldn't* she issue a "restraining order" on the redistribution of her porn flick, on the publication of her nudies in both *Penthouse* and *Playboy*, the year was '79 (Before AIDS), Hamilton Jordan was deftly counseling Jimmy Carter on "Human Rights," Madonna was an eighteen-year-old tyro called Louise Ciccone, slim but breasty, brown hair and lush bush and sexy hair on her belly and lots under her arms, her "look" Lower-East-Side-sulky, even then she was religious as heck, in her way, only Diane Keaton among the bigs voted Yes on Madonna's application to live in the San Remo, perhaps on the grounds of sisterhood, I can only speculate, perhaps on the grounds of charity, we are in the grip of BAND AID, aid to the strife-torn in Africa, if only those Marxists would let our dollars get through to the folks that need them: the good poor (in Matthew Arnold's father's phrase), Poverty Sucks, like the bumper-sticker says, but isn't it just the incentive you need to get rich, a buffer (I mean poverty) against getting poor, as AIDS discourages congress with Haitians, homos, hemos, so wear your necktie munch on irradiated bean sprouts phone your broker *don't* bend over, "Like a Virgin," Madonna's first mega-smash, has got it all if you alter the words, while inserting Mother Teresa in her habit for Madonna in her confection of silks, no big deal, not with our technology, I think of the poor when I eat Tandoori, you wouldn't believe how many Indian/Pakistani restaurants there are throughout the U.K., Sikhs though scarce, evidently because of their continuing dispute with India, because of their stubborn insistence on possessing their skins, tough for a male Sikh to hide when you think of it, appearance isn't everything, well, it's darn close, take Madonna's navel, truthfully I prefer reading about her navel from a distance, the U.K. isn't distant enough, and I'd prefer reading about her in another language, Basque, say, or Punjabi (as spoken by the Sikhs in northwest India), Gosh, she's the very reincarnation of Marilyn Monroe, a tramp with style, a composite of styles, a xeroxed composite of apparent styles, a xeroxed composite of apparent styles accessed, video'd and transmitted via satellite, take the incessant rain in London, filthy weather and the thing is we have the technology to do something about it, the Brits though would like it both ways: the Queen Mother at Ascot and the creeping Americanization on the telly, "Dallas" reruns are all the rage, "MERRY MPs DANGLED A TOPLESS GIRL OVER THE RIVER THAMES IN A STAGGERING EARLY-HOURS RAVE-UP" (this wasn't Madonna though it might have been), "ONE LABOUR MEMBER SWUNG THE GIGGLING GIRL OVER THE EDGE OF THE COMMONS TERRACE WITH HIS ARMS ROUND HER LEGS AND SUDDENLY HER CHARMS POPPED OUT," according to *The Sun*, but why Madonna rather than video'd chanteuses like Blondie or Sade (pronounced "Sharday"), well, consider her hair, I think of Bernini's St. Theresa in her passion, and Barbara Stanwyck in a '40s betrayed-husband flick with moody camera angles, polymorphous perversity, A.C.-D.C. and whatever other C's you come up with (these *are* the pluralistic, pentecostal '80s), Madonna's hair — I want to put this plainly — is, like Ahab's doubloon, everything to everybody and nothing, like the foamy head of my draft Guinness, without the draft, now if we can only convince our Secretary of Defense, who, like Madonna, as of this writing, is on a bad roll, he's an honorable man, a proud man, and when he closes his eyes to respond to a question we know that the teleprompter on the inside of his eyelids will be American-made, without Japanese anything, I imagine the unwinding of a bloody bandage and underneath, red and never not festering: *Communism* (reads the teleprompter) in *Our* hemisphere, when the talk turns to politics Madonna and her entourage commence to yawn, and who can blame them?, like that enduring silliness about what does the Scottie wear under his kilt, here in Inverness where I'm nursing my pint (it's late morning but raining bullets), I scan the Ox-Bridge weeklies wherein the splenetic-exotic Scot is as ever good sport, as the Hindus under the Raj, as the "kaffirs" to the Afrikaners, but note: there is, as the intelligent writer demonstrated conclusively in a *New Yorker* article a while back, a distinct though subtle difference between fashion and style, that latter as you might expect being the more refined species, where then would you situate Madonna?, don't answer too quickly, don't answer

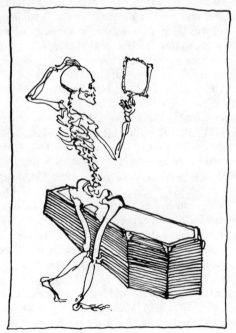

Gerald Burns

surely on the basis of Madonna representing "low" as against "high" culture, I'm tempted to quote the playwright Tom Stoppard but compositionally I can't fit him in, here he is: "There's an essential distinction between countries where the abuse of human rights represents the system in triumph, and the countries in which it represents the failure of the system," Stoppard of course is clever and wealthy, and clever about being wealthy, but beneath the neat formulation resides the oak-panelled soul of OxBridge, Sandhurst too, I remind you that it was not in benighted Moscow nor in Pretoria's whited sepulchre nor in Managua Nicaragua, but in the demotic Big Apple that they denied Madonna, oh well, it's Thursday and I'm off to the National Film Institute to see Joseph Losey's remake of Fritz Lang's *M*, and what can one say that hasn't been said about the ringworm of child molestation, is it really happening?, is it lurid imagining erected on lurid imagining in the service of classic-formula COKE and the New Old Vigilance?, Losey did his *M* in '51, twenty years after Lang, with (improbably) David Wayne in the Peter Lorre role, Losey, you recall, an American who did most of his strong work in England, best known for his collusion with Pinter in *The Servant*, Pinter incidentally just back from Turkey where he and Monroe's ex, Arthur Miller, were sent by PEN to make certain queries about the systematic violation of certain Turkish artists' human rights, Pinter didn't hit it off with the American ambassador, in fact exchanged vivid Pinteresque insults, slinging at each other from a stagey distance, the ambassador with the provisional last word: Pinter was incapable, he put it, of seeing Turkey's policy "in the round," which evidently is how our Secretary of Defense's position, judging from his recent teleprompted remarks re Turkey's "alleged" genocide of Armenians, the Secretary's guiding principle/missile here being Turkey's good will re U.S. bases in Turkey to bolster defense against Communism world-wide and intergalactically as well since the Soviets are, please remember, Asiatics, possessing that Asian mentality derived from Attila, limitless aggression, absolutely, Madonna about the eyes is Asian, dancing in circles like a benign ringworm, like a houri or Odalisque, she doesn't touch us like Mary Pickford, touch is scarcely the point, nor is the coolness Garbo's with its insinuation of depths, Madonna glitters like neon viewed from the wrong side of the scope, she's there and not there, making contact with our nervous system like an electrified dentist's implement tap-tapping our tooth, no longer "the victim's information, but the *victim*, that torture needs to win — or reduce to powerlessness. By expanding the types and frequency of torture, by acquiring and exploiting a more exact knowledge of psychology and neurology, torture in the late 20th century has become able to inflict an immense variety of relatively graded degrees of pain upon anyone" (Edward Peters, *Torture*, Blackwell, '85), here in the U.K. there are only four television channels (though satellite dish antennas are making their bid) but any number of labels of beer, what happened to that honest mug of English bitter that is not ice-cold after the American fashion?, lets' face it, short of cauterization (large-scale), homogenization American-style (Japanese-accented) is irresistible, and, yes, it is up to the artist (the who?) to extract, extrapolate, extort the esthetic principle no longer orbiting neck-deep in contaminant, such an immense variety of flavors, besides you can blend them yourselves, Madonna is (grant me this trope) a dervish, her mobile navel, slender, spike-heeled feet administering delicately graded degrees of pain, her Asian eyes, polymorphous hair, (since shorn), her broader and broader wake of agents and investment advisers, which is probably the toughest job of the lot given the wild fluctuation of the dollar, mind you, I'm not implying that there aren't good, sound, economic heads in control: rock-solid Volcker of the Fed, the incorruptible Stockman man who was a peace activist in the Sixties and recently left the administration for Wall Street and a real salary (seven figures allegedly), Reagan's *Doppel* Regan (exorcized in the wake of "Irangate"), the estimable Meese (he's at Jusice but ranges widely), who then are our torturers? Well, I'd like to cite Arendt's banality of evil (you thought I'd have something off-the-wall up my sleeve), in fact it's more appropriate than ever, dissociate while administering pain hi-ho, in front of the console, phoning your broker, stroking your hairless leg, "evil" itself can stand redefining, which perhaps I'll get to, though in a roundabout way, since it is harder than ever to be plain, that is, *you* are "plain" but is it plain that's received?, heck no, the language all unstuck, thus Madonna and her whirling navel will describe a broad sphere of effluence, so to speak, and if this seems elusive, take heart, there are these constants: dollar and power, though their acquisition and implementation signify a more various collusion, collusion in what?, in keeping the good poor good and poor, in keeping the electrified wire (now wireless) hooked to your genitals, yes yours.

U.K., 6.85
U.S., 9.86, 8.87

THE OLD PROFESSOR'S SONG
by James Broughton

Because I lost my logic
in my sixty-seventh year
I bump my way across each day
and never see things clear.

Did my brain evaporate?
Did it fall behind?
Did it sink into a think
that made it lose its mind?

Without my fixed opinions
I'm slackly going to pot.
Instead of fame to light my name
I disreputably rot.

O murky world, O Nietzsche,
O shivering underwear!
I daily crawl from wall to wall
and never know I'm where.

MOZART
by Terry Jacobus

leave me! he said
only Mozart can comfort me now

RICHARD BRAUTIGAN: FREE MARKET EUTHANASIA
by Ed Dorn

The sensationalism surrounding the death of Richard Brautigan has been odd. It has met all the qualifications of *National Enquirer* prurience — calculation, decay, disease, drek sexuality, and a fate conveniently beyond explanation. Richard would have enjoyed that part of it because he was drawn to such style of coverage, and, in fact, might have had it in mind, since he arranged for his body to rot for several weeks before the likelihood of discovery.

The first thing to understand about Richard's mind was that he idealized the common intelligence. That's why he was abruptly popular, and why, in the end, he was systematically forgotten: The people who were surprised by him never abandoned their hatred of him, and the ones who loved him, never a large number, never abandoned him. Even toward the end you could meet people who thought *So the Wind Won't Blow It All Away* was the truest account of growing up even written. The only trouble with his admiration of the *National Enquirer* audience was that they never heard of him. He was condemned, and he knew it, to be one of us.

Last fall, when the news of his suicide came through the wire, there was a blizzard of speculation. A lot of the turbulent guesswork was simply the confusion of the strange man's friends. They felt the triumph of an adversary's death. And in fact, it was a strong coup. Literary personalities overwhelmingly die in the presence of at least one other person. To die as he did, with calculation, with everything working — lights, radio, telephone machine on in a house with a Do Not Disturb sign — was a disturbing after thought to a public not yet accustomed to free-market euthanasia.

The comparisons with Hemingway are quite erroneous: Brautigan was not a shotgun man. The pronouncements that women drove him to it are equally off the mark. He mostly got along with women better than with men: he was more confidential with them and more friendly toward them. The fact that he was disappointed in marriage had to do with his alienation from humanity in general on a constant basis. He looked to men for the kind of respect that the exclusiveness of marriage denied. The aesthetic which led him to prefer Japanese women was at the heart of his essential lack of interest in domestic routines. His views on these matters are very eloquently expressed and recorded in *Sombrero Fallout*, a deeply lyrical presentation of the contrast of American and Japanese traits.

He was a roamer, always looking for the odd sign and the direct encounter, and he was naturally dubious of explanation and analysis, because he felt the phenomenon itself was complete. And so did his readers, during the early years of his success. He didn't write fiction so much as observation, honed and elevated so as to catch the light emanating from the most presumably insignificant of details. The only respect in which he was a Christian was the interest he shared with Christ in professional women.

He was a true macho in that his challenges were thrown at men. He loved sharp argument, the nastier the better. He craved for verbal contest to reach a point where he was compelled to say "Watch it! you're going too far." Those who knew him well, and who played that game with him, took it as a compliment if that theater of combat was reached. Although his writing is not violent, there was no end to his search for the bounds of violence. To Richard Brautigan, the idea of fate itself was comic. That attitude has always made as many enemies as friends.

He had no history of morbidity. All his writing — the lonely, wry, preoccupied, lapidary miniatures he published as poetry, or the spare boldness of his micro-prose — was devoted to coaxing life to live up to its obvious possibilities. Death was a fact to him, not just another attraction. Richard could be vicious, but he was not sour. He had too much pride for that.

Brautigan saw himself and often referred to himself as a humorist. That's a designation not much used about anyone anymore, since everybody in the whole nation has become a comic. But it has been a rare thing when an artist has identified with any tradition in this century. There is a distant similarity between Brautigan and Twain. It consists almost solely in a natural innocence in regarding the evil disposition of mankind. But whereas Twain's treatment of the condition is streaked with acid intelligence, Brautigan's is amazingly tolerant, if not gleeful, and resembles an anthropologist's understanding more than that of a literary man.

Contrary to what is often claimed, Richard spoke easily of his childhood and its tribulations. He was without recrimination, so his stories were saucy versions of the School of Hard Knocks. His work appealed to those who had decided not to mock their chains but to pick them up and carry them out of the hippie slums of the West Coast back to the Rocky Mountains, much as the disappointed seekers of '49 gradually made their way following silver rather than gold to the East again.

One night in August 1980, Richard delivered a little talk and read from his work at the Chautauqua Auditorium in Boulder [Colorado]. There were about a thousand old-timey people from the hills to hear him. He was very impressed that forerunners like Billy Sunday and William Jennings Bryan had spoken there. He like those old echoes. The audience of freckled, ginghamed women and their freckled, ginghamed children with their homespun fathers obviously loved him, and he openly returned their regard. It was a touching reunion filled with gentle, reflective laughter.

That summer in Boulder was special in a number of ways for Brautigan, and he was fascinated with the town itself. It respresented many elements of the new life, the untested but already discernable motion of the '80s at the brink. He was impressed with the liberal sprinkling of beautiful women in the crowds. He stayed at the Boulderado for about a month and felt at home in the ornate, turn-of-the-century ambience. In 1980 the hotel was still a little rough-edged, although some of the present amenities were in place then. The heyday of the hotel in Richard's terms would have been slightly earlier, in the '70s, when the clientele was a loose traffic of waywardly successful odd-balls with specific intentions if they could "get it together."

It was while he was staying at the hotel that he met Masako one evening at a party in his honor given by Ginger Perry. Perry had apparently managed to find the one Japanese girl in Boulder that summer. Masako was very young and very Japanese. She called him Lichad.

Boulder became even more absurdly intriguing in his estimation. He glowed with possibilities and talked about new writing projects. Fishermen came and went. There was a fair amount of talk about fishing the intown course of Boulder Creek. And then, eventually, he took Masako off to Montana. they didn't live happily ever after, but they were very happy for a while.

His second wife, Akiko, has related how she saw him inadvertently in North Beach very shortly before his suicide. The sight of him was so affecting she followed him along the street and into Vanessi's, an old and still classy Italian restaurant on Broadway, near the crossroads with Columbus Avenue of San Francisco's bohemian quarter, the haunt of sailors and internationalists, and except for the Spanish Mission and Presidio, the oldest inhabited part of the city.

She stood there by the door, she said, until Richard saw her. He closed his eyes. In this sign she thinks he saw her as a ghost. But as everyone knows, if you're lucky enough to see a ghost, you open your eyes. What Richard actually saw, from the testimony of his own records, was yet another instance of the distortion of the dream he had had. It was the final judgment of the truly poor that everything be perfect.

TAURUS RISING   Liz Henderson

FROM THE E.C.°CHAIR

A reader suggested that we lengthen the Corpse by ½ inch every issue. Eventually, you would drape it over a chair, or (if we increase paper weight) prop it behind the door like a surfboard. In either case, whether flaccid or erect, you would have a growing Corpse in your hands, a Corpse harder and harder to mail but more and more obvious. This reader was obviously flattering phallometric editorial fantasies. We have no intention of lengthening what already throws a substantial shadow. A few weeks ago, a letter bemoaning the poetry avalanche in the office went out of here. It went out over the Editor's signature, but it was written by an impostor. We beg you to disregard it: we are once again in love with poetry. Tom Clark, who knows, writes: "Don't blame poetry for the crimes of bad poets." OK. But we still have a beef with Art. We believe that art is doing fine, but that all artists are dead. A longer Corpse anyone?

CHER CADAVRE EXQUIS

LETTER TO THE *CORPSE*

re. Hakim Bey's "Pornography" in the Nov/Dec issue:

my hunch is that the kind of poetry the Persians or North Indians are responding to is either ancient texts or something close to song lyrics. Evangelic enthusiasm is probably the closest we come to the former; as for the latter, most song lyrics do not hold up on the page. In North Amer-

ica at least, if the audience responds immediately to something it has never heard before, chances are what it is hearing is less than poetry.

It seems to me that paradoxically the American poet is blocked as effectively as the Russian poet. There you are forced to lie to be able to publish; here you can say anything and it does not matter. It is like being in a theater in which a poet smells smoke; is it worse to be gagged at that moment or to only be able to shout "fire" in Bulgarian? Beyond these difficulties, however, meaningful art is being made in Russia and America, which in effect argues that the self is not subject to any society.

I agree with Bey that poetry must be reconnected to the body but I don't think pornography is the answer (nor must Bey, as he offers a three-minute film, and not another kind of poem, as a way to "unchain Desire from its bondage"). Most pornography is imaginatively limited by a compulsive sadism directed against the self or the other, and is an icy symptom of the extent to which imagination and body are split in our Protestant society. In my own experience, I have found that gratified desire leads to imaginative vision and work, that orgasm stimulates fantasy, that there is an antiphonal swing between making art and making love. To put it this way, of course, does not mean that as a consequence of such a view my art accomplishes what Bey calls for. It does suggest to me that a poetry connected to the body does not necessarily have sex as subject. Bey's proposals all center around the performance of poetry, as if immediate audience response is the "test." While, as I mentioned before, I distrust *audience* approval, during a Cecil Taylor recital several years ago, I began to fantasize about a certain kind of "poetry performance" that might be physical, serious, and audience-engaging.

Taylor did two long improvisations, and in each there was a marvelous combination of thematic passages and seemingly spontaneous detours. I was never sure what was going to happen next, while at the same time I never felt that I was just listening to noise. It occurred to me that what Taylor was doing had parallels in the writing of a heterogeneous range of poetries: Antonin Artaud, Clark Coolidge, Vladimir Holan, Robert Kelly, for example — and, would it be possible for a Coolidge, say, to "write" out loud before an audience, improvising sounds, words, phrasings and image-chains with a similar precise discontinuity to that of Taylor's? Any poet who could success-fully do this would have to train like an athlete (Artaud's vision of actor training for his "Theater of Cruelty" comes to mind) — for a combined mental and physical stamina would be needed. And I am not just describing a kind of "rapping" — I am thinking of an explosive, fully voiced "Bop prosody" that at no point would relax into conversational language.

Several months after hearing Taylor, I was in Donte's, a North Hollywood jazz club, where a drummer friend, Frank Severino, was playing with a quintet. During a break, Frank suddenly said, "Hey man, why don't you do a poem?" I was not sure what he had in mind, but I decided on the spot to give my "Taylor fantasy" a try and impro-vised for 3 or 4 minutes. I just started with the first word that came to mind once I faced the mike. I can't recall here what I actually said, but it started off something like this:

the block the rock a flock of rocks a brain
a grazing brain bitter bile balls
peals of balls Niles of balls can a
cannibal have a ball can he engown his brother
can a brother brain his lathe
can a symptom sneer at a spore a flock of
    knaves
a knife of leaves a feel a feel for gourds
gripping gourds gourds of coral of
gleet of guided pistols of mimosas
wrapped in pads of braided gore

The challenge of having to second by second dodge *and* accommodate the predictable, with the feeling that any moment the jig could be up, gave me an eerie, exhilarating sensation of "running on empty." I was so conscious of physically being there, that *that* noticing created a stronger sense of resistance, which was also a goad, than the mental pushing ahead. I felt like my head was in a vise, that words were being screwed out of me — at the same time that the space itself — the club — felt relaxed, even limp. As a kind of physical mentality turned its bore against my mind, my body seemed to float. As Charles Olson wrote (in a different context) "The poetics of such a situation are yet to be found out."

— Clayton Eshleman

HEADSTRENGTH UPHELD

Back to the Good Book, and Rodger Kamenetz's claim that "a glance at Exodus 32:9" will show how I have "completely distorted" the Exodus story.

As Exodus 32 opens, the Israelites, forever grumbling, think that Moses (who's gone up the mountain) has abandoned them. Finding themselves without a leader and without a god — Yahweh had communicated to them through Moses — the people decide to create their own. Everyone donates their gold jewelry which is melted down and molded into the Golden Calf. Then "all the people sat down to eat and drink and afterward got up to amuse themselves." In other words, in-stead of an authority imposed from above, the peo-ple — each contributing according to his abilities! — collectively create their own leadership. And, after the hardships endured wandering around the desert under the Moses-Yahweh regime, the Golden Calf signals a time for some heavy partying. Mean-while, up on the mountain, Yahweh tells Moses what's going on. Yahweh wants to wipe out the whole lot, but Moses dissuades him. Instead, Moses descends the mountain and reinstates his authority by strengthening the priesthood and purging (mur-dering) 3000 Israelites. Exodus 32:9, to get back to Kamenetz, states in its entirety: "Yahweh said to Moses: 'I can see how headstrong these people are!' " This, I think, reinforces rather than refutes my reading: "headstrong" means "unwilling to sub-mit to my authority." Yahweh, remember, always refers to the Israelites as "my people," indicating possession. The injunction "You shall have no other gods except me" is not, as is commonly thought, an assertion of monotheism. Yahweh recognizes the existence of the other gods, but makes it clear that the Israelites can have only one Numero Uno. I stand by my characterization of Exodus as a "Stal-inist manual on the suppression of dissent." The Golden Calf is not, as Kamenetz says, "a return to slavery," but rather a spontaneous revolt, an affir-mation of life against both the Egyptian and the Mosaic slaveries. That such celebrations of life end in bloodshed is a fact tirelessly repeated through history. The Church and State can only stand so much life. When writing to *EC*, it's always wise to leave the last word to a Rumanian exile. Here then is what Mircea Eliade has to say about the god of Exodus: "He demands absolute obedience from his worshippers, like an Oriental despot...The intolerance and fanaticism that are characteristic of the prophets and missionaries of the three monotheisms have their model and justification in Yahweh's example."

— Eliot Weinberger

SACRIFICE DENIED

Kirby Doyle confuses the religion of Judaism, which abhors human sacrifice, with the myriads of early religions — Celtic, Greek, Aztec, Pawnee, Shang, etc., etc. — which included such sacrifice in their rituals. As Dr. Turney-High states in his *Primitive War*, "one of the greatest values the captive could serve has been as human sacrifice to a god who demands such immolation." The God of the Jews, the God of Christ made no such demands. It is those who promulgate a lie which has caused and may still cause countless, obscene murders who are favoring human sacrifice. Being a poet is not enough to wash the blood off one's hands.

— Theodore Wilentz

SHED POUNDS

In response to Mr. Kamenetz's very timely & necessary piece:
IT'S TIME TO SHED A FEW POUNDS!
The rest of the magazine, tho certainly not devoid of particles, brings to mind a unity — 'to care'. I found an exquisite corpse last summer, a dragonfly husk sucked dry by heat, exoskeleton of the void. But the Wings! Four nets cast to the wave of windows still catching light! Keep up the good work.

— Paul Piper

SWEETEST GUY WHO EVER SLIT A THROAT

It seems that warring letters to editors is developing into a form of legalized slander or at its best into an aspiring art-form. Upon being attacked, one would better take on the tone of a Paul Valery, or his extension as per your narrator in Valery in America. I liked Kamenetz' riposte to Weinyber-ger, and "SORRY, SUKKAH" indeed. It occurs to me, if we claim that "everyone is a Jew" then no one is, and that goes for poets as well. W. sounds fairly afflicted by his sense of Judaism, outraged even, while K. is intrigued. Different ball games. Was at the Pound symposium at San Jose State. Pedantry flew slow and thick as a brick wall trying to take off. A conceptual language exiled from particulars and trying to make a mythology in a barren waste. Much less interesting than poetry — in fact, opposed to it. The frozen vs. the flow. These academics make their living off "explicating" the Cantos made up of swathes of literary gossip and streaks of lyric genius. The guy was a consummate mimic: from paranoid schizo to Daniel Arnaud. Ford Madox Ford described Pound as the sweetest guy who ever slit a throat. Sounds right on. Would take years of scholarly industry to iron out all the ironies, n'est-ce pas.

— Jack Marshall

IRATE CANADIAN FICTIONEER

I guess Ray Johnson taught me this about The Word: write letters to one person, but for ever. That article, which provoked yesterday's obscenity-strewn monologue on this same machine (at least when I handwrite, the words may be illegible, but I think they're spelled right, this fucking antiquated bulldog does not correct) that article was yours to publish. I chickened out, that's all. I included a similar challenge to Jewish writers of my age to define their Judaism in an article on the Objectivists, but everybody told me it was an evil idea, so I deleted it. The article, which may appear in *The Little Magazine*, unless they grow fearful from my five-page contributor's note — the article ended by being neither religious nor sociological but uh musical. (When I play the flute, men run, neighbors complain, cats stare etc...When I play the harpsichord, Robert Buecker loses his temper.) I remember in Richard Kostelanetz's *End of Intelligent Writing* there were lists of various young intelligent writers. There were many long lists. I bet Richard doesn't even remember if I made Promising Young Critic and Promising Young Editor list. Richard's now a friend, if I were to list my friends, he'd definitely be on the list. So there's a list. And if I were to do a second list, People Who are Jewish, Richard would be on that list, too; and so would you. I could say the three major modernist painters are Matisse Picasso and Cezanne (Miro?). The three major Jewish modernist painters are Modigliani Soutine and Chagall. The three major abstract Expresionsts are Pollock, Kline and de Kooning. The three major Jewish abstract Expressionists are Kline, Rothko and Reinhardt. You could say that Reinhardt is more important than Kline, but. . . well it's all opinion. Lists about quality are opinion. But lists of religion, like lists of nationality, are not matters of opinion; or are they? I'm Canadian. I'm in an anthology, Contemporary American Fiction. I don't consider myself a fictioneer. I think what I'm talking about is evidence, as in Seidman's *Collecting Evidence*. My friend David Shapiro does not limit himself to facts, but loves opinions, and it, as a practical matter, gives him more to say, more to write. Seidman's silences and Shapiro's rap drive different people bonkers. I happen to enjoy both. Jerry Rothenberg on the other hand bugs me. Please forgive me, Jerry, but it's true. I don't know why. I'd sooner read Jerry than have dinner with him. If you were to publish this letter, then I'd almost certainly never have to have dinner with Jerry again. Why would you publish this letter? Is Judaism not a principle then of *cadavre exquis*? Is *Cadavre exquis* as good a game as *Plain Implications*? Do you think your agent could sell Plain Implications to Parker Brothers? I'm afraid to talk to my agent — about anything. You see. . . but it's a long story. Oh well I must pay some bills and I must read some of the other articles in the current issue of *EC* besides my own. They couldn't be as upsetting.

— Michael Andre

been captured by the *Southern Review* mavens and have been put on a diet of poontang and biscuits in sawmill gravy? I hope one of *EC*'s minions will be remarking on Lorine Niedecker's FROM THIS CONDENSERY. Whether Robert Bertholf (truculent, blue-collar technocrat that he is) got all the poems and got them right is a matter for him and Cid Corman and Lisa Faranda and Jenny Penberthy and Peter Quartermain to argue out. JARGON SOCIETY hopes there will be demand for a second edition and we'll correct any errors and omissions. But literati are such a nest of adders. It is wryly amusing to know that Zukofsky almost without doubt passed off several of Niedecker's country musings as two of his best poems. And Basil Bunting was amazed to find one of his early efforts hidden away in Patchen's THE JOURNAL OF ALBION MOONLIGHT. The stuff of dreams, etc. It is sad to find out at a venerable age that poetry gives you leprosy, herpes, AIDS, lumbago, and terminal boredom. I.e., I hope you are enjoying the Funless Eighties amongst the glitzers and the grunts more than I am. Keep under cover. Eat yur grits!

— Jonathan Williams

REMODELED *ZONE:* APOLLINAIRE MOVES ON

You're tired at last of the ancient world — and of the modern one too

— Jim Brook

HIGHLANDS DISPATCH

A new copy of *EC* having filtered into Highlands from Outer Cosmic Infinity, we assume you have

Alice Codrescu

THE ROMANCE OF CITRUS
(Sectional Version)

by Christy Sheffield Sanford

Oranges *(Jamaica)*	A cloud of esters escapes as Elena splits an orange. She takes each half and on hands and knees scrubs rhythmic circles. She is cleaning the floor of the restaurant after closing. Her husband Eddie bought the oranges from the market woman who is his mistress. A baby cries in the background.
Lemons *(Atlantic City)*	On TV the movie star, Susan Sarandon, cuts a lemon and rubs the flesh of the fruit over her bare breasts and arms. She stands at a sink in front of her window. Burt Lancaster watches from across the way. Now Eddie grins as I remove a lemon segment from the fridge and rub it over my belly.
Grapefruit *(Miami)*	Eddie's redheaded lover arranges hors d'oeuvres, and as she rounds the kitchen counter with a tray he squeezes her black velvet bottom. "A fanny like ripe grapefruit," he says to his son, age 7. Rachel smiles, but a sudden impulse to slap Eddie's face frightens her. Then he grabs his bongos, dedicates a jazz improv to her and her cunt throbs.
Limes *(New Orleans)*	On the verandah Eddie and I check our plane tickets to Guadalajara. Beside purple bougainvillaeas we sip Lime Rickeys under the stars. Gazing at the lime rind in his glass, Eddie tells me how after school he used to lick limes, sprinkled with sugar. He flinches when I say, "What we're doing is very dangerous."
Tangerines *(Guadalajara)*	Eddie puts my feet on his shoes and dances me about — like my father did when I was 8. My daddy taught me to foxtrot to Bob Eberly singing "My heart belongs to Tangerine." I held his waist; he held my shoulders just below the curls. "Eddie," I say, looking at the high cheekbones I love, "would you mind if I changed my name to Tangerine?"

DREAMS OF SNAKES, CHOCOLATE AND MEN

by Christy Sheffield Sanford

Snake	On Captiva Island I sit on a ledge beside palmettos; a blue and green snake sticks its head through pine straw. I lift the reptile, thin as my ring finger, and it expands to a gray, puffy-cheeked, diamond-backed rattler the length of a bed. Trembling I sling the snake onto snapping twigs.
Chocolate Bar	Hmmm, my bittersweet addiction. A waiter serves me a dark, satiny chocolate bar, lumpy with peanuts like a Baby Ruth, but with a few bites missing. My teeth clamp on something hard. I try again. My jaws ache. I shove the confection off the table. The dessert plate breaks.
Snake, Chocolate Bar	A viper slithers over an inedible candy bar. I tear aside the skin, do a cross section on the bar — discover only a teleidoscope of rich designs. Even under the microscope candy looks alluring. Yet the surfaces within surfaces confound me.
Man, Snake, Chocolate Bar	A swarthy man wears a violet shirt and eats pink watermelon. A purple snake shifts in his black hair, slides across his chest, intertwines our legs. He peels a wrapper from his chocolate bar, munches the candy, passes it to me. I taste. "Theobroma — food of the gods," he whispers. A delicious spasm ripples through my pelvis.
Chocolate, Snakes, Man	Last night the chocolate factory exploded and burned. The smell of scorched chocolate permeated every room in my house. The lost luscious promises. In the surrounding woods some snakes fled underground; others died of smoke inhalation. And in the plant a man eating watermelon on his break perished.
Chocolate, Men Snakes	Even now in the Orinoco basin, harvesters with machetes reap cacao pods for me. My brain still carries the chemicals chocolate and men trigger. All over the world men in violet shirts split watermelons and toast me with their juicy sections. Racers, whips, cobras and kings wait, ready to weave through all my dreams.

SKULL-SIZE AND WORLD PEACE

by Kirby Olson

EXAMINE THE PORTRAITS OF BAUDELAIRE AND POE CLOSELY

They both wore their hair the same length and in the same style, with heavy dark eyebrows and sunken faces, moustaches over their top lips, thick

Edgar Allan Poe

Baudelaire

silk scarves or ties wrapped around their necks, otherwise wearing perpetual black. The look on each of their faces is that of a child who has not been invited to a party that everyone else in the neighborhood is going to attend. They were both cut off by their military-minded stepfathers, financially and emotionally, from the security of the family nest. Perhaps this accounts for the gloom stamped indelibly on their faces. They both gambled away youthful fortunes. Everything got away from them. This may account for their choice of women in their later lives: Poe chose fragile, extremely young women who would lean on him for support, Baudelaire chose a black actress that he could manipulate with what little money remained in his possession. There is no doubt that they loved their women (if anything, they loved them *too* much), but they also liked the fact that they could possess them by keeping them in a marginally crippled state, so that they wouldn't get away like everything else. All these resemblances are superficial, however, when one realizes the true reason that they have their curious sympathetic vibration. Literature is an unregulated harmonium, the poets being the glasses filled with water. Very rarely are two glasses not only of the same size but filled with the same amount of spirit. Baudelaire and Poe may have come closer than any two other poets. A singular music emanates from ev-

ery skull in the history of literature. Like a bell-jar, when it is rung, it will cause other bell-jars of the exact same shape to ring at the same pitch. The true reason that Baudelaire and Poe are so closely linked is that their skull sizes were *exactly* the same. Now that we have examined and explained how writers respond to one another, let's move on to how readers respond to writers. As the number of writers grows, the number of readers declines. These numbers are directly related. The more writers there are, the more readers are disconcerted at trying to find an appropriate voice that they can respond to. I recommend that each writer and each reader have his head examined. Readers can then pick up a list of writers who share their exact skull size. Then they can give this slip to the bookstore manager who can go into the back, like a shoe salesman, and find the appropriate books. The bookstore representative can return with a pile of possible fits, and the potential reader can choose the book or books whose style most appeals to him or her at that moment. Once the world has discovered the truth of how readers and writers respond to each other, no reader need ever feel alienated from literature ever again, and no writer will ever again have a problem finding his audience. Of course, there will be certain head sizes that won't be well-represented by writers, but this is the same in the shoe store, as well. It is hard to find a size three or size sixteen, but rather easy to find a size ten, for example. Those who are left out by their heads being too small can always try mind-expanding drugs. For those whose heads are too big, they can always go to a shrink. Or they can try the most tragic step: becoming their own poet. "But I won't have any readers!" I hear them shout. Well, no poets do at the beginning. With a little help from evolution, however, they might become as widely read as Shakespeare (meanwhile, poor Shakespeare might become as little known as them). The chances for world peace are the same as the chances that everybody's skull, readers' and writers' alike, will some day be, if not identical, at least in some harmonic relationship to one another, creating an aleatory Mozartian arrangement. Until that day we will have to selectively attune to those skulls similar to our own on this discordant planet, to keep from being driven mad by the bells, bells, bells, the tintinnabulation of the b.e.L.L.s.

THE ROSE OF MARION

for Harold Talbott

by James Schuyler

is pink and many petalled:
it rests on the rim
of a shot-glass on the desk
in my room in this
Eighteenth Century house in,
of course, Marion, Cape Cod,
Massachusetts (for
further details, see Thoreau
or "The Outermost House" by
what's-his-face).

The window is filled
with leaves! So different
from my urban view
in stony-hearted New York.

I love leaves, so green,
so still, then
all a shimmer. Would
I like to live here? I
don't know: it's
far from friends
(for me) and others
I depend on. But
it's awfully nice to visit,
a whaling port,
like Sag Harbor, Long Island.

Pink rose of Marion, I
wish I knew your name.
Perhaps one day I will.

BUREAU

NEW YORK: LOOKING FOR LOVE

by Hariette Surovell

It had all the makings of a classic weird evening. Walking east on Fourth Street at twilight, I heard a neighborhood kid asking, "What do it be, man? Do it be a pig, a dog, or a chicken?" I figured I would shortly discover what they were talking about, and, sure enough, when I got to the corner of Fourth and Second Avenue, I saw it in the gutter — a large, four-legged hairless animal fetus deposited next to a parked cop car. The sight was too nauseating to inspect. So when I got to the lobby of my building, and ran into my neighbor, Joey, an accommodating and worshipful janitor, I requested, "Joey, go to the corner and tell me what that thing is that's lying in the gutter, please." He returned grinning. "I don't know, Hariette, but it make me want to throw up." I went upstairs to shower and dress — my sarcastic buddy Louie and I were off to a party uptown. I had received a xeroxed invitation to this particular soiree. The hostess, whom I had met briefly, hailed from eastern Europe. I wasn't sure if this fact — or a possible enrollment in an EST seminar — accounted for the wording of the invite, "Do your commitment and come experience this party with me." On the door of her apartment was taped a notice: "Come in and hang up your coats. There will be a midnight surprise. I love you all. Oxana." "I *love* you?! What the fuck is this — a Back to the Sixties Be-In or what?" sputtered Louie. "I forgot to wear my fringed vest and my pinstriped elephant bells." "Oh wow, I'm peaking," I enjoined. "Doesn't she know that this is the '80s and we're all supposed to hate each other? Maybe we should just go back downtown to the weirdos and the winos." "Let's stick around for the midnight surprise," I demurred. Together, we conjured up fantasies of illicit substances, exotic dancers, Rambograms, performance art tableaux, chocolate cake from the Erotic Bakery. The teeny livingroom was so crowded that Louie compared the experience to "being trapped in a subway fire." Oxana appeared, wearing a silk suit, and gave us both exuberant kisses. Louie and I separated to seek out potential love interests and dance to the incessant dj-created music. The music was great. A Columbia University neurophysicist was witty and surprisingly hip, but in the final analysis, not my type. A Yugoslavian violin student had mythic Ivo Pogorelichian beauty. He asked someone for a cigarette. They proferred a pack. With a cunning expression, he snatched two. "What makes you think you're entitled to two cigarettes?" I asked, wary of Yugoslavian greed ever since my love affair last May with a penniless Slovinian with an enormous appetite. "Because I am special," he replied, without skipping a beat. It was 12:15 and there was no surprise in evidence. "Could we have missed it?" Louie asked. After all, the two jazz musicians who perform on Fifth Avenue wearing ape masks had arrived in full regalia and whipped out their instruments. But Oxana, eyes sparkling, assured me that the big moment was yet to materialize. Then, at 1:00 a.m., the music stopped. Oxana stood in the middle of the room. She had made a costume change, and now sported a long black lace scarf which was wrapped around her short punk haircut, and she had opened the buttons of her frilly blouse to reveal a moderate-sized camisole-encased bosom. "I have an announcement," Oxana said gravely, "I am the surprise." There was scattered, half-hearted applause, and someone yelled, "Take it off, baby." "I have something to share with you. Three years ago, when I came to this country, I thought I was crazy and I cut off my hair. Now, three years have passed and I know I am not crazy." The dj resumed her duties with Stevie Wonder's "Spiritual Walkers" from his latest LP. I wished he had instead chosen the cut, "Go Home." Oxana was hugged by five or so good sports...or fellow "graduates." Louie already had our coats in his hands when he found me. "She *thinks* she's not crazy," he hissed. The next morning, Joey knocked on my door. "Hariette, I have news for you. It was a pig. It was a pig that wasn't borned yet, and I found out one of the homeless guys from the men's shelter, he stold it and took it back to the shelter wit him."

The following Friday, I attended a party to celebrate the opening of a new neighborhood restaurant. Caribbean food served in a punk ambiance — street art on the awning, waiters with blue hair. Neighborhood residents were convinced that this endeavor was doomed. Each previous restaurant in this location had died a prolonged painful death, as if the very space inhabited was endowed with bad karma. But, in my opinion, there were concrete reasons for those failures. The dank health food restaurant served millet pilaf with its omelettes. Then there was the unpretentious Fench bistro. They served meals French peasant style — lots of long tables, like picnic tables, with benches. In this case, it was obviously poor judgment, not bizarre culinary concepts, that led to this establishment's demise. How could anyone assume that New York strangers want to sit at the same tables and eat together in a public place? Each time I passed the empty restaurant and espied the mournful but stoic faces of the owners, I wanted to cry out, "Use your *tetes*!" I have never really understood the mentality of wanting to own one's own restaurant. When friends occasionally enthuse, "Wouldn't it be wonderful if, one day, we could all get together and open up our own little cafe?" I reply, "No." Possibly my friends are more extroverted and sociable than myself. Of perhaps the desire to feed strangers is indicative of one's need to nurture. It is because of this possibility that I always feel enormous sympathy for humiliated restaurateurs. Anyway, in this particular case, the skeptics were way off base — the joint is jumping every night. In fact, I dined there recently and there was such a long wait to eat that a nervous gay man on a date with a fussy adolescent bribed the maitre d' $10 to get seated. I thought, "Now really! Right here in the East Village! A $10 bribe when the entrees are $6.50!"

PARIS: RUE DU TEMPLE

by *William Levy*

"no good ever comes from being too polite."
— Jean Rhys, *Quartet*

As we walked down the stair
I noticed a spec of cum in your hair:
Zarathustra, the teacher of nimble dances
teaches us to encourage steep slopes to form
abysses above which one may dance...
Oh dancing girl who loves the
worn narrow streets of Europe
Having taken the name and
abandoned the husband who loved
her in New Zealand.
I crave and fear two forms of madness:
One is for the love of God;
In that scenario I see myself
Praying in front of the Wailing Wall
until the end.
The other is for the love of a woman:
That I call my Blue Angel syndrome
where I chase sleazy strippers
Wind up holding the coat of her male
callers as they retire to the bedroom.
At that Lubischer kosher pizza parlour
on the Rue des Rosiers I look up,
not surprisingly startled to see photos of men
Praying in front of the Wailing Wall
And you beside me wearing a red feather boa.
After giving a predatory vernissage roar when I
    baptised
a resident expatriate literati "the unprattling
    rodent";
the boyfriend she calls Poopsie as "ultimately
    pouncey"
You asked: Please. Don't make me laugh while
I am putting on eye makeup.
Merely nodding to your colleague Salomé you
Shuddered when seeing Gustave Moreau's
painting of Prometheus, on the wall opposite:
His uncomprehending stare as the vultures
peck his liver eternally.
And didn't deny it when I asked:
Do you too want to defy the Gods?
But asked two other Talmudic questions:
Do you mean — as well as other things?
Or, just like yourself?

Maybe that was in answer
to my question about kissing,
Standing on tiptoes stretching
to reach your lips for a kiss:
Soft kisses, serious stares, scarlet smears.
If I hadn't lost my bottom front teeth
I might have been able to grasp
the string of your tampon,
Pull it out slowly
Kissing the pink in Paris.
And the next morning
(there is always a next morning)
You got dressed and musically announced:
No tampons. No toilet paper.
I'm going out with a coffee filter in my twat.
I wish there were more places
on your body to touch
that each time we made love
I would find a nerve
not known before.
When you touch me
it's like
Witnessing the crucifixion:
It causes me to tremble
And glow in the dark.
You knew I would swoon when you said:
I had heard of the silver Tiber
And the golden Arno,
But only the Seine pleases me as a river;
It has grace and solidity.
In the elevator which only goes up you spoke
Of my filling the nine holes in your body.
You can treat me rough — use violence, you said.
"Miraculo!" I cried waving arms dancing about
    amiss.
On cloven hoofs not quite plunging us down
    the dark
    abyss.
When I ran out of money you dropped me;
I returned to Amsterdam
with the crabs
and a broken heart, sitting here
Thinking...
Oh disco chicken decaying in the Marais
on a rapidly diminishing inheritance.
If your heart
weren't so empty
You'd have bigger breasts
What we used to call *the annointed*
We now call *a survivor.*

ARE YOU READY TO DIE FOR THE SEXUAL REVOLUTION?
by Charles Shively

Recently, Jerry Falwell brought his M&M road show to Cincinnati and demanded that the gay baths be closed immediately because of AIDS. (As it turns out, no gay bath — although advertised for years — has ever been able to open in Cincinnati.) His call coincides with some elements in the gay community — who seek repentance and forgiveness for what they understand as their sexual sins. They believe that they can sacrifice their sexuality and be granted everlasting life. Such nonsense. Everyone is going to die; giving up sex will only make the remaining life less joyous. During the bubonic plague of medieval times, crowds would do penance in the streets and whip themselves and promise to be "good" if only their deity would remove the plague. Or the Greeks before Troy believed their plague was brought on because their commander fucked a priest's daughter.

Even supposing that the pagans and the Christians were correct that sex causes AIDS, I would then ask, why should people not be ready to die for sexual liberation. Better dead than locked in our rooms, terrorized by the doctors, the priests, the politicians. There are risks in sex — think of all the rapes and queerbashing — but gay liberation should struggle to remove those risks, not succumb to our enemies.

Many gay "leaders" are now calling for us to put our faith in the medical profession, but that profession itself must bear major responsibility for making our sexuality more dangerous than it need be. They tell us to send our hundred million dollars to the Centers for Disease Control (CDC), but that center does more to maintain than to control disease. Look at their history. In 1932, they began an experiment on six hundred Black men, which was only discontinued when the press uncovered their crime in 1972. (Caspar Weinberger was then HEW Secretary.) Four hundred of the Black men were watched to see what the effects of untreated syphilis would be on their mortality rate; the other two hundred were used as "control subjects." Even after the "experiment's" rapid termination in 1972, treatment for the surviving men was delayed almost a year. The Centers for Disease Control, as one newspaper reported, "sees the poor, the black, the illiterate and the defenseless in American society as a vast resource for the government" (James H. Jones, *Bad Blood, the Tuskegee Syphilis Experiment*, 1981).

But the CDC has been hardly more trustworthy in dealing with straight white people. In 1976 — after Gerald Ford had pardoned Nixon and needed to refurbish his own election campaign — the poli-

Bruce Hutchinson

ticians attempted to restore faith in the government by creating a Swine Flu Panic. (They had planned an epidemic.) When their flu vaccine began killing people, their political ploy flopped and the Swine Flu Crusade dropped into the dustbin of history with the Ford. But in the process, the drug companies who manufactured the vaccine made a good profit, which they shared with the Republican Party.

There is, however, a frightening likelihood that AIDS has been funded all along by the federal government. If the theory of Jane Teas (Harvard School of Public Health) is correct that AIDS is caused by a virus related to the African Swine Fever Virus, then there is evidence that the CIA itself is responsible for introducing the disease in the western hemisphere. A *Newsday* article reprinted in the *Boston Globe* (1/9/77) reports that CIA operatives received the virus at Ft. Gulick (a CIA biological warfare training station in Panama) then travelled to Navassa (a U.S. controlled island just off the coast of Haiti) and then to Guantanamo — the U.S. naval base on the island of Cuba — where the virus was spread to Cuban pigs. From there it spread to the Dominican Republic (1978), to Haiti (1979) and reappeared in Cuba in 1980. According to James E. D'Eramo, the African Swine Fever Virus in Haiti initially "killed 80 to 100 percent of the pigs in a given location, but as it spread from one pig feeding lot to another the mortality rate of the pigs decreased to a mere 3 percent." Currently, according to Dr. Teas, "the Canadian, Mexican and U.S. governments are in the process of destroying the pig population of Haiti in an attempt to control the current African Swine Fever Virus infection, with the United States footing the $18 million bill" (*N.Y. Native*, #64). Would it be possible that — given $100 million — the doctors would just decide to kill all the queers, Haitians, and intravenous drug users exposed to AIDS?

The African Swine Fever Virus theory would suggest that the CIA effort in Cuba got out of control, spread to Haiti and then to people. A newly published book (*A Higher Form of Killing, The Secret Story of Chemical and Biological Warfare* by Robert Harris and Jeremy Paxman, 1982) suggests a more sinister possibility. In their epilogue, the authors point out the chemical and biological warfare and research continue in the United States under the Department of "Defense" — known as the Department of War before 1947. The current one and a half trillion dollars allocated for war leaves plenty of room for circumventing the rules of international law. In testimony before the House Committee on Appropriations in 1969, a military spokesman explained: "Within the next 5 or 10 years, it would probably be possible to make a new infective micro-organism which could differ in certain important respects from any known disease-causing organisms. Most important of these is that it might be refractory to the immunological and therapeutic processes upon which we depend to maintain our relative freedom from infectious disease." Further, a 1975 military manual promises forthcoming "'ethnic chemical weapons' which would be designed to exploit naturally occurring differences in vulnerability among specific population groups" (pp. 240-41). AIDS sounds just like such an ethnic weapon which knocks out the immunological defenses of the individual. Certainly

if such research has been pursued in the Department of War/Defense, they must already know a lot about how to turn on and off the immunological defenses. The U.S. Military attitude towards lesbians and gay men should be well known: they claim we are unfit for service.

Agent Orange (with its dioxin component and relatives) should be studied closely for parallels or links with AIDS. The U.S. government has certified that Agent Orange is harmless — an excellent example of manifest dishonesty and unreliability in medical research. The International Symposium on Herbicides and Defoliants in War (Ho Chi Minh City, January, 1983) found that dioxin toxicity includes "1. chronic hepatitis; 2. disturbances in immune function; 3. disturbances in lipid and porphyrin metabolism; and 4. neurological abnormalities, sometimes associated with a toxic neurasthenic syndrome." One of the significant discoveries of Vietnamese scientists has been that dioxin causes damage to the sperm similar to nuclear radiation. Sperm has, of course, been suggested as an agent in AIDS transmission; also one of the primary effects of Agent Orange is rapid and premature aging, another part of the Acquired Immune Deficiency Syndrome.

The difficulty with AIDS is only superficially medical. True, we don't know the cause or the treatment for the disease. But for syphilis we do know the cause and we do have an effective treatment and have had since the 1940s. For religious reasons the disease has been retained in order to punish people for their sexual liberties. We allow this because too many people feel that what they call "promiscuity" inevitably leads to its own punishment — death, disease and destruction. The CDC doctors (all white men) called it "Bad Blood" and some even after the relevations of 1972 believed they had been smeared by the press despite the good work they were doing.

Instead of checking out the CIA, the CDC or the medical-pharmacological establishment, too many gay people readily surrender to the lie that our sexuality is crippling us. They say our sex is adolescent, compulsive, retarded, irresponsible, sinful, and dreadful. Such teaching has encouraged the spread of syphilis and such teaching will surely impair our struggle against AIDS. We must not trust doctors, politicians or other professionals to do for us what we must do for ourselves. We cannot let others (however well-intentioned) speak for us. ☙

THERE'S SOMETHING ABOUT STUPIDITY
by James H. Hopkins

Pincus-Witten, New York art critic, has written a stupid book called *Maximalism.* It is full of super-ficialities and the mindless jargon of contemporary art criticism. No doubt it will quickly fall into the abyss of ten cents bargains at the Bryn-Mawr book sale, but before it does I believe it offers a good opportunity to reaffirm some simple truths which he so glibly dismisses or ignores. There is a mildly amusing picture I've seen somewhere of a group of Boy Scouts sitting around a camp fire each with his hand encircling the erection of the boy next to him; all of the boys are staring straight ahead with huge grins on their faces; it is entitled "Circle Jerk." This picture is the art world as seen through the eyes of Pincus-Witten. Contemporary art is produced by a kind of mutual masturbation; the artist's main con-cern is to imitate previous styles or invent new styles which are in turn to be imitated. Pincus-Witten suggests that it is the sole occupation of the artist to chase a "style bus," and after a mad dash to grab the pole and swing aboard only to discover that the "style bus" terminates at the next block, he has to leap off and start all over again. Now, this perhaps does have merit as a kind of intellectual gymnastics,

and may indeed be an accurate reflection of Amer-ica as a country devoted to conspicuous consump-tion, waste and superficiality, but it is my conten-tion that it is not the way art is made here or anywhere else. Just as surely as Mr. P-W is a con-noisseur of the most obscure and transitory styles in painting, it is just as sure he is master of obscure and transitory English. First, take his term *"Max-imalism."* (Try saying that aloud and you'll see what a mouthful it is.) The sense of the word is so indef-inite as to be meaningless. Maximalism? Maximum paint? Maximum size? Maximum color? Maximum ideas? What the hell does it mean? I'm afraid not much. Or try this one: "Schnabell's primary formal concerns address the question of how to apply paint to disruptive and 'sociographic' surface-art for arts's sake. All of his 'iconography' and 'iconology' is pre-textual. Nor is this necessarily a failing. Such mat-ters are purely neutral." Thank God they are neu-tral! We'd be in a hell of a mess if they meant something. Or take this next which is quite typical. "There is the difficulty and disagreeableness of il-legibility of image, the disjunctive and near hap-hazard character of the work; then again, there is the conjunctive character of the visual intelligence which is capable of missing — as an act of will — two layers of visuality. The 'support' may be more properly seen as a kind of 'depth of field'. And paint-ing becomes not an action on the surface, but ac-tions perpetuated within an arbitrary relief-like cor-ridor of space." (Why does that last remind me of Luke Skywalker in *Star Wars*?) But I should have known what I was in for when words like "inter-face," "acculturation" and "attributed content" be-gan cropping up. The whole thing carries me back

GRAVITATION

Lucian Popescu

to my original image however, with the added observation that maybe this time the masturbation is more like private "self abuse." There is something really perverse about P-W's definition of a successful art critic. A good critic he says, referring to Clement Greenberg, is one who champions artists whose work survives. I always thought a good critic (if there is such a thing) is one whose good judgment and taste allowed him to pick the wheat from the chaff. But finally, let us turn to the really disturbing void in Mr. P-W's arguments. I say void because only once does he mention the missing aspect, and like his scientific brethren dismisses it as irrelevant. He says early in his book, "Astonishing as it may be, many people still haven't gotten around to admitting that 'quality' most often means the attribution of a specious transcendency to work that merely corresponds to an *a priori* set of features concerned wholly with formal components. More, such attributions are probably no more than a nostalgic sentimentality inescapable of dying bourgeois aestheticism." Poor Pollack! Poor Rothko! You really were only tormented by formalist bugbears and not a vision of a spiritual reality as you thought! That last sentence is tired Marxist jargon. In another context (his introduction, which is uncharacteristically pretty clear and vigorous) he says: "that is, 'art as religion,' (is) something one either believes or does not. It is a matter of faith. I do not say I lack this faith. I only say it is futile to pretend that articles of faith can rationally be discussed in other than a historical way, as a branch of history of religion. All transcendental defense, like religion, ends up with the belligerent 'my book is better than your book.' " Now again it would take me a long time to adequately deal with all of this but I only point out that to say the transcendental aspect of art cannot be discussed does not refute transcendental arguments, it only refuses to discuss them. The whole attitude strikes me rather like the husband who says to his wife, "I don't want to talk about it!" when she brings up the subject of the other woman.

Well, in spite of P-W's *caveat* I will discuss the metaphysical aspects of art, because art without transcendental value is little better than Aunt Tillie's snapshot of Niagara Falls raised a notch by technical facility. In what follows I will be forced to use simple words long current in the language and possibly with religious overtones, but at least I do not mean to be sectarian and hopefully the terms will be accepted in the common sense way they are usually used.

The fundamental void in P-W's views of the artistic process is precisely his refusal to discuss the fact that the success of a work of art is dependent on the degree to which the work of art is a communication between two human souls. An artist who lacks this fundamental element of soul may indeed be forced to build the substance of his art on permutations of previous art, or the invention of new "styles" as P-W contends. (We are tempted to ask in passing where P-W thinks these new styles come from.) Now, I am not denying the importance of the historical process, but if there is anything that has been proven by the perspective of time, it is that art which is motivated by looking backwards is dead art. What else? While it is true that every artist reviews his own art history and to a more limited extent art history outside himself, if he is not responding either consciously or unconsciously as a human being to the *world outside of art*, he is simply a snake eating his own tail. Not only must the artist react to the world he lives in outside of art, but he must struggle to bring something into being which will arouse a response in another human being that will communicate something about the human condition in this world outside of art. Oh, I admit that one of the responses to a work can be an appreciation for the evolution of styles as P-W contends, but it is only one and a decadent one at that. Indeed, there are dozens of other responses possible of greater or lesser merit than the consideration of style. But I submit that the one that is most profound, and likely to endure, is the recognition between the artist and the viewer, of the spiritual dimension of the historical age they share and the spiritual commonality of being human. It is true that the artist uses his artistic means, or style, to communicate, but, what he communicates is not style but this transcendental experience. To maintain less is to suggest that love is sex, happiness is in material possessions and the immeasurable universe is only a mathematical puzzle. Let me pick as a first example to illustrate my meaning the Raphael Madonna in the National Gallery. I don't think that even in those who today profess to being Christian that the "iconography" arouses the reverent response it did when the picture was painted. This, granted, is obvious, and also it is obvious that the art-historian who points out St. John hanging about the corner doesn't help either. So where does this leave us? Does it reduce us to saying that the "style" is what endures? I think not. Rather it is that we respond through the superb technical means of the painting to the profound spiritual experience of the artist that guided and motivated him in making the picture. We vibrate, in harmony with the painting, as if hearing a melody vaguely remembered that makes us smile privately and for a brief moment feel a unity with all things and there is no pain. It seems to me that if we do not make this connection, our response will be limited to admiration for style and the painting becomes more related to the skills of the circus than to those of art. Let me add to this, lest it be misunderstood. The response I've described to the Raphael painting is only one possible response, as the human spirit in its spiritual longing is multifarious, I will even admit that the response I have described is "poetic," transcendental if you will. In which case let us take a more direct example. Our appreciation of the painting of Edvard Munch must respond to the angst and suffering of this tormented man on some level or his paintings do not "work" for us. Unless we do, there is little left because as P-W himself points out, Munch was not a particularly skillful painter. The poor bastard, though. I fear that most people who saw his show, never really touched the raw nerve of the paintings which form their heart and soul and which drove Munch to the insane asylum. What these observations point out, obviously, is that it is the spiritual insight and sensitivity of the artist that ultimately determine the quality of his work and not his mastery of a particular style or even the invention of a "new" style. I could compound the list of examples. Even Matisse's desire to mollify the tired businessman is more a spiritual desire than a materialistic one: or consider Cezanne and his monastic existence: poor Gauguin, do you mean to tell me that the demons that pursued him to the ends of the earth were problems of style? And Mark Rothko, saying that if "people understood his paintings, the world would be at peace" is only a formalistic concern? I wish it were as simple as P-W thinks. To imitate or invent a new "style" in the sense he means is easy compared to the real thing. Then, to quote P-W quoting a fellow critic, it's only a matter of "making it to the store first." We hear so much about the "artistic struggle" that it becomes a cliche to be sneered at, yet of the artists I admire, known and unknown, and that the world seems to revere for their enrichment of human life on this tortured planet, the vast majority did indeed struggle and persevere against incredible odds, against all rational sense, to pursue their own vision. And I submit that these were intensely personal, transcendent dreams and nightmares, and that their styles, gleaned from their own searches and experiments and the outside art that surrounded them, was a means of communicating this vision and not an end in itself. I must believe this. I must have faith that this is so; that art is a means of awakening a spiritual response in another human being. I believe this for a quite simple reason — because the alternative offered by P-W is so shallow as to overwhelm me with horror and revulsion and would make my life and life in general, meaningless.

HELEN VENDLER'S BUTCHER SHOP
by William Corbett

The Harvard Book of Contemporary American Poetry, edited by Helen Vendler (Belknap/Harvard University Press)

Helen Vendler's anthology proclaims the Age of Lowell and ten thousand men of Harvard (Harvard University Press at least) want victory today! Believe me I tried to kill the impulse to write that sentence, but any other tone seemed inappropriate to such a silly book. Harvard University Press may now claim for itself a piece of the pie long in the hands of The Oxford Book of and Vendler's canon will surely become gospel for a few, but contemporary American poetry has been so mauled in the process it is nearly unrecognizable. There is so much more to American poetry of the last forty-five years that what Vendler has left out mocks what she has seen fit to include.

Nowhere does Vendler come right out and state that she is promoting Robert Lowell to the head of the class, but his name dominates her preface. She begins with a quote from his poem "Epilogue" and goes on to claim that the poem "best sums up the aesthetic predicament of our present poets." To make the case for Lowell's dominance, and for the significance of all the poets she has chosen, Vendler redraws the map of recent American poetry so as to exclude the Black Mountain school, the Objectivists and all but eliminate William Carlos Williams. Such a snap of the fingers seems contemptuous of the very rich nature of the poetry with which she seeks to "charm" her readers.

Olson, Creeley, Dorn, Duncan, Levertov and Wieners are absent from the book. Zukofsky, Reznikoff and Oppen might just as well have written in a foreign language. Not only are they absent, but no poet who bears the mark of their influence is in this book. The place that Williams might occupy in the history of American poetry Vendler gives to Wallace Stevens. Vendler does so not because she has written extensively on Stevens, but because Stevens "flowered late" and "is the chief link between the earlier high modernists (Eliot, Pound, Williams, Crane, Moore) and the later poets." Reading this, it is difficult to keep a straight face. Stevens is a great poet, but it is possible to imagine 20th century American poetry without him. It is simply impossible to imagine American poetry of this century without Williams. It is one of the glories of Stevens' poetry that it does *not* connect with that of Eliot, Pound or Crane. If there is a link Williams is it, and that link runs through *The Descent of Winter, Spring and All, Paterson* and "Asphodel, That Greeny Flower." Lowell himself read Williams closely and in his last poems arrives at a measure of Williams' freedom.

After Stevens the anthology is arranged chronologically by birthdate beginning with Langston Huges (b. 1902) and ending with Rita Dove (b. 1952). The period it covers is roughly 1940 to the present, and since there is no date of closure the implication is, beyond. Few will quarrel with many of the poets Vendler includes. Ammons, Ashbery (third behind Stevens and Ginsberg in number of pages), Bishop (rescued from "The Fish" and "Roosters" — a fine selection), Hughes, O'Hara (skimpy), Jarrell (no more than a nod in his direction), Rich, Roethke, Simic and James Wright will have a place in any comprehensive anthology of this period. Her exclusions aside, there are few surprises here. Only Howard Nemerov's inclusion surprised me. Since Vendler's taste does not accommodate the mavericks of recent American poetry, Jack Spicer, Philip Whalen, Kenneth Rexroth (Gary Snyder represents the West Coast on Vendler's map), Lorine Niedecker, Robert Kelly, Sterling Brown (a maverick by virtue of neglect) and Hayden Carruth do not belong.

The blandness of this book comes in part from Vendler's disregard of small presses. Only Allen Ginsberg and Albert Goldbarth (b. 1948 and the only poet in the book new to me) have made their reputations publishing in small presses. Vendler depends, as she has as a critic, on the books published by New York's large commercial publishers. Were she making this anthology in 1935 Pound and Williams would find themselves on the outside.

As for her choice of poets born during and after WWII Vendler has passed her hand over, and is gambling on, Dave Smith, Louise Gluck, Albert Goldbarth, Michael Blumenthal, Jorie Graham and Rita Dove. If I were them, I would not be flattered. Blumenthal, Dove and Goldbarth have barely begun their careers, and they may wonder why they were chosen over Bernadette Mayer, Ron Padgett, Alice Notley, Michael Palmer, Bill Knott, James Tate and August Kleinzhaler. In extending her canon into the immediate present, and placing bets on the future, Vendler is out on a limb as uncertain as the Stevens one which broke under her.

Part of Lowell's prominence for Vendler must be that she sees him in such a flattened landscape. The poets she allows the reader to measure him against are Ashbery, Bishop and Ginsberg. The field is so limited that the race has been decided beforehand. When she compares him to Pound Vendler argues that Lowell as a chronicler of history calls Pound's history into question. Perhaps, but the sonnets from Lowell's *History* she selects put the artificial "weighty blocks" (her phrase) of that work enough in this reader's mind so that he remembers Lowell's history as Kings, Queens, Napoleon, wars, power and violence — textbook history. Her selection emphasizes the personal side of Lowell's endeavor, but this is only a part of that monotonous drumbeat of a book. If, as she claims, Pound displays "artificial helplessness" before the past is it a strength of Lowell's that he turned centuries of history into sonnet after sonnet like sausages?

When I first looked at Vendler's anthology I was somewhat outraged. What other response can there be to Amy Clampitt's (b. 1920) three poems that glug like heavy cream poured from the bottle and seem written to be paraphrased and no Olson, no Niedecker, no James Schuyler or Barbara Guest? But my outrage quickly became bemusement. Something of American poetry is indeed here, but I can only be bemused, even as the image is horrifying, at the surgeon who saws, hacks and sutures a healthy body to claim life for a hank of hair, piece of bone, lung and elbow. That there *is life* here despite all that has been cut away suggests how robust American poetry has been over the past forty-five years. But to get a clear idea of just how robust, peculiar, contrary and vital that poetry is we will need a doctor other than Vendler.

JIM GUSTAFSON & IVAN SUUANJOFF

Mircea Eliade is dead. He spent his life investigating the history of the eternal return. He was a poet of the mysteries whose mysteriousness he brought home to us like food. He was a great warrior for human beings in an increasingly mechanical world. His writings point to the possibilities of a defense, based on the endlessly generative power of myth. The modern world, he warned us, suffers from ontological amnesia. Eliade reminded us constantly of our original mandate. In one of his dreams, he saw his coffin flying across continents and oceans, coming to rest at last in his native village in Romania. In one of his stories, a young soldier's soul wanders about confused amid the surge of many other dying souls. There are rumblings of War this sweet Spring, and portents of a mass exodus of souls from the planet. We don't know which loop of the eternal return carries the soul of Mircea Eliade in its journey, but we call on the Great Spirit to quickly return him to us. If possible, we'd like it to fill us with Mircea Eliade. We'd gladly make ourselves host to his great soul.

CHER CADAVRE EXQUIS

ROLL YOUR OWN ANTHOLOGY

Helen Vendler's anthology did seem kind of silly, at least based on looking at the table of contents while browsing books in Harvard Square. I feel like I have been enough a part of "Contemporary American Poetry" for the past decade to know that an anthology that proclaims itself to contain that artform between its covers has to be catholic in its taste. I have also been a part of this game long enough to know that anthologizing poetry is an art in itself, one with few successful practitioners. I'll take Bill's word for it that Vendler fails. I didn't think I would admire her taste, and she does not seem to share mine when it comes to who to include or exclude from the required reading list. It is, after all, a question of who you respond to as much as anything else. But I am not writing to argue over names. Instead I offer a suggestion and a tale. Suggestion: If you don't like *The Harvard*

Book of Contemporary American Poetry make your own. The impulse is there, so why suppress it, particularly in this age when nothing sells and anyone can be a publisher.

Tale: In the spring of 1982 I was working at fabled Harvard University as a catalog editor. I had a student visiting me from the college I had attended, one Kenyon College where both Poetry and Plato were considered to be a Big Deal. This student was a pleasure to work with, and an English major as I had been. So we got to talking about poetry. Of course Kenyon is the other college that Robert Lowell attended, when Harvard applied a little too much mental pressure on him. When the National Guard started shooting students at nearby Kent State in 1970 one Kenyon English professor pulled out *For the Union Dead* in an attempt to appear relevant. Robert Lowell was taught and I remember being not impressed. It was Allen Ginsberg, Robert Duncan, and Gary Snyder that we read among ourselves, and it was these people that I went to see and hear. I was curious if any of the people I had been reading when I was in college ten years before (not reading in English classes but among my peers) were still on the minds of English majors. You people who teach college these days will not be surprised to hear that the answer was no. My visiting student didn't know anything about Jack Spicer or Charles Olson, had not heard of Frank O'Hara or Gary Snyder. I wanted to remedy this and give her something to read. I had been introduced to these poets by anthologies published in the 1960s: Donald Allen's *The New American Poetry* and the Kelly/Leary *A Controversy of Poets* were primary sources. I was looking for an "updated" version of this, but it wasn't there. So I thought I would do my own. By that summer I was working at a part of the university where I had access to a large computer system which included a text editor, formatter, and a high-quality laser printer (which in 1982 was big, rare, and expensive). I also wasn't too busy that summer so I set to typing work by my favorite poets. Who do you include? Well, right away I was able to free myself from the greatest barrier: representing a period. All I had to represent was what I had and continue to respond to in poetry. I didn't have to pretend, as I assume Helen Vendler did, that what I chose represents the period, a period in which American men and women of various political, sexual, cultural and economic orientations have been using poetry as a means of expression. I looked over my collection of books, read through the ones I read over and over again, and found that I was compelled to include work by 13 poets. In my case these were limited to members of the generation I had learned from, and so they did not include any poets born since 1940. What do you include? Well, there were a couple of things that became clear. Again there was nothing to represent except the poet's strengths, so the poems were simply the ones that struck the deepest, whatever their form or length. And the true acid test was in the typing. I did a magazine for a few years, a pleasure shared by a large number of *Corpse* readers and contributors I suspect, and this magazine was produced from mimeograph stencils that I produced on my typewriter. I learned there that typing a poem is a special kind of reading. You can't type and proofread things you don't like, unless you're getting paid for it. So I produced *A Personal Anthology* that fall. It was 120 pages, including a short bibliography of what books the poems could be found in, and was printed "on demand" on the laser printer for anyone who was interested. The technology that I used has changed a great deal in the past few years. Many writers now have some kind of computer available to them. The amount of information that can be stored cheaply on these machines is equal to many hundreds of book pages. The cost and availability of the kind of printer that can produce a page worth reading has improved. They now cost a few thousand dollars, rather than $860,000, still too expensive for most people. Hopefully they won't be too expensive for long. But to keep our eyes on the future I must add that I find myself this year working on an example of the ultimate anthology-building kit: a collection of all of classical Greek literature. In this case the typing has all been done by someone else. We have the full text of all the writers who wrote in Greek, from Homer to St. Basil, already entered. It's already indexed by word, author, work, chapter, and verse. It even includes *Anthologia Graecae*, but then with the aid of the computer you can make your own and print it out in a few minutes. So here we have the equivalent of the Loeb Classical Library plus a lot of indices, and it can all fit on a single compact disk the size of an open palm. These are the same compact disks you now see in the record stores pressed with the ultimate high-quality digital recording of your favorite music. And unlike the situation in 1982 the

collected poems of many of my favorite thirteen, such as Olson, Ginsberg, Creeley and Blackburn, are now in print. If someone was willing to do the typing we could put them all on a single disk, along with everyone else's favorite thirteen. In fact we could put recordings of your favorite thirteen reading your favorite poems on the same disk with the poems themselves, and you could choose to read, listen, or read and listen at any particular time. We could put picture in too, but then it would end up looking like the talking heads of the *American Poetry Review* which is pretty boring. Better to contemplate the profound sarcasm of Ed Dorn's text, and then if you're in the mood, listen to it.

So the plan for the 1990s is we'll let Penguin or Oxford or Warner Communications put everything on a compact disk and then anyone can program their own anthology, which is after all just a body of literature filtered through somebody else's sense of taste. I propose that we start distributing the body; let the body be public and maintain taste as a personal thing. There's room for Louis Simpson and Joanne Kyger, as long as someone's willing to type them in. If someone loves Louise Gluck's work, she'll be there, don't worry. Then those of us who want someone else's taste can go down to the store and pick up *The Harvard Filter of Contemporary American Poetry* by Helen Vendler. The rest of us can roll our own.

— Paul Kahn

"ANOTHER SLIM VOLUME OF MODERN ENGLISH POETRY!" SHRIEXED JACOBSEN

MESOZOIC MUCK SLAMMED

I'm not sure that having an excerpt from a letter of mine in the *Corpse* deserves sending me 5 copies, but thanks. Letters are some of the more entertaining things in *EC*. For instance, Eshleman's. Takes him two self-serving columns to inform us: 1) that "orgasm stimulates fantasy"... Hey, that's big news! Hark and take heed, everybody. And only a few thousand years late, while any adolescent with a hand will yawn with boredom at the obvious. But that's the forté of all self-important yakkers: belaboring and beating off platitudes as though they were mind-boggling perceptions. Where would we be without such urgent updates on the use of our equipment? And 2) as per later in the issue, what can't be supplied of sensory immediacy is glued and spittled together with shreds of caveman wallpaper bloated into aggrandized claims of which he knows nothing, not having been there... or are we to assume he's a reincarnation of Freddie Flintstone? — but no, Fred's much funnier. There seems to be a law which governs perceptual laziness: lay all inane grand claims in the general vicinity of some prehistoric bog for mythological reference when you're lame on particulars; softens the focus, also the brain. But anything to legitimize the baby-babble of which he is so fond and adept. Of course. If one believes that the mind is a liability, then losing it becomes a positive plus. And as for his "Taylor fantasy" (even entitles turds)... a real breakthrough in banality. Am sure Cecil would love to hear it; could do wonders for him. So, word is out. So, should we presume, in the murky light of his orgasmic insight, is Clayton's pecker? Out there right now solemnly "gratifying desire," waggin for dear life? Wag away, man, wag away, and thou shalt be granted subsidies to wag furtheraway in thine Mesozoic muck.

— Jack Marshall

CHRISTA DID NOT DIE IN VAIN

Eschatology certainly is catching — a live body each minute of the day at least. Funerals are our perhaps finest form of entertainment. Note our noblest efforts at rhetoric after the fiery death of seven aspiring human angels. Reagan doesn't even approximate Pericles' oration but it served the pur-

pose: tears of the pleasure of sorrow. It helps form us as a nation of pleasure seekers in the riskiest unknown. We already have drugs, pornography and smoking. Christa did not die in vain.

— David Ignatow

CAN BOB DYLAN TAKE CARE OF HIMSELF?

Clayton Eshleman's letter was interesting (in my case, fantasy stimulates orgasm), but I disagreed with a few of his points — I'm not even worried about song lyrics — I figure Bob Dylan can take care of himself — but I was concerned about "if the audience responds immediately to something it has never heard before, chances are what it is hearing is less than poetry." Wait a second!! What about humor?? Is an audience supposed to be a collection of minors to which the Artiste contemplates his or her Bomber Self?? Lighten up, Clayton. Poems are supposed to be funny (not to mention silly). (After one of my readings, this girl told me she really liked it — she said, "I laughed my ass off" — that made me feel good — it meant we communicated at a level greater ((and lesser)) than mere words — real poems are invisible — the words aren't important — the communion with other souls is.) The only poems in this *EC* I really liked were the ones by Christy Sheffield Sanford. I definitely want a longer Corpse — & I want it every week (watch out *Newsweek!*).

— Chris Toll

HAT-SIZE AND WORLD PEACE

I read with great interest and amusement Kirby Olson's essay "Skull-Size and World Peace" and it occurred to me that world peace may not have to wait the millennia required for enough mixing of the human gene pool to achieve uniform skull-size. Such an event is unlikely anyway as some environmental force would be necessary to make one particular skull-size a desirable evolutionary trait. If we could just make sure that the negotiators representing the USA and the USSR at the Geneva arms control talks have the same hat-size we may be one step closer to world peace.

— Michael Byers

POEMS BY JANET GRAY

I DECIDED NOT TO BURN DOWN THIS CITY AND MYSELF IN IT, or, DIDO RECONSIDERS

(after Rich & Beefheart)

Whoever works in this room could work
   anywhere.
On the wall: a photograph
of this person working in a car —
bare knee, scrunched satin gown, headless
   shoulders,
flamingo arms and hot dog fingers
working under the dashboard of the car
on a tropical night.

Whoever works here is a hot dog worker.
The obligatory mess: black trays
spilling paper, several scungy mugs,
typed pages piled unblemished
at the edge of the light:
these are for sale.

In the black book in the triangle of light
are the pages not for sale:
you don't work in this room
without thinking of poetry as the guerrilla night
   life
of someone who fights to be passable...
poems as fruit
hurled at a blank page bound to other pages.

Thinking of the young girls who go out at night
to hear men sing. Of lovers parting.
The man with a destiny
in the striped light of a city
the woman home with inflamed marrow.

I have worked to prove I could
in spite of my crazy secret:
that the helpless lust, the cities
are absurd. I will not
step out into the striped light:
I will stay in the triangle.
But I will not allow my bones to ignite.

*   *   *

It was simple to deceive you, simple to keep you
believing I was not what I am. You
were the night monster singing in the hot light...
There we met. Simple (when we were alone)
to tell you I loved you and take your jeans
in my hands...love was enough bribery.

What was hard: because you thought
I was a man you became like me
and I less like myself. Nights
with your softness, some gift,
a blue toy, your wordless pleading. Waking
to a charred world with no people in it.
Not remembering...who left, why,
what I did about it. Whether I had
anything to do with it.

Knowing I was the lover,
you a visitor who resembled me.
The throb I loved before
in you was mine: *I want to live.*
I want to make instruments scream.

Come out, young girls, come out.
I am the monster tonight.

* * *

It's simple to rise from work to a world
without people, sleep, rise
and work again. It isn't simple
to rise a thief with a blue rose frozen
in your brain, beyond seven doors, behind
a wall of ice. And the princess waiting.
Tropical payday and what do the women do?
I burnt down Carthage
but not myself in it...

                             I made these.

I want to say I made the walls that stood here
before the fire.
My body was immune to sacrifice.
The patterns of need were in disorder and fought
for space on the edge.

THE EVIDENCE OF THE PINK DETECTIVES

You have to deal with the
evidence of your sense, though there
is other evidence — conversions, little disasters,

back pain. I hear
an assortment of things!
The light bill going up,

and what we love so
much — foreign music & coffee water —
I hear them on borrowed time.

The Pink Detectives are on TV tonight.
On the table is a navel orange.
Beyond that, the answer is no, no, no.

AMNESIS MANIFESTO
by Nicomedes Suárez Araúz

The totality of human existence is circumscribed by amnesia. Our collective amesia (that immense void in our universal history) is paralleled in our individual lives: in the absences in our memory of birth, first years of life and the myriad forgotten incidents of daily life. As Cesare Pavese expressed it, "We remember instants, not days."

Amnesia is part of every gesture, every look, every attempt we make at remembering and thinking. It is not unconsciousness; it is a stalking presence that erodes, shapes and refines our lives. Each one of our thoughts and memories has been molded and subverted by our amnesia. The world of amnesia and absences is a universe coexistent with the realm of memory and presences.

W. B. Yeats noted our longing for what passes away, saying that "Man is in love, and loves what vanishes." Our amnesia, both personal and collective, implies a continual loss of everything that is ours or is near us: a world of irrecoverable lost objects. The scribes of Loén wrote about this:

Found Objects may surprise us with their revealed qualities; Lost Objects pain us with the resplendence of their absence. The history of the world and of our lives is largely a process of discarding: we live on little details, we die on little details and we burn to live. Those shed objects glow with the incandescence of our inner selves. Our greatest loss has been the millions and millions of years, unrecorded by history, touching on infinity: a vast expanse of immemoriality or amnesia. This amnesia encompasses the enigma of the arts of lost objects. As such, these works of art are *letters to amnesia* — their intimations recover for us the sense of the infinite. They, like messengers of amnesia, flutter with the melancholy and joy of things that have become invisible.

Without an awareness of amnesia the arts do not have a complete vision. We are, in large measure, what we have lost and can never recover or recall.

The history of amnesia as a theme is a vast crevice in time. It extends quietly and implacably across the thoughts of men and women who struggled to uphold the presence of their creations, of their expanding memory: their history.

Many of those who have believed in a world previous to our birth often believed in a limbo of amnesia — a state or stage through which we all pass or enter at the moment of our birth. For the ancient Chinese, it was a passage through the gates of Hell. There Lady Mêng compelled all souls re-entering the wheel of transmigration to drink the Min-hun-t'ang, the Broth of Oblivion, which would erase all the memories of their previous lives and knowledge.

Plato, in the 4th century B.C., amazingly coincides with this belief in his notion of *anamnesis*. For Plato, amnesia offers an epistemological explication — our learning in life is the shedding of the forgetfulness that overtook us at birth. All knowledge is a remembrance of the ideal realm which our soul knew before it came into this world.

Another writer (or keeper of memories), Plutarch, in the 1st century A.D., lamented how oblivion turns every occurrence into a non-occurrence. In the 16th century, Michel de Montaigne bemoaned the aberration of memory caused by forgetfulness. In 1726, Jonathan Swift in *Gulliver's*

Travels depicted a group of decadent men whose memory does not outlast the movement of their eyes from line to line of text — hence, they are condemned never to enjoy the pleasure of reading. Six years later the epigrammatic Dr. Thomas Fuller clustered in a phrase a fact everyone suspects or knows: "We have all forgot more than we remember." (*Gnomolia*, 1732)

In the 19th century, William Wordsworth revives in memorable verse Plato's notion of amnesia: "Our birth is but a sleep and a forgetfulness." ("Ode to Intimations of Immortality") Some years later, Charles Baudelaire, following a long mystical tradition, would speak of the physical world as "a forest of symbols" whose meaning we have forgotten but that the poet can rediscover by means of his imagination. In the 20th century, from the world of *Ulysses*, James Joyce tells us that "the idiosyncrasies of the poet are concomitant products of amnesia."

The last four decades offer several examples of writers who have treated the theme of amnesia. Among them we find Jorge Luis Borges who, in his short story "The Immortal," presents men condemned to immortality, decrepitude and final oblivion of language. Gabriel Garcia Marquez in *One Hundred Years of Solitude* (1967) presents a void in memory from which language emerges and to which it returns. Milan Kundera in *The Book of Laughter and Forgetting* (1978) turns the theme into a gashing tool of political protest — we have forgotten because those in power have willed our oblivion by altering recorded history, by erasing traces.

The elegiac tradition in poetry often dwells on the theme of forgetfulness. We find it in poets as diverse as Mimnermus of Colophon (7th century B.C.), Sextus Propertius (1st century B.C.), Chang Chi (8th century A.D.) or, in modern times, John Milton (17th century), Johann Wolfgang von Goethe (18th and 19th century) and, in the 20th century, Rainer Maria Rilke and Pedro Salinas.

Evidently, the theme abounds in all eras and, in modern times, it has overflowed from literature into films, which use it primarily as a device to multiply the possibilities of the plot and to create or heighten mystery and suspense. The theme is ubiquitous, but its application as *structure* — as well as theme — of artistic works is unique to the Amnesis movement.

The history of amnesia is not only what has been written or created, but also what is present in us at every moment. Facing it, our mind is compelled — like an actor without a script — to improvise to feed the continuum of our existence.

We cannot remember, so we create. Our fictions can be products of our forgetfulness. We cannot remember our beginnings so we fabricate them with images and theories: Matter emerging from spirit; a Prime Mover; the Big Bang. (1) As Robert Jastrow has said, the cosmologist grudgingly recognizes that a curtain has been drawn — perhaps forever — to our possible knowledge of the inception of the universe and its early development. The theologian smiles with pleasure, seeing in that fact a proof that the eternal and the divine cannot be apprehended by reason.

At every turn in our lives, a crevice in our memory: Last Friday a full moon was shining. Or was it Thursday? It was a light yellow coin. Or did it have a greenish haze? An orange glow? Because you said it was going to rain the next day. I can't remember.

We'll have to construct it against a pearl black sky, out of cartilage and glass, wire and papier mâché, a coin, a white shadow, perhaps with thistles, yellow and ashen. And it will be there — a gap. A round hole on which we have constructed our moon which will evoke that absence — that lacuna in our memory.

Creation is brought forth by amnesia as much as it is by memory. Bertrand Russell in *The Analysis of Mind* (1921) postulates a world created a moment ago, populated by beings who recall an illusory past. (Freud called the fabrications of false memories by the psyche *paramnesia*.) *There* is the perfect creative amnesia: out of the present, an illusory past. A fiction.

We who recall you, Mnemosyne, Goddess of Memory, recall your daughters, the nine muses who feed on memory. Without memory there is no presence, there is no art. But memory is the form, that which the hand and the mind recall. Rhetoric is an aggregate, the remembrance of the gestures and efforts at creation of so many who came before us.

Memory is the form; amnesia can be the content. Amnesia seeps like a many-tongued fire between the firm fingers of traditional forms. Memory is essential to paint in a certain style, to cluster words in certain rhythms, to dance with certain body movements — all growing from the past.

Amnesia can be the content and can also inspire forms that memory helps to forge. Amnesia is the anti-Mnemosyne, a whirl of shadows, of crevices that enter and disperse everything. Amnesia crumbles the geometry of things and creates a world of strange relationships and dissociations in space and time.

To enter the kingdom of amnesia is to enter a world where names have been displaced by water and shadows. It is to find oneself again speechless, with one's heart beating without words. It is to face a tree, a house, a street, a cloud, a bird, a song — a world we cannot gather beneath the marble domes of traditional forms or labels from the past. It is to enter a world forever marvellous.

The creations of the Amnesis artist are *letters to amnesia*, messages to our individual and collective states of amnesia. (2) Without an awareness of amnesia, we cannot have a complete vision. The poetry, the painting, the music, the ballet, the theater of amnesia: forms of forgetfulness resonant with allusions, polyvalent in meanings, aesthetic objects that illuminate life.

But, what is the color of amnesia? What is the form of amnesia? What is the sound of amnesia? What are the gestures of amnesia?

We cannot know, but can imagine them. For example, we can imagine the visual forms of forgetfulness (as the plastic artists of Amensis have done) as parks full of images that resist being gathered into symbols, trees cut in half, ghost images of objects, lost alphabets, ephemeral gestures. Emblems and presence of the landscape of amnesia.

Giorgio de Chirico wondered at the possibility of entering a world where the links, the associations of memory have broken down. In his book, *Metaphysical Art* (1919), he writes: "I enter a room, I see a man sitting in an armchair, I see a bird in a cage, I see a painting on the wall; a bookcase with books...But now let us suppose, that for a moment the threads of memory were broken completely, since illogic is predicated on the loss of memory, who knows how I might then see the room. Who knows with what astonishment, what terror or what possible joy, pleasure and consolation one might view a scene in which one's memory was severed. How would the room look without memory?"

Facing amnesia, as the scribes of Loén say, "the artist, like the proverbial amnesiac of Eretria, fabricates stories to cover the voids in his memory ....The stories of the artist are those that lend themselves to the paint brush, to marble, to the

movements of his body, to music and to writing." The fables of the arts of amnesia are testimonies to the absences in our mind.

What words can represent the form or formlessness of amnesia? (3) Expressions (such as those written by the scribes of Loén) with an indeterminate semantical focus, or others composed in a fractured rhetoric, stories that makes us feel and understand the confusion, astonishment and vision of amnesia.

The theater and ballet of amnesia enter the realm of absences and presences that conforms amnesia. From light to darkness, from the visible to the invisible, from presence to what is hidden, from variety to a nuance that approximates uniformity and sameness.

Memory and amnesia are as much a part of music as sound and silence. A melody depends on remembrance verging on amnesia. The music of amnesia, like the *zikr* of Middle Eastern music, pursues the purest silence, which cannot exist in reality, but only in our psyche as a *forgotten* sound.

In the plastic arts, particularly since 1982, the expression of amnesia has rapidly expanded in the work of the artists of Amnesis. Surprisingly, aside from Giorgio de Chirico who hinted at the possibility of seeing amnesia as a creative premise, plastic artists throughout the ages have gathered beneath the shadow of Mnemosyne or Memory.

All art movements depart from certain assumptions or premises. Surrealism maintains that the deeply-embedded memories of the subconscious can be expressed, without rational control or esthetic and moral constraints, through formal approaches that range from the blob to figurative representation; Expressionism claims that the distortion of perceptual reality can reveal the soul or inner world of beings and things; Abstract Expressionism affirms that color has an affective and mystical quality; the attitudinal art of Marcel Duchamp assumes that the nominative act by the artist can render a common technological ware into an *objet d'art*.

The plastic arts of Amnesis assume that amnesia is immanent to the psyche, that our mind invents "fables" when confronted with forgetfulness, that the notion of the Lost Object is integral to aesthetic amnesia. Amnesis affirms that the "fables" of amnesia can be given a spatial dimension or structure much like mnemonics (techniques to assist and develop memory) attribute to memory artificial spatial arrangements (images set within invented *locis* or places). An Amnesis artwork succeeds to the extent that it enjoins us into an awareness and understanding of amnesia and its diverse implications.

The works of art of Amnesis adopt a symbolic representation (in the sense that a minimal spot of paint can act as a symbol). They include singular combinations of spatial and temporal planes, the indeterminate use of signs and self-reflexive fictionalization. It is an art the content and structure of which is fundamentally molded by the notion of amnesia and absence and not by presence and memory (be it conscious or, as in Surrealism, subconscious memory).

The essential elements of this art are:

(a) An anesthetic atmosphere allusive to amnesia created by the formal elements of the works of art — in painting, for example, by the allusiveness of perspective, line, form and color.

(b) The Lost Object as an emblem for the absences of amnesia. Such symbol may be an absent image or silhouette, a half-image, a fractured image, a ghost image, etc.

(c) The incongruous organization of disparate icons that suggests the bewilderment and dissociative effect of amnesia and that can lead the viewer to a singularly polyvalent semiotic reading.

(d) A sense of ahistorical or undifferentiated time. Memory operates by association in space and time (it has a geometry and a chronology); amnesia dissociates the normal arrangement of both. Some Amnesis painters represent this quality by a suitable manipulation of spatial planes.

(e) A sense of ephemerality implied by the notion of amnesia and often embodied by the transient nature of certain works of art and media.

(f) The link between linguistic elements (titles, letters, phrases, etc.) and the theme of amnesia.

The totality of human existence is circumscribed by amnesia: the amnesia of a *pre-history* entirely unrecorded, and the amnesia of a possible (thereby in itself a presence) *post-history* when the human race, by its own hand or because of a natural catastrophe, would be extinct.

The written history of mankind began barely five thousand years ago. From that point back to the inception of the universe we have a vast gap in our collective memory. And now, after that fateful August 6 in Hiroshima, we are overwhelmed by the visible threat of the possible annihilation of every human being and of all human memory. Our hand has added on a greater weight to that of the Biblical prophecy of an apocalypse. (4)

The problem of memory appears in large measure resolved. Writing and modern mnemotechnical machines, such as photo cameras, tape recorders, movies, videos and computers, scrupulously document our lives, dreams and fears. Yet, the waters of amnesia that run beneath us, as the scribes of Loén state, will always be with us. Our words, our gestures, our dwellings and all the supranature we have built will always be set on a sea of amnesia.

Amnesia can be considered, as the scribes affirm, as something terrifying and destructive, comical and beneficent, as a state of emptiness or a state which poetically alludes to all things. Amnesia is a psychical phenomenon and implies a metaphysical entity. There is something divine, something that frees us in forgetfulness. If we had flawless memories, our existence would be unbearable. On the other hand, the interior world of an amnesiac is one of confusion, bewilderment and terror. A world we cannot completely imagine but which we can intuit in our daily life.

Amnesia is a certainty; it is an undeniable presence and essence of our personal and collective worlds. It evokes — particularly in our days — the human condition, more than ever so tenuous and precarious. The arts of amnesia are an exaltation of the miracle of human life which survives, as the scribes say, "as a leaf on a sea of amnesia." To see that leaf vividly, we must look at the waters of forgetfulness. Thus we will pierce the blinding dome of our technological supranature, that thick covering of presences and memories, of facts and documentation which can prevent us from conceiving ourselves in the total context of the universe.

Amnesia can erase all things, as Plutarch said, and all things can be within it. It suggests the elemental void of the *creatio ex nihilo*; for some, it may evoke the vacuity of nirvana, but these notions are fundamentally colored by inhuman or superhuman implications. Amnesia is everything and nothing; qualities which have been attributed to divinities. But this divinity (unlike Mallarmé's mystical silence) does not dwell in a distant or recondite heaven but, rather, within us. She is the anti-Mnemosyne: a void and a plenitude in our lives. Memory emphasizes our differences; amnesia illuminates our similarities. Amnesia does not imply the negation of our memory; it implies the expansion of our consciousness.

The written record of mankind is the work of amnesia as much as it is of memory. A weave of words, of images and traces. Testimonies and fables. Amnesia has always been relevant to our destiny. History records references to psychological, historical, social and cultural amnesia.

Through the webs of memory, we can see the fables of the fountains of amnesia, fresh and sublime, humorous and joyful, traditional and new. A new vision of art, language and reality.

We who feel inspired to write, paint, create music, act, dance, produce films with the gestures of everything we have lost and can never recover or recall, sign our names as testimony of everything that has vanished in us.

(1) *Hans Vaihinger, in* Philosophy of the "As If" *(1911), influenced by Kant postulates that the fundamental concepts and principles of natural science, mathematics, philosophy, religion, ethics and jurisprudence are fictions which, although removed from objective reality, are useful instruments to act upon the world. In* Cours de linguistique générale *(1931), Ferdinand de Saussure, the founder of modern linguistic, insisted on the "arbitrary" character of language and its divorce from reality. This tenet dismantles the belief — suggested by our common sense — that there is a direct correspondence between word and thing, signifier and signified. The skepticism as to our ability to apprehend reality directly or of arriving at ultimate truth reaches its extreme conclusions in the work (since 1967) of the poststructural linguist Jacques Derrida.*
(2) *A "letter to amnesia" obviously cannot expect an answer: its very presence can be said to be its answer. On the one hand, the creations of Amnesis can be conceived of as open works (a term coined by Umberto Eco). That is, they are creations that are self-reflexive and indeterminate in meaning. In them, there is a free play of signs: they do not project a "message," but rather proliferate menaings. Paradoxically, however, these creations are also closed works since they are conceptually fixed on the notion of amnesia in all its implications. As open works, they delve into a questioning of the relationship be-*tween expression (all types of means of communication — phonetic, visual, etc.) and reality. As closed works, they embody a concept applicable to the human condition and destiny. The poetics of amnesia — like Hegel's dialectic or Aristotle's notion of infinity — can be seen as a pure mental construct and can be applied to external reality. In Vaihinger's conception, it is a useful fiction. The notion of a creative amnesia can prevent us from falling into the vagaries of extreme transcendence since amnesia is an immanent quality of our psyche.*
(3) *The reader will find a more detailed discussion and exemplification of amnesia as a creative premise in literary works in my introduction to the anthology,* Amnesis: The Arts of Amnesia and the Lost Object, *which Lascaux Publishers will present in 1986.*
(4) *The reader can imagine the overwhelming feeling of the Earth as a lost object, as the ultimate lost object. The concept of amnesia as an inspiration to artistic creation is intended, among other things, to emphasize in our expanding awareness of ourselves the preciousness and precariousness of human existence. It therefore acts, dialectically, as an exaltation of life and of the Earth. This humanistic aspect of Amnesis led R. Buckminster Fuller (the well-known architect and philosopher and key advocate of global self-determination) to support the Amnesis project in 1982.* ☠

Stephen Parlato

CLOSED FIGURE
by Stefan Brecht

1

His crazy gogo dancer's mask
reveals the high heels' wear, & neath it nakedness is strewn
for a delight of dumbness, but she
plays chess:
she fucks with all the earnestness of some young girl dressing before a date,
a perfume of sheer air ascending the shivering margins of her slender stretched-out figure,
in sublimation far indeed
— her charm like all charm infinite & sad —
of the gyrational machine, the bone mill, at her center, she
in energy of nothingness the stubbornness, a thermal abnegation, life
as shimmer: who is not nothing? but queerly, splendidly suspended
(her flanks from armpits to her thighs are sweaty)
like paper, glory-hued & Oriental of high-borne kites
above the splintry tossing crate wood of their cross staves:
her framework lines that never meet, her cunt gives to her bone cage
veracity:
while from behind her dancing shield she shoots her arrow into the darkness
beyond her lover's shoulder.

2

I am an old man now upon the count of time
and yet the flower grows upon my belly
on the occasion, on the occasion of this slender gogo dancer's naked craziness
inborn with grace, a picture drawing of delight:
a gift of time that with a playing child's intensity her drive devours
in growing earnest, my surprise, of giant eyes
& steady greed of belly. I am an old man now: upon the count of time
I'm here, provision of forgetfulness, not even quite as grateful (glory be)
as I might be were not this dancing waif so grandly generous:
unstinting in her labor, her face a blind of charity, her silence fire: gorgeous.

3

I make love to her cunt before we have sex.
She lets me but she would just as soon have me hold her and kiss her on the mouth.
Her cunt is small and neat
and nearly odorless.
I lick her not to get her ready
but because I love her cunt.
It is the center of her person
and it stands for all of her
and for all in her
that is open to me.

Faye Kicknosway

4

In trust she bloomed a flower on a tiny stage of light
and gave to men herself and their desire
and loved them, better: liked them
and was liked, and gaily counted
the crumpled bills in utter innocence and conscience
a little high, a little stoned, inebriated
by the exchange of gifts, until inevitably
hatred, exception foreordained, out of the darkness reached
and plucked her and crushed her, her confidence
betrayed.

5

In a classic confusion,
the victim instantly seeks
the identification with the perpetrator
seeks him out as co-conspirator,
bleeding yet, the face deformed
by the blow, forms an intimate alliance with him
and commences plotting, bringing him food and flowers,
a like deed against one unscathed as yet
that will prove she could not possibly be the one hurt,
that this could not have happened to her.

6

Having fucked her, though with many pauses, for three years, I find,
now that she's left me for another, her face, body & spirit interposing themselves
between her and her possible successors, so that, comparing, I cannot quite see them
or seeing them, solid, behind her picture in the air, measure them by their divergencies,
and count these deficiencies unacceptable. Thus to the panic of my old age is joined
a deep uneasiness that I may have made a mistake: too confident in my ability to go on & do better,
too fearful to take her up on her offers of a commitment,
too pettily critical of the expressions on her face and of her conversation,
unappreciative of her spirit, brutal in my fear. When I see her these days,
trying to free myself I greedily grasp the evidence of her aging. But I find her
incomparable.

7

The colors are fading from this long-stalked flower
that in a dry glass I have kept high above my desk
for now over a year long after
throwing out a good round half dozen
of roses, mistletoe, violets, gardenias,
the blue of its two flame-like stringy heads gracefully shaped
now very close to the parchment brown of the clusters,
high on its strident narrow stalk, of its leaves, so that now on this thistle, a present to me,
        the last one,
this difference that once made for its beauty is a gap
no greater than that between any two epochs in one's life
which is to say an instant and the next, a reminder
almost only, withdrawing, and with something like an antagonism toward me
the great structure of this one-time plant rises in my room's air
a strident diagram of life's beauty.

MIRROR SONG
by Edward Field

When you look, fierce face, in the mirror
    mornings,
is it absolutely necessary to groan?
It's not that you're ugly really, just old and
    ravaged
with, wouldn't you say, haunted eyes?
Well, you alone know what they've seen.

If your life has turned you into this, remember,
you've worked hard not to make it even worse.
Think of all the talking and screaming
therapies you've tried, not to mention
    acupuncture,

diet cures, years of yoga exercises,
and, as good as anything really, prayer.

Instead of hating your face, shmeggege,
can't you dredge up the least compassion
for what you've gone through? Tenderness
    perhaps?
Don't scorn yourself, give yourself a medal,
    pops —
it's been a long haul out of the pits, if you are
    out yet,
and you look it.

RECENT BORING LITERARY PASTIMES

by Diane di Prima

missing dead poets
dishing dead poets
wishing He had or hadnt fucked them
pretending He had when He hadnt
pretending He hadnt when He had

hating the language poets
hunting them thru wet streets
  thru cemeteries full of dead poets
  whose hats fell off in the rain

understanding the language poets
misunderstanding the language poets
hating linguistics because of the language poets
reading literary criticism or refusing to read it

getting lots of books & magazines in the mail
not getting books & magazines in the mail
reading the books and magazines you do or dont
  get
   throwing them out
   giving them away
   using them to prop up the frig
  (in whose freezer is the dismembered
   corpse of a dead poet)
reading the books but not the magazines
reading the magazines but not the books
not reading anything but the village voice
not reading anything but cereal boxes
not reading anything but sumerian doggerel
not reading anything anymore
not reading
reading incessantly at home in the rain

reading in dirty coffee shops
pretending to read in dirty coffee shops
  while seeking the ghosts of dead poets
  or their wives
  or mistresses
  or their grown-up punk kids
who kiss ass for publication in new age quarterlies

or who kiss ass for recording contracts
or who dont give a fuck & skateboard on South
 Van Ness
  waiting to be hit by a truck
  so they can become dead poets

deciding that poetry is political
deciding that poetry is an art
deciding that art is or isnt political deciding all
  artists
are dead & arent political

eating yr words
eating yr hat
eating the wet hat of a dead poet
in a cemetery full of dismembered freezers

remembering the 40's
remembering the samba
remembering rubbing elbows w/obnoxious dead
   poets in filthy bars in unmentionable
      neighborhoods

remembering shooting up w/dead poets
remembering ripping them off
remembering being ripped off & falling asleep
   w/yr chin in a portable royal typewriter
wishing dead poets were here
comparing them all to Lew Welch
or Jack Spicer who never heard of language poets
telling Ted Berrigan stories
pretending Frank O'Hara never said anything dull

admiring poets for being or not being gay
admiring poetry for being by or about women
   or indians, blacks, latinos, jews, et cetera
admiring ethnic poets of obscure sexual
  preference
   who probably stand hatless in the rain

AUTOINCINERATION OF THE RIGHT STUFF

by Ivan Argüelles

mambojive collapse of occidental managerial class system
all hands on deck throttle-down or throttle-up
autojam fluid sands icicle coated metal verbiage
the sun that living star is now matched in brilliance
by deity of the rose splendor of liquid fuel tensions inviolate
mining the air of the gods sarcophagus and luminous mummy
unquiet republic of the stars diamond planet rosicrucian destiny
"what will this do to our our program to reach JUPITER?"
who are these — methobapterian religious freaks? catholics? scientologists?
founding fathers of television stoneage democracy rubble
"for at least forty-five minutes debris kept falling from the sky"
to go with violence is not asking for but taking license to destroy
telekinetic molten riot it is noon everywhere in orbis stellarum
instamatic incineration of biogenetic code up in flames
feathers of the eyes of the gods who always suffered man's
walking on the lake of air and the darkness that proceeds
from the marginal leaf of supersonic literature in despair!
join me friends in arabic alembic prayer wheel top-siding
into magnum of eternal water the beaches are never free!
we eat our sandwiches with intact hands revolving our eyes into
celestial spheres where enigmatic buddhas automatic and impotent
exchange masks wives children automobiles electrodes DNA RNA
we suffer these things imagining swiftly the immediate demise of imagination
take my fingers off feed them to the impossible fish of URANUS
I hear their music their moons their clouds of insane love
THE MASTERGUIDE IS NO MORE IN THE NAME OF YAHWEH APOLLO AKHNATON
the supreme eye burns itself just as the numinous mouth devours itself
jazz cycles of infinity repeated on eternal screen Dan Rather
who will count the children? who will walk the dog? where are we?
suddenly air is impact the heaviest thing we can ever know

Jan Gilbert

THE CORPSE STORY
by Deborah Salazar

The first naked man Mrs. Hernandez ever saw was a corpse. The story is one she likes to tell in pieces; she usually begins by describing the black nails on the blue fingers or the dots of hair on the shaved head, and then she tells about the beautiful young doctor. Sometimes she leaves the doctor out. Not telling the whole story makes Mrs. Hernandez feel tender, womanly, enigmatic. She never tells the part about the love affair.

One spring day, not very long ago, Mrs. Hernandez was standing with her two mildly anorexic teenage daughters at a Wendy's salad bar. The girls were chattering about whether or not photographs of naked men turn women on as much as naked lady pictures turn men on. "I can't stand it if the guys are all hairy," Rosa, the younger one, was saying. "The darker they are, the hairier they are — I just can't stand it." Mrs. Hernandez reminded her girls that her first naked man was a dead man. He was all purple and parched to the bone. She told them that in her two years at the medical school in Guayaquil she'd never seen a fat *cadáver*.

Rosa heaped a spoonful of chickpeas onto her plate and told her mother to quit being gross. Piedad, the one with a booksack clung over her shoulder and Sylvia Plath biographies brimming out of it, wanted details — did the corpse have a hairy chest or a hairless chest? Mrs. Hernandez said she couldn't remember. But the anatomy professor at the Universidad de Guayaquil was young and handsome, she said. He had long black eyelashes and full red lips. He was her first great, utterly debilitating crush.

"Your first?" Rosa was surprised. This bit of information had never been included in the story before. "How *old* were you?"

"Eighteen, and very innocent. Also, very terrified." Mrs. Hernandez tried to explain to Rosa (who was fourteen and simultaneously in love with a jr. high track star, all her sister's boyfriends, and Al Pacino) that terror brings on the greatest passions. "I was scared of sex and I was scared of death," Mrs. Hernandez said. "When the sea heaves and the sky turns black, every woman falls in love with the captain of the ship. A Spanish proverb," Mrs. Hernandez said. "You girls should learn them all, know them by heart like me."

Three of the walls in the dining area of Wendy's were all glass. When Rosa, Piedad, and their mother sat down with their salads, they sat at a bright orange table in the middle of the sunlit restaurant. Mrs. Hernandez, sipping her iced tea, flashbacked to the familiar part of the story; she told her daughters that when her parents had seen that she wasn't going to grow up pretty enough to marry a doctor, they decided that they may as well allow her to go ahead and apply to the medical school. Rosa was listening dutifully, but Piedad pushed back her plate of plain lettuce (on which only a tiny peaked teaspoon of diet dressing had been applied) and pulled a spiral notebook out of her booksack. She licked the tip of her pencilpoint. "Please tell me about the dead man, Mama. What did the genitalia look like?

Mrs. Hernandez told Piedad to put away the notebook and eat her salad.

"But Mama, I'm going to write a poem." Piedad had decided to become a writer. The decision was one week old. Mrs. Hernandez liked the idea of her daughter writing poems. The activity seemed to go with the girl's thin, mournful face.

"I tell what parts of the story I want to tell," Mrs. Hernandez said.

"That's OK," Piedad said. She was tapping the eraser butt of her pencil on the table. "A poem isn't like a story. I can start any place I want."

Alright then. Mrs. Hernandez put down her little white plastic salad fork and began to tell about how her hands were pinched inside surgical gloves, about how sweaty she was — she was hot and breathing hard behind her surgical mask. She was terrified to pieces.

"This is wonderful," Piedad said. "You were a bride, weren't you? Behind a mask and everything."

Rosa was chewing her chickpeas and looking glum. "I don't get it," she said.

"What about the doctor?" Piedad wanted to know.

"You never say a whole lot about the doctor. You had a big crush on him and . . . ?" Piedad's voice lilted sweetly upwards on that last syllable.

Her eyes widened.

Mrs. Hernandez jutted her chin out a bit and heaved a sigh, the way she always did before beginning to talk about the young doctor. It was a gesture she'd affected after seeing *The French Lieutenant's Woman* for the first time. She kept her chin in the air for a while and tried to remember something lovely and true about the young doctor that she could tell her children. She didn't believe in inventing parts of her story; she believed that the most effective truths, not unlike the most effective lies, were ones that were not too detailed, not too knotted up with *extravaganzas*, indulgent fictions or desperate facts.

"He had this way," Mrs. Hernandez finally said in a slow serious voice, "of cupping one hand in the other when he was restless or bored. This way of touching himself carefully, the backs of his fingers stroking the cupped palm over and over." One night, when she'd walked in late to a lecture being given by a visiting professor, she'd looked all over the dark auditorium, over the unidentifiable lumps of heads of the audience until she spotted them — those restless hands, those small plump hands touching one another. Yes, *plump* hands. They were broad-palmed, and the fingers were short, tapered like a woman's. The nails were rosy, more violet than pink. More blue than violet. Yes, *blue*. And the veins on the backs of his hands showed clearly — they were blue too. One would think the hands would be cold, but they were not. Did he rub them together to keep them warm? They were not cold hands. "I *know*," Mrs. Hernandez said, "because he had this way — like Phil Donahue — of touching a woman on the elbow to emphasize a point." Or gingerly taking a hand. Oh, he wasn't slick. He was anything but. His kindness felt genuine, his touch was arm.

Piedad hadn't lifted her eyes from her notebook. Her pencil was doing double-time across the page. Rosa was poking at her last leaf of lettuce with a fork. When she spoke, it seemed to Mrs. Hernandez that she spoke in total aimless innocence: "Mama? Who was your second naked man?"

"Your father," Mrs. Hernandez lied. "Piedad, please eat your salad." ☙

THINGS TO DO AT 453 SOUTH 1300 EAST, WINTER '86
by Anselm Hollo

Read ten thousands lines
by the poets of Finland

translate two hundred and twenty-six

then sit & stare
across to where sky meets dead sea
out beyond the polis
of this valley

Think of SIERRA PLUG "The Ecological Chaw"

see hundreds of erstwhile
(*very* erstwhile) trees go up in smog
from the assholes of fast little vehicles

get up and eat some fast little vehicle

That mixed choir's really raving away on the
     radio

Now contemplate the wish baskets in the Xmas
     tree
slow down past the speed of light

see them go up & down up & down
floating across the desert & over the mountains

Feel gentleness invade you with the thought of
her who brought you here

& here she is   no need to write now

THE PAST BEING LIVED NOW

by Carol Bergé

The dear radical socialist anarchist poet
living in a two-room walkup in Bensonhurst,
near the Lebanese, Russian, Orthodox Jewish
colonies, near the Arabs, the streetmarkets.
Taking the subway to Manhattan for readings
once a week at least, saying very earnestly
"I used to be married but she died long ago"
to watch the compassionate faces near him.
Listening to Stravinsky and Rachmaninoff,
Mahler and the Schubert String Quintets,
reading Marx, Freud, Chomsky and Goodman.
Growing grey at the temples and the pate.
Joining the Writers Union when one comes by,
becoming an officer by unanimous election.
Submitting triolets and villanelles to many
magazines staffed by three violet lady muses,
hoping to meet one of them by candle-light

some day in the past, some day in a future —
Fiddlehead, Gusto, Blue Unicorn, Pendragon,
American Haiku, Goblets, Kudzu, Poets Monthly.
Some socialist lady living at Boston's fringe
reads his poetry, writes him a scented letter
on the qualities of his political love-poems.
They meet and are far too shy to consummate.
She was Daddy's girl, an only child, lives
with three cats and plants, has never been
married, has two advanced degrees from some
formidable schools, found herself in Borneo
once, for ten years, did complex translations
of their lifestyle poetics, was published by
a state university press, became famous for
them, for a year, then faded. She smiles
at our hero, her hero, basks in candlelight,
his admiration, red wine or espresso at a
Greenwich Village cafe, Mozart background to
lend luster to their halting intellectuality.
Will they marry? He is allergic to her cats.
He doesn't know yet about her inheritance.

BUREAU

COPENHAGEN

by Gregory Stephenson

Passing the statue of Soren Kierkegaard on my way
into the Royal Library, I salute as always. He smiles
dreamily under a dunce cap of snow. Kierkegaard is
still very much a presence in this city (more especially on winter days). You can visit his grave in
Assistens Churchyard (his name means churchyard
in Danish), read his letters and touch his furniture in
a museum, drink beer in an old café that he frequented. I see Danes reading his books on trams and
in cafés and parks. Other famous ghosts in the streets
of this city are Gauguin, Lenin, Joyce, Céline, Christopher Isherwood and Robert McAlmon, all of whom
lived here for a time. None of them seems to have
liked it very much though. The Danes are too ironic,
too introverted and melancholy for most tempera-
ments. Joyce, who could read and speak Danish
fluently, concluded that Danish was a "a weeping
language and the Danes a nation of weepers, of wild
men with soft voices." (On two occasions I've run
into Max Pedersen, who tutored Joyce in Danish in
Paris. A frail old man now, he remembers Joyce with
great sympathy, referring to him still as "that poor

boy.") The subtle and elusive anguish that Danes
nourish in their spirits has something to do with
light, with the extremes of daylight from winter to
summer, and the gray half-light of so many days.
There seems to be more than a casual connection
between meteorology and metaphysics. In winter
the clochards of Copenhagen like to hand out in the
city library on Kultorvet, where they doze in their
overcoats with books open on their laps. The real
saints of the city, though, are the old ladies who feed
the birds, the gulls and pigeons of the squares, the
ducks and swans of the canals and parks. The birds
recognize these thin, birdlike ladies who bring them
bags of seed and suet and breadcrumbs day after day
and at their approach there is great avian jubilation.
The winter days are cold, gray, dim, brief. Children
skate on the frozen lakes. On winter afternoons I like
to sit on a bench beneath the dome of the glass
hothouse in the Botanical Gardens and breathe the
warm, humid air among the tropical plants, the tall
palm and banana trees. In warmer weather I follow
through the streets a man with parrots on his shoulders, a girl with rings on her toes, a fat woman in
grimy finery pushing a baby carriage filled with her
strange possessions. There are so many mysteries in
the city, while on every corner tourists consult their
maps searching for "The Little Mermaid."

The Corpse wants you to remember. We've brought you unadulterated venom and indiscreet joy for over three years now. We have been called everything from "anarcho-trash" to "the *New Yorker* of the avantgarde." That last one really hurt, but we dodged it and shimmied on. We made impostors suffer and let the splendid shine. Our demise was always imminent but, for generic reasons, impossible. Nonetheless, periodically we despair. This is one of those times. Despite partial help from LSU, and quite a few new subscribers, there is barely enough cash to draw the bolt on the grave. We publish 3,000 Corpses every two months (more or less) and we still call ourselves a "monthly" because we hope to be, and being "avantgarde" we already are. But we need help. We need the renewal of your subscriptions. We need your (still) tax-deductible contributions. We need angels and heavenly subscribers. We need investors: we've proven that we can do it. There is no telling what we can do with a little slack. Will you dance with us? You *can* take it with you. Give it to the Corpse.

KAHN'S COMPUTER KNOCKED

I have several questions for Paul Kahn. Uno/ is your computerized *corpus litterarum graecorum* in Greek? in translation? or both? ditto indices? Duo/ how portable? is there a solar-powered three-pound reader? As Walt sd, where you read is almost as important as what you read. I like to take books to the shore, the mountain. *"Read these leaves to my-self in the open air, tried them by trees, stars, rivers."* Tre/ who was the visiting student reading?

— Sam Abrams

QUEST

I am writing a biography of Saul Zabar, founder of the Upper West Side's foremost smoked fish emporium, entitled "On Wings of Novy," and I would be pleased to hear from any in your audience who knew Zabar before his present ascendency, or patronized his shop. For "The Knife of The Times," a chapter on dermatology, I would also be interested in guidance, help, advice, and correspondence.

— Atlas MacShane

THE NINETIES GLIMPSED

We live in an era when both Bob Dylan and Ronald Reagan can subscribe to the visions of St. John the Divine, the apocalyptic revelations of Armageddon. What, I ask myself, does this mean? In the latest cross fire concerning the Ezra Pound controversy I find it once amusing yet scandalous that the Old Geezer has been dead for sometime and yet, as we all know, it is easier to kick a dead dog around, wherever and how ever he lies, than to contend with the menacing pit bulls that live and thrive in these most perilous of times. The eighties have brought on a mishmash of miasma and there are plenty of fronts to take on both derriere and right guard. Past year's P.E.N. Conference serves as perfect example as to how low we have all sunk. In that moment where that old literary sow herself Ms. ("all writing is pigshit") Cynthia Mac Donald thanked that literary necrophile, His Highness Norm Mailer (who, incidently I can't help but point out has made a killing exploiting the image of that ever-Exquisite Corpse Marilyn Monroe) for "raising the money." A moment both right and left, pro and con, feminist and chauvinist were so moved as to applaud.(!) What better theatre could serve to exemplify the bottom line to the current wave of Kulchur makers on all sides? And who will bring to trial those criminals who have committed the worst crime one can commit against poetry, the crime of subsidizing mediocrity? Thru the seventies we all witnessed that bizarre phenomenon where farmers were paid by the state to grow nothing. In retrospect it is easy to see that the state also made it a policy to pay the poet to say nothing. Such are the excesses of Capitalism. And if "Poetry is the Crown of Thought" (B. Peret) then one would have to conclude that many in the current wave would serve humanity best by turning in their crowns for dunce caps. When the President of the U.S. can sacrifice needed funding not only for the mouths of poets, but for AIDS research, depressed inner-city landscapes' crumbling structures of society — capitalism be damned! Let them eat MX missiles! Three and a half billion dollars anted up for defense! Beatniks and politics aside I hereby nominate Bob Kaufman's AMERICAN SUN POEM the poem of the decade. Who else has bothered to state the obvious? His Ancient Rain descends on us. And like Chicken Little we're left with yet another exquisite corpse whose last words might very well have been, "The sky is falling." Praise be Amitabbha! And if I dig E.P. for one thing it was his bitter pronouncement that the death culture is dead. And serves as no mean apology for *his* embracement of fascism. Not unlike our current President who has shown by his actions that a White Supremacist by any other name is still a Nazi. Yes, here are many fronts and it will be interesting to see how the decade will play itself out. The 90s will be a whole different ball game. No doubt about it. As nine is six upside down let me tell you fellow poets and fat cat culture makers at large, the nineties are gonna make the sixties look like a cake walk. Number nine is a higher vibration and for those of us who do survive these fated grim years I know I won't be the only one tortured by the disappearance of reality.

— Surya

THE EXCURSION: OR, O COLUMBUS!
by Thomas McGrath

This morning is the morning when Mrs. Murphy's treasure chest opens.

All the ladies of the town get out of bed: naked:
Except for their life-preservers — it's a Significant Day!
They put their brassieres on backward.
Then: oilskins. And: rubber boots —
Using old garter belts for the proper nautical effect —
And they shinney up their husbands' mainmasts to get a brief look at the weather,
singing a snatch from Brecht's poem "Ballad of the Pirates":

> "Oh heavenly sky of streaming blue!
> Enormous winds, the sails blow free!
> Let wind and heavens go hang! But oh
> Sweet Mary, let us keep the sea!"

Then, just as husband is trying to box the compass, (surprising
Weather, *he's* having) or get a bead on the sun,
The women are off! In marine splendor! They are going Garage
Sailing!

Sometimes on lakes, sometimes on rivers, sometimes
In ditches, and latecomers surfing on the last of the morning dew!
Tacking and turning seaward to scud the bright blue briny!
A beautiful day for garage sailing!

And the bay is full

(Or has its fill) of them. And they are so joyful!
Splicing their mizzens and shivering their delicious timbers,
And contriving, by Great Circle lingo, to thwart their neighbors' avasts!

And what garages! Ranch types, terraced with cows and their cowboys;
The Bride-a-wees: vinecovered, their roofs cloudy with Datsuns
Mewing in Japanese against the perilous flood!
There are Swiss chalets, chateaux and simple salt-boxes
Confounding the whelming tide with that good old Puritan jazz,
And the cineramic Protestant rectitude of Increase and Cotton Mather!

Some, captains of gothic garages, are ringing their bells and gargoyles,
While others, late starters, only now, on the meadows of plankton,
Are reviewing their troops (or Old Salts as they may be called),
While the Earlies, Msss. Flotsam and Jetsam, in pelagic disaster areas
Are seeking the spangled lamp whose dome is deeper and darker
Than any sea dingle or oceanic boudoir or barranca,
Or trying to catch or ketch a bald barnacle on a plate of blue fish,
Or snatch the black pearl of desire from the dens of the iniquitous Deep.

But Mrs. Murphy's treasure chest has long — alas —
Been emptied: by early lovers, couth and uncouth, by kith and kind,
By kindred candid and unkind, by talking heads, heedless
Of her need or nod or now't or naught or nix or nonesuch:
And so the poor woman's bereft — a soul in the dark night
Sailing toward Nowhere among the long black boats of the dead.

Still, here's a drowned dictionary, everything illegible
Except for the words *water* and *salt*. But, as they say,

Who needs it?
The ladies mount their garages.
They sail

Back to their homes in Plague Harbor
Meanwhile the dictionary

Dries.
And the word "salvation" appears in the margin!
Hot

Damn! It's Mrs. Murphy's map to the Enchanted Isles!
But, the ladies have gone home again to their own treasures:
Beer cans, children, husbands, mortgages, bills, adultery —
Home Sweet American Home!
The garages are no longer sailing
And the seas fill with sharks of Auld Lang Signe.

E. M. CIORAN: A THINKING SAINT
by Sanda Stolojan

translated from the French by Claudia Ancelot

In his *Conversation with Chestov*, Benjamin Fondane quotes Chestov as saying that the best way to philosophize is "to walk alone," without the guidance of another philosopher or, even better, to talk about oneself. Further on, Fondane adds: "The typical new philosopher is a private thinker, Job sitting on his pile of manure." Cioran belongs to this breed of "private thinkers" and has indeed walked alone. For years, he was disregarded or snubbed by specialists in philosophy, known mostly to lonely thinkers, misfits, poets, mavericks, read by students rather than by professors. Today, Cioran is "in," translated and frequently quoted. To refer to the author of *Syllogisms of Bitterness* is to display oneself as a free spirit, a non-conformist, at odds, particularly, with Parisian received wisdom; to call on his all-embracing skepticism as the prophet of the death of a civilization and, of course, to revel in his style and humor of this strange negator. Characteristically, Cioran leaves no one cold or indifferent.

Some are irked by his paradoxes or his cartwheels; others are amused, delighted by what has been called his "endless facetiousness." His genuine readers experience a curious feeling of euphoria on the brink of an abyss, like that young Lebanese woman reading Cioran while the bombs were falling, in a Beirut cellar: his wit, she says, gave her a lift, his black and corrosive humor was a kind of tonic in the midst of disaster. And there was this Japanese woman who wanted to kill herself but who, in the nick of time, chanced on Cioran's writings about suicide and began corresponding with him. She had discovered someone haunted by the same thoughts and her act was turned into a written observation, her obsession into an exchange of words about suicide.

Those who approach his writing discover the "Cioran effect," that gift of his to draw you into an adventure which is all but bookish. They discover that special tone which he himself defines as "something you cannot invent, something you are born with . . . an inherited grace, the privilege of making others feel your organic pulse; tone is more than talent, it is the very essence of talent" *(The Trouble with Being Born)*.

Cioran has always rejected theory, he has been listening to the obsessions rising from his own internal sources: "I have not invented anything, I have merely been secretary to my own sensations." The paths of culture have always turned him back towards his own self, back "among the living, stumbling across those ancient miseries he trampled in his race towards detachment." He has nurtured this skepticism, grafted it unto his quivering temperament. "What a philosopher leaves behind is his temperament . . . the more alive he is, the more he will let himself go," says Cioran in *The Evil Demiurge*. A master of paradox, of negation and denigration, a "courtier of the void" (an expression he might have coined himself) he is indeed a living paradox: a skeptic who has not turned his back on life. Cioran's first essays written in Rumanian already portend the way in which he is rooted in his own pulsions and moods. Today, in the light of his work, it is interesting to peruse those writings from the remote thirties.

Read in relation to Cioran's works in French, those youthful essays shed some light on the way he is rooted in the experience of his obsessions and on his path once he had gone over to French lock, stock and barrel, that is with his own self as he was at the end of the thirties: a Rumanian intellectual, part of a brilliant and anguished generation, steeped in Kierkegaard and Chestov, Spengler and Kayserling, with Ecclesiastes and the Book of Job as bedside reading. Those essays show us what he got rid of, the "old man" of his youth and the "new man" he became after his providential encounter with the style and essence of the French language.

His first essays published in 1934, *Pe Culmile Disperarii (On the Peaks of Despair)*, already vibrate with the color, the colors of Cioran's accord, constantly restated, amplified, modulated, subjected to the rigor of French, but whose echo still resonates in his latest aphorisms, proving that their characteristic tone does indeed stem from his roots.

The very title of his first collection of essays *On*

Jean-Jacques Passera

the Peaks of Despair (this without a hint of irony) typifies the original Cioran and stands in contrast to the striking name of his first book in French, *A Handbook of Decay. On the Peaks of Despair* is the lyrical title of a book which contains *the stuff* of Cioran's future work on the form of despair. *A Handbook of Decay* is a title which goes down well in French with its double entendre on the meaning of "handbook'" and in which "despair" has given place to "decay," a cruel and harsh word in tune with what is expected of a modern work.

By the age of twenty-three when he published *On the Peaks*, Cioran had already read everything and discovered his subject: himself, alone, grappling with himself, with God and creation. From the very outset he had turned his almost monstrous lucidity against himself: his *Thinking against Oneself* and *The Lover of Paroxysm* are already contained in *On the Peaks*. The titles of those first essays are revealing: *No Longer Able to Live, The Sense of the End and of Agony, Grotesquery and Despair, Forebodings of Madness, Melancholy, Ecstasy, Apocalypse, Monopoly of Suffering, Irony and Anti-Irony, Commonplace and Transfiguration*, etc.

Everything is already in place: the feeling that life is beyond repair, beyond remedy, worry, an-guish, the sense of nothingness, the praise of silence. And even his personal quirks: insomnia, nocturnal walks, his laziness, his passion for music, the obsession with suicide. On his twenty-second birthday he concluded an essay with these words: "How strange it is to feel that at this age I am a specialist in death." *On the Peaks* sounds the theme of metaphysical exile: "Isn't life an exile and nothingness our homeland?" — a theme he reverted to forty years later in *The Trouble with Being Born*: "I shall have lived all my life with the feeling of having been snatched from my true place. Were the term 'metaphysical exile' to be devoid of meaning, my own life would suffice to confer it one." In *On the Peaks* we encounter a lyrical and expressive Cioran who insists on "the lyrical resources of subjectivity," who holds "lyricism to be a barbarian form whose virtue is to be nothing but blood, sincerity, and fire," who has a horror of "refined cultures frozen into forms and frames," of people "who will go on posturing even to the brink of death just to make an impression." (Later on, in *The Temptation to Live* he picks up this idea and this image in his portrait of the French, described as a nation of actors, "great specialists in death." In a telling essay he compares despair which is rooted in one's being to doubt which is something more intellectual and he proclaims that psychologists usually end up as skeptics. While rejecting his youthful lyricism, while adopting the doubts and ironical smiles of the French moralist, Cioran does not shed his obsessions, his manias, and tics.

FRACTURES
by E. M. Cioran
translated by Leonard Schwartz

Each new development is but one more ill omen. From time to time however an exception that the chronicler magnifies in order to create the illusion of the unexpected.

That envy is universal: the most striking proof of this is that one finds it again with the lunatics themselves in their brief intervals of lucidity.

All the aberrations attract us, and foremost of all Life, aberration par excellence.

Standing, one admits without drama that each instant which passes vanishes for ever; *stretched out,* this obviousness appears so unbearable that one desires never again to rise.

The Eternal Return and Progress: two equally meaningless expressions. What remains? Resignation to surprises which are not surprises, to calamities which would like to be original.

"You often speak of God. That is a word which I no longer make use of," an ex-nun writes me.
  Not everyone is lucky enough to be disgusted with Him!

All these nights in the midst of which, in the absence of a confidant, we are reduced to Him who has played this role for centuries, for millennia.

To have invented the murderous smile.

What is marvelous is that each day brings us a new reason to peter out.

Since one remembers only the humiliations and the defeats, for what will all the rest have served?

To interrogate yourself about the essence of everything gives you the desire to roll on the floor. It is in any case in this manner that I formerly responded to the capital question, to the questions without response.

Chaque événement n'est qu'un mauvais signe de plus. De temps en temps pourtant une exception que le chroniqueur grossit pour créer l'illusion de l'inattendu.

Que l'envie soit universelle, la meilleure preuve en est qu'on la retrouve chez les aliénés eux-mêmes dans leurs brefs intervalles de lucidité.

Toutes les anomalies nous attirent, en premier lieu la Vie, anomalie par excellence.

Debout on admet sans drame que chaque instant qui passe s'évanouit pour toujours; *allongé,* cette evidence paraît à ce point irrecevable qu'on souhaite ne plus jamais se lever.

L'éternel retour et le progrès: deux non-sens. Que reste-t-il? La résignation au devenir, à des surprises qui n'en sont pas à des calamités qui se voudrait originales.

"Vous parlez souvent de Dieu. Voilá un mot dont je ne me sers plus," m'écrit une ex-nonne.
  Tout le monde n'a pas la chance de s'en être dégoûté!

Toutes ces nuits au milieu desquelles, en l'absence d'un confident, nous en sommes réduits à Celui qui joua ce rôle des siècles, des millénaires durant.

Avoir inventé le sourire meurtrier.

Ce qui est merveilleux, c'est que chaque jour nous apporte une nouvelle raison de disparaître.

Puisqu'on ne se souvient que des humiliations et des défaites, à quoi donc aura servi le reste?

S'interroger sur le fond de quoi que ce soit vous donne envie de vous rouler par terre. C'est en tout cas de cette manière qu'autrefois je répondais aux questions capitales, aux questions sans réponse.

Opening this manual of pre-history, I fall upon several specimens of our ancestors, lurid to the extreme. Without any doubt, so they were. From disgust and from shame, I quickly reshut the book, all the while knowing that I will reopen it each time I wish to reflect on the genesis of our horrors and our dirty tricks.

Life secretes anti-life, and this chemical comedy, instead of making us smile, gnaws at us and makes us panic.

The need to devour oneself dispenses with the need to believe.

If rage were an attribute of the On-High, I'd have left behind my mortal status ages ago.

Existence would be able to justify itself if each behaved as if he were the last one living.

Ignatius of Loyola, tormented by scruples on whose nature he did not expatiate, recounted that he had dreamed of destroying himself. Even him! This temptation is decidedly more widespread and deeply rooted than one thinks. It is in fact the honor of man, ere it becomes his duty.

He alone is disposed to work who deceives himself, who ignores the secret motives of his acts. The creator that becomes transparent to himself no longer creates. The knowledge of oneself makes the *demon* grumpy. It is there that one must search for the reason why Socrates wrote nothing.

That which discredits arrogance is the fact that we can be wounded by precisely those we scorn.

In a work admirably translated from the English, a sole flaw: the "chasms of scepticism." The translator should have used doubt, since scepticism is a word which in French admits of a nuance of dilettantism, indeed of frivolity, inassociable with the idea of the abyss.

The taste for formula goes along with a weakness for definitions, for that which has the least connection with the real.

All that can be classified is perishable. Nothing lasts but what is susceptible to several interpretations.

To grapple with blank paper, what a Waterloo awaits me!

When one meets with someone, as high as his merits may be, it must not be forgotten that in his profound reactions he differs in nothing from the common run of mortals. One must handle him with prudence, since, like everybody, he cannot bear frankness, direct cause of the quasi-totality of quarrels and of grudges.

To have brushed up against all the forms of abasement, including success.

Not one letter from Shakespeare. Didn't he write any? One would have loved to hear Hamlet complain of the superabundance of the mail.

The outstanding virtue of slander is that it creates a vacuum around you, without your having to raise a finger.

One is almost always outstripped by events. One only has to wait in order to realize that one is guilty of naivety.

The passion for music is in itself a confession. We know more of an unknown who gives himself over to it than of someone who is insensible to it and approaches us every day.

At the utmost point of nights. No longer anyone, nothing but the society of minutes. Each one pretends to keep us company, and then vanishes — desertion upon desertion.

Never to take sides testifies to a disquieting perturbation. Who says *living* says *partial*: objectivity, late phenomenon, alarming symptom, is the first step towards capitulation.

One must be as little in the know as an angel or an idiot to believe that the human escapade can turn out well.

Tout ce qu'on peut classer est périssable. Ne dure que ce qui est susceptible de plusieurs interprétations.

Aux prises avec le papier blanc, quel Waterloo en perspective!

Quand on s'entretient avec quelqu'un, si hauts que soient ses mérites, il ne faut oulier à aucun instant que dans ses réactions profondes il ne diffère en rien du commun des mortels. Par prudence, on doit le ménager, car, à l'égal de tout un chacun, il ne supportera pas la franchise, cause directe de la quasi-totalité des brouilles et des rancunes.

Avoir frôlé toutes les formes de la déchéance, y compris la réussite.

On ne possède aucune lettre de Shakespeare. N'en a-t-il écrit aucune? On aurait aimé entendre Hamlet se plaindre l'abondance du courrier.

La vertu éminente de la calomnie est de faire le vide autour de vous, sans que vous ayez à lever le petit doigt.

Si on est presque toujours dépassé par les événements, c'est parce qu'il suffit d'attendre pour s'apercevoir qu'on s'est rendu coupable de naïveté.

La passion de la musique est en elle-même un aveu. Nous en savons plus long sur un inconnu qui s'y adorne que sur quelqu'un qui y est insensible et que nous approchons tous les jours.

A l'extrême des nuits. Plus personne, rien que la société des minutes. Chacune fait semblant de nous tenir compagnie, et puis se sauve — désertion sur désertion.

Faire la part des choses témoigne d'une perturbation inquiétante. Qui dit *vivant* dit *partial*: l'objectivité, phénomène tardif, symptôme alarmant, est l'amorce d'une capitulation.

Il faudrait être aussi peu dans le coup qu'un ange ou un idiot pour croire que l'équipée humaine puisse bien tourner.

The qualities of a neophyte are heightened and reinforced under the effect of his new convictions. That he knows; what he ignores is that his shortcomings increase in proportion. From there are sprung his chimeras and his pride.

"My children, salt comes from the water, and if it comes in contact with the water, it dissolves and disappears. In the same way, the monk is born from the woman, and if he draws near to the woman, he dissolves and ceases to be a monk."

This John Moshus, of the 7th century, has the air of having understood better than much later Strindberg or Weininger the danger already signaled in *Genesis*.

Every *life* is the history of a debacle. If biographies are interesting, it is because their heroes, and their cowards just as much, have obliged themselves to innovate in the art of toppling over.

Disappointed by all, it is inevitable that one comes to be by oneself; unless one began there.

"Ever since I have observed men, I have learned only to love them more," wrote Lavater, contemporary of Chamfort. Such a remark, normal to an inhabitant of a tiny Helvetian Village, would have seemed of a simplicity indecorous to a Parisian familiar with the salons.

French: ideal idiom for translating delicately ambiguous sentiments.

Bach in his tomb. Like so many others I have seen him there, thanks to the indiscretion of grave-diggers and journalists, and I often think of his eye-sockets which contain nothing original, except that they proclaim the Nothingness that he denied.

To have nothing in common with the All, and to ask onself by virtue of what derangement one belongs to it.

Les qualités d'un néophyte se rehaussent et se renforcent sous l'effet de ses nouvelles convictions. Cela il le sait; ce qu'il ignore, c'est que ses travers augmentent en proportion. De là découlent ses chimères et sa superbe.

"Mes enfants, le sel vient de l'eau, et s'il est en contact avec l'eau, il se dissout et disparaît. De même le moine naît de la femme, et s'il approche d'une femme, il se dissout et cesse d'être moine."

Ce Jean Moschus, au VIIe siècle, a l'air d'avoir compris mieux que plus tard Strindberg ou Weininger le danger déjà signalé par la *Genèse*.

Toute *vie* est l'histoire d'une dégringolade. Si les biographies sont tellement captivantes, c'est parce due les héros, et las lâches tout autant, s'astreignent à innover dans l'art de culbuter.

Déçu par tous, il est inévitable qu'on en arrive à l'être soi-même; à moins qu'on n'ait commencé par là.

"Depuis que j'observe les hommes, je n'ai appris qu'à les aimer davantage," écrivait Lavater, contemporain de Chamfort. Une telle remarque normale chez l'habitant d'un patelin helvétique, aurait semblé d'une simplesse inconvenante au Parisien familier des salons.

Le français: idiome idéal pour traduire délicatement des sentiments équivoques.

Bach dans sa tombe. Je l'aurai vu donc comme tant d'autres par l'indiscrétion des fossoyeurs et des journalistes et depuis je pense souvent à ses orbites qui n'ont rien d'original, sinon qu'elles proclament le néant qu'il a nié.

N'avoir rient de commun avec le Tout, et se demander en vertu de quel déréglement on en fait partie.

IN PRAISE OF JAMES BALDWIN
by Anthony Barthelemy

In June 1963 New Orleans Assistant City Attorney Edward Pinner filed charges in Municipal Court against Frank Rossitter and George E. Deville, the manager and assistant manager of Doubleday Bookstore, for displaying and selling obscene material. The obscene matter was James Baldwin's *Another Country*. New Orleans District Attorney Jim Garrison, much to his credit, refused to take the case to court. However, in January 1979 the Internal Revenue Service and the Supreme Court seemed able to do what Mr. Pinner and the New Orleans Police Department were unable to do: rid the country of *Another Country*. In a decision in favor of the Internal Revenue Service (*Thor Power Tool Company vs. the Commissioner of Internal Revenue*), the court allowed the IRS to access and to tax the value of publishers' backlists. Such taxation, of course, makes it costly for publishers to keep large supplies of books in their warehouses. The book burnings feared by Jim Garrison in 1963 actually began to take place in 1979 as publishers sought to rid themselves of books that were unlikely to enjoy an immediate surge in demand and sales. One reason to complain is that for too long getting even ten copies of a couple of important novels by Baldwin was impossible. In the Fall of 1983 I ordered ten copies of *Giovanni's Room* for a course. The order could not be filled. In the Fall of 1985 I ordered ten copies of *Giovanni's Room* and *Another Country*. The bookstore could not locate a single copy of *Giovanni's Room* and only four used copies of *Another Country*. I thought that in another year or two *Go Tell It on the Mountain* and *The Fire Next Time* would be the only two books by Baldwin easily available. Things looked better and better for Mr. Pinner. Then in December 1985 and February 1986 Dell reissued ten titles by James Baldwin: *Another Country, Blues for Mister Charlie, The Fire Next Time, Giovanni's Room, Go Tell It on the Mountain, Going to Meet the Man, If Beale Street Could Talk, No Name in the Street, Nobody Knows My Name,* and *Tell Me How Long the Train's Been Gone.*

No other book captures the narrative power and finesse of Baldwin so well as *Another Country*. Although not generally considered his best work, *Another Country* is a superb example of the modern American realist novel. From its attention to detail (cigarettes, ice cubes, plastic wrapping on pork chops) to its hip street talk (the kind that Mr. Pinner finds obscene) and nitty-gritty sex (all kinds, gay, straight and [N.B.] interracial), *Another Country* captures with grace and style the struggles, deaths and triumphs of black Americans in the New York City of the early '60s. (Camelot was on the Potomac, not between the Hudson and Harlem Rivers.) In some ways the novel's hyperrealism dates it, and when it attempts to be most hip, it appears — from our contemporary perspective — most tired. But to dismiss *Another Country* because what was jive (remember that word used to mean "with it" and "cool") now is jive, would be like condemning *Madame Bovary* because the medical profession has changed. More importantly, Baldwin's story of Rufus and Ida Scott remains as gripping and as pertinent in 1986 America as it was in 1964. Rufus, a jazz musician bursting with talent and anger, struggles to maintain his dignity and identity in a savage world that remains suspicious of black men. Although Rufus knows the comfort of family and a true friend, when he hits bottom, unable to find work, unable to demonstrate his worth, he surrenders to circumstances rather than allow his family to see him broken and defeated. He becomes Baldwin's invisible man, symbolic of the invisibility of black men (gender specific) except as emblems of terror for white America. Ida, Rufus' beloved and loving sister, must understand Rufus' fall and disappearance. She must also comprehend *beyond the intuitive* what it means to be black in America and what happens to black men in America. Baldwin's choice of sister Ida, blues singer, as the *trouveuse* of the novel, emphasizes the importance of the black chanteuse as the articulator of the anguish, despair and triumph of black life. The blues and jazz singer reaches her black audience in sorrow and celebration. She celebrates poetry from the familiar hardships and misery. Additionally, this female was uniquely able to break through the cultural barriers, and her voice and *words* could be heard in white America. Perhaps the message went unheeded and uncomprehended, but her voice penetrated and sometimes permeated that other culture. (God bless the child who's got his own.) Perhaps the greatest evidence of Baldwin's craftsmanship in *Another Country* is the fact that in this story of a black man and of black men, they remain invisible. There is only one major black male character in the novel, and he vanishes from the narrative after the first seventy-eight pages. But here Baldwin reveals the paradox of black invisibility in America, for everyone knows black men are a vital part of American consciousness and American mythology. (Seen Bill Moyers lately or Bruce Willis in *Moonlighting?*) Yet *Another Country* is not a hopeless novel.

Neither light nor hope nor sympathy escapes *Giovanni's Room*. In this, his second novel, first published in 1956, Baldwin creates a bleak and cold underworld in which gay men live, couple, hate, kill and die. When one of its denizens does seek escape in light and love, he encounters contempt and malice from his compatriots who scurry to enthrall more securely the would-be escapee. Love, we learn, is the only release from this grim and painful world, yet love finds little nurturing in *Giovanni's Room*. The novel's young narrator, David, a white American hiding from himself, his family and his countrymen in this Parisian *demimonde*, cannot love because he has not set his "heart free of hatred and despair." And his hatred is set most severely against his own heart. Loved by the young Italian Giovanni, David never forgives Giovanni or himself for his emotional and sexual needs and desires. Unable to love himself "totally without rancor," he despises everyone and everything, especially Giovanni and Hella, David's unloved but loving fiancee. The hatred swells until David destroys Giovanni and perhaps Hella too. Embittered and embattled, David never learns that love could have set him free and saved those who loved him from falling victim to his struggle against himself. "Love him [Giovanni]," David is warned by a weary yet wise citizen of the *demimonde*. "Love him and let him love you. Do you think anything else under heaven really matters? And how long, at best, can it last? Since you are both men and still have everywhere to go? Only five minutes, I assure you, only five minutes, and most of that *helas!* in the dark. And if you think of them as dirty, then they *will* be dirty — they will be dirty because you will be giving nothing, you will be despising your flesh and his. But you can make your time together anything but dirty; you can give each

other something which will make both of you better — forever — if you will *not* be ashamed." Now the question arises: "Is *Giovanni's Room* a gay novel? It does not sound like a black novel. Is it a black gay novel or a gay black novel?" Well perhaps it is all of these things and none of them. We all know that such descriptive adjectives are frequently treated as restrictive adjectives, and such terms as "black literature" or "gay literature" or "feminist literature" tend to allow the literary establishment to marginalize the literary efforts of a particular — and usually unpopular — group. Authors themselves, and particularly those who consider themselves to be "major" authors like to avoid such classifications because they do not wish to marginalize themselves or limit their appeal or audience. Consider Baldwin's condemnation of Richard Wright's *Native Son* for being a "protest novel" and his equally ironic condemnation of André Gide's *Madeline* because Gide does not keep "hidden from us" his homosexuality. This notwithstanding, such descriptive adjectives are useful when they are purely descriptive. The cases of Faulkner and Southern literature and the Bible and Hebrew literature or even the very term "English literature" are instructive. No novel is more southern than *Absalom, Absalom!* but we feel no constraints in identifying it as a great American novel, a great modern novel, *and* a great novel in English. The same applies to *Giovanni's Room*. Clearly Baldwin's sense of himself as a member of a politically oppressed minority informs his portrayal of Giovanni. However, the most pertinent descriptive adjectives for *Giovanni's Room* are beautiful, gripping and finely wrought because the novel surely is all of these.

Similarly *Another Country* is an Afro-American novel, an American novel and a modern novel. Each description is useful *and* neutral; it only prejudices the book to an already prejudiced mind. Perhaps we can attribute this condition to Mr. Pinner who described *Another Country* as "the most filthy and pornographic book I have ever read."

There is much to be found in all ten titles published in this collection. *The Fire Next Time* and *Go Tell It on the Mountain*, Baldwin's autobiographical first novel, are two other works in this collection that enjoy continued popularity and critical attention. As always with Baldwin, there is a relentless, uncompromising inquiry into problems that every thinking person has pondered.

WHAT THE SHADOW KNOWS
by Sandie Castle

He was one of those men who prided himself on understandin women. He said, "I know them inside out." He sounded like an asshole ta her but she was much too tired ta tell 'im and he'd stopped listenin weeks ago anyway. He would bring books ta the house by the dozens, mostly about socialism and the women's movement. One day when he came ta visit she was drawin a picture of a man who had a single hook where his hand shoulda been and it was reachin for somethin clean off the page. When he asked her about the significance of the image, she said, "It don't mean nothin."

The next time he stopped by he was actin all excited. He said, "I brought you a wonderful present. You're gonna *love* it, I promise." Lookin really tickled with himself, he handed her a book called *Trotsky on Literature and Art*. All she could do was sigh in disappointment. What she really wanted was a television. He said, "Look you don't understand what this is, this guy is great, he'll show you just where you're coming from. I think that's just what this country needs, more art from the working class and I for one want to encourage your creativity." Oh Christ, she thought, just what I need and God knows I always wanted one. She used it to prop her window open.

Now whenever he came by she would complain about a clock tickin. He became annoyed with this after a while and attributed the noise to her preoccupation with self. He said, "You have too much imagination." He asked ta see more drawings but she refused ta show him, they'd gotten so strange that she didn't like seein them herself.

While standin in front of her mirror, he said, "You know a lot of people have told me lately that I look like Che Guevara." She was watchin him stroke his mustache. "What do you think?" he said, striking a pose. She laughed, replyin quickly, "Henry Higgins." "What?" Then repeatin herself with pained exactness, "Henry Higgins." He walked away pretendin he hadn't understood.

He was fascinated by her poor white background, strewn with prostitution and drug addiction. She was trying ta figure out why anybody with a college degree would feel like a hero for makin a conscious decision to work in a factory. She had never been fascinated by factory workers and knew damn well she never would be. The only hero she'd ever had was Peter Pan. "Now there's somebody fascinatin," she'd say. She had always loved the androgynous quality of his nature and the clothes he wore. She was convinced that Peter could fly simply because he'd never looked between his legs. Some-

times she wished she hadn't, today was one of those. She had a backache and her head hurt and not bein able ta fly still depressed her from time ta time. She confided all this ta the man layin next ta her, who professed ta be solely concerned with the human condition.

Now this here man was real busy at the moment tryin ta get laid so he hastily reminded her that people somewhere right now, at this very moment, were fallin down dead in the streets from hunger. It was another "count your blessings" lecture. By now she realized she was gettin her period and wondered if she should use a sanitary napkin or a tampon. She felt empty and inserted a regular. He was not amused by her earthiness as she licked the blood from her fingers. She was fully aware that this made it taste much better. She wondered if this habit of hers would be discussed with his therapist. Imaginin the conversation gave her a great deal of pleasure. However, she was not pleased by the fact that he was payin some guy fifty bucks an hour ta listen ta the same shit she had ta hear for nothin. Some guy who never slept with him and his goddamn politics, who she was sure had never believed in Peter Pan. His patient hadn't given her so much as an orgasm and she knew that this wouldn't ever be the topic of any conversation they had.

Tonight *the patient* was angry because she could not come up with anything sufficiently warped or freaky in her past to satisfy him. He said, "There must be something you left out, just think about it for a minute."

She tried ta remember some incident which he might find arousin but this whole thing was startin ta get on her nerves. "I just can't," she said. "That's your whole problem," he said, "you just repress things." She was wonderin why they couldn't do it regular. She asked again if he heard a clock tickin. He just shook his head.

The only complaint she'd ever voiced to his face

was that he was not a good cunt eater. This distressed him ta no end. He was so bitter about it that ta get back at her he said quite smugly, "Real women are responsible for their own orgasms." She did in fact think about this and then took a woman as her lover, she felt much better and told him so. He did not appreciate her interpretation of responsibility, he told her that lesbianism was a dangerous form of political separatism and sexually immature. He suggested she grow up.

The tone of his voice changed as he ran his hand along her thigh. He began talkin about the last demonstration he had been to. By the time he got ta the part about the folksinger he was hard. She wondered whether it would help things if she played Cuban music on the record player and covered the bed with propaganda pamphlets.

He rubbed her breasts roughly and told her that she did not deserve ta have such a nice body because she never exercised and drank and smoked too much. She thought about this and lit a cigarette. He accused her of bein cruel and manipulative. As he positioned himself above her, he said, "You use your sex as a weapon." She put her cigarette out and blew him. When he came he wrapped his hands around her hair and pulled her head so close she was afraid she'd smother or choke ta death. She swallowed hard and thought she tasted metal. She had performed like a good machine and for this it was hard ta forgive her. The accusation from time ta time was that she was too professional.

As soon as he recovered he began ta talk about the problems connected with oral gratification, mumbled something about people always havin high expectations, thinkin things always have to be reciprocal. It was the "thought that counts" theory. She heard the clock tickin again, this time it was much louder. She decided not ta mention it. She went ta brush her teeth, he followed her. Standin in the doorway watchin her spit into the sink, he began tellin her how much he loved her. She lit another cigarette and started fillin the tub with water. He was capable of workin himself up ta quite an emotional pitch without her assistance so she chose ta ignore him.

He was cryin now and sayin that she had completely misunderstood his motives for bein with her. The only thing she thought a person needed a motive for was murder. She lowered her body until her ears were underwater. Now he was screamin that she was an ungrateful, calloused and ignorant

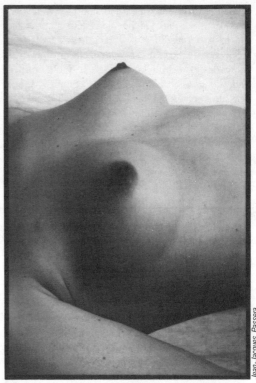

Jean-Jacques Passera

bitch and one day she would regret this and understand that he had only tried ta help her, but then he added that it would be too late. She closed her eyes tightly and thought about her mother.

By the time she started dryin herself, he had calmed down completely. "After all," he said, "you're just a victim. What could I expect? Just a helpless victim of a classist capitalistic society, reared with the wrong set of values, however honest." Of course he would forgive her, he would even say he was sorry. "There now," he said, kissing her on the top of her head, "isn't this better than fighting?" He was actually smilin. He reminded her cheerfully that after the revolution things would be different. She was sick ta the stomach at the thought of it. She let the water out of the tub and, applying her eyeliner ever so carefully, agreed. He chattered away in the background while she studied herself in the mirror. She was glad her eyes were green, she was glad that this was over.

He said he would call in the mornin so they could examine what had happened. She walked into the bedroom with him trailin behind her. Now he was talkin about the positive energy of anger. She handed him his lunch box and said, "Have a good session." She could tell he was feelin great as he left, he was whistlin.

She laid in bed for an hour smokin, masturbatin, readin. It was the latest book he'd left, entitled *Understanding Fascism*. She kept readin little sections aloud and laughin. Che Guevara, indeed! She got up, washed her hands and threw the book in the trash can. She began ta dress as if she were on a mission. Pullin on tights and blouse, caressin suede boots that she'd saved for a special occasion. She felt ten years younger already. She went in search of scissors, cut her hair as short as possible, pulled the tampon out, stuck it into a vase and watched it bloom. The blood trickled down her leg. She could hear her mother's voice sayin over and over, "You'll never grow up, you'll never grow up. I just don't understand it. What's wrong with you? NEVER NEVER NEVER NEVER!" The clock began tickin so loudly that the voice disappeared. She knew she had to hurry. The belly of the crocodile hadn't ever seemed smaller than now. Removin the book from the window, she stood on the ledge, took a deep breath and jumped. She hoped Tiger Lily would remember her. And never never land? Why it had never looked better. ☠

SENSATION
by Victor Serge
translated from the French by James Brook

for L.

("Don't be sad. . .")

After that splendid Notre Dame inverted
in the pure Seine of the vagrants' remorse,
after that trembling rose window
    blooming in the black water
where the stars spin out their inconceivable threads
through the profiles of sea horses through foliage
            as real as mirages.

what is there, O madly reasonable spirit,

what remains inaccessible to the awakened sleeper
who follows, down these dark quays,
        from one Commune to the other,
the hopeful cortege of his executed brothers?

Gerald Burns

BIRDER'S LAMENT
by Philip Lamantia

Robin, rare Robin at my window
below the introduced tree, pecking black seeds
Blessed be, this
otherwise difficult day
gracious vision, Robin, of your mandibles
to counterbalance the Killdeer birds crushed
on their nests by giant tractors at Crissy Field

POETICS BY PLUTO
by Philip Lamantia

The dendrophobe across the way just demolished nests
   of finches sparrows other possible birds

Wild in the city with green teeth up through the pavements Phoenix is that bird
From ashes of the kali-yuga
      another root in the great tradition
through caves of animal fetishes Cernunos in the lap of Diana
      A wee chance
      Better falconry
than the definitive end Better the poetry of the birds
Up from salty deeps, Dianas, to rule us and reweave a scallop shell sacred to Venus
      There's a cleavage possible
Mother Shipton's prophecy that the end of the cycle is not foretold
but only the end of insane mankind
                    Read it here before amnesia
the superior salt maneuver
in the language of chirping finches

     is that bird, Diana

In a late Goethean mode happiness ignites its grand illusion
Timeless all that old cant about the hermetic art
opens a poetic fundament deep into the pyramid The processional colors
of finches repeat ritual doorways in aura of instant death
the poet No Name by chance seering open pavements of Ol Frisco
the Barbary Coast from carpets of brown dust to Twenty-ninth and Courtland Avenue
a crustaceous wind from ancient oaks off the *E-chi-lat* River
      near a minor fault line but active in the nineties
off the semi-wild park which will have a monument to Isadora Duncan
      where I ran and danced with youths of frenetic romance
lash of the bay below
curving geology with two-thirds of a whole number
to tip the dragon of summer
into transfigured space of thin peninsula
      Costanoan triblets from San Bruno to San Juan Bautista
Mockingbirds are returning to Frisco
to lift the ancient taboo
hummingbirds by the milliards at the feeder stations
Meanwhile empires are vomiting
not some nineteenth-century phano-sphere of coming blight (trotting castles) but
sudden death for a whole continent of forest here & everywhere
      sparrows strangled in midair with the last condors
situate Acid Rain and the Green House Effect
      plague-lined trees oil-slick birds
There's little time left for geographic enclaves to form Aquarian islands
(from them only could I be reading you)

If (as Hegel proved) poetry is a rare assemblage
a Watts Tower transmuting junk
how over-quantified to vanishing the prosaic is

       "I always thought there was something funny about
       our generation, now I know why, it's the last one"

Violent flashes to each other words become cancerous with meaning
The hood of horror has actually come back those mornings insane
mankind signs all the prose of the world
The gods first craze those they decide to destroy
Think *nous, ment,* ithyphallic Min
to project sensibility
How do I feel? rotten, misnamed 'hysterical' who calls freely for the Annulment of Nuclear Physics
as if technē were the issue and
not a cosmic catastrophe
Ask those who put the sacred animals in niches at Altamira
and those who call up the beasts in islands of new forest

Now there's mostly monolithic media noise
       on the inner cliff a shadowy figure who announces
the Admonition, again
but certainly some attempt at statement, flying wild to the polis, is proportional to our destruction as
  a species
When does the winged bridge appear on this terrified earth?

Somewhere between Walpi and New York as they are Another world Whether others see it or not is
  aleatory
but the emerald vision persists, a bygone reformed off serpentine rocky shores
transmitting abalone shells at midnight all the way from New Ireland
'Dances of the Pheasant and Quail societies are generally attended'

Pluto retrograde five degrees into Scorpio
      Radioactive rain days
Will dejection ever end for incantators
once the mysteries of falconry join the old art of an inner dance?
      Frisco was like that
There are thirty species of birds feeding Telegraph Hill
          Site of appearance
          visible light
                The Invisible Light
          and the night of gold: imaginable
          origin of language
          Quotidian humming
          gradations of vocables transmitted
          among the very few

Dripping pine needles generate geometric thought Is there any other?
On this language island night's my day
Empires are still rotting A Sandpiper trapt in oil slick

FROM THE E.C. CHAIR

When Ronnie Burk, and then Ira Cohen, suggested doing an issue on Julian Beck I wasn't so sure. I never knew the Becks though I knew their successors, the San Francisco Angels of Light, rather well. Part of The Living Theatre cast stayed with us in 1968 in Detroit after a successful performance of *Paradise Now*. They came to breakfast . . . naked. That was both shocking and pleasant as things often were in those days, and it is in memory of that pleasant shock that I decided to go ahead with this homage to Julian Beck, anarchist, poet, and founder of The Living Theatre. Ira Cohen gathered a great many pieces for us: we were only able to print a few. We apologize to those we had to leave out.

Sadly comes the news of Darrell Grey's death. Darrell, poet, essayist, above all friend, died miserably of poverty and drink in an Oakland flophouse. His body wasn't found for three days, and when it was, his parents, summoned by phone, told the landlord to throw out everything in Darrell's room, and to sell what he could "for his trouble." So out went Darrell's poems, his novel, his collages, his photographs, his thousands of letters from his friends. He died twice, the second death more brutal than the first. We are asking all his friends to check their files for work by him to send to Allan Kornblum, Coffee House Press, Box 10870, Minneapolis, MN 55440. "To do to things what light does to them," said Darrell paraphrasing Guillevic in *The Actualist Manifesto*. He did to us what light does: illuminated and transformed. Adios, poet.

Ira Cohen

JULIAN BECK AND JUDITH MALINA IN *SIGNALS THROUGH FLAME*, 1983.

JULIAN & THE APOCALYPSE

by Tom Weigel

Julian Beck's impact upon both theater and society would never have been the thing it was without the available specter of the A-bomb. This, added to America's long involvement in the Vietnam and Cambodian wars, enabled the Living Theatre to reach out to a growing audience, already stirred to protest. In this climate, Beck's confrontational approach to theater would always make the stage seem secondary to its purposes. The Living Theatre's first compulsion was to call up and enact in proto-shamanistic Artaudian frenzies of emotion its commitment. That commitment was to the premise of an always renewable oppressor and the ever-available oppressed. The repetition of this theme was relieved only by the effectiveness of Beck and the company in choosing to address their audiences in a direct manner. This approach often saw him and players carry the play off the stage and into the audience. The interaction was deemed essential. On the surface, its success towards the encouragement of our active rejection of the predatory-natured society was dramatic in itself. This impression seemed substantial in view of the enormous crowds they enjoyed at the outdoor performances of *Paradise Now* for instance, both in the U.S. and Europe. How much sincerity in its principles to be later demonstrated by others is still a question. Quite often, Beck suggested through the Living Theatre's example that madness endemic to Artaud's theory was a way to confront the oppressor, who was "the power broker" then. He would appear to have had considerable success in this department. We now come to the new power brokers of today, who have become unmentionable among no other than the Living Theatre's progeny. To say who really controls *who* among our "struggling masses," mainly poets and "performance artists" is too sensitive for controversy. Oppressors, (*first rule of thumb*) whether yours or theirs (though always the people's), must come from the outside, never from within our own ranks. Given this, the nuclear and post-nuclear periods, or *ages* if they must be, have only to run out of print paper before being eulogized. The world was topical for the Living Theatre and Julian Beck. He undertook nothing which did not pose the social oppression and bondage, out of which comes grief, war, atrocity, genocide, death and destruction. As such, corruption was another coveted concern of this didactic impulse, as it was for Brecht's Berlin Ensemble. That corruption was only seen to be manifested among the ruling classes, of course. This predominant view, humorless at heart and drunk on Apocalypse (now the oldest wine in the history of social outrage) appears irreversible. No opposite views of the intelligent sort are to be had. A strange proposition this, which might say more for the depth of propaganda itself. There are only opposite conditions like apathy, escapism, delusions and fascism. Another view might see a need for more insight. For instance, if the now taken for granted psychology of opposites gives us nothing but the defined polarizations of Right and Left, which we've all come to breakfast and sup upon, it would suggest only the Revolutionary can have the better part of humanity's welfare at heart. It is also a premise that anyone who would move among the new power brokers could scarcely afford to treat with scepticism. And so, for only a moment, I have the pleasure to dream about what present day arts and letters would be like without our long nurtured fetish of thoughts upon apocalyptic destruction. For it would seem that the Revolutionary cause has long presupposed that the oppressor looks forward with great appetite to those glorious nightly orgies and banquets in chic airconditioned climes of private interest-free fallout shelters. It's either this, or we must accept their propensity for self destruction, along with genocide, suicide and manic depression. Then to suppose that Apocalypse is the final issue, and being such, it might be free of further implications for the rest of us, it's the final bid for the most esteemed page of art's moral register. There's a nightmare of guilt for both oppressor and oppressed. Here another veritable "abomination" rears its ancient monks' head in the fiery arena of true blue agnostic concern. Goodbye Julian — goodbye Living Theatre, though we'll never really be through with you. Indeed, you were right, the Apocalypse *has* won and we are all exquisite living corpses.

TOO MUCH, I THINK

by Taylor Mead

Julian Julian Julian — I have mixed emotions about the Living Theatre which of course was Julian. Why did they preach love and socialism and commune-ism and the World as one and behave so badly and rudely in restaurants, screaming at the waiters and owners of little innocent side street ristorantes in Rome, etc? Why were their rehearsals so often a study in mental S & M? Was it because Julian was tolerant to the point of absurdity, or sainthood? I never saw Julian behaving "badly" but I was only around occasionally and was often giving the theatre a hard time myself. Screaming at them during performances if they repeated themselves too often. For instance during a performance in Cassis, France, where they were performing Mysteries in a theatre my friend Jerome Hill had erected for them at the cost of several hundred thousand dollars in a great setting opposite a glorious cliff across a Mediterranean inlet. They kept saying (I believe Julian) "We must end the war in Vietnam . . . we must end the war in Vietnam" while everyone in the company ran around dying of a plague or war or something — in a very cliché fashion — they were so "deep" into how to die it all came out very communal to the point of sameness. In any case I believe something repeated enough transvalues itself — it reached this point for me and I began yelling "a bas les intellectuels" . . . "Vive la guerre de Vietnam" . . . "Vive president Johnson" and over and over *almost* as many times as Julian was intoning "we must end the war in Vietnam." At some point a member of the mostly French audience yelled "queue de poisson" and I left the premises — to rejoin the actors and audience in a celebration down the hill in the town port — Judith and Julian were very forgiving and said they wanted to stimulate their audiences in such a fashion. Members of the troop had other opinions. "We were frozen" . . . . "It was horrendous." A pompous French critic wrote in a major magazine that the whole thing was an insult to Cassis which was "a flower in the buttonhole of Provence" and my friend Jerome tore down the wonderful theatre. But I have seen many things of the "Living" that I wholly approved of in performance . . . some of the crowd-pleasers or critic-pleasers like "The Brig" and "The Connection" and *parts* of most of their other pieces. I even like the last presentation at the Joyce Theatre in New York where the critics went savage: "They ain't got no respect" as Rodney Dangerfield would say, and they have no sense of history or aristocracy either. Besides I thought it showed an interesting change of direction for the Living and a refreshing sense of humor about themselves, and of course Julian's acting was superb. Judith and Julian are great actors. In fact it's hard to tell when they're acting in real life or other. I never quite bought the great tax revolt when they picketed and even broke into their theatre on Sixth Avenue and 14th Street after the government seized it for non-payment of taxes. In the first place, someone who everyone in New York knew was a "box-office thief" was operating their box-office. Were they doing rehabilitation social work on him or what? He walked off with a huge percentage of their box-office receipts for extremely successful plays, far more than tax money. Did they just turn this into a chance for noble social protest against government taxation or what? But then I suspect Jesus too. So who am I to know? Little me? Speaking of acting — Judith Malina in William Carlos Williams' plays I considered a great discovery in the realm of Bette Davis and such and I was a little disappointed she didn't stay in the at least near commercial stream of theatre. No, they had to intellectualize and "think" about everything . . . too much, I think . . .

Love 'em.

Julia Demarée

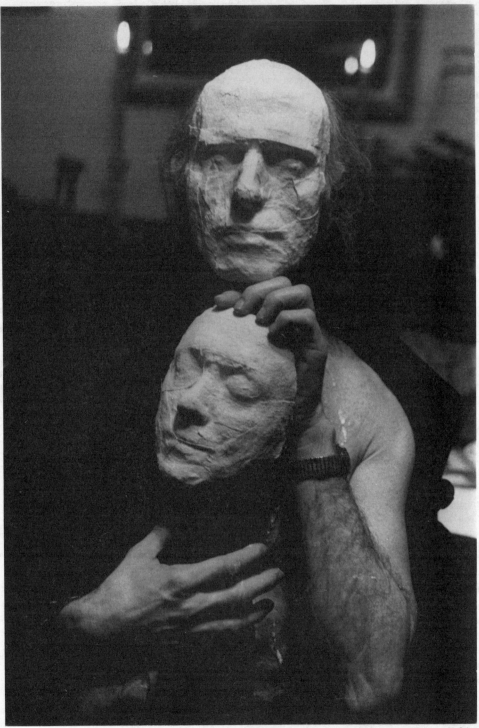

Ira Cohen

POEMS BY ALLEN GINSBERG

YOU DON'T KNOW IT

In Russia the tyrant cockroach ate 20 million souls
and you don't know it, you don't know it
In Czechoslovakia the police ate the feet of a generation
        that can't walk
and you don't know it, you don't know it
In Poland the police state double agent cancer grew large
        as the Catholic Church Frankenstein the State
        itself a Ship in Goloush
and you don't know it, you don't know it
In Hungary tanks rolled over words of Politicians and Poets
and you don't know it
In Yugoslavia only the underground partisans of the Great
        Patriotic war
Fought off the Great Patriotic Army of USSR
and you don't know it,
you know Tito but you don't know it
you say you don't know it these exiles from East Europe
        Complaining about the Gulag in Nicaragua
Cause you don't know it was the party card intellectuals
        of Moscow Vilmirs Minsk Leningrad and Tibilisi
Saying "Invade Immediately" the curse on your Revolution
No you don't know it's not N.Y. it's Moscow Prague Budapest
        Belgrade E. Berlin
saying you don't know it you don't know it
It's Bela Achmadulina in Candlelight saying "American poet
        you can never know the tragedy of Russia"
Nor you Borge Cardinal Rodriguez you say you don't know it
you Can't know it you're busy with war the Yankees Worse
        than memory of Stalin
That you know it, yes you do know it
But you don't know it but you will know it
yes you will know it Lenin said
the first time History is Tragedy the second time repeats
        it's Comedy
or was it Trotsky?

Non passaron the whispers from the Elbe, the intellectual
        skulls shattering teeth on Danube, Vistula
the Churchbells drowning in the dammed Waters of Volga
The Taiga woodsman weeping over the "boring pamphlets" his
        forests provided
the Kulaks rattling shells & bones to seed a new millennial
        agriculture by 1980 90 2000
with the ectoplasm of Lysenko providing ammonia to grow
        Kasha —

STALIN SIGHTINGS:
Photos by William Levy

You don't know it Castro the intellectual in Power Chair
                a quarter century
biting fairies' nuts off, sneaking into Manolo Ballagra's
                desk to read my love letters
Making Padilla eat your shit you don't know it's
a frou frou among French intellectuals whose magazines
                you glance at
between Wars from the North Yanquis and banquets with Pork & Rum
after TV evening news —
                You don't know it
Madam Mandlestom's thick books of gossip, Mrs. Ginzburg's
grey prisoners shitting on each other in the hull of the boat
on frozen sea out of Vladworstak going with the million
Card Carrying Party members old Bolshevik friends of Lenin
to the frozen puddles and hungry banks of Kolyma
Where skeletons hit each other to keep alive you don't
know it

And they Don't know it, Absionov Sfwaretsky, Romain Rolland
                Eherenberg Fedorenko Marhov Yevtuchenko
don't know the midnight club of Death Squads on Cobblestone
                no
they don't know the ears cut off, heads chopped open in
                Salvador don't know the million
Indians in Model Villages Guatemala

Don't know the 40,000 bellies ripped open by the D'aubuisson
                the Salvador Hit man for Death Politics
don't know the yanquis exchanging money from the Duane for Chinese opium
Trading Bananas to Europe for Tax control in Managua & Shanghai —
Don't know the holocaust in Salvador 25 years ago 30,000
shot one week for thinking Left Pink triangle
                yellow red headband lie on peyote
Don't know Pedro Petrie, Einstein engenado, street Rap & indian Hi Sign
Don't know the leap of Imagination like a frog in a communist Monastery Pond
Don't know how to Confess like a worm turning in a matchbox full of Salt
Don't know Solitude, the lesbia Capo ordering the Movie Star Princess to expose her
——— and her delicate pink ——— and her firm round ——— to
                the false dogs of Ideology Fart Yowp with a big prick
                Whip Blip Blip Blip —
Wrap it up in Dynamite they Don't know the Marines in your
                mother's toilet
No you don't know it we don't know it only the stupid
                American USA knows it intolerant gasbags ascend
with millions of Copies of *Reader's Digest* & the Moravian Bible
Just like a photo enlargement of a thumbnail translation
Put in my tieless shirt pocket in a sweat eyes closing as
                the enemy approaches
to fall asleep & snore Don't I know it

                February 17, 1986 2:00-2:12

VELOCITY OF MONEY

I'm delighted by the velocity of money as it whistles
        through the windows of Lower East Side
Delighted by the skyscrapers rising and old grungy apartments
        falling on 84th Street
Delighted by inflation that drives me out on the street
After all what good is the family farm, why eat turkey by
        thousands every Thanksgiving
Why not have Star Wars? Why have the same old America?!?
George Washington wasn't good enough! Tom Paine pain in the
        neck, Whitman a jerk!
I'm delighted by double digit interest rates in the
        Capitalist world
I always was a Communist, now we'll win
as usury makes the walls thinner, books thicker & dumber
Usury makes my poetry more valuable
my manuscripts worth their weight in useless gold —
Now everybody's atheist like me, nothing's sacred
buy and sell your grandmother, eat up old age homes,
Peddle babies on the street, pretty boys for sale on
        Times Square —
You can shoot heroin, I can sniff cocaine,
macho men can fite on the Nicaraguan border and get paid
        with paper!
The velocity's what counts as the National Debt gets higher
Everybody running after the rising dollar
Crowds of joggers down Broadway past City Hall on the way
        to the Fed
Nobody reads Dostoyevsky books so they'll have to give
        passing ear
to my fragmented ravings in between President's speeches
Nothing's happening but the collapse of the Economy
so I can go back to sleep till the landlord wins his
        eviction suit in court.

        2/18/86 — 10 AM

THE FATAL ATTRACTION

by Elinor Nauen

he's depressed he's shopping he's in great pain
I've destroyed his life with my fatal attraction conquest
femme fatale she who never
what he wants what is it he sees
I don't I shouldn't but I want I can't but
chatter on your book my book
a most unhilarious life

the one I meant to have & pushed too far & here we are
miserable & hard & nervous
I remember everything you ever said
I forget all the promises you think you made
& the anger I deserve
you are my only mother, Mom
see the stigmata on my tongue?
I'm biting back retorts
patient as sea glass   huddled by the ocean
I speak   translucent & smooth
he wants me   in some way   I don't   I turn
to drama melodrama some say
I'd rather live alone than with you
but I'd rather live with you than without you
but will you hate me till Wednesday please so I can get a little
more work done?
he buys 4 bright tank tops (old men's undershirts)
& a pair of purple shorts
in the curtained dressing room we almost
I stagger against the wall when he slides his hand
under my shorts   dizzy
terror — would this never have happened?
he's trouble I'm trouble I know it I'm in trouble
let's go to your house
("our house" I say to myself)
& we do & make love then I don't
go with him to Sasha's play & he won't tell me he loves me
why not why not I scream but he's late & just says
you know
of course I don't   eat   I do
clip   my red toenails go to the movies say nothing
about anything to my friends the 2 dykes who come visit & adore
me or don't
this week I'm into adoration
last week hypochondria was my hobby
this week abasement to him & desire from everyone else
(the office heart-throb & one other)
in 5 years I'll remember the passion the intensity the fatal
attraction & think   this was a good time
but right now I'm a jerk who fakes seizures
plus I want to step back behind the curtain
keep my life inside itself
its old routes   I get lost
going to work if I swerve the least bit

THE GARDEN

by Hayden Carruth

It is anywhere, but always America, always an exact
  encompassment
of his consciousness, as this lower end
 of a southward-sloping field,
  this order in
disorder, these rows of little carrots,
 corn, beans, squash, with a spatter
  of weeds as they
might be flung from a heedless hand among
 the attempts of culture. He
  is anyone,
any poet, perhaps, wishing he could
 be anyone, which really
  is what he is,
any poet grown old and gray, paunchy,
 his fingers stiff that try to
  grasp the weedlings,
inflamed eyes from the natural pollen —
 oh, not his mind, his body
  rejects the world,
not his spirit but his flesh, which he is —
 and his vision is misty.
  A patriarch
of his tribe he would be now if the tribe
 had not gone off in sorrow,
  dispersed and lost.
He is alone. He is accustomed to
 talking to no one, the great
  no one that is
everywhere unknown, the mythic consciousness in which his own is as
  a scared owlet
in the parliament of swans and larks and
 thrushes. The garden, it seems,
  is a map, a
crazy-quilt of shapes and colors, the weeds
 already flowering, chick-
  weed, heal-all, purs-
lane, planted marigolds for protection
 among the cabbages, and
  sweet william, and
nasturtiums, a scattering of little fierce
 states and nations; or it is
  a funnel for

the whole medley of the field, whirling the
 storm of history, many
  voices, many
deaths "Love is like a faucet" sang a black
 and beautiful and ravaged
  lady, "it turns
off and on." Evil and good. How the pro-
 cedures of time are an un-
  avoidable
disorder, here in the garden. His mind
 repeats over and over
  many names, but
most, now and for many years: Allende —
 there, as if from the fringes
  of the forest,
from the wisps of clouds, Allende, the name
 of sorrow, of misery,
  of hopelessness,
and of humiliation, too, and great
 despair, for that death was made
  in treachery
by the poet's own civilization,
 yes, reject it as he may!
  In Chile are
his thoughts brought all together, the storm's whirl
 of circumstances, where evil
  previls always,
it being of the nature of the storm.
 Señor Presidente, please
  do not forgive
me, not ever. The poet stands now. Pain
 in his knees. He staggers, and
  the misty blaze
of hawkweed and daisies above him in
 the field sweeps him in tumult
  back, down and back
to the garden. He kneels again, voiceless,
 defeated. A kingfisher
  speeds down the brook
below him, like a projectile
 under the arching alders
  and birches, their
tunnel, flinging harsh derisive laughter
 as he goes, but it is not
  a projectile,
not a tunnel, the laughter is only
 the sound kingfishers must make
  in their species,

evolved for who knows what reason — but not
  a reason, only the flung
    random effect
of random causes. Another sound would
  serve as well. Imagining
    has made only

devices that self-destruct — great Villon,
  Vallejo! — abruptly in
    the swish of a
machete. Kingfisher, careen once more
  through the storm. *O mi Presidente,*
    never forgive.

THE WET CORPSE WAVES AT
THE WORLD SAYING: EXODUS
by Edward Mycue

Mental agility, fleshbound, wrapt, justified in strange beauty exploding in the glands, seaweak slips within the sliding light trembling, lurching into dripping sleep as the body exhausts the mind. Caught in a wave of worlds, gape-drunk, fingers spread beside the face, tentacling fugues of the scents of the uncontrollable theaters of skin slanting to the foot that dangles, drifting to a distant bed. This uncertain swim through night turns in pursuit of the pavilion and wakes our brittle sleep of unfinished contemplation. Or I might have said only "my" if you don't want to be included. Because it is there for a time that time is in the corner with sandy night horses, ghost dancers   each weighted like the rose and each the same, the same and variable — as Apollo flowers in the sacred stream of our foolish, frantic, anxious, hot, moist, crazed, burning and aching swims (— would you rather I say "MY" and only my, mine alone?) through night. Then time gets up out of the corner and moves. Stories skitter like rose smoke or acknowledged manners or even unacknowledged manners (and you know who I am) that I sew on like doubt over dark. Then when my own motives brim over with secrets, regrets — that suggest dark the great restorer and light just a chalk block — time gets up again out of the corner it somehow got back into and moves on out of the earth and back into it like a megadream arc-welding tool and sails up gusting over the memories that are a hedge of scars spanning the indifferent face of afternoon. Now, here I stop to meditate the sealed gates of preference: why I chose to be the man I am: for I love freedom.

IF I EVER GROW OLD:
GRIM & GLEEFUL RESOLUTIONS
by Elinor Nauen

after Swift

To be grumpy, grouchy, petulant, paranoid & mean: to hit out with my cane from my wheelchair at passersby
To clutch my chest, turn red & be allowed everything
To insist upon senior citizen discount
To constantly remind the whippersnappers that if it was good enough in my day it's fine (too good) for them
To remind the Young that I knew them when younger
To make children kiss me on my withered cheeks & if it makes them cry because I smell funny to snap a sharp slap for disrespect
To make them push me fast in my wheelchair but if they tip me they should've known better

To tell my great anecdotes as often as possible, to hone them for the historians
To scare the wits out of the Young: It goes so fast, one day you're young, the next you're like me, old & feeble, how did I ever get to be so old, it'll happen to you. To never let them forget this
To give up shopping & dressing, as no one wants to fuck me so why bother
To expect plenty of the strong & healthy, to poopoo their feats
To make gossip supreme: to call as I do now, Steve & Maggie & Alice daily
To help, with the accumulated wisdom & authority of my years, all those who suffer
To cut off mercilessly anyone who interrupts
To become extremely set in my ways, obsessive, hypochondriacal, opinionated, argumentative, obstinate & indomitable
To remind One & All of my various former loves & enumerate those once infatuated with me: nessun maggior dolore che ricordarsi del tempo felice nella miseria

CHER CADAVRE EXQUIS

CORPSE USE RESTRICTED BY OLIGARCHY

I would like to call your attention to a disturbing state of affairs here at the University of Wisconsin-Madison library. *Exquisite Corpse* is kept here in the rare book room, which means that access to it is quite restricted. First of all, the hours are limited. Second, the procedure for getting something is a bizarre bureaucratic nightmare of filling in forms, putting all your possessions in a locked compartment, obtaining special acid-free paper and special pencils, and reading a two-page list of rules and regulations about care of materials, behavior in the rare book room, and other matters. After this, the librarian fetches the material from the safe, but she has to know the volume number. As I simply wanted to browse through some recent issues, I was a bit at odds with the standard procedure. I managed eventually to explain the concept of browsing to the librarian, and simply ignored her when she said, "You mean you don't know which issue you're looking for?" Perhaps all of this may not concern you, as it might lead some to give up the fight and buy a subscription. However, my guess is that consignment to the rare book dungeon keeps the journal from many potential subscribers and many potential readers. It might be considered an honor to be classified with antique manuscripts and crumbling folios, but I'd prefer to be in the periodical room, which is designed for reading.

— Larry Cohen

BECK TRIBUTE MOVES

Your tribute to Julian Beck moved me as it must have moved many, many others for whom the Living Theatre is an unforgettable part of what we have experienced. I first saw Julian and Judith some years before I met them, when I was drawn to small uptown lofts by their presentations, if memory serves me right, of Pirandello and Strindberg, playwrights who were exciting to read or read about but whose plays seemed impossible to find produced. When the Living Theatre established itself, precariously but magnificently, on 14th Street and 6th Avenue, it became one of the most vital scenes for the happenings of the time, the plays being part of the happenings as were the intermissions where so many movers and shakers mingled in the large and extraordinary lobby. It was probably through James Spicer, a major domo of sorts to Julian, Judith and the Living Theatre, that I came to know Julian and Judith. I never knew them closely, except by the strength of their personalities and by their creations and by all one absorbed from what was in the air and what one heard from friends who mattered. I last saw Julian at the St. Mark's Poetry Project celebration for Allen Ginsberg's *Collected Poems*. I knew he was a dying man but in the few words we exchanged was the living intelligence and gentleness and strength that transcended the physical.

— Ted Wilentz

ZIKR MEANS REMEMBRANCE

In his otherwise-charming essay on Amnesis in the last *Corpse*, N. S. Araúz made something of a blunder in linking amnesia to the sufi technical term *zikr* or maybe he was just being too subtle for me. "The music of amnesia, like the *zikr* of Middle Eastern music, pursues the purest silence,. . .a forgotten sound." But *zikr* actually means remembrance, as in the Koranic verse where Allah says, "Remember me and I will remember you." Some sufis have actually identified the term with Plato's anamnesis. Now it might be said that *zikr* comprises a sort of magick language, mantric, consisting only of divine names & of pure sounds (rhythmic breathing) which "contain" the essence of those names; & that in this sense *zikr* constitutes a sort of forgetting of ordinary language with all its lineal arbitrariness, its failure to achieve *meaning*. In order to remember the Self, one forgets all that which impedes realization. If that's what Araúz meant, then of course he is correct.

I've always been anti-amnesiac, & Araúz has forced me to rethink my position — always a pleasure. However, I *still* hate novels which begin with the hero waking up with amnesia — an exceedingly cheap plot device. And here's an interesting point: do you actually *know* anyone, personally, who ever suffered from clinical amnesia? Does Araúz know anyone with amnesia? Probably not. And yet I've read scores, maybe hundreds of works of fiction based on the concept; & I've always felt this disparity as yet another example of the way most fiction fails to intersect with reality on any level actually experienced by me or anyone I know.

It's only appropriate that the only lit'ry magazine in the world that *admits* to being a corpse should in fact be the only one that provides real animation, vril, elixir vitae & spunk. I wish I could bail you out of your financial sink — but I'm already mired in too many moneyless Kulture-ventures as it is. But I'll pray for you, for your mortal bones. And for your amusement here's some recent bumpf from the Association for Ontological Anarchy.

— Hakim Bey

POEMS BY DEBORAH SALAZAR

AT CROSS PURPOSES

Structure could become a panacea;
what words chase after in pantomime
is a feminine form in each idea
I can't pin down with a masculine rhyme.
Adam names the animals; each name fixes
itself at my mouth like a muzzle.
If Christ is the Word, no logic prefixes
a logos lost in the crossword puzzle.
It's sick mathematics; forms diversify
with each thesaurus we add to the shelf.
You want me to be plain, but even if I
named you, you would not recognize yourself.
Like, "Lamb of God" is a pet name and yet
it's a password, a code, an epithet.

I'm pressed for a secret I've overheard,
a fact I've forgotten, a gist I've missed.
But I don't say much; I've got a word
at the tip of my tongue like a eucharist.
A host of synonyms muttered like quips
that you should be equipped to understand
are changed to lies when they pass my lips.
Our words are poor traitors; they turn on
    command.
And though nothing adds up, one myth is about
a cross in the shape of a squatty plus.
Definitions evolve until they're x-ed out,

but this formula doesn't suit either of us.
What stands for your order is minus mine:
a plus like an omen, a negative sign.

TAKING PAINS

for Elise Blackwell

It's so dark in there (in the caviar jar)
"The history of Russia" (whose black well?)
A white slash of sweat (at the crook of your arm)
and a very young wine (it's pink and warm).

Sure, women have a long way to go but
men came too fast (what csar outlasts the crown?)
You fall over, riddled — the jokes dart in.
Each is crucial, short-lived, masculine.

It smarts. What pain can outsmart a husband?
What other daughter can touch you, Elise?
If most pains are feminine, quiet and chronic,
your body's a cure, your poison and tonic.

I feed us fish eggs and artichoke crowns.
We laugh about daddies of black-eyed girls.
Each rival head's blonde (but it's just not fair)
so we walk ourselves home (it's dark in there).

BODY LANGUAGE

by Stan Leventhal

Looking down at the dry stain on the blanket, Roger remembered spitting out the semen and saliva after Charlie came in his mouth. Recalling the foul taste, he handled the blanket at arm's length, as though it were diseased. Folding it, making sure that his fingers did not touch the soiled part, he tucked it into his laundry bag. Roger had planned to suck Charlie's cock. All of the gestures and signs he had developed to attract attention to his own cock were sublimated so that the focus would be on Charlie's. The message was obvious, the language — though silent — clear and direct: I want to suck your cock. Tease it, devour it, feel it grow. The pleasure would be mutual. Roger would enjoy making Charlie writhe and groan, as Charlie would revel in feeling his cock harden, the nerve endings stroked until almost numb, the tension and release of a satisfying orgasm. But Charlie tried to take what Roger wanted to give, and a gift is robbed of all meaning if it's stolen. Charlie had not understood, was unable to distinguish between two acts which look similar but are completely different. Cocksucking may look like facefucking, but anyone who's tried either knows that they have little in common. A cocksucker takes the active role by manipulating his partner, who remains passive. A facefucker ignores the artistry of the cocksucker by thrusting his cock into the mouth and throat as though it were merely a convenient orifice with nothing special to offer. Roger and Charlie had knelt on the bed, face to face. Bending, Roger embraced Charlie's cock with his lips. He provided saliva, worked his tongue, created vacuums, caressed with his cheeks and palate. Charlie responded by seizing Roger's hair. He rammed his cock into Roger's mouth. Forcing him to lie down on his back, Charlie straddled his head and pumped his face like a jackhammer. Roger did not resist. He could not bring himself to deny Charlie the pleasure of an orgasm, even though he suddenly found himself not enjoying what had, a few moments before, been sublime. To explain the difference between giving and taking, sucking and being fucked would destroy any vestige of propriety, mystery, sensuality. The sperm, which would have tasted pungent and creamy was rendered bitter, slimy.

The mouthful that Roger had planned on savoring and swallowing was instantly spat onto the blanket in disgust. Roger locked the door and slung the laundry bag over his shoulder. Leaving the building, walking up the street, he could still recall the awful taste on his tongue. He exchanged the bag for a ticket at the launderer's, wishing he could erase the memory from his mind as easily as stains can be removed from blankets.

SEMEN

by Ronnie Burk

Ammonia
Ascorbic acid
Ash
Calcium
Carbon dioxide
Chloride
Cholesterol
Citric acid
Copper
Creatine
Ergothioneine
Fructose
Glutathione
Glyserylphosphorylcholine
Inositol
Lactic acid
Magnesium
Nitrogen
Phosphorus, acid-soluble
Phosphorylcholine
Potassium
Pyruvic acid
Sodium
Sorbitol
Vitamin B-12
Sulfur
Urea
Uric acid
Zinc

— Thaddeus Mann, *The Biochemistry of Semen and of the Male Reproductive Tract*

POEMS BY ANNE WALDMAN

ALL THINGS CONFINE

after Hadewijch
(Dutch, thirteenth century)

All things
crowd me

but I am wide
wide
I am wide

After that "other"
I grasp
bigger world:

Always this is
my love
& joy

but when
I catch "it" (world)
once in a
while
it flings
me wide

"Me" is too narrow
All else is
my joy

It is this other
kicks me
further & wide

All things confine
but
the poem, the
matrix,
dear man-or-woman
energy-I-fuck

The poem
arises from
you, Other,
& from you,

the world
widens

the world
widens

TRAVEL BEING LOVE

I awoke in an ancient country to you
You smelled of lilac, of musky dew
& tasted of salt & sex
I heard you moan like a beast
The arrangement of your limbs was intense
I was reading the life of a dead poet
You pretended to be asleep, ha!
The bracelet on your arm over face hid a blue
  eye
I saw you quiver & expect something
I smelled your lemony hair
I heard a far car swish like a fish
& someone yell "Frankie!"
I heard the motor hour go by
Then caught myself touching you
I can't help it
You want me to, don't you?
You didn't want any words or places
Where we hadn't yet met
Managua? Sri Lanka? Halifax?
Listen: we sat in The Black Rose near the
  Aquarium
where an Irish lilt filled the air
Sweet guys & girls off boats
at the next table were drinking & smoking
& you said "Vrindaban!" & "Night's a switch"
These lines are swift arrows
I smelled that you had been hiding many years
& invited you to this restaurant
where blinds clattered
The light again shifts
A man coughs loudly
Your face hesitates on the border between us
While a green oilcloth shines in a new light.

THE CURIOUS DISPOSITION OF BODY PARTS, 1800-1850: COINCIDENCE OR ROMANTIC IMPULSE?
by Sterling Eisiminger

In the Museum of Natural History in Florence, Italy, Nathaniel Hawthorne once saw in the room dedicated to Galileo a forefinger of the seventeenth-century astronomer preserved and "fixed on a little gilt pedestal, and pointing upward, under a glass cover." Hawthorne added, "It is very much shrivelled and mummylike, of the color of parchment, and is little more than a fingerbone, with the dry skin of flesh flaking away from it; on the whole not a very delightful relic; but Galileo used to point heavenward with the finger, and I hope has gone whither he pointed" (*Notes of Travel,* IV, 1900).

Hawthorne sounds slightly disgusted and surprised as he describes the keepsake someone took from Galileo's corpse but, in fact, taking and preserving part of a body at or shortly after death has been customary in many cultures for ages despite numerous taboos. In the Middle Ages, bodies were often boiled to remove the flesh in order that the bones could be saved and safely transported. To insure that their bones would be taken to their homes in case of death, the crusaders took large cauldrons with them to the Holy Lands. During the same period, if a person achieved sainthood and the popularity of Thomas à Becket, for example, his bones were distributed widely. Despite the emphasis on burial in Hebrew and classical writings, the bones, hair, and organs of Christian saints have been kept in reliquaries for centuries. These containers "may be rings enclosing a small fingerbone, or even a bone chip behind a crystal cover; gold cases for limbs; jewelled sarcophagi; or for very popular saints, whole cathedrals" (Barbara Jones, *Design for Death,* 1967).

During the English Renaissance and Restoration the practice of saving body parts seems to have gained in popularity as a grief therapy, as a memorial for the dead, and as an expression of political opposition. The heads of Thomas More, Henry Grey, Walter Raleigh and Oliver Cromwell, and the heart of Anne Boleyn were all removed after death during the sixteenth and seventeenth centuries and preserved usually for political reasons. However, for reasons that are not entirely clear, the practice became especially widespread among the artists and intelligentsia of the romantic era. Joseph Haydn (d. 1809), Ludwig van Beethoven (d. 1827), Frédéric Chopin (d. 1849), Percy Shelley (d. 1822), Lord Byron (d. 1824), Jeremy Bentham (d. 1832), and Napoleon Bonaparte (d. 1821), had parts or all of their bodies preserved for a variety of reasons after their deaths.

The reasons for the preservation of Haydn's skull are indeed strange. It seems that after the composer's death, two phrenologists, men who believed that the conformation of the skull revealed the mental capacity and character of the owner, paid a gravedigger to decapitate the corpse. When Haydn's body was exhumed outside Vienna for transfer to Eisenstadt, where the composer had lived for many years under the patronage of the Esterhazy family, Prince Esterhazy noticed the absence of the head and ordered the police to conduct an investigation. The phrenologists were located, but they were out of the police's jurisdiction. The Prince then offered to buy the skull, but the clever thieves sent the purchasers another skull which, nevertheless, was buried with the body. It should be noted that the motives of the phrenologists, who had been friends and admirers of Haydn, were honorable, not ghoulish: they wished only to preserve a skull with the configuration of musical genius in order that other skulls might be compared to it. When the last of the two phrenologists died, he bequeathed the skull to the Vienna Society of the Friends of Music; to this day Haydn's skull lies alone in Vienna while the rest of him is in Eisenstadt with another man's skull.

Because of Beethoven's deafness, there was also considerable scientific interest in that great composer's remains. On March 27, 1827, the day after Beethoven's death, an autopsy was performed by Dr. Johann Wagner who was particularly interested in the cause of Beethoven's deafness. In the postmortem examination, the temporal bones were sawed out for closer scrutiny. These were displayed for years in the Vienna Anatomy Museum, but they have since disappeared.

The remains of Chopin are similarly separated, although the locations of the parts are known. His body lies in Père-Lachaise Cemetery in Paris while his heart is beneath a marble bust in Warsaw's Holy Cross Church. Chopin was a native of Poland and, although most of his mature life was spent in France, he never lost his affection for his native land. In fact, throughout his years in France, he kept a silver vessel filled with Polish earth, which was sprinkled on his coffin during the funeral ceremony. Just before his death, fearing a premature burial, Chopin asked that his body be opened and that his heart be removed for return to Poland.

Perhaps more popular is the legend of Shelley's heart. Of extraordinary size and durability, the poet's heart survived several days in the sea, the devastations of lime and sand, and finally the cremation fire itself. Edward Trelawny, friend who had arranged the pagan funeral service because he felt Shelley would have liked it, finally snatched the heart from the ashes but lost it in a wrangle with Leigh Hunt. Lord Byron and others imposed on Hunt to give the heart to Mary Shelley who, when she finally got possession of it, preserved it in wine for a while, then dehydrated it, and kept it with her in a silken shroud the rest of her life. It was finally buried with Shelley's son Percy in a silver case.

Lord Byron, who played such a dramatic role at Shelley's funeral, and who died two years later during the Greek war of independence, was also opened after death in order that an autopsy might be performed and that the inhabitants of Missolonghi, Greece, might have more of the man they loved than they already had. The Greeks were given Byron's lungs, which were placed in the Church of San Spiridioni, and the rest of the body was sent to England where it was buried in the Hucknall Torkard Cemetery in Nottinghamshire. The urn containing Byron's lungs disappeared during the continued fighting in Greece. As Leslie A. Marchand notes in his biography, Byron, who used a skull as a drinking vessel, probably would not have objected to the distribution of his parts because he once wrote apropos of the eviscerated body of Lord Guilford: "Conceive a man going

one way, and his intestine another, and his immortal soul a third! — was there ever such a distribution?"

The body of Jeremy Bentham was also eviscerated, but the parts were not distributed. Instead Bentham gave explicit instructions in *Auto-Icon* on the disposition of his body. It was to be mummified, dressed, and seated in a glass box in the dining room of University College, London. Bentham stated:

If it should so happen that my personal friends and other Disciples should be disposed to meet together for the purpose of commemorating the Founder of the greatest happiness system of morals and legislation [namely Bentham], my executor will from time to time cause to be conveyed to the room in which they meet the said Box or case with the contents there to be stationed in such part of the room as to the assembled company shall seem meet.

Unfortunately, the method that Bentham had hoped would preserve his flesh failed, and a wax head had to be placed on his shoulders. His actual head now rests in the box between his feet.

Napoleon had no desire that his body be preserved, although he did request an autopsy. After his death, however, according to Jeremy Beadle, his head was shaved and the hair distributed to the former emperor's admirers. Napoleon's heart was removed along with his stomach, intestines and penis, and preserved in the customary reliquaries. Professor Beadle reports that the intestines were destroyed in a 1940 German air raid on London, and the penis "was offered for sale [in 1972] at Christie's but failed to reach the reserve price" (David Wallechinsky et al., *The Book of Lists,* 1978).

In addition to the seven men discussed above, all of whom died between 1800 and 1850, two other prominent men who died much earlier were exhumed during this fifty-year period. For two very different reasons, sundry body parts were removed and saved during these exhumations.

During the French Revolution some Frenchmen took out their wrath on the aristocracy by disinterring the body of Louis XIV, who had died in 1715, and plundering his heart. The organ was later sold to an English connoisseur of rare foods who ate the embalmed heart.

In 1813, Sir Henry Halford, the English Royal Surgeon, performed an autopsy on the remains of

King Charles I, who was beheaded in 1649. The surgeon saved the king's fourth cervical vertebra, which the executioner's ax had cleanly severed, and used it for thirty years as a saltcellar until Queen Victoria ordered the bone returned to the tomb. Victoria's failure to be amused effectively rang the death knell on the general practice of saving body parts. However, it must be said that in 1903 the U.S. Patent Office did grant a patent to an inventor who had devised a technique for preserving all or just the head of a corpse in a block of transparent glass. No models were submitted with the patent application.

Among the nine men discussed above, there are few patterns. Five of the men were prominent artists of the romantic era, but only Chopin and Bentham requested the disposition of their body parts; only three and possibly four dispositions were illegal, and only two of the men now rest with all of their body parts in the same location. Parts of four of the men are lost, and there is no pattern among the parts of the nine that were saved: four hearts, a set of lungs, a skull, a skull portion, locks of hair,

some intestines, a stomach, a penis, a vertebra, and an entire body. Six of the post-mortem incidents can be attributed to romantic impulse and three to science or pseudo-science. The impulses can be subdivided according to nationalistic fervor, fury, love, and individual disregard of authority or accepted social norms.

One cannot expect the wishes of the dying and the grief-stricken to be consistent and rational, but their desires are not always irrational either. The dying often wish to remain among the living or leave something of themselves as a hedge against oblivion, and those who mourn the dead, quite understandably, want to retain a memento. Caretakers of the Protestant Cemetery in Rome, for example, say that it is still impossible to keep violets on John Keats's grave. Most people, however, are satisfied with a dried flower, a gold watch, or a ring. But for about fifty years, several people wanted to hold on to a good deal more, and several coincidences combined with the impulsiveness of a politically and emotionally turbulent age seem to be the best explanation for these curious events. ☠

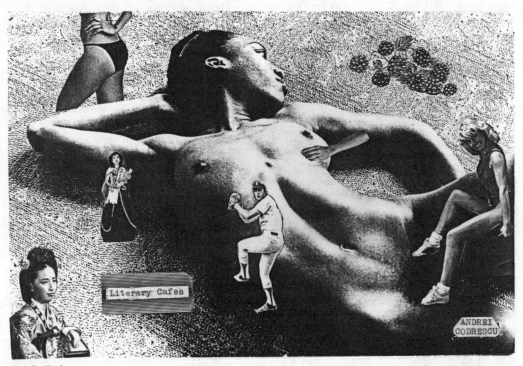

Rudy Burckhardt

POEMS BY EDWARD FIELD

IN THE MIRROR

It's in the bathroom that I loudly groan
    over my incandescent foolishness —

When I think of what I've said and done,
especially tonight at the dinner table —
    O why did I have to blab like that
among those grown up literary people?

You are a jerk and never will be other,
and right thou art to know thy estimate:
    it's written all over your silly face.

And therefore, you may well invoke
    The Eternal Fraternal Principle,
a cry resounding down the ages

to Gods and man alike,
    from Job to Christ-on-the-Cross to you:

O Brother!

ON REFLECTION

I couldn't have admitted it then
but it wasn't so much being horny as
if I didn't want sex
what else was there to do —
everything else in life was boring.

If nobody wanted me
what good was anything:
The only turn-on in fact was
if somebody wanted me.

The royal proof of that, the clincher of course,
is a hard cock,
waving in the air, sliding down your throat,
surely worth a moment, or decades, to adore.
It's what nine-tenths of the world, a genius* wrote,
would crawl on their bellies for.

*Alfred Chester in *The Exquisite Corpse*

YOOHOO

by Laura Rosenthal

Women are collapsible
& can be taken anywhere
on three strong legs but
they aren't stupid
They break off
whispering in the kitchen
when the men come
they break engagements
on the phone   break
code   wind   nails
& still they break up
in all the right places
at the old jokes
at the bowl of broken eggs
you opening her
zippered necklace
Years later waiting
tables they won't regret
the drinks they spill
the fits of temper
they are prone to

LADY FATIMA'S HAND

by Denyse du Roi

for Nina Zivančević

In the midst of matter we are in magic,
traipsing those living star-points of the quotable
quote. Everything comes eventually & somewhere
Cocteau says, "Angels fly because they take themselves
lightly." And we grow lighter too, stuffing jewel boxes
with salty mythologies, growing our tummies on a canvas
too stained with irises not to notice. It's a secret
how these next fifty years'll elapse, canals & bridges
still open to the flâneur, impressionable, yes, but
gradual knowledge of cities, gargoyles over Brassai's
naughty Paris & empathy for nightlife, for your glossy
helmet with wings under afternoon tea hats & (incidentally)
flashing Minus Three prescription sunglasses culled from
the sea. Welcome to such a lovely head this little hand
says in a mighty gesture & trembles below the ear's plushest
part. Tonight we are rich, Nunzio, before an elusive body
of work, detecting these erogenous zones so that the poet's
mouth forms purple feathers, rapturous to say the least.

ONCE UPON A TIME TO COME
by André Breton

translated from the French by Bill Zavatsky and Zack Rogow

Imagination isn't a gift but par excellence an object of conquest. *"Where,"* wonders Huysmans, *"at what time, in what latitudes, in what waters could this immense palace actually rise with its cupolas soaring to the clouds, its phallic columns, its pillars emerging from a hard, mirrory pavement?" (En rade).* A totally lyrical, totally pessimistic way of erasing everything one thinks, everything that should be, as fast as it happens. This palace was *rising, palacing*...That imperfect tense, that useless splendor tending to reject with quasi-legendary gratuitousness the need one feels — those *phallic columns* — to behave, be it only from a sexual standpoint, otherwise than one behaves, bearing witness to a sinful lassitude and to an inadmissible doubt concerning the real powers of the mind. The lamentable formula: "But it was only a dream," whose growing usage, among others cinematographic, has contributed more than a little to the rise of hypocrisy, hasn't been worth discussing for a long time. Why not say it? Huysmans knew very well that the kinds of visions he had — as one can have them: outside time — were no less destined to carry the world "forward" than "backward." What good is it, unless one is going to gloomily retire to a safe refuge, what good is it to accord to that which, once again, should be, the frightening faculty of having been and no longer being! I know the argument against this: "But at every step the mind stumbles into vestiges of certain times and places. Its images are slaves to the greater or lesser emotions which those vestiges gave it. Crazy fetishist! What we conveniently call the past catches it, undeniably, on its weak side. Saint Anthony's nights, Mexico before the arrival of the Spaniards, a photograph of an unknown woman dating from the last century: you over there, if you move try not to make too much noise."

But where are the snows of tomorrow? I say that the imagination, whatever it borrows from and — for me this remains to be proved — if it really does borrow, need not cringe before life. More particularly, there will always be, between the kinds of ideas we call clichés and ideas ... who knows, which will become clichés, a difference susceptible to making the imagination mistress of the mind's estate. It's the whole question of the transformation of energy presenting itself once more. To mistrust as one does, beyond all bounds, the practical virtue of imagination, is to try to deprive oneself at all costs of the assistance of electricity in the hope of bringing hydro-electric power back to its absurd waterfall consciousness.

The imaginary is what tends to become real.

Apropos of which, I'd like to rent (I'll say nothing of buying) a property in the Paris suburbs. (All I need is the money.) Nothing spectacular. Only about thirty rooms with, insofar as possible, long hallways, very dark, or which I'd undertake to darken. Ten or twelve acres of wooded land all around it. A few streams or, preferably, one or two ponds would not be unwelcome. Naturally I'd want to make my own judgment about the security of the place (when I speak of security, thieves will do me the honor of believing that I'm not thinking of them.) Let it be possible for whosoever it might be — the various people whom I'd agree to meet — to enter and leave there night or day without causing any scandal. In a word, all these preconditions easy to meet.

An underground passage, whether or not it needs to be dug, not presenting any further difficulties.

From the outside: rather than a hotel or an inn, so it makes you feel completely disoriented, a coach house. But from the inside, as you'll see, a coach house where those who, according to me, have the right to be there, could always come and hear tiring ideas in exchange for tired ideas.

Meals will be served regularly and *on time* to ... let's say three girls who will be invited to spend time at this place, these girls being the most recent to have achieved renown in a scandal about some haunted house. We'd begin by putting them at ease by persuading them that they're really "at home." In case of any manifest deficiency on their part, replacements would be found for them as soon as possible. In case of an emergency, additional aid could be brought to them. (One might even call on a young man who involuntarily specializes in these kinds of things, though never on more than one young man at a time.) As occasional companions for these young persons we will provide several other girls and several young women who are incidentally in a position to present interesting mediumistic phenomena, or who are unusual for the strangeness of their minds or beauty.

In each room, a large clock made of black glass will be set to ring midnight *particularly* loud. It will be strictly forbidden, on pain of immediate and permanent expulsion, for whomever it may be, despite all provocations to which one might be exposed, to perform, within the walls encircling the grounds, the act of love.

Hardly anything will be there except little desk lamps with green shades, very short. Day and night the blinds will remain closed.

The reception room, whitewashed, will be illuminated only by indirect light and will contain no other furniture than two authentic Merovingian chairs except a stool on which will sit a perfume bottle, tied with a pale ribbon, inside of which steeps a discolored rose, its stem and leaves equally lifeless, which can be seen today, June 9th, in the south window of the pharmacy at the corner of the Rue Lafayette and the Rue du Faubourg Montmartre.

So much for the arbitrary.

But the flock of butterflies set loose by nature will be caught by a man later on and *commented upon*. We shall see, in the end, if bedsheets are made to serve as an envelope for the bodies of men and women (what address would you put on them?) or if, with their incomprehensible height when spread out, they are made to turn imaginary a body which may or may not be imaginary so to prove that the human mind, whatever one says about it, *escapes with something more than a fright*. (Recently I was told this charming ghost story: two men, dressed in the usual costumes, had fun scaring ignorant people several nights in a row by walking around a cemetery. Finally one night a "hardy soul" discreetly snuck up behind them at a bend and took it upon himself to follow them. Aware of a presence at their backs, they high-tailed it out of there. I prefer the first two men to the third.)

A "wishing well," a pure and simple replica of the one at Luna Park, though on first sight less *free*, but diverse, more insistent and much prettier.

Five rooms, with their windows and doorways boarded up, access to them rendered almost impossible without compromising the oath taken to not try and look into them. In the first and, I suppose, the largest one, the finest specimens of mannequins and wax figures will have been gathered, not all piled together, nor with each one playing a part, but arranged in such a manner as they might have appeared before the walling-in, to create the greatest spirit of abandon. In the second, eccentric suitcases, large sunflowers, and spiritual party favors will be thrown together side by side; its walls will be completely papered with love letters. In the third, which we will attempt to make the most luxurious nursery in the world, only a cradle, lacerated and decorated in the proper place with a dagger, will list, like a ship in distress, over a floor of waves that are too blue. Necessity dictates that I be the only one who knows what will take place in the fourth, and that just one trustworthy man should know the true purpose of the fifth, without possessing more than myself or anyone else the ideological key to the whole. (A little puerile? All the better.) The worst is that the first room, from the outside, will not be the slightest bit distinguishable from the second or fifth. The work of setting up the house will be carried out so as to eliminate, *a priori*, any possibility of indiscretion.

Desiring to limit myself today to a simple outline, I won't enlarge uselessly on the decorating scheme of the rooms that are to be occupied. This could only be, of course, absolutely austere — the disparate extremes within the whole corresponding much more to necessity than to capriciousness. As to the rest, one may trust our taste.

The most stringent regulations regarding physical hygiene will be scrupulously observed.

Actually, I still don't know if we'll decide to keep on the premises two white greyhounds or two white terriers of very pure pedigree, or if we can get along without these animals.

What, above all, I wish to defend here is only the guiding principle of a fellowship whose advantage would be to place the mind in a position which seems to me poetically the most favorable. The matter at hand, right now, is not to delve any deeper into the secrets of such a community. I repeat that, while writing these lines, I am momentarily leaving out of consideration all other points of view than the poetic, which doesn't in the least mean that I accept the judgment that I'm thrashing about in utopia. I'm content to point out a source of curious *movements*, to a large degree unforeseeable, a source which, once one consents to follow its angle — and I bet that it will be accepted — would be, for overturning mountains and mountains of boredom, the promise of a magnificent stream. One can't help but think this way and look ahead, faced with today's blind architecture, a thousand times more stupid and revolting than that of times gone by. How bored we'll be inside it! Ah! You can be certain nothing will happen there. But if, suddenly, a man heard, even in such a domain, that something had happened! If he dared to venture out, alone or almost so, over lands where chance has struck? If, his mind defogged of those stories which as children delighted us while beginning to hollow out a place in our hearts for deception, that man would risk snatching out of the hands of the past its mysterious prey? If that poet himself wanted to penetrate the Lair? If he was, himself, truly resolved to open his mouth only to say: "Once upon a time to come..."?

Thomas Willoch

NORTH FROM SAN DIEGO: REAGAN'S AMERICA

by David Stoesz

Driving north from San Diego, I suddenly found myself in Ronald Reagan's America. The discovery was unexpected. As a critic of his presidency, I had failed to see much coherence in his thought or logic behind his actions; neither seemed relevant to the needs of the nation. Raised in the Midwest and educated in the East, *I* had a sense of America — the land, people, their customs, and *my* reading of what the country was about had consistently been at odds with the pronouncements that came from the White House. But, as the golden hills, the brilliant surf, and the streaming traffic slipped past Interstate 5, a buoyancy of spirit surged and, shedding years of angst and protestation, *finally* a catharsis. Not only had I unraveled the President's master plan for the nation — I was in it.

Southern California is a land of simple symmetries, inhabited by gallant aviators and sneering officers from the Immigration and Naturalization Service (INS), by Dionysian adolescents and complacent retirees, and by cheap help that doesn't talk back. It is a corner of the country that has never failed (because it has never been tested), where the people are content (because the discontent have no voice), and where culture is fashionable (because anything authentic has been merchandised). Here is a *style* of life which has never been confounded by the past, leaving people with little wisdom with which to prepare for the future. The result is a state of mind that insists on infinite possibilities yet fails to recognize its insistence as hubris. These views are reflected in our present standardbearer, a stoic somnambulist who believes that everything here is ideal and finds anything somewhere else incomprehensible. This is the home of the President and for no other reason it is the prototype for the rest of the nation: southern California.

So, what *if* the president's vision of the country is southern California? After all, this outpost on the postindustrial frontier features a protean economy that has lured millions from dustbowl and rustbowl alike. Yet, most Americans who built the nation by stamping steel and harvesting wheat would find the prosperity here strangely unsettling. They might wonder if what's happened to southern California *is* good for the rest of the country.

The old economic base of southern California, truck farming and fishing, has given way to industries of the service and military sectors. Having avoided most of the costs of industrialism — a rotting infrastructure, escalating taxes, and urban underclass — southern California is able to convert incoming capital, dollar for dollar, into economic growth. With the revenue rush provided by tourists, retirees, the armed services and its subsidiaries, the growth has been spectacular. Precisely what comes out of the mad pursuit of growth for the sake of growth is another matter. The local service sector has given the world McDonald's; the military sector helped film *Top Gun*. If southern California shows us anything it is that an economy dominated by service and military produces a false sense of progress and a false sense of security, but nothing concrete.

Out of this abundance, the Good Life has taken a surprising twist. Rampant self-indulgence has given way to neo-puritanism southern California style. After cultivating a reputation for hedonism, the natives were chagrined to discover that nirvana has one great drawback: with little hardship naturally available, it becomes necessary to erect artificial obstacles in order to prove one's mettle. Under these circumstances virtue is most easily displayed by denouncing pleasure, and southern Californians are having a high time with being prudent. In fact, a tyranny of health and good thinking has emerged: no drugs, no smoking, no pornography, no promiscuity and, above all, no fat. With this code, southern California will never produce a Gertrude Stein or an Ernest Hemingway — nor even a Studs Terkel.

As the traffic began to slow along interstate 5, I recognized how appealing the caricature of southern California has become to a nation losing stature. Great nations, the President instructs us, evince a bounding economy, military strength, and moral integrity. Of course. But these are less cause than effect. The President leaves a question begging: whence do these derive? The true sustenance of a nation is its people: it is their heroism that makes a land great. Unfortunately, on this subject the President is inexperienced, mistaking media hype for human fortitude. Heroic proportion is shaped by more humble and enduring qualities than those piped by the President. Carl Sandburg knew that when, one afternoon along the Desplaines River,

he stumbled upon "a crowd of Hungarians under the trees with their women and children and a keg of beer and an accordion." And John Steinbeck knew it when he wrote about the Joad family migrating from Oklahoma to California. These people knew the meaning of hard work, fought when they got mad, and celebrated life with occasional debauchery. *These* were the people who made the America we long for.

By this time the traffic had almost come to a stop. Cars crowded each other as four lanes narrowed to two. Ahead, another feature of southern California. Fiscal and military policies of the Reagan Administration have placed severe pressure on Latin nations. Hundreds of thousands of their people have fled across our border in a migration as great as those that brought us the Irish and the Italians, then the Jews, Hungarians, and Poles. But escape from the Latin economic gulag is not easy. San Diego is saturated with illegal aliens, and work opportunities lie to the North. And, at San Onofre, the route constricts, the Pacific on one side and miles of rugged Camp Pendleton on the other. The Immigration Service has taken full advantage of this coincidence, establishing a facility to intercept Latinos seeking liberty and opportunity in the United States. As the traffic crawled past, the INS officers methodically scanned vehicles for unwanted immigrants. Those apprehended were marched off, hangdog, to the line of green and white vans for the trip back south. Then it was my turn. Framed by two glaring Immigration officers I realized that my trip had left me at the doorstep of the ultimate contradiction of free-swinging, sunny California. Behind the facade of prosperity and opportunity lies a terrible truth that we should ponder if we insist on emulating southern California. In order to protect ourselves from desperate people we will have to erect many more barriers such as this.

As Americans we belittle the political gangsters who would trample the courageous impulses of freedom-loving peoples. "Oppressive methods cannot work," we cry, "the people will triumph." And in our mind is a symbol of the inhumanity of the State: government automatons, concertina wire, blinding floodlights — checkpoint Charlie. ☠

The *Corpse* went to New York for the twentieth anniversary of the St. Marks' Poetry Project and had its faith renewed. Everyone is dead, although several savage poets with the night in their teeth tried to prevent attempts to attach poetry to critical discourse like a firecracker to the tail of a dead opossum. As the boring crawled back to their "texts" the truly dead went dancing.

COMMENTARIES BY ANDREI CODRESCU
as heard on National Public Radio's "All Things Considered"

NOUVELLE EROGENY

Flossing and kissing can give you AIDS. This fact, one among many, from my morning paper. Actually, any wet contact between humans can spread the virus. Animals were not included in the report — but since monkeys have AIDS too, it might be cautious to include your pets in the general injunction. No more tongue-kissing your cat. Clearly, our erogeny needs rethinking. Instead of wet-to-wet contact we must make wet-to-dry contact and vice versa. The skin is a very good prophylactic except in places where it leaks and these should be sealed shut with latex. Eyeglasses are also an excellent prophylactic. I have been using mine for years to keep my eyes from making reality pregnant. Plastic surgeons should consider removing all the seven openings of the body to a single area — to the top of the head, let's say. That would make it possible for a good hat to cover all the mischief. Another suggestion is that we give in to our true nature, which is masturbatory. Sex is an invention of the media: no one really wants to do it, but it's hard not to when you read in the paper about all the sex everyone's having. If we didn't have to keep up with the Joneses, we could all be doing what we like best anyway: go back to the fifties. The music was better then, we had patriotism, and we masturbated, on the slightest pretext, to bra ads from the *New York Times*. With all of one's openings clustered at the top of the head under a hat it would be easy to masturbate by just nodding in time to fifties bop. This way we could save the world, and still have fun. I'm not suggesting implementing all of this at once: we might begin by drying up a little every day, and visualizing the new body, and the nouvelle erogeny which, like nouvelle cuisine, is mainly in the mind.

THE LORD'S CORPORATIONS

There are psychic disturbances in the world, big winds that blow through the collective consciousness gathering strength. Our humble souls are racked by it. What is one to make of the TV ministries of the Lord looking to swallow one another like deregulated airlines? Are the Lord's airplanes stalled on the airports of the media? Are the religious wars raging elsewhere about to break out at home in front of the children? Preachers retire to towers to fast until death unless they make millions. But what if death isn't enough and upon dying they find that there is bad news in the next world too? Dying used to be a sure way to meet your maker. But now with so many dying for religious reasons in Iran and elsewhere, there might be a big traffic jam with believers of all sorts fighting to get to different levels. There may even be, God forbid, a whole class of agnostic spirits who fancy themselves scientific, and won't believe in anything — even dead. Of what avail is death to a dead evangelist if he finds that the postmodern spilleth into the postmortem? Another man of God confesses to having sinned in a motel room with a woman while yet another threatens to expose him. Some say the devil is playing fast and loose with the wealth of the faithful. Others say that it's only capitalism reaching at last the heavenly realms on ladders of cash the way McDonald's reached infinity on mountains of burgers. Still others say that the new corporations of the Lord came out of nothing and are about to return there. They were made ex nihilo like the world. But the faithful and the humble like ourselves, who have neither towers nor TV satellites to turn to, feel only the blowing of the winds of insecurity and fear. The day of reckoning may be at hand: first the preachers are borne on the wings of evil, then the soap operas stop showing up. Truly will darkness then descend upon the world.

ATTACK ON VOODOO

The Fifth Estate, a Detroit newspaper, reports on the persecution of Voodoo practitioners in Haiti. Following the fall of "Baby Doc" Duvalier hundreds of voodoo priests have been hacked and burned to death. A Haitian writer told the *New York Times*: ". . . this has been a fanatic crusade . . . like the Inquisition, with people dragged off to church or lynched." Called "shango" in Cuba and Trinidad, "macumba" in Brazil and "hoodoo" in parts of Louisiana, voodoo is an old natural religion of earth spirits brought by slaves from West Africa to the Americas. The natural religions of Europe have all but disappeared before the onslaught of Christianity. In this country, the religions of Native Americans are closely watched, and all potentially threatening offshoots, like the Ghost Dance Religion, have been quickly suppressed. There is more at stake here than a simple religious conflict. The old religions taught communion with otherness, with nature and animals. They were in direct conflict with the centralized, hierarchical authority of the Christian church which mediates the experience of the divine for the individual. Industrial and post-industrial civilisation fear the old gods because they intoxicate human beings with the possibility of ecstasy. The current persecutions in Haiti, aided, incidentally, by U.S.-funded evangelical Radio Lumiere, are part of a long string of wars against the old religions. One can now add Haiti to the growing list of religious conflicts in the world. The paradox of religious war at the end of the twentieth century, this most "technologically" advanced century, will not yield easily. The Marxists try to explain it away as class warfare. Capitalists in search of markets hope it will go away when opportunities develop. Well-meaning technocrats put their faith in bigger and better machines. The military reassures itself with its missiles. And yet, as soon as the logic of the obvious seems firmly in place, the werewolves come out of the dark and begin the old dance.

COMMERCIAL POEM
by David Zauhar

William Carlos Williams, an old man
now, over one hundred years old,
is forced out of retirement and death
and endorses frozen produce
for companies catering to upwardly
mobile America, or so it seems after
I watched the late movie last night
and saw this ad for waffles that opened
with an old woman who was probably
Flossie reading a note she found
on the fridge out loud, saying
"this is just to say
I have eaten the waffles
that were in the fridge
and which you
were probably saving
for brunch: forgive me,
they were so fluffy and
light, and very inexpensive" but
she could have been anybody, an actress
playing Flossie, not necessarily her.

Then he appeared, William Carlos Williams,
over one hundred years old and tired,
saying "this is one pure product
of America I go crazy for" and trying
to smile, pretending the earth under
our feet is the crust of some huge American
apple pie, and I groaned when I saw
him on TV and wished the commercial
would end, but the image lingered on
the screen, all night he was there, smiling
at Flossie with no life in his old
physician's eye, and an ache in his
gypsy heart.

Brian Swann

KANTIAN CONSIDERATIONS ON CATS

by Edouard Roditi

Consider, for example, the empirical judgement 'This is a cat', which is easily transformed into 'This purposive whole serves the purpose of being a cat', or, in somewhat technical language, 'This purposive whole has as its final cause a cat's having to be'.
— S. Koerner, *Kant*

We invade their privacy and insist on stroking their back when they would rather lick their crotch, adopting postures that remind us of a musician handling precariously an invisible but exceptionally unwieldy bass-cello.

All through the Middle Ages, Jewish pawnbrokers were obliged by some German municipal laws to keep cats as a means of protecting goods left with them as pledges against the depredations of mice and rats. Cats have thus acquired a hereditary fear of pogroms in the course of which their ancestors were also victims, in the ghettos, of the violence of hooligans. As soon as a cat now feels at all threatened, it still seeks refuge beneath the nearest bed or sofa.

Surreptitiously, cats are apt to steal inferior meats rather then eat the better ones that you offer them.

They distrust you, but make sudden demands on you when they want attention or affection. If you neglect these demands, they may punish you by pissing in unexpected secret places in your home.

They treat each other as ruthlessly as if they were handling mice, but demand of you the most gentle and tender handling.

You sometimes find some of their discarded fluff in your scrambled eggs, and then wonder if this is a revenge and for what.

They sniff contemptuously at your fruit salad and make you feel a fool for wanting to eat it, but they stretch a furtive clawed paw, as soon as you turn your back on them, towards your costly imported *pâté de foie gras*, though certainly not because the truffle that it contains looks so much like their own snout.

You sometimes dream of avenging yourself on them for their many misdeeds, but you have no proof of playing in turn the victim's part in their utterly mysterious dreams.

Some nations are known to have made a practice of mummifying them after their death, and some people still believe that they can reappear to haunt you as ghosts.

Do they really exist, or are they figments of the imagination of lonely widows and old maids?

Watch a cat drive her kittens off with her claws, when she feels that the time has come to wean them. It's an education in education.

I sometimes wake up wishing I were, instead of a human being, a cat's crotch. It must feel good to be licked so often and so assiduously.

Give a cat a ball of knitting wool and it will produce a tangle that has nothing in common with what is called a cat's cradle.

They have no conscience and no categorical imperatives, and their being is anything but purposeful. Their legendary nine lives are always unpredictable and infused at all times with a random quality of their own.

If you really have a purpose, purr, Puss!

Alice Codrescu

WHAT IS THE MYSTERY OF POETRY?

by Max Martins
Translated from the Portuguese
by James Bogan

The mystery of poetry is what's left:

after the Academy dusts off the poem
after the poem is used for a mop
after the poem wins the big prize
after Police-Censors slam poet and poem in prison
after the pope blesses the poem
after the literature professors extract the metaphors, tropes,
   and scaffolding from the poem
after the poem is entered in the Congressional Record
after a robot recites the poem
after the President quotes the poem in his Inaugural Address
after they don't pay for the rights to the poem —
   or even if they do
after they say, "Wow! What a poem!"
after they say, "Oh! what a shit poem!"
after the thief steals the poem
after the poet counts syllables on his fingers and toes
after they use the poem for toilet paper
after the reporter asks, "What is the mystery of poetry?"
after the poet betrays his own poem by saying:
   "The poem is hungry for itself."
after Octavio Paz is devoured by the poem
after the psycho-critics isolate alienation and perversion
   from the poem
after the State fixes the value of the poem
after the Directory of Syndicated Poets takes charge
after B. Dalton puts the poem in the window
after a reader encounters a poem face to face
then erases it because he knows he doesn't
know how to explain what he knew in the poem
after the oral poet asks the tape recorder to keep his
   poem
after the poet turns himself off and signs his
   name in white at the bottom of a blank page.

Michael Neff

at the end of rage

Jayne Lyn Stahl

> "Truly we are here
> on the roof of the world."
> — *J. M. Coetzee*

Maybe a flight back east
will cure,
a sidewalk surrounds me like rain
it is night like a dumb beast
I want only future.
I watch as pain becomes a sneer
on the face of contempt.
city you are my mother
you are unfinished I am restless
it is not for me to judge
the city of my birth.
like a devout atheist
I am waiting to be disproved
on elizabeth street a red ambulance struggles
like red brick your children   little italy
grown old with fear your women in designer
    despair.
I hear the long, solitary notes of a ripe flute
from a cracked tenement, new york
you are my mother
though old and battered
your wisdom defies you
like an empty mirror
in a crowded room
you remind us of our infirmity
like a nagging wife
you are an ancestor
in spite of yourself.
how I love your passion
Manhattan where survival is the ultimate revenge.

in San Francisco I speak broken italian
with a lost sailor from naples
where streetlights of hunger
hide men without roofs
from the sun.
a blind man sits outside an autoteller
on montgomery street with his coin cup
he swears your gates are open
his cup is empty.
on grant street fat chickens hang
in windows of chinese merchants there is chatter
and fast feet.

I watch this city as the other
we are all cities waiting
to be watched.
at the end of rage
like a full beast
I must wander to stay awake
where are your vowels?
like a swollen nerve on a vital bed
there is no denying it —
there is no relief
but to stalk the streets
demanding only what is
alive and true.

far above the hills
we make love to ghosts we never knew
and awake with the taste
of sweat on our thighs.
O city where is your anger
asleep in the last car
of the last train out of penn station.
where is your anger
in a dumpsite collecting uranium
in sudden rifle of a lone lunatic
in macdonald's blitz in the terrible eyes
of a child on a bus O city
where is your anger?
we make love to ghosts
we never knew.
let the dead stay where they are
they will only go back to shadows
on the sheets ironic as the hot sun
on a cold hearse.
your ghosts walk
but they do not move strange city
your massive nerves protruding
through a suit of ivory.
I am waiting to be disproved.
your ghosts walk
but they do not move.
give me back my rage O city
in uneven rhythms on drunken streets.
I will dance for you
read like a warrior
red with beginning.

DO SWEETLY DOOM ASKEW

by Ralph LaCharity

tucked asleep against their lovers
    poets swale sweetly askew

  night rolls round
             this globe loony & tuneful
       in a wide band kicked off by sun

& lo! the poets who have lovers
       swale sweetly tucked, rolling

blessed breathy resonance reigns
  these are those wee hours
    poets who have lovers know
       & who sleep with lovers have, aye
blessed are the tucked against
  whose easy breathing reigns askew
  whose true plight heaves sweetly
  whose global glaring wearies, in love
blessed are the poets, their wakeful rage
      precisely bent nightly down
          & close
  their tuned terrors fleshed, merciful
wet & torqued & rhymed & fat
    blessed & hard & naked & fading
  softed & close, sleepful   gone

for yes it is death to wake a sleeping poet
      is death to bring certain sun to bear there
      & tis death to sing the bitter wake lovelessly
  o tis death   tis death
     to plight soundless   wordless & alone

blessings on the poets
     who sleep love's sleep
  their solitary plights softed aware
  softed aware as night rolls
         as danger nods
    as sweetness weaves
such brevity drains & o!
    that such charm find thee, sweet bitters

who come here sans sunny praise
dire comisery
lucre
or loony tunes
sleep tucked, o rolling nod-weavers
tis danger-loving death ye despise
aye, all premature dawn
& a moon that cannot rock us

sleep tucked, nod weavers
bend precisely nightly down

we come bereft of policy praise
our thoughts hum
we are penniless
choked by jokes
unfocused
limp & newborn
noddy tuckers
loony bayful bawling ones

o ye plight-bound livid Okies
        distend ye   aye, disperse
        dispel this stiff blind
        stink & go slick
           dye whole days in shade
         damn doomers
      lick hug
        die another birth already
        defie decline   go down
          bend nightly
    mock a moon that cannot rock us
       nightly down, doomed
plight nodly, loon
       do sweetly doom askew aye, do

We're taking back the beaches. As you read this, *American Poetry Since 1970: Up Late*, published by Four Walls Eight Windows, should be in your bookstore window. Edited by the *Corpse* editor, it is a massive, 105-poet assault on the rotten parapets of the status quo. As well as being a splendid tome of poesy. In the same window this Fall you should find Ronald Sukenick's *Down & In*, a history of American bohemia that argues for its irrepressible actuality. Anne Waldman's two anthologies, *The Next World* and *Homage to Ted Berrigan* are imminent as well, making this window into a space ship. Our ear picks up the trembling of revolts in the body social as well as the body poetic. The word reaches us that bureaucrats everywhere are warning against a new cycle of student activism. Yeah.

CHER CADAVRE EXQUIS

LETTER TO *EXQUISITE CORPSE*

There is a city in Europe bisected with a deep ravine. Even at noon you can hear crows calling down there among the green activity on both sides of a tiny stream. The cliffs are high and blend into ancient fortifications whose ruins are by now almost parts of nature. Or they are parts, as we are, looking at them with thoughts in our heads like Limestone, Crows, Catacombs, Small Countries and their Endless Wars. Above these forlorn battlements are perfectly ordinary handsome nineteenth century houses and commercial buildings, streets busy with the polyglot and friendly population, cars from France, Portugal, Germany, the Soviet Union.

This is what a magazine should be — a fertile and dangerous cut across the streets of our complacent enterprises, an old person displaying her wounds, a young man sniggering, sexy almost adults chasing each other down narrow streets lined with costly shops and named for saints, a surprise and a discontinuity. That is it, the thing a magazine must be: a weapon of acute discontinuity.

Above the city I have in mind stands its best-known symbol: a broad hipped woman gilded, upright atop a column. The Golden Woman. Only a few years ago this apparently ancient patronne was set up, restored after decades in hiding after someone feared a greedy and ferocious occupying army would abduct her, symbol as she was of an independence. We don't like anybody, the man said to me, we are kind to everyone. We use friendliness as a means of independence, a golden woman, not an iron tower. Her hips shine!

— Robert Kelly

PETER STUYVESANT REQUESTS PERMISSION TO EXPEL JEWS FROM NEW AMSTERDAM, SEPTEMBER 22, 1654

The Jews who have arrived would nearly all like to remain here, but learning that they (with their customary usury and deceitful trading with the Christians) were very repugnant to the inferior magistrates, as also to the people having the most affection for you; the Deaconry also fearing that owing to the present indigence they might become a charge in the coming winter, we have, for the benefit of this weak and newly developing place and the land in general, deemed it useful to require them in a friendly way to depart; praying also most seriously in this connection, for ourselves as also for the general community of your worships, that the deceitful race — such hateful enemies and blasphemers of the name of Christ — be not allowed to further infect and trouble this new colony to the detraction of your worships and the dissatisfaction of your worships' most affectionate subjects.

Samuel Oppenheim, "The Early History of the Jews in New York, 1654-1664," *Publication of the American Jewish Historical Society,* XVIII (1909).

Ed. Note: *St. Marks' Church in the Bowerie whose frontyard contains the mortal remains of Peter Stuyvesant should take note. We propose that Stuyvesant be disinterred and Ted Berrigan buried there instead.*

TOO HOT FOR *LIFE OF CRIME*

Startling revelations have come to light about the Language poets' connection a secret Aryan brotherhood. Members are identified by the "-an" suffix on their name, hence Watten, Harryman, Silliman, Perelman, Robinson, Hejinian, Amnasan. (Slight variations are calculated to evade detection.) An attempt to bore Robert Duncan to death and then install him as their patron saint failed due to his outboring them. Meanwhile new light has been shed on the origins of the group from the work of Cooligen and Bromigen, well-known inert gases. Bromige has tried to throw suspicion off himself by suggesting Michael Palmer is actually Michael Palmerston.

In other developments, the Languish siblings continue to hold their mock-seances in the manner of their peers' Langton Street atrocities at the home of the young Michael Amnasan. Their house organ, *Jimmy & Lucy's House of K*, has already produced some immemorable neo-Wattenspeak in the work of "Dr." Shiedlower, Jed "Tabula" Rasula, and Michael "Forget-me-not" Amnasan, who are all establishing themselves as boring pseudo-intellectuals.

Life of Crime, however, has adopted a soft on L=I=N=G=U=I=C=A stance since their attacks have resulted in favorable publicity for the Lang-gang and real ignominy for Nolan (obviously a closet Linguicist himself).   ☠

FRESH OUT OF NODLAND
by Barbara Barg

It's a heavy narcotic we've pledged our genius to — the uncelebrational idea of total self-control. The insanity of expecting it to be in constant siege upon our newly human brains. We are oh, we are so ungenerous with our pointlessly tamed selves, so relentlessly cultural! So demonically emotional! It's so embarrassing. I would really like to be able to talk to a bird, or a snake, and highly recommend the human experience. But the way things are now, I'd just appear the forest fool. Even though.

I've had a good life.

It isn't nearly e-fucking-nough.

I need something to explode the chill off my senses, something to give zing and punch to the notion of being alive. Some release from the tension of my tiny universe of human habits, release that realigns me with my potential charm.

I mean *real* release. Not the bullshit designated by Church and State and some other tight-asses addicted to power. Not the patronizing *ritual* release of a Mardi Gras or a Superbowl where the idea is to get blotto and pretend we still know how to be wild. I've been about as blotto as I can get. The horrors, the ghosts, the howling persons, the longnecked men. Yawn. Snooze. I'm bored with reliving the pouting destinies of the Poes, the Charlie Parkers, the Kerouacs. Art History is full of people who couldn't survive past middle age without brain damage. They should have learned to play the piano. Then they would have seen that if all ten fingers press down at once, there is no melody.

The Ditch of the Dead. I'm sick and tired of it.

I'm bored with 4ths of July when we celebrate beer and gunpowder. Bored with the doctrines of crucifying the flesh in order to resurrect the soul.

Bored with these trifling customs (all in the name of the pursuit of pleasure) that would dull the hardest of stock — those obligatory lounge drugs, dentist office rock and roll, and especially that cemeterial adventure of cold sex on an acre of genuine extra-genital disinterest . . . cabbage patch fucking located squarely in the centerfold, while the rest of the body slumbers away in a grinding gloom, senses and psyche doped, escaping the moment through fantasy, or otherwise pardoned so we can blur the knowledge that it isn't enough.

Some sweet dreams, huh? For the supposedly most-gifted lifeform on the planet (and here the snakes forever snicker). Is it my imagination, or has any other gifted lifeform noticed the disappearance of subsoil in Joy's neck of the woods? Does anybody feel like *humming* anymore? Where has all the personal power of youth gone? Are we too cool, too directed, too mature to do anything but dismiss Marx as a misguided man who spent most of his life sitting on boils in a British library? So he didn't get it exactly right. Who does, do you? He was passionately (Yeats was not entirely correct about the passionate) concerned with wealth being counted in currency other than a Gross National

Product. Disposable time to the citizens, that was his kind of currency.

It's so like us with our hunger for pleasure and our reality of boils. We are alienated from one and led to the other through the daily activity of resignation to our powerlessness, for which we are blandly rewarded with ritual release. Coffee break. God I'm so bored full of longing. Candy bar. Have a baby, a career, a cigar. A toast to Life, whatever that is. A drink on the House. Smoke a joynt, fuck your brains out, shoot a speedball to your brain (subway to infancy), write a book, come around to a way of thinking, make it easy on yourself, get comfortable, be responsible, do what you're so posed to do and stop trying to rebel against the world or save it, look, grow up. Celebrate a job well done.

Where is my personal power?

Where is my truce of mind?

Where is my passion, my pulse?

MALTHUS IN THE TWENTIETH CENTURY:

There's a whole lotta people on this planet.

MUST?

Look, this isn't new. How many thousands have we been rehashing this? Unless some sudden environmental or genetic or galactic groove-changer swings in soon, we're going to shrivel up and blow away. Must we be slaves on the wheel of Darwinian karma? Over-specialized in post-agriculture culture? We've been breeding out pleasure and breeding in power. Not personal power, the stuff of well-being and intensity of existence. You know the power that pits us human vs. human. The power that demands national, indeed global steadfastness of purpose and preaches denial of our most enchanting impulses.

Who makes the world what it isn't? What kind of world demands a human to control herself? Why aren't we panicking?

THE DESIRE TO DOMINATE:

Sleep, that's the easiest thing in the world. Just close your eyes — on the subway or lumbering down a street, or standing in line to ask if there are any trains going your way — and snooze without alarm for as long as you like...forever if you like. And who is to say that's not living a life as well as anyone else? I'll tell you the truth. Just thinking about all this makes me want to walk right out

my front door onto 12th Street, cross over and buy a syringe and a few bags of dope. Then I don't have to worry about what I'm going to do tomorrow. Sleep. It's as easy as falling in love.

A DREAM OF THE MARVELOUS:

I dream of a planet glowing with lovely tones. Persons alive! Not mere ornaments of air. They laugh. They enjoy each other's company. They don't hustle or overcongratulate. Their past isn't everyday. They know how to dance on feet of bliss. It's in the music — in the voices. Rhythm captivates the spine! A joyous noise in the afternoon. Pulse.

BEHAVIORAL RIGIDITIES:

That's what we're missing. Pulse. What we have instead is ego. Ego is a slave to the rules of conduct, rules which were agreed upon for us before we were even born. Rules which are not threatened by our rights to vote in our laughable democracies, or by our revolutions in our laughable totalitarianisms.

Unfortunately, the experience of pulse so confuses and alarms that ego usually is in need of "a good stiff drink" after such an awakened moment. That's what culture, left to its own devices, has led us to. Any triumph of life independent of "the rules of conduct" requires immediate blotting out by ritual oblivion. Any public show of pulse and people will immediately think you one of the homeless. Who else would burst into spontaneous song in the middle of the afternoon under the arch in Washington Square Park?

Oh we are routinely aware that we *have* a pulse, and we do have some dim recollection that pulse has some relation to being alive. When we fear we're too close to death, we even bother to *take* our pulse (so unfamiliar with its existence are we, we have to go looking for the damn thing). But we have long forgotten pulse's address — which is not the wrist, but the *moment*. The enlightened don't have pulses, they *are* pulses, beating. Being and beating with no ulterior motive. It makes doing dishes a helluva thing.

BRUTAL STRATEGIES:

Maybe that's why shooting coke was so attractive to me. You pull back on the hammer, see that blood flow into the syringe, then slowly push in till all the liquid disappears into my vein. A few seconds later BANG! Mountains on the move! I spend the next minute totally conscious of the only moment that ever was, is or will be. Then I spend the next fifteen minutes wondering if I'm going to die. Then I spend the next five minutes fixing up another shot with very shaky hands and eyes. Then I spend the rent. Then I howl the deep and rumbling howl of a heart tight like a fist, choking on self-pity, wasted pale and inconsolable. I let myself become a lonesome girl tormented by such self-control. Veins swollen on my black and blue arms. Surrounded by dark walls, needles and spoons. Don't you just love those long, rainy afternoons?

THE ELEMENTAL VIBRANCY:

It is the heart which illumines this firmament. And pulse is the very center of heart, the nerve of heart. The mind is an unclear mirror, but the heart, it beats! Is it ever the case that the mind is alive when the heart has ceased beating?

I reject you too hip bulldozers of doom. My feet no more go down to death. Snakes are smiling, birds breathe deep, even insects are radiant with life, and I know how to laugh again.

When is the soul?

The being has made friends with herself. Eyes once dull now shine. Each act is her own and not a pantomime. She does not feel separate. She no longer dreads the trouble of examining her morning head. There is a day today and she is in it. And it's okay today to treasure up this elegant kiss of soul.

I have obtained a soul. It's in the center of my heart. Don't let it make you uneasy, friend. It's got nothing to do with a crusade.

Don't you see? It's just the elemental vibrancy. Shining. Singing. Beating. It needs no other meaning.

If you don't think I love you, Baby, look what a fool I've been.

SUPRANATIONAL GOALS AND VALUES

When we look into the smoking mirror of History, let us remember that two open wounds at eye level is not like seeing. Let us visit each other all of our lives and create a common language other than war. Let's stop trying to preserve the unpreservable.

Each day brings its own identity.

Let go.

Let go.

The soul is perpetual syncopation; rhythmic, tonal, melodic.

I've been down low
I've been traveling blue
I've been cool too long.

Life
is the hot concept.

MOOSE GROIN, MINNESOTA
by David Zauhar

Rumor has it in this great northern neck of the rural woods that *Corpse* editor Codrescu has publicly expressed dissatisfaction with the city of Minneapolis on one of his recent N.P.R. broadcasts, claiming that the city is too clean and the population, shall we say, too monochromatic and bland. Now, I have no way of verifying this rumor since I live in an area without public radio, but if he did in fact say these things I would like to go on the record by wholeheartedly agreeing with his alleged assessment of our state's largest city. Minneapolis is boring, no doubt about it. To be blunt, the city is a great lukewarm bowl of urban oatmeal, drab, flavorless and perfect for cold weather. People should realize, however, that there are parts of Minnesota which are bursting at the seams with creative energy. My current home town of Moose Groin (pop. 4,964) is one of the many rural communities which offer something beyond the usual Minnesota fare of fishing holes and mosquitoes. Groinites display an active interest in all types of artistic endeavors. For example, our public library is especially proud of its holdings in modern and contemporary poetry. Furthermore, the annual Moose Groin Public Library Reading Series has recently featured such poets as Tom Clark, Philip Lamantia, and Lyn Lifshin. While Clark refuses to come back to the state until the Minnesota Twins once again play baseball in an outdoor stadium, most of the poets who have read here were quite pleased with their reception and with the artistic environment in general. I should also mention that the poet Ed Dorn visits Moose Groin every year for the opening of walleye season in late April. His free workshops have long been a popular way to pass time while waiting for opening day. Finally, the local

Literary Guild awards the Robert Bly Inflated Urinary Tract Award each year to call attention to the most pretentious volume of poetry published anywhere in the United States. The visual arts, while not yet as vibrant as their literary counterparts, are also coming into their own. The most famous example, internationally known by now, is Christo's monumental creation, Gopher Wing Lake. Several thousand train loads of water from Hudson Bay and Lake Superior were required to fill this abandoned open pit mine, and as a finishing touch, Christo provided the usual element of controversy by purchasing 17 Dave Smith sculptures and dropping them from helicopters into the newly-created lake. While New York and Minneapolis critics still occasionally gripe about the fact that only scuba divers and cold water fish can view this portion of Mr. Smith's corpus, the locals are rightfully proud of their contribution to the creation and display of avant garde art. While fully devoted to nationally and internationally known artists, Moose Groin also advances the cause of regional artists as well. The most curious example of this is taxidermist Elrod Weatherbee. Billed as "The World's Only DADA Taxidermist," Weatherbee constantly explores and advances the dimensions of his art. His work includes such creations as "Northern Pike With Head of Rat," and of course the grim mobile, "Hung Jack Rabbits With Fangs." Both pieces are currently on display at the Kimball Museum in Fort Worth, Texas. His most talked-about work, however, is still taking shape in his studio. It reportedly involves the body of a famous deceased Hollywood actor who left his body to Weatherbee with the specific instructions that it be used in the most monumental taxidermic project ever undertaken. Presumably, Weatherbee intends to graft the head of a sheep and the forelegs of a bear to the body, and then to display it in a traditional wildlife setting. Tentatively titled "Studies in Specie Combination XXIV," the work is scheduled to be revealed next year during the Fourth of July Celebration at Gopher Wing Lake. Poetry and the plastic arts are clearly thriving here. Perhaps the only cultural activity in which Minneapolis currently maintains any sort of an edge over Moose Groin is music. However, this little town is not about to rest on its past accomplishments. Mayor-elect Wyatt Lundgren has promised to attract top-flight music to The Groin. Along these lines he is currently negotiating with Ed Sanders for sole rights to The Fugs' Family Archives, to be housed, barring complications, in the refurbished East Wing of the Gus Hall Museum of Social Consciousness. Should this deal be completed, Moose Groin will be a well-rounded cultural center, comparable to Paris and New York, snow and mosquitoes be damned. I hope I don't sound too much like a Chamber of Commerce brochure when I talk about my home community, but I think it is important that people recognize the aesthetic and cultural advantages which can be found in rural Minnesota, not to mention the lower cost of living. All of these factors make Moose Groin a perfect town for aspiring artists, and an exciting place to visit on your next family vacation.

— David Zauhar
Commissar of Culture and Chief Custodian
City of Moose Groin, Inc.

P.S. Please find enclosed three poems about my career as a janitor. Normally, I would send them to *CUSTODIA: A MAGAZINE OF VERSE*, but like other small and specialized poetry mags, it has fallen on hard times, publishing only once a year, and even then sticking to the well known janitor-poets, so that we younger ones don't have much of an outlet any more. Thank you for your time.

POEMS BY BILL KNOTT
CHILDHOOD:
THE OFFENSE OF HISTORY

Scraping a poised enough patina of voyeur
From your eye I spread peanut butter on my
Groin and let the ocean waves wash it off —
Hey, nice cosmic microdots. For afters we'll

Listlessly memorize the Smith wing in
The phone book or try to hump Empty Dumpty:
    vain
Efforts that crud up what we have done
In obscure countries driven by passion

Out onto balconies to address the
Populace with our love, false solution
For their poverty which is based on

The art that the dirt in my heart is white.
Crammed mad, thoughtmotes in a themebeam:
He has a shiv grin. The soap he uses is ugly.

BRIGHTON ROCK
BY GRAHAM GREENE

Pinky Brown must marry Rose Wilson
to keep her mouth shut about the murder
which the cops don't know wasn't no accident —

Pinky has a straight razor for slashing,
a vial of acid for throwing into,
a snitch's face. He dies in the end. The end

of the book I mean, where, on the last page,
Rose shuffles home from church praying
that her Pinky has left her pregnant . . .

Now, this kid — if he was ever born — joined
a skiffle group in '62 called Brighton
Rockers, didn't make it big, though,

just local dances and do's. Rose,
pink, brown, all nonelemental colors, shades
of shame, melancholy, colors which, if you

get caught loving too much you could get send
    up
to do time — time, that crime you didn't,
couldn't commit, even if you were or weren't

born and even and if your dad he died with
his sneer unshaken, his punk's pure soul
    unsaved . . .
Every Sunday now in church Rose slices

her ring-finger off, onto the collection-plate;
once the sextons have gathered enough
bodily parts from the congregation, enough

to add up to an entire being, the priest substitutes that entire being for the one
on the cross: they bring Him down in the name

of brown and rose and pink, sadness
and shame, His body, remade, is yelled at
and made to get a haircut, go to school,

study, to do each day like the rest
of us crawling through this igloo of hell,
and laugh it up, show pain a good time,

and read Brighton Rock by Graham Greene.

MALE MENOPAUSE POEM

How as to lean my non-eon on autumn's roan
Undoing, to smile while the stymies crawl
All over me and the prismatic blindfold
Around my testicles creaks: guess this house

No longer knows which door I am. The window
We were — does it remember its view? You-or-I
saw so little out there; what future only
Catnap glimpses of our furtive nightmare.

Doorknobs worn to doornubs, grey stubble on
Gaunt armpits, lists like that litter this earth.
A lattice of graves greets me or is kind to me;

My hair plowed with parents, their protracted
Smoothings of some poor, tuckablanket bed.
As said each road I find in your face is fled.

THE GOLDEN AGE

Is as it were a confession — won by endless
torture, which none of our interrogators
bothers to record — all the old code names
and dates, the hoarse data of sandpaper
throats, even their remorse, are ignored. Far

from which a late (not lost) messenger stares,
struck by window bargains or is it the gift
of a sudden solicitude: is she going to
lift up her shadow's weight, shift hers
onto it? She knows who bears whom. In

that momentary museum where memory occurs
more accrue of those torturers' pliers, than
lessened fingernails or eyes, teased to a pulp,
we beg for closeups. Ormolus, objets d'art!
A satyr drains an hourglass in one gulp.

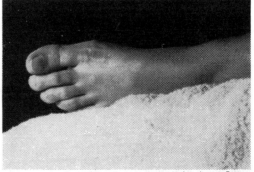

Jean-Jacques Passera

GRANITE

by Joel Oppenheimer

we can trace the word granite
back and back and back

it means 'a hard stone'
and its name appears
in the language
in the seventeenth century

it comes from
the italian word
granito
     which means
a speckled stone

granito is from
the italian *granire*
'to reduce into graines'
hence to speckle

and *granire* comes from
granum
     the word for
corn in latin

all this history
reason enough perhaps
to take *cum granum salis*

that is
     with
a grain of salt

the proposed crystalline
repository in the
cardigan pluton

listen to the language
for god's sake
     a
crystalline repository
which means a place
in a particular kind of rock
in which to put things

in other words
a radioactive dungheap

listen to the language

where the deep root
of the word granite —
that sound uttered by

our oldest forebears —

is *ger*

gee ee are

which meant
to ripen or
to grow old

related to the same ger
in geriatric
as well as grain

all words sprout meaning
if we track them far enough
all words tell us the truth
if we allow them to

pluton's root is
pluto
     from pleu
pee ell ee ewe
the word for flow

waters flow
     riches flow
even the word
pulmonary
     the lungs
the place where the air flows
and all the flight words

but what help is the language
with what flows from plutonium

we are talking about
to ripen
     to grow old
to be allowed to flow
to be allowed to fly

and in the name of imperfect technology
imperfect because science is used
by men who don't understand it
and cannot admit what they do not know

they make up answers for what they do not know

and in the name of imperfect democracy
imperfect because we had no say
and despite this hearing

must be cynical about ever getting that say
beyond the saying of some simple words

in the name of those abstractions
and your imperfect use of them

you would waste us

well he said this is all
perfectly safe and not only that
it's really necessary
and who's to argue with necessity
or bring up emotional responses
when science is involved

in the book of the secrets of enoch
written two thousand years ago
god speaks to man

i curse ignorance
i promised all life
i do not turn from and blight
i did not spoil man or earth
or whatever else i made

i do damn his fruit
when it is rotten
when what he does brings on darkness

it is not easy to speak as a poet
in a culture which trusts only technology

still i know that what you do
brings on darkness

it is not easy to trust technology
in a culture which sees itself being destroyed

but your fruit is rotten
it brings on darkness

i know too that each time technology fails
we retreat again to the myths
because it is the myths gave us life at first
and allowed us to understand the universe
and it is the myths sustain again

when christa died thrown against the universe
by perfect technology
                oh yes it was perfect technology
all your colleagues assured us
and still do
                only the human element failed
as always as always the human element
fails precisely because it is human

and to blame perfect technology's mistakes
on human error or element is wrong
in a human universe
                which i beg
to tell you is here where we live

so when christa died thrown against
that wider universe
                it was the myth we turned to
to give us solace and understanding

there are indeed more things in heaven and earth
than are dreamed of in your philosophy

so we have to keep saying no

we do not believe in your philosophy
which eats even granite deep beneath us

i would remind you too
you have a team working right now
of your mythographers
linguists semioticists anthropologists
seeking to build a myth to keep our children's
children's children's children away from your pit

do not sneer at the myths

they tell us more truly our births

and we do fall back on them
battered by your logic that is no logic
and your facts you still can't prove
and your technology that kills flesh

and i want this granite
still tied to ger

i want to ripen and grow old
as i want all of us to

and i remember that god told enoch
i do not turn from and blight
i did not spoil man or earth

Susan B. Taft

THE NUDE MANIFESTO

by Rudy Burckhardt

Doesn't everyone like looking at a nude?

Remember, a young woman or man in the street is nothing but a nude with clothes and shoes on. When Botticelli painted one of the first nude figures in the Renaissance he called her a Venus or Aphrodite, after the Greek and Roman Goddess of Love. It was a true liberation from the Middle Ages, when a young woman in a picture had to be a Madonna clothed in many-folded drapery. It soon spread to France, Spain, Germany, the Netherlands but not England or Switzerland. Before long a reaction set in; a fierce monk, Savonarola, took over in Florence and burnt paintings of nudes in the public square. He was burnt himself a few years later, and the struggle between prohibition and the freedom to paint nudes has been going on to the present day. In Rome around 1830, Nathaniel Hawthorne, upon seeing a great many Greek, Roman and Italian statues, thought there was really no call for so much nudity, since one saw only clothed people in daily life all around. In 1890, Thomas Eakins had to put a hideous black mask on the face of a model so she wouldn't be recognized, and then was expelled from the Philadelphia Academy for letting young ladies have a glimpse of a nude male. However, since the Sixties Revolution and Philip Pearlstein's many paintings, our liberation is complete — well almost — we still get charged with sexism and what Rackstraw Downes calls ogling. What is ogling? It's an old English word meaning to look at something with an ulterior motive. What is an ulterior motive? Something not quite above board unless two consenting adults have it at the same time, which is rare. Ah, if only we all could look at a nude figure the way my son Jacob did at age two in the Uffizi in Florence. After passing through many rooms with Madonnas and Child, upon seeing Botticelli's clear and lovely painting of a standing Venus, delighted he said: look, woman nice and clean — no baby. I'm not a dirty old man, I take a shower every day.

The expense of spirit in a waste of shame
Is lust in action, and till action, lust
Is perjured, murderous, bloody, full of blame
Savage, extreme, rude, cruel, not to trust

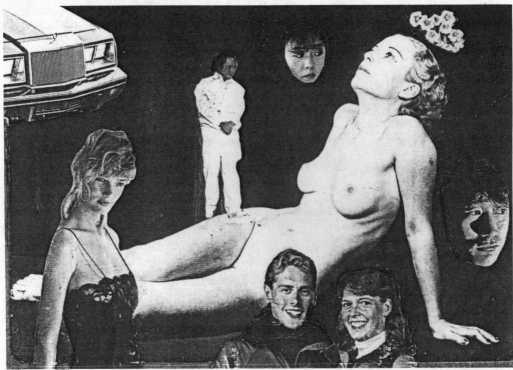

Rudy Burckhardt

Enjoyed no sooner but despised straight
Past reason hunted and no sooner had
Past reason hated —

Well that's how Shakespeare must have felt on the morning he wrote that sonnet. What makes a Venus contemporary?

Humorous
Disturbing
Adorable
Satisfying
Conspicuous

Untouchable
Indifferent
Like Hawaiian music
On top of you
Distant
Concupiscent
Exemplary
Plain

This list cannot go on. Nudes are in the eye of the beholder. There is no right way to look at a nude. A glimpse may be too much, a longer view improper. When in doubt, just close your eyes.

THE SHARING OF ANTHEIL'S WEIGHT
by William Levy

The music and life of George Antheil may be understood as a (wobbling) pivot around which the balance of many a dynamic motion of twentieth century art turns. As a pianist, composer and author, he embodied the artist in revolution. Revolving, motion in orbit or circular course or motion around an axis or center. Rotation, complete change, great reversal. Fundamental reconstruction. Nature's vital breath is the spiritual energy of male and female principles with their ceaseless permutations of expansion and contracting; uniting, they constitute the beginning of things. Man Ray's famous photo-portrait of George Antheil reveals an evil innocent with the timeless quality of a beautiful androgyne. Marlene Dietrich, David Bowie, young Mick Jagger, old chairman Mao, Charles-Henri Ford. The triumph of interiority and magical realism over social naturalism and positivism.

Antheil's autobiography is a yuppie handbook on how-to-score glittering prizes in the international art world, a *What Makes Sammy Run* as written by Sammy Glick, himself. This kind of promotional display also has become *l'air du temps* of the late eighties; sense bearing vectors gliding eloquently from voice to voice.

George Antheil had twenty-six personalities, one for every letter in the alphabet. In "H" for humor he alienated his patrons and supporters and like many true artists, fled from success while seemingly pursuing it.

The twentieth century is the sound of ideologies clashing in political and cultural Isms. George Antheil joined as many as he could. "Illustrious persons, however, did not always come to my house first," he wrote. "Sometimes I was first invited to theirs." George Antheil would have made an excellent dinner companion.

George Antheil was a futurist magnet for three different writer/promoters who later took up the Axis cause. A networker caught in his own web of contacts. Ezra Pound: he gave him access to Jean Cocteau and the important Parisian salons and introduced him to the Anglo-American world of letters with his pamphlet *Antheil and the Treatise on Harmony*, broadcast wartime radio speeches over Radio Roma. Jean Benoiste-Mechin: he organized the early concerts of George Antheil's *succès de scandal* Ballet Mechanique and put himself into print in the leading French magazines and wrote and published a book simply called *Antheil*, became a prominent minister in the Vichy cabinet of Admiral Darlan. Hanns von Stuckenschmidt: he introduced George Antheil to a German reading public, secured for him the most influential music publisher and then became a prominent figure in Third Reich cultural organizations. Is this auspicious and meaningful? Utter nonsense?

We are all still trying to unravel the quest for the absolute, that unprecedented generosity of conceits prophetically proposed by pre-W.W. I Russian and Italian Futurism: their political foster children, the Soviet and Corporate State. "We are witnesses of the greatest Moment of summing up in history," Sergei Diaghilev wrote in 1905, "in the name of a new and unknown culture, which will be created by us, and which will also sweep us away." In music it was the wireless imagination of Luigi Russolo's *L'art dei rumori*, a manifesto on the art of noises first published in 1913. "We must break out of this restricted circle of pure sounds and conquer the infinite variety of noise sounds," he demanded. "We want," Russolo continued, "to intone these varied noises and regulate them harmonically and rhythmically." He envisioned an orchestra which would produce the most complex and novel sonorous emotions, not through a succession of noises imitative of life, but through an imaginary association of these various timbres and rhythms, where every instrument offers the possibility of changing tone. George Antheil exhibited a similar impulse toward this new aesthetic.

If, as Lenin claimed, communism is socialism plus electricity, then our postmodernism is all the cultural cataclysms of "between the wars" — plus the silicon chip. George Antheil's music is concerned with time, not tone. For him melody did not exist; rhythmic power was the important thing to develop in music, harmony was and is, after all, a matter of what preceded and what followed. Ezra Pound paraphrased this into: "There is nothing sacred about the duration of a second . . . Not the number of vibrations but intervals, the proportion of a note to some other note." That is to say . . . asymmetrical duration.

PHYSICAL TIME CONCEPT

Time is *order, form* of experience
Time *measures* events
Time is divisible into equal parts
Time is perpetual transience

MUSICAL TIME CONCEPT

Time is *content* of experience
Time *produces* events
Time knows no equality of parts
Time knows nothing of transience

George Antheil gave attention to instruments and their aesthetic possibilities. There is the often told story how the violinist Olga Rudge got an audience with Mussolini for herself and the pianist of a just performed Antheil composition. The pianist complained that the composer took the piano for a percussion instrument. "So it is," agreed the dictator. "So it is!"

George Antheil risked saying: "I am a *classicist* at heart." Like Schubert, in his string quartet "Death and the Maiden" he wrote notes for effect, rather than to be played. Only the wind knows the voice of his violin parts. In an era before tape-recorders and computer sound-sampling, George Antheil had a mimetic ear, the ability to transcribe natural sounds making many of his compositions a kind of recognizable acoustical stenography. George Antheil's music is a parade of themes, circuits of fragmentation and continuity, an intersection of singularities as a way of creating discourse. They make one think. Quotations abound and are never — well, almost never — flawed by cerebral aridity. One hears Dvořák, Jelly Roll Morton, Stravinsky's *L'Histoire d'un Soldat*, street sounds as well as Arabic zither rhythms he encountered in Tunisia (from the enigmatic Baron d'Erlanger) right before composing his Second Sonata.

He collaborated with other artists, other arts. He conspired. Ever ready to play the trendy artist hangabout during his two main periods — as an outlaw modernist in Europe and as a populist prince in Hollywood — George Antheil did produce a remarkable body of musical compositions. The catalogue of his music lists over three hundred titles. Piano music, of course. Vocal music, including songs for the cinema. Chamber music. Works for solo instrument and orchestra. A few symphonies. Operas. Musical theatre. Ballets (choreographed by George Balanchine and Martha Graham) and film scores. Scores for television series and for the radio. Inspiring other writers, he wrote much himself. This avid reader eagerly awaits a collection of George Antheil's essays on music. Also a reissue of his glandular detective novel, *Death in the Dark*. He set to music the poetry of William Blake, John Keats and Percy Bysshe Shelley. George Antheil was more than mimicry and osmosis. He was blessed with that rarest of gifts, the desire to entertain and the ability to do so.

My research reveals George Antheil to have been behind two splendidly memorable events while I was a teenager. I was taken to a Broadway revival of Gershwin's *Of Thee I Sing* in the early fifties, and the mixed-media stagecraft, then new to me, of using film within an opera, and also the satiric view of American politics seemed challenging and innovative. At the time I was unaware that the story of *Of Thee I Sing* was borrowed from the poet Walter Lowenfels's earlier play *U.S.A. with Music* — for which George Antheil wrote incidental music — and the staging was strongly influenced by Antheil's opera *Transatlantic* — for which Lowenfels revised the libretto. Later, at university during the cold war era, I had compulsory military service. Twice a week at eight in the morning, dressed in the blue Air Force uniform, I tried to sleep through lectures droned by washed-out colonels and majors, by priests with small determined mouths brought in to justify war. We were all required to view a series of films under the heading of Air Power. The one about the Allied bombing of the Ploesti oil fields of Romania — Hitler's last source of natural petroleum — made a lasting impression on me. Now I know why. George Antheil, who wrote the "Airplane Sonata" in 1921, wrote the musical score for this film in 1955. All of it time-binds for me in 1987.

As Thomas Nashe — that true child of the iconoclastic sixteenth century, so reminiscent of our own — is seen as minor where major among Elizabethan writers means Shakespeare, Spenser, Marlowe and Jonson, George Antheil can be considered minor where major among modern composers might mean Igor Stravinsky or Miles Davis. To be sure, Nashe and Antheil have much in common. Both shocked their contemporaries. The elements of Bad Taste in both have confused scholars. In both there is merit ignored. Major modern writers, however, like Wyndham Lewis and William Burroughs openly acknowledge their literary debt to Nashe. And in a few hundred years from now — if I can make a hopeful guess — Antheil too will astound, incite, radicalize other musicians, composers and poets, because art is often one huge struggle with the shape of death.

Further reading:

Antheil, George (1945) *Bad Boy of Music* (Garden City, N.Y.: Doubleday and Doran). Reissued (1981) with a new introduction by Charles Amirkhanian (New York: Da Capo Press, Music Reprint Series).

Pound, Ezra (1978) *Ezra Pound and Music*: Edited with commentary by R. Murray Schafer (London: Faber and Faber).

Whitesitt, Linda (1983) *The Life and Music of George Antheil: 1900-1959* (Ann Arbor, Michigan: UMI Research Press).

BOOKTALK BY ANDREI CODRESCU

A History of Modern Poetry, by David Perkins (Belknap/Harvard University Press)

Critics couldn't exist without literature, but few of them like it. When they do, it is because the writers have read critics and, this being evident in their work, critics can converse with other critics through the writers, a bit like guests at dinner shouting at each other over the heads of their hosts.

David Perkins, the John P. Marquand Professor of English and American Literature at Harvard University, has written a history of modern poetry in English that is dedicated to the proposition that poetry, like all things, has been getting worse since the days of the gods — in this case, Ezra Pound and T. S. Eliot, but mostly Eliot. This isn't hard to prove if one follows the conventional path carved by academic consensus in the past forty years. It is a path that leads from Eliot to his conservative epigones of the New Criticism, which included John Crowe Ransom, Allen Tate, and Cleanth Brooks, the author with Robert Penn Warren of a student bible on the appreciation of poetry. From there the road goes to a drunken village of poet-professors of the fifties inhabited by folks like Ted Roethke, Robert Lowell, John Berryman, Sylvia Plath, and Adrienne Rich, and then it becomes a series of footpaths, the most promising of which leads to a campfire tended by the neo-primitivists Robert Bly, Gary Snyder, and James Wright. Another path leads to Dr. Perkins' own favorites, John Ashbery and James Merrill, two poets different and difficult enough to be unassailable. It's a neat picture. The only thing about it is that it's all wrong, ignoring as it does the other facts of the American poetry scene: its tremendous vitality in performance, its experimental forays, and the genuine popularity of much of it. When Dr. Perkins encounters a stubborn (i.e., organized) fact, he steps lightly out of the way. He has not heard of American Surrealism, and he has probably never watched MTV. No matter. As Anselm Hollo once wrote in a poem called "The Musicians": "You missed them./They didn't miss *you*." Dr. Perkins bemoans the anxiety of poets working under the shadow of the dead gods, T. S. Eliot, that is. How would he know? I know hundreds of poets. Not one of them worries about Eliot. They rarely think of him, in fact. You may do the same with this book. 🖋

SEVEN EPISODES IN ALIENATION
by Virgil Nemoianu

All kinds of things are being redeemed or rehabilitated nowadays: ferocious animals, once the enemies of mankind, are declared worthy of protection and love, ugly monsters are presented to us as kind and cute, and strange-shaped aliens are reckoned to be brotherly and benevolent creatures. But is this vast movement towards the abolition of suspicion and intolerance and hate truly sincere? I will be so persuaded only when I see the determined hostility against alienation and absurdity beginning to abate, only when we begin to talk about the loveliness of alienation.

Far from inventing or discovering the absurd, our century merely invented ways to hate it. Great writers and journalists will start shaking in their boots as soon as they hear of alienation — Catholics and Marxists and Existentialists alike — yet they keep taunting and cursing its absurdities and disorders, smell it out in remote nooks and crannies, hunt it down with relentless abhorrence. Intolerance, what else? Absurdity and alienation are parts of the human condition, as even their most desperate detractors will have to admit. Where then is now Baroque mansuetude, where Romantic humor, which had always provided the means for a leisurely coexistence with it? Remember one Erasmus of Rotterdam, who could point to absurdity, laugh a little, pat it on the back protectively, and go on about his business. Unlike him, we keep badgering alienation, we pursue it with cruel determination. Small wonder it starts fighting back, pushed to extremities as it is. Like Moby Dick, chased to the ends of the earth, alienation turns on us and will then, only then, become truly dangerous and ugly. What do you want, any species must defend its right to survive!

Let's all make some New Year vows: friendly meekness towards the absurd, indifferent smiles towards alienation, dignified relinquishment of these biases, no more invidious carping at alienation's small prerogatives. Alienation can definitely be tamed: the harmony of our universes is well in need of it.

II

In Romanian the most basic and obscene cursing word is this: "du-te-n pizda ma-tii" or else "te bag în pizda mâ-tii." It means "go back into your mother's womb" or "I'll push you into your mother's womb." Actually, it's not "womb," but "cunt." So, I'll stick you in your good mom's cunt, is what the angry, vengeful fellow is telling his neighbor, go

commit incest, return to your sources and origins. Yes, he is yelling, why don't you recapture original innocence and unity, go back where you started from, that's where you belong, in the womb, in primitive utopia, in your ecstatic unity with the all-embracing slimy *Urgrund*, with the Great Mother. You are not a human being, our exasperated Romanian thunders, back to the maternal womb with you, back to happy commonality, I curse you the most terrible curse I know or can imagine, I curse you to lose your alienation.

III

You watch this great tennis match, you watch Lendl, or Connors or Borg, or some other grand master. Serving an ace, responding to a backhand, skimming the net, changing the balls. Once in a while you see them pacing behind the lines of their own side, they look neither right nor left, neither up nor down, they stare at their own rackets; they count the strings on the rackets with concentrated attention, they seem to have discarded the rest of the world, they are no longer mindful of the rest of us. What are they doing, I have always wondered? What thoughts or feelings occupy their minds? Lendl is no longer a predator in those seconds, McEnroe no longer the ambitious, demanding brat, they seem to be inhabiting some kind of elsewhere, briefly they have abandoned their social role as entertainers and competitors, they are estranged from their work and from their fellow human beings. Why these seconds of deep and blissful alienation? Very simple: alienation is restful. Communion and communication with people and with your own labor means strenuous effort, it is — dare I say it? — not natural, not my original state. My original state of nature is the only one to which I am allowed to return completely only in short moments of blissful repose — it is alienation. In sleep, in the serenity of self-absorption, in prayer and meditation, in the disregard of my neighbors, in loneliness and contempt, beatific smiles settle on our faces. Oh, the happiness of alienation! Oh, the scarcity of alienation!

IV

Alienation is merely the lack of humidity. Some societies are damp, soaked and warm: you see them full of visceral crawlings, with few rules and intense love relationships, places of sincerity and intenseness, places of letting go, where you can freely wrong those you love. You don't keep your shirt on, you let yourself go in the sound and the fury, constipation is not very likely, people slap each other on the back with big wet fishes. It is very cozy and warm and sweaty and innocently cruel and murderous, among these old-country drunk Russians, sleazy Romanians, oozing and huddling Italians and Jews, in *shtetls* and *izbas*, among sheep-reeking Balkan shepherds. Impotent rage, utopian schemes, bizarre rumors and panic-filled hysteria are passed on first in whispers, then surge in inarticulate loud moanings, like froth on the top of clashing billows.

People hate each other too much to bother with a divorce, they get both mad and even, they boil in their resentments, brains turned to mush, and look with desperate hope towards a world of alienation. The stars on their firmament are cheap glittering products, they pray for loneliness and for the quibblings of the detailed contract, they yearn for the dry sun of apartness, taciturn remote neighbors seem the apex of elegant distinction. Dare we hope for more? What? Actual indifference? Wow, I swoon, I come! Wet societies feel swampy, degraded, and morbid, they aspire towards a seat on waterless rocks under the glaring, pitiless rays of desiccation. They passionately love alienation, they have been known to stage revolutions for it.

V

A short theory of flag-waving. Few things are as absorbing as to notice a thin silken flag, with its strong vivid blocks of colors, caught in a light strong breeze, hit by it obliquely (from right to left, from down to up) and slowly and thus unpredictably moving in either nervous flutterings or unfurled in full majestic openness. Think by comparison of fires in that open hearth. Much more variety, there, of course, frisky mischief, a little inhuman, childish

or demonic perchance; those capering flames call and lure you though not like the sirens or the sea or the ghosts of the deep. The fire in the hearth does not ask you to join it, to be *with* it, just to be and do *like* it: ritual self-immolation, spasm and consummation. Burn, baby, burn! Spread far and wide the universe of fire!

Not so the banners in the wind. Don't do like them, don't follow them at all, think of them as an analogy to who-knows-what, the object of substantial and fruit-laden contemplation. Agitated or solemn, the flags' movements are not really playful. I cannot foresee them, I cannot count or order them, yet I know they will never compare to the range of movements and shapes that live inside the flames, the waves of the ocean, even of the wind-swept grass. These flags: they belong to human society, they are dry, a little dignified, perhaps reasonable. Good enough for me, though, they keep me guessing in delight, as they keep rustling and swishing and prancing their comic pretense. You think you proclaim community, the triumphs of war and peace, keep them waving, they signal the beauties of alienation.

VI

Compassion above all, for everybody and everything, fair enough. But how do you show compassion to tough, sly, illusionless Alienation? How do you actually go about it? Well, there are ways and means, I suppose. You look it hard in the eyes and you give it a firm handshake. You give it a swift kick in the pants. You place it under long and loving observation, poke tubes into it, guide your lenses and telescopes on it. Or give it some tattered old clothes, Goodwill rejects and the like and teach it to join society, like a bewildered middle-aged immigrant in the streets of New York. Make alienation useful, teach it a trade, let it engage in some new business, help it buy a car and a house in the suburbs, watch TV, and send its kids to a posh private college, do some jogging and vote for Joe Biden. Be compassionate to alienation, be understanding, open wide your doors to it. Don't worry at all, it will gladly join the rest of us — it will become alienated.

VII

And now, finally, myself: I am much more afraid of allineation than of alienation. ☠

AS AN EXPERIENCE
by *Tsunao Aida*

translated from the Japanese by Hiroaki Sato

LEGEND

When crabs
crawl up from the lake,
we tie them to ropes,
go over the mountain
to the fair
and stand by the pebbly road.

Some people eat crabs.

Hung by the ropes,
scratching the air
with ten hairy legs,
the crabs turn into pennies;
we buy a clutch of rice and salt
and return over the mountain
to the lake side.

Here
grass is withered,
wind cold,
and we do not light our hut.

In the dark
we tell our children
what we remember of our fathers and mothers
over and
over again.
Our fathers and mothers,
like us,
caught the crabs of this lake,
wept over that same mountain,
brought back a clutch of rice and salt,
and made hot gruel
for us.

Ikeda Katsumi was in Shanghai. It was Kusano Shimpei who introduced him to me. I became acquainted with Kusano in Nanking. On the day we met, Ikeda took me to a small restaurant in a grubby alley. On the way he bought crabs from a crab vendor. I say crab vendor, but he would just stand by the roadside and give you live crabs, tying each to a rope. Ikeda had been in Shanghai before

me, so he knew exactly what he was doing: he bought four crabs, went in a small restaurant, had them boiled there, and ate them while drinking. So that you may know what kind of man Ikeda was, I'd like to tell you an episode. His wife was a young actress with an old film company — Shinko Kinema, was it — and a beautiful person. Ikeda said something clever to her, lured her out, put her on a train, and seriously threatened her at a door, saying, "Marry me. If you don't I'll jump right out of this door and kill myself," so she had no choice but to give consent — she volunteered this story when I went to see them at their house in Shanghai. Ikeda had such a devil-may-care yet somehow calculating look and was at the same time a considerate and very loveable man. Here is one of his poems. Young poets today may find the piece lacking in something, but I believe even now it's a good poem:

You are of my age
but you have a magnificent mustache
you are skinnier than I am
and taller by three to four inches
your Japanese has no conjunctions
but since you are a poet
your Japanese is pure
and all poetry
"I am clumsy poetry, I have a long way to go,"
   you say
but as we walk, you say
"The four legs that walk on history"
in front of the innumerable jars of *lao chiu* at Ma
   Shanghou you say
"Each one of these jars is a line of poetry"
China's literary leadership, which has grown too
   old, will despise you
you aren't sad about it
rather it just makes you square your skinny
   shoulders
when I say so-and-so is good
you hasten to ask:
"Is he still better than I?"
you believe in your sole self terribly adequately
but that isn't your arrogance
it is loyalty to heaven's principle that there's always
   only one beginning point
you say you now have ninety members for your
   Poetic Territory
you urge subscriptions, collect money, and buy
   paper

saying you'll put out a 300-page book of poems
your calculation will probably go wrong
but your skin, which doesn't stop renewing itself for
    a second
will remain
so you feel bright
ah every thing, every phenomenon, is poetry for
    you
I trust you for your being busy
"Since Japan and China had a quarrel I went
    Hankow. I go Changsha. I go Kweichow. I go
    Yunnan. Then it's Indochina, Hong Kong"
your wandering
your return home
you now put it boldly:
"Twentieth century, farewell
"Poetry, farewell
"Literature, farewell
"Shanghai, farewell
"Earth, farewell
"There's no culture. There's no hope. There's no
    light
"There's no Chinese literature, now"
parting is your courage
despair is your "departure"
your eyes, the slits, are
murderous swords to me
at the tip of your walking stick that you never part
    with
I sense the sad anger of a young China
you trampled upon the decorum and manners
of the aged great country
the realist China
you put your fist to your mouth grateful for "Ching
    ching"
and still
at my word, "World poetry will come from Japan"
you say stubbornly, "World poetry will come from
    China"
ah who in the world knows
of this childish dispute in Asia
on a day when the earth is disturbed
fifty-five yuan Bamboo Leaf Green
sixty-five yuan Carved Flower
our two wallets good enough only for another chin
you are poor
I am poor
your child is often ill
my two children often cry
but what abundant talkativeness of you and me
we don't talk about politics

but we've said enough
you love China obstinately
I love Japan obstinately
you are our friend
you and we are full
your youth with a mustache is beautiful
your droll, desperate face
is very good
yes it's very good
Soon,
again like our fathers and mothers,
we will carry our bodies, grown thin and small,
lightly
lightly
and throw them in the lake.
And the crabs will eat our sloughs
to the last bits
just as they ate
the sloughs of our fathers and mothers
to the last bits.

That is our wish.

When the children fall asleep,
we go out of our hut
and float a boat on the lake.
The lake is half light
and we, trembling,
make love
gently
painfully.

I got the idea of "Legend" toward the end of 1940, when I was twenty-five years old and I volunteered and joined the Nanking Special Service, a special administrative organization that belonged directly to the military. Assigned to it, I was, to use the phrase of those days, a military civilian, and a military civilian had to read aloud what they called the military civilian's oath in front of the director of the Service. You had to stay, no matter how hard it was. As soon as I joined it I disliked it, but I endured it for two years. The Service had some soldiers who took part in Japan's assault on Nanking, and some members of the pacification unit, the predecessor of the Special Service. The Japanese army committed genocide in Nanking. Some of the people had seen atrocities with their own eyes and told their vivid recollections of it. After one of these stories, I heard this: crabs during the war were extremely delicious, and that it wasn't something the Japanese said, but it went from mouth to mouth among the people whose land was occupied, who were slaughtered. That's what my colleagues at the Special Service told me. The crabs harvested during the war were delicious, they said, because the crabs ate the corpses of those killed and thus had a lot of fat. I have never checked whether or not crabs actually eat human beings, if not as they are, but in the decomposed state when they are as gelatinous as planktons, but I think they probably do. They may not eat them thinking 'these are human beings we're eating,' but I'm sure they do eat them. It is because of this, I think, that the Chinese did not eat crabs during the war except in extreme circumstances. Not a single one of the Chinese I associated with ate crabs in front of me. The talk of crabs eating the people killed in the war got stuck in my head, but I didn't see crabs in Nanking. After I was freed from the Special Service, I went to Shanghai and ate Chinese crabs for the first time. On the grubby streets in Shanghai, there were a number of grubby small restaurants. They were run by Chinese. I said small restaurants, but they were more like bars, and on the streets where the bars were, crab vendors showed up. I'm not quite sure where they got them. It was close to the Yangtze, so they got them either directly from the Yangtze or its tributaries or from the marshes connected to them; they were large crabs, and they were delicious. Toyoshima Yoshio was a good writer with the soul of a poet; he liked sake and seems to have come to Shanghai from time to time, since before the war, and the reason he came to Shanghai was that, though the sake there was good enough, the crabs were even better, so he came there to eat them. The poet who told me how to eat them was Ikeda Katsumi, who died since then. The people who recognize his name are becoming fewer, but after the war he put out the poetry magazine called *Hana* ("flower") and later started the magazine called *Nippon mirai-ha* ("Japanese futurist group"). *Nippon mirai-ha*, though Ikeda died, is still published by the original members of his group, and like *Rekitei* ("historical process"), to which I belong, has a large family, and it is, I think, one of the influential "association magazines" of poetry that represent the postwar era well. In any case, I became friendly with Mr. Lu I, too, and I think Ikeda introduced me to him. I drank with Lu I at Ma Shanghou, which is mentioned in the poem, and sometimes at other places, too. There's one thing I can't forget. At a restaurant in Wumalu, when the three of us — Lu I, his younger brother Lu Mai, and I — were drinking Carved Flower, chatting, I inadvertently ordered crabs. As soon as a waiter brought the crabs, Lu I's eyes became a little sharp and he clearly said, "I wouldn't do it, I don't eat crabs." I knew at once, but pretended not to know, and asked, "Why?" "I've hated crabs since I was a child, I don't like the way they look, I don't even want to see them" — he explained. Lu I didn't eat crabs because he didn't think it quite right to eat with a Japanese the crabs which were said to have become delicious by eating the flesh and blood of his compatriots, slaughtered by the Japanese. I can say the poem "Legend" was made as my own requiem for the tens of thousands of people who were shot by the Japanese army and dumped in the Yangtze, and for people such as Lu I who associated with Japanese in Shanghai during the war, were troubled, yet kept writing poems. "Legend" is a piece already fifteen years old and far from my present mentality. Basically, there's something about the poem that makes me feel that Ikeda Katsumi, Lu I, Kusano Shimpei, to name a few who were close to me during the war, and countless other friends and comrades, guiltless people, Shanghai, Nanking — these things were more or less unified in the form of the poem, "Legend," and that with the unification came a sort of relief.

Bruce Hutchinson

POEMS BY ANNIE SILVERMAN

SEVENTEEN YEARS AFTER THE FIRST MEN WALKED ON THE MOON

Sitting side by side
Watching Jung on the screen
arms barely touching
breathing in unison
each of us holding hands with ourselves
instead of attempting the unmatched pair

Collectively our consciousnesses
watch the film
yet listen for the other

Even at 34 and 41
The archetypal
first date

AFTER THEIR FATHERS DIE

The bodies of middle ageing girls change

They wake up and see in bathroom mirrors
Mustaches growing above their lips

They feel new sets of wrinkles
Carved deep into their hearts

Their bowels develop minds of their own
And subvert years of careful schedules and
   training

Their periods change as tears
Fall down inside and travel through
Unexplored regions of their geography

They feel perfectly normal most of the time
Until those thoughts about forever
Crush and pull their insides out
To make them feel that emptiness
All over again

Being called "little one," or "peanut"
Could easily fill the holes inside
These middle ageing girls
But they will never hear themselves
Called these names in
Just the right way again

CLOSER TO GROUND

by Pat Nolan

The past examples
the future events

we build on what we remember
forgetting is what we do best
the world a reminder of that
how close we are to earth
as we distance ourselves

mammal fungus

"ain't nobody here but us ants"
(oldest work force known to man)
"insect" still insults
nothing but contempt for survivors
their myriad permutations
the compromise we can't make

that's the narrow view

gone in the time
          it takes
                    a nerve to twitch
grand illusion spark
as with Newton
          cosmic ideas bear fruit

warm breeze
a nectarine drops

Julia Demarée

ANATOMY OF THE SOUTH

by Fred Hobson

The compelling sin of the South is no longer racism. It is public relations, image-making, which is perfectly understandable since the image of the late Confederacy was so bad for so long. Now, each Southern state boosts itself, seeks its identity in tags and labels, slick and polished. Virginia is for lovers; Atlanta is the "the City Too Busy to Hate," And so on.

But the labels I like best are anatomical ones. I live in Alabama, for example, and one who lives in Alabama cannot long escape the claim, announced annually on the state's license plates, that Alabama is the "Heart of Dixie." I am also a student of Southern history and literature, and one who reads about the South for long must at some point come across a reference to North Carolina, in particular Chapel Hill, as the "Mind of the South."

"Heart" and "Mind" — bodily parts displayed geographically — led me to consider, in a more general sense, the South as living organism, as body not only spiritually and politically (as in "body politic") but indeed physically; led me, that is, to construct a sort of anatomical map, an "Anatomy of the South." Not anatomy metaphorically but anatomy in fact: certain Southern parts do serve certain physical functions.

One has, first, to visualize the South as animal — a grotesque, misshapen creature, quadruple amputee (befitting a veteran of the War Between the States) with an oversized head; a creature lying on its belly, beaten down (under the North's oppressive weight), facing East. Then one sets about to construct the "Anatomy of the South."

One begins with the givens. Alabama is the "Heart of Dixie" and North Carolina the "Mind of the South." The Tar Heel State has long provided intellectual leadership for the South: Howard W. Odum and his social scientists in Chapel Hill, Gerald W. Johnson, W. J. Cash and any number of journalists and social critics have shaped Southern thought. North Carolina has always considered Dixie rationally, not viscerally.

As the "Heart of Dixie," Alabama is visceral, corporeal. It has, traditionally, thought with its blood, which generally runs bright red. Alabama rushed into the Civil War; North Carolina waited and considered. The intellectual detachment of North Car-olina it finds impossible, and its politics bear witness.

But to return to the upper coastal South, the head and face of the creature called Dixie. If North Carolina is the mind, Virginia is above it and serves as well a cerebral function. Virginia is for lovers, yes, but in an ethereal, metaphysical sense. Lovers of the true and good and beautiful. Duty, Devotion, Sacrifice, Chivalry, Noblesse Oblige; these are qualities Robert E. Lee embodied and Thomas Nelson Page illustrated and defined for the rest of the South.

Virginia was the Platonic ideal to which the Deep South aspired, the image from which the rest of Dixie sprang. Alabama, for instance, built mansions on the Virginia model, adopted chivalry and noblesse oblige. But there was always something missing; Alabama, still frontier in the 1840s and a rough, aggressive place, lacked the gentility of the land from which its forebears sprang. To the present day, the manner of the older South, of Virginia, is mixed with a frontier vitality in Alabama, expressing itself mainly in championship football. (The Upper South — the Atlantic Coast plus Kentucky — plays basketball.) Alabama then, a strange admixture of manners and football, both more or less than the real thing, not a true Tidewater but — in deference to rule by pigskin — a sort of Crimson Tidewater.

If Alabama is heart and North Carolina and Virginia the faculties of reason and imagination, South Carolina — located on the lower part of the face — represents the mouth of the South, Dixie's voice. It works both spatially and historically. The greatest Southern orators, Rhett and Yancey, Calhoun and Hammond, came from South Carolina. The inflammatory rhetoric that led to the War Between the States came largely from there. South Carolina deserves its anatomical function.

And if South Carolina is the voice, mouth, Tennessee is backbone. The Volunteer State, rough and ready in the old days, still proud, rock-ribbed and uncompromising, is Dixie's spine. The Southern animal is lying on its belly, remember, facing East. If Tennessee is backbone, Mississippi is the guts of the beast, the stomach with a Bible Belt wrapped around it. Forget, hell! Mississippi, like Alabama, is visceral.

The rest of the South is anatomically more difficult. Only Louisiana stands out, with its winding, intestinal river emptying the waste of the mid-continent into the Gulf. And Florida with its pleasure function and profile geographically misplaced but suggesting new Sun Belt priorities.

Georgia remains. The state Mencken believed indisputedly the worst in the South now considers itself the best. It has Atlanta. It elected a president. It is the chest of Dixie, covering the heart — the chest thrust out with pride, cocky, challenging — the South triumphant.

STUDIES IN ABUSABLE COLOR

by Jim Gustafson

There was a sadness hanging in the air like spurned telepathy. You'd received a telepathic memo from Rothko in purgatory while you were in your tree house dangling high over the Pacific. You were given a box of light, a cloud of your choice, a book of photographs of duststorm variations, and some sketches called STUDIES IN ABUSABLE COLOR. "I felt petty annoyance with bottle green, so I eliminated it (& all the sports cars that color) and made the universe a much safer place." Sure you did. That was a color that was real big with the coconuts for breakfast crowd, and the riot that followed its vanished sent the ice machines into a mad rebellion all the way to Imperial Beach. Everywhere you looked assholes were patting the ground wondering where their wheels went. "I melted all those Porsches down and sold them to the devil who said he was going to make wrought iron fences out of them." Only seems fair. "And sweat boxes for troublemakers." There is no room for atrocity in an ideal world. There too many mysto-mutts running loose without collars. Anything that keeps the universe from devouring its own shadow is within the regulations. Look it up.

I SMOKE THIS CIGARETTE FOR YOU

by Elinor Nauen

My poems are in love with your poems
Can you see me? when you take
Off your glasses
Do you see me with your total body?
The poets push their love into my
Body & it comes out my mouth
Take your shirt off let me see
Your darkness my red bra your hands that see
What my words remember only while I sigh
When I wear my red bra
I always need to take off my shirt
But honey it's the same underwear

FOR ROBERT DUNCAN

d. February 3, 1988

by Tom Clark

How the arm moved
throwing the poet's
ashes out of the boat
how it all comes back

How the whole story
form of telling curves
the story around
these cosmic corners

How the stars swam
how the moon
was dying down
out over the water

To loosen out into
those big quiet waters
little pieces of
us all are floating on

INDEX

CITY LIGHTS PUBLICATIONS

Goethe, J. W. von. TALES FOR TRANSFORMATION
Hayton-Keeva, Sally, ed. VALIANT WOMEN IN WAR & EXILE
Herron, Don. THE LITERARY WORLD OF SAN FRANCISCO
Higman, Perry, ed. LOVE POEMS FROM SPAIN
    AND SPANISH AMERICA
Kerouac, Jack. BOOK OF DREAMS
Kerouac, Jack. SCATTERED POEMS
Kovic, Ron. AROUND THE WORLD IN 8 DAYS
La Duke, Betty. COMPANERAS: Women, Art & Social
    Change in Latin America
Lamantia, Philip. MEADOWLARK WEST
Lamantia, Philip. BECOMING VISIBLE
Laughlin, James. THE MASTER OF THOSE WHO KNOW
Laughlin, James. SELECTED POEMS: 1935-1985
Lowry, Malcolm. SELECTED POEMS
Ludlow, Fitz Hugh. THE HASHEESH EATER
Marcelin, Philippe-Thoby. THE BEAST OF THE HAITIAN
    HILLS
Masereel, Frans. PASSIONATE JOURNEY
McDonough, Kaye. ZELDA
Moore, Daniel. BURNT HEART
Mrabet, Mohammed. THE BOY WHO SET THE FIRE
Mrabet, Mohammed. THE LEMON
Mrabet, Mohammed. LOVE WITH A FEW HAIRS
Mrabet, Mohammed. M'HASHISH
Murguía, Alejandro, ed. VOLCAN: Poems from Central America
O'Hara, Frank. LUNCH POEMS
Olson, Charles. CALL ME ISHMAEL
Orlovsky, Peter. CLEAN A POEMS
Paschke, Barbara, ed. CLAMOR OF INNOCENCE: Stories
    from Central America
Pessoa, Fernando. ALWAYS ASTONISHED: Selected Prose
Pasolini, Pier Paolo. ROMAN POEMS
Poe, Edgar Alan. THE UNKNOWN POE
Porta, Antonio. KISSES FROM ANOTHER DREAM
Purdy, James. IN A SHALLOW GRAVE
Prevert, Jacques. PAROLES
Rey-Rosa, Rodrigo. THE BEGGAR'S KNIFE
Rigaud, Milo. SECRETS OF VOODOO
Saadawi El, Nawal. MEMOIRS OF A WOMAN DOCTOR
Sawyer-Lauçanno, Christopher, transl. THE DESTRUCTION OF THE
    JAGUAR: Poems from the Books of Chilam Balam
Sclauzero, Mariarosa. MARLENE
Serge, Victor. RESISTANCE
Shepard, Sam. MOTEL CHRONICLES
Shepard, Sam. FOOL FOR LOVE & THE SAD LAMENT
    OF PECOS BILL
Smith, Michael. IT A COME
Snyder, Gary. THE OLD WAYS
Tutuola, Amos. FEATHER WOMAN OF THE JUNGLE
Tutuola, Amos. SIMBI & THE SATYR OF THE DARK JUNGLE
Waley, Arthur. THE NINE SONGS
Wilson, Colin. POETRY AND MYSTICISM